John Lewis Dyer

The Snow-Shoe Itinerant

An autobiography of the Rev. John L. Dyer

John Lewis Dyer

The Snow-Shoe Itinerant
An autobiography of the Rev. John L. Dyer

ISBN/EAN: 9783337015633

Printed in Europe, USA, Canada, Australia, Japan

Cover: Foto ©Raphael Reischuk / pixelio.de

More available books at **www.hansebooks.com**

THE

SNOW-SHOE ITINERANT.

AN AUTOBIOGRAPHY

OF THE

REV. JOHN L. DYER,

FAMILIARLY KNOWN AS "FATHER DYER,"

OF THE

Colorado Conference, Methodist Episcopal Church.

———

ILLUSTRATED FROM DRAWINGS BY MRS. HELEN H. CHAIN,
DENVER, COLORADO.

———

CINCINNATI:
PUBLISHED FOR THE AUTHOR BY CRANSTON & STOWE.
1890.

Copyright by

JOHN L. DYER,

1889.

Words Introductory.

It were easy to have edited Father Dyer out of his book. But, dressed in my diction, he would have been a sorry masquerader. The survivors of The Fountain and Buckskin Joe would not have recognized him. The placers of Fair Play and the diggings of Breckenridge would have turned their backs upon him. All would have been disappointed to find the conventional minister where they had the right to expect the unique individuality of the frontiersman. "Next to the biography of Peter Cartwright," says Prof. S. W. Williams, who has edited more manuscript than any man in our Church, "this is the most interesting in the annals of American Methodism." I trust that Father Dyer's hosts of friends will enjoy the story even as they love the story-teller, and see and hear him in every chapter; that his worthy successor in the Colorado Conference will catch the fervor of his dauntless spirit; and that his artless narrative will contribute somewhat of value to the History of Rocky Mountain Methodism.

I have gone over these pages alone, and with my venerable and beloved brother, until their personality has possessed me, and I and the Snow-shoe Itinerant seem to be one. But now his snow-shoes are to bear him in one direction, and I am summoned in another. As for him, I have no fears. The same good Providence which has guided him safely from Santa Fe to North Park, and through the gulches of the Sangre de Christo and the passes of the Continental Divide, will gently lead him "Over the Range" at last, on whose yonder sunny slopes he will meet the companions and friends of his youth, that son whose untimely taking off dashed his cup with bitter sorrow, and, best of all, the Divine One, on whose altar he has laid an unselfish and noble life. As for me, I doubt not that the editorial pen will write in more heroic character for the example of Father Dyer, the Cartwright of the Rockies, the pioneer hero of Frontier Methodism, with whom I hope by and by to sit down in our Father's house in heaven.

DAVID H. MOORE.

EDITORIAL ROOMS,
WESTERN CHRISTIAN ADVOCATE,
December, 1889.

CONTENTS.

Chapter I.

Ancestry and Early Youth—How his Great Grandfather got to America—Life in Virginia and Kentucky—Blazing the Way into Ohio—The Darbys–Dyer's Mills—The Fosters—Freeborn Garrettson—An Evil Prophecy—"Tom" Corwin as a Temperance Lecturer—An Old-fashioned Family Altar—Apprenticed to the Plow—Pioneer Preachers—Two Notable Camp-meetings—Bascom's Manly Beauty—Finley and his Indian Converts—"The Jerks"—Youthful Sports—'Coon-skin Currency—A Normal Case of Buck Fever—The Winter School—Barring out the Teacher—Glade Run *versus* Big Darby—Mathematics in the Big Woods—The First Sunday-school in Georgeville, ... **Page 11**

Chapter II.

Unites With the Church—Dread of the Class-meeting—Conversion—"Innocent Amusements"—The Family removes to Illinois—The Wilderness—Hunting a Home—Caught in a January Storm—Primitive Hospitality—His Father in Peril—Black Hawk War—Volunteers—"Westerfield's Defeat"—Ross's Escapade—End of the War—The Crash of 1837—The Church survives—Full Salvation—Praying for Death—Made a Class-leader—Brings up the Preacher's Salary—Marries Harriet Foster—Death of his Wife, 1847—A Sad Mistake—Divorce—Lead-mining in Wisconsin—Made a Local Preacher—"Brushed" at the Old Stone Church—An Unexpected Revival—Jonah—"Hoist"—Surrenders—A Supply on Wingville and Lancaster Circuit—A Rowdy at the Mourners' Bench—Admitted to Wisconsin Conference and sent to Elk Grove Circuit, ... **25**

Chapter III.

Admitted to Conference—Tragic Death of the Divorced Wife—Salary of $100—Fond du Lac Conference—Franklin and

Wingville—Lincoln the Shouter—A Singular Dream—Dividing the House—"This Place belongs to the Old Lady"—Chauncey Hobart's Ague Fit—Fayette Circuit—Cholera—An Awful Experience—A Successful Thief—Cold Comfort—A Hospitable Infidel—A String of Fish—"I have made up my Mind to go"—Prayer Answered—A Warning—A Fight at Camp-meeting—Suckers—The Beautiful Country, PAGE 48

CHAPTER IV.

Richland Mission, Minnesota—Marriage of Rachel—On the Road—Bethel—Tragic Death of Robert—Revivals Everywhere—Trip to Wisconsin—The Second Camp-meeting in Minnesota—The Crash of 1857—The First Conference held in Minnesota—Caledonia or Preston Circuit—Surety—Pastoral Visiting—"How long does Thee intend to hold these Meetings?"—Running from a Shouting Wife—A Pioneer Temperance Crusader—"The Most Industrious Little Mill I ever saw"—"The Fifth Time, it went off"—Conference at St. Paul—Anecdote of Bishop Morris—Austin Circuit, ... 69

CHAPTER V.

En route to Austin—Swimming Root River—A Bare-footed Sermon—A Mischievous Immersion—Stuck in a Slough—Moses Mapes—The Black Horse and his Rider—A Revival Cloud-burst—Specimen Converts—A Liberal Baptist—The State-line Broken—The Three-cent Seeker—A Providential Haul—Conference at St. Anthony—Crossing the Zumbro on a Raft—Camp-meeting on the Chippewa—Prescott Conference—Chauncey Hobart—Rice Lake and Chippewa Squaws—Indian Bargain—Menominee Mills—Captain Wilson—Whisky—An Irate Father—North-west Wisconsin Conference—Security Debts, ... 87

CHAPTER VI.

Off for Pike's Peak—Retrospect—Great Loss—Ox-train—Preaching *en route*—Dog Soup—Ox-gad *versus* Rifle—"Cut Off," or "Cut On?"—A Mad Boss—The Last Night on the Plains—Denver in 1861—Byers's Printing-office—Patriotic Sermon—Off for Buckskin Joe—Dyer's "Short Account"—A Year of Strange Adventures, ... 117

CHAPTER VII.

On Foot to Denver—Colonel Chivington—Anecdote of Bigelow—On the Blue—Bachelor's Hall—Turn about with Gamblers—Deputy Assessor—Snow-shoe Accident—"Not Quite Handsome Enough for me to dance with"—"You can stand that or make a Temperance Speech," . PAGE 138

CHAPTER VIII.

Winter Exodus—The Pioneer Theater—Revival at Gold Run— No longer a "Supply"—Up the Blue on Snow-shoes— Origin of the Names Tarryall, Buckskin Joe, Fair Play, Mosquito, *et al.*—The Espinosas Raid—A Run for Life— Baxter Hung—Last of the Espinosas—Tom Tobin the Avenger, ... 148

CHAPTER IX.

Traveling the Circuit During the Raid—A Bad Scare—A "Fearful Porcupine"—Bishop Ames organizes the Colorado Conference—Typical Instances of Rough Characters in Rough Camps—Practical Effects of Dancing-schools . . 156

CHAPTER X.

Organization of the Rocky Mountain Conference, 1863—Presiding Elders Willard and Slaughter—Sent to South Park Circuit—Flour $15 per Sack—Funds exhausted—Carrying the Mail on Snow-shoes—Laden with Gold—Traveling Companions—Life-saving—An Unwilling Mail-carrier— Lonely Trips—A Perilous Leap and a Lightning Slide—A Pack-cow on the War-path, ... 162

CHAPTER XI

Agent for the Rocky Mountain News—The Express robbed by "Secesh"—A Rebel Rising invited, but not accepted— The Chase—Experience as a Volunteer—The Robbers Captured and "Lost"—Corn 13 Cents a Pound—Indian Scare— Building a Fort in Denver—Joking with "Old Chiv."— Sand Creek from a Colorado Stand-point—The Snow-shoe Preacher a Bishop *pro tem.*—Chivington's Great Speech— A Year with Five Quarters—A Cattle Baron—The Southern District—Prospecting New Mexico for Methodism—Trini-

dad—Crossing the Rattoon—An Unexpected Wedding—
Maxwell's Grant—The First Protestant Minister in New
Mexico—Judge Watts—Birthplace of Montezuma—The
Pueblos—The Penitentes—Mexican Hospitality—Supersti-
tion, ... PAGE 178

CHAPTER XII.

Conference of 1865—Bishop Kingsley — Conference Photo-
graphed—Presiding Elder again—Grasshopers—Sad Con-
tribution to the Union—A Fruitless Quest—A Run to New
York and Boston —Robbed—Enough of the East—$125
Stage-fare Atchison to Denver—At Work again — Modern
Revivals — Conference at Empire, 1866—Bishop Baker—
Acting Bishop—Bishop Baker rests at Mr. Burton's—South
Park District—Fort Garland—Tom Tobin—Father Machbœuf—Saguache—The First Shout in the San Luis Valley—
Old Chief San Juan as a Comforter—Poncha Pass and California Gulch—Unhorsed in the Arkansas—A Bare-foot Ser-
mon—Wilderness Distances—Alma Camp-meeting—" Stack
your Chips and give us a Hearing!"—On Snow-shoes
again—In Peril—Delivered—Sam Hartzell's—Uncle Jesse
Frazer's—Hard Times for Preachers—All Night Ride with
Colored Soldiers—Little Denver—" Be it ever so Humble,
there's no Place like Home," 196

CHAPTER XIII.

Winter of 1866-67—The Veiled Prophet—" Did You bring me
any Tobacco?" — Salt-works—Among the Red-skins—Cy
Hall as Stage-driver—Lost in the Snow —Sledding in May—
Bishop Ames and the Conference of 1867—Early Settlers of
Colorado City — Camp-meeting Conference — Delegate to
General Conference—W. F. Warren's Good Record—Bishop
Ames's Travels over Part of my District—Incidents of the
Excursion—Ministerial Courtesy—Off to General Confer-
ence—Shoveling Out—Taken for my Father, ... 216

CHAPTER XIV.

General Conference — Committee Work—The Indian Question—Battle of the Giants—Boundaries—Colorado Conference—Bishop Simpson, ... 231

CHAPTER XV.

New Mexico District—Kit Carson—Mad Indians—Illustrative Episode—Sheep Cheese—An Abiding Wonder!—Shutting the Mouths of Owls and Wolves—The First Class-leader in New Mexico—Rev. Thomas Harwood—Whole-souled Miners—Lone Rocks—In a Texas Corner—Wine-press—Fort Selden—Indians!—Fort Craig—A Strange Presentiment—Mrs. Harwood—Fort Defiance, Arizona—Rev. Mr. Roberts, Presbyterian Board—The Navajoe Thieves—Fort Stanton—An Improvised Warming-pan—A Timely Wedding—Dangers—Boska Grande—Fort Sumner—Fort Bascom—Fort Union—Ten Thousand Miles on Horseback in Two Years—A Bit of New Mexico History, ... PAGE 240

CHAPTER XVI.

Conference at Central City—Bishop Kingsley—Conference of 1870—Pueblo—Bishop Ames—Divide Circuit—Married to Mrs. Lucinda P. Rankin—Lynch Law—Elbert County—Benediction and Dancing—Wm. Bonafield's Close Call—Was it an Assassin? — Miles Madden shot—Father's Death—Evans, Platteville, and Fort Lupton—A Severe Accident—Geo. H. Adams—Sister Williams—Then and Now—A Pleasant Visit—A Difficult Backout—Conference, 1873—Greeley and Bishop Andrews, ... 260

CHAPTER XVII.

A Three Weeks' Jaunt—Smashed up—Service at Father's Grave—Wash-burn Creek—Dyer's Mine—Patient Burro—Brave Maiden—Sunday at Alma—Back to Erie—1874 Conference—Colorado Springs—Bishop Bowman—Monument Circuit—Bowling Alley Parsonage—Building—1875 Conference—Central City—Bishop Haven—A Joyous Fourth—Assassination of my Son Elias—Cast down, but not forsaken, ... 277

CHAPTER XVIII.

Lake County—Judge of Probate—Early Strife—The Case of Elijah Gibbs—A Mob—"Come out and be hung like a Man"—The Attack—The Successful Defense—Gibbs's Flight and Pursuit—The Committee of Safety—Elias Dyer Judge—

Offends the Committee—In Peril—Hardin murdered—From Bad to Worse—Trials for Law—Brave Andy Wilson—The Arrows of the Lord—The Judge murdered, ... PAGE 285

CHAPTER XIX.

Report of the Tragedy in the *Rocky Mountain News*—A View from the Inside—Letter from J. McPherson—Correspondence of the Fair Play *Sentinel*—Item from the *News*—Extract from Country Paper—Letter from Judge Dyer—Another Letter from the Judge—Letter of James H. Johnston—Last Letter of Judge Dyer—Dispatch in the *Rocky Mountain News*—Extract from a Country Paper—Another Letter from McPherson—He is appointed Probate Judge—My Son's Estate administered upon—Sale of Dyer's Mine—Reflections, ... 297

CHAPTER XX.

Conference of 1876—Boulder and Bishop Harris—Fair Play and Alma—A. J. Smith—Governor Bross's Doxology—Dumphouse of the Dolly Varden—The First Preaching on Mount Lincoln—A Marriage in *High* Life—Supernumerary in 1877—Conference 1879, Bishop Merrill—1880, Bishop Warren—Ignorance or Worse?—Indian Scare—A Moral pointed—Father Meeker—Smut—Success—Breckenridge—First Church on the Western Slope in Colorado Conference—Lessons in Prospecting—The Warrior's Mark—How Stockholders are swindled, ... 322

CHAPTER XXI.

Sister Van Cott at Breckenridge—Conference at Leadville—The First "Fifth Collection" all mine and for the University of Denver—Ranchero—Wife's Tragic Flight—Cloudburst—To Denver—Chaplain of the State Senate—Breckenridge again—"Hair-hung and Breath-shaken"—Religious Beginnings of Denver, ... 341

CHAPTER XXII.

Gold and Silver Mining in Colorado—Smelters—N. P. Hill—Governor Gilpin, Crank or Prophet; Which?—Coal—Iron—Hot Springs—Climbing for Life—*The News*—Governor Evans, ... 350

SNOW-SHOE ITINERANT.

CHAPTER I.

YOUTHFUL YEARS.

MY friends, both in and out of the ministry, have for years urged me to write the story of my life. At last I have come to think that I ought to do so. I am assured that but a few days remain to me, and that what I do must be quickly done. God has wondrously led me, and what I write I consecrate to him. May his Spirit guide my pen!

The name I bear—so far as our records go—begins with my great-grandfather stepping on to an English ship, when a lad, without leave of the officers, bound for America. With others, he was sold out for a specified time to pay his passage. But he fell into good hands, and his apprenticeship was worth all it cost. He became the owner of a desirable tract of land in Pendleton County, Virginia; married; was blessed with two sons—Roger and John—and a daughter. His eventful career was cut off by the Indians before he reached middle life. His widow married a Mr. Cravens, and bore him several children. One of these was the Rev. Wm. Cravens—better known as Billy

Cravens—a Methodist, fearless and determined, dealing still-houses and dram-drinking fearful blows, and certainly the boldest anti-slavery man of his age.

John, the second of the two boys named before, was my grandfather. He married Miss Jane Morrel. The third of their nine children, Samuel Dyer, my father, was born in Pendleton County, Virginia, March 23, 1786. In the spring of 1788, the family moved into Kentucky, and settled within six miles of Lexington. Ten years later, in the spring of 1798, they moved to Ohio, not yet a State, and made their home at Station Prairie— a stronghold against Indians—below Chillicothe. In 1800 my grandfather moved to the junction of the Darbys, in Franklin County, where he built the first grist-mill in Central Ohio, on a tract of land containing six hundred acres. It is still known as Dyer's Mills.

Grandfather was quite a character in his way. He had a saw-mill, also, and when a fine cherry-log was brought one day, he selected enough of the planks into which it was sawed to make him a coffin, stored them in the loft of his log house, and when he died they were used as he intended. He was not a Church member, but was anxious to hear the Word. Learning of a young Methodist preacher who had come within eight miles, he sent an invitation for him to preach at his house, which was declined because grandfather was not a member! Nothing discouraged, he sent for Lewis Foster, who came gladly, and who, when grandfather died—January 12, 1812—preached his funeral sermon. My grandmother died in great peace a few years later. She was a Methodist of the old stamp. Her memory is precious.

As my mother was a daughter of this Lewis Foster, it will not be out of place to present him to my readers. He was a native of Baltimore County, Maryland; married Miss Ann Davis, and spent a long and happy life with her and the large family which blessed their union. He was converted in early life, and joined the Church under Freeborn Garrettson. I heard him state that he thought Garrettson was the best-looking man he ever saw, when he would ride up to his father's to preach, and say: "Boys, feed my horse well, for he has lost two holes in girth since I was here last."

His father was a local preacher before him, and he was but twenty-two when he began proclaiming the gospel. In 1800 he moved his family from Pennsylvania to Ohio, blazing their way, his wagon being the first that ever made the journey from Wheeling to Chillicothe. He made his settlement in Madison County, where West Jefferson now stands, and labored for the Church as a respected and successful local preacher.

On one occasion, probably 1820, when I was a small boy, father took the family to a camp-meeting, where Russel Bigelow presided and preached one of his most wonderful sermons. Strange to say, my grandfather was called on to follow him, although there were eminent ministers present. After the preliminaries were closed, he rose tremblingly and said: "I can see but one reason why I have been called on to speak at this hour, and that is, if I fail I have but little to lose." It was later in life I learned the full force of that expression. Suffice it to say that, before he was through, the people were carried away above preacher and angels to Christ Jesus. Such a rising and shouting for joy and crying for mercy I have seldom if ever witnessed from that day to this. I dwell on these details with fondness, for I am proud of my Methodist lineage, and of the fact that I can trace the ministry in our family back through grandfather to great-grandfather Foster.

In October, 1810, at the Foster homestead in Madison County, my father, Samuel Dyer, and Cassandra Foster were married. I was born March 16, 1812, at the junction of the Darbys, near the old mill, and named John Lewis, for my two grandfathers. My father was justice of the peace, and among the men that frequented his primitive court was a Mr. T., who was generally half-drunk, and would persist, when in that condition, in shaking hands with me, although I was scarcely more than four years old. On one occasion, seeing him coming, I hid behind mother as she sat spinning flax on her little wheel, and said: "He is drunk, and I will not shake hands." But he saw me, and when I drew back, he said: "What is the matter with that child?" She told him what I had said. That raised his Irish. He stamped his foot, and said: "That child will make a drunkard as sure as he lives. I have never seen a child that hated a

drunken man but would surely be a drunkard."
I was badly frightened, but never forgot his angry
prophecy. I was born with a love for whisky. I
can not remember when, at the smell of it, water
did not gather on my tongue. But whenever I
tasted it, the thought of old T. came into my mind
and terrified me.

Not long after, another event occurred which
helped to save me. Father was laid up with
rheumatism, and the young people of the neighborhood gathered to pull his flax. As the custom
was, he provided a quart of whisky and a bucket
of water, which I sat in the shade to dispense.
Never did anything look so tempting. I thought
I could mix the whisky with water, so that it
would not strangle me, and drink all I wanted and
nobody know anything about it. So mixing up a
half tin-cup full, I drank until it did not taste good
any more. The next thing I remember was looking toward the house over a small field of wheat.
The stalks seemed to be about seven feet high,
and the heads nearly a foot long, and they all appeared to be pitching over each other. So I thought
it impossible to get home, lay down, and was carried to the house. That was my first and last
"drunk." When I had grown to young manhood,
I heard "Tom" Corwin deliver a temperance lec-
ture. His experience and arguments captivated
me, and I signed the pledge, and ever since have
practiced temperance closely and advocated it earnestly. Old T.'s prediction, thanks be unto God,
was never fulfilled.

I could not have been more than six years old when I had a great trial. My father made a profession of religion. He asked the blessing before eating, which seemed to me a great waste of time. He had family prayers night and morning. But a few days passed before some friends came to see us. All the afternoon I thought, Father can't pray like a preacher, and, if I were in his place, I would put off praying till they leave. But he never quit while he lived. Mother's heart was full of joy. She had been a professor since fourteen years of age. Now her husband walked with her, and all was gladness. Memory lingers on our old-fashioned family altar. My mother had never learned music, but she knew the tunes to the good old hymns. How appropriate her songs were! In the morning,—

> "Awake my soul, to meet the day;
> Unfold thy drowsy eyes."

Or,—

> "Once more, my soul, the rising day
> Salutes thy waking eyes."

Her sweet voice put life into the hymn; and the prayer that followed was surely heard in heaven.

As we had a farm, the clearing was hard, and I was kept close at work early and late. Almost as soon as I could reach the plow-handles, I was set to plowing. If I had not gone at least two rounds across a ten-acre field before sunrise, it was thought a late start.

This was before we ever heard of a Sunday-school, say in 1820. At that early day the Methodist preachers were almost our only expounders of God's Word. They faithfully followed the settlers, thirsting for the salvation of souls, almost regardless of pay. And what men of God they were!—John Collins, John Sale, Robert W. Finley, James B. Finley, his son, and many others of that noble stamp. Known almost as far as they could be seen by their saddle-bags, in which most of their valuables were carried, they traveled large circuits, often swimming swollen streams and enduring all manner of hardships, preaching almost daily, receiving only food and clothing. They were not hirelings, but shepherds caring for the sheep, and looking for their reward at the great day. I hope to see them crowned after the resurrection with crowns made by God's own hands.

In those times, the quarterly and two-days' meetings were institutions of Methodism. The fourth quarterly meeting was a camp-meeting. They were looked forward to with prayer as seasons of revival. I shall never forget my first camp-meeting! Henry B. Bascom was there in his youthful vigor. He was called "the Kentucky preacher;" was supposed to be the finest-looking man then living; was surpassingly eloquent, and fully baptized with the Holy Ghost. He preached the 11 o'clock sermon. The people for miles around were present, and made an immense crowd. I remember the man and the scenes better than the discourse. There was a death-like stillness, while both preacher and Spirit seemed to work upon the hearers. At the close, there was a call for seekers. The altar was filled with penitents, and others in groups all through the congregation were crying aloud for mercy. An old man and his wife find two sons and a daughter at the altar, crying, "Save, Lord; I perish!" The sons had persecuted the father, who now kneels between them, exhorting them with a voice almost like thunder to surrender all to God; the mother meanwhile equally engaged for her daughter. After a hard struggle, the blessing comes, and the prayers of children and parents are turned into praises. Add to this scene scores of similar ones, and the reader may have some idea of a camp-meeting more than sixty years ago.

Stimulated by the example of the Methodists, the Presbyterians, I believe, held series of services which they called "protracted meetings." Our protracted meetings were called "revivals." It is a blessed fact that our meetings were never "protracted" without becoming revivals. The coming of the presiding elder and the quarterly meeting was the sign of Pentecost. What wonder that this announcement came into general use: "We will begin a revival at this place at the next regular appointment?"

The presence of converted Indians fixed another camp-meeting indelibly in my mind. It was held on Big Darby Creek bottom, in the Chenoweth settlement. James B. Finley was presiding elder, and was in charge of the Indian Mission at Sandusky. The announcement that he would bring seven or eight converted Indians, called together an unusually large number. The first I saw of the Indians was when the horn sounded for morning service. The eight came out, clothed as white men, their long black hair combed down upon their shoulders; and, taking their seats, began, without book or notes, to sing, in their own tongue:

> "O how happy are they, who their Savior obey,
> And have laid up their treasure above!"

The long hymn was too short; for it was a feast to hear them sing. Those Indians had given up that part of the country, and now they were back, singing, with the spirit and the understanding, those hymns that were afterwards sung in every settlement, and called "the Indians' tunes."

One of the eight was a preacher; and was called up into the stand to preach. A Negro was interpreter. I do not remember much of the sermon. When interpreted, it seemed to come second-handed. Since then, several times I have tried to have my own talks interpreted to Mexicans, but the result was never satisfactory. The fire and power of the original, such as it was, never appeared in the translation.

This camp-meeting was a season never to be forgotten. Finley, just in his physical and spiritual prime, preached at 11 o'clock, and all through the day he seemed to move heaven and earth. The Holy Spirit was poured out, and scores were crying for mercy, and as many others shouting the praise of God. Some were stricken down with conviction, and lay like dead men, but would come to life again, shouting happy.

Scenes like this were common. The "jerks," a peculiar physical phenomenon connected with religious excitement, had mostly ceased. They began in Kentucky. At Cane Ridge Camp-meeting, held by the Presbyterians and Methodists, men fell by the scores. A physician thought he could raise them. He was called, and with his preparation of hartshorn went to work. But no sooner had he reached the fallen men, than he fell himself.

I remember to have seen but one case. It was that of a good woman—an own aunt of Hon. W. N. Byers, of Denver—who was strangely exercised. As two women held her, she jerked her head so violently, that her long hair became loosened and snapped like whip-crackers. Some called this "the falling fanaticism;" but, with others, I have thought that the times required some strange thing to awaken the Church and arouse the people, who were just out of Indian wars, almost without books to read, sadly neglectful of the Bible, and forgetful of God.

As I stated before, we had plenty of hard work; but mixed with it were the amusements peculiar to pioneer life. Among these was hunting. The forests abounded in raccoons, wild turkeys, and deer. Every boy was familiar with the use of the rifle—old-fashioned muzzle-loaders, powder-horn and charger, and patch and ball, and flint-lock.

When acorns failed, the raccoons ravaged our

corn-fields. That made sport for us boys. It was night-work, and all the more interesting on that account. My brother Robert and I would take a horse and our 'coon-dog, and seldom return empty-handed. We used no guns; but would tree the 'coon, climb after him, shake him off, and leave the dog to make the finish, which was not always an easy task, as the 'coon was capable of making an obstinate fight. On one occasion, we treed two on the same tree. As I climbed the tree, one jumped off, but the dog chased him up after me; so that I had one above and one below me. I succeeded in shaking them both off, far more easily than I have shaken off book-agents since then, and the dog quickly dispatched them. The same night we treed another on a large honey-locust, too full of thorns to climb. But there was a hackberry-tree by its side, by which I climbed above the worst of the thorns, and then got over on to the locust. The coon was at least sixty feet from the ground; but I followed him to the top and shook him off. He proved to be the largest one we ever caught. Never did I look to the top of that tree in day-time but the blood tingled to the end of my toes. I could not have climbed there in daylight. Money was scarce in those times, and 'coon-skins were almost currency at twenty-five cents apiece. So when we counted seven as the result of a single hunt, Robert and I felt "passing rich."

Deer-hunting was more to my notion, although my first experience was not calculated to inflate my pride. I espied a noble animal at a short distance, and was undiscovered. Never had boy a better chance; but a strange sensation possessed me. I was not frightened, but shook as in ague. I could not aim my rifle, or hold on the broadside of the deer, or even pull the trigger. The last I managed somehow finally to do, and at the crack of the gun the deer looked around to see what was up. I fell to loading again, but was unable for my shaking to bring the powder-horn and charges together. This brought me to my senses and settled my nerves; but the deer tired of waiting, and ran off.

In a little while there was another opportunity. This time it was a large buck. The fever did not come back. My nerves were steady. I took good aim and fired. The buck fell. I ran with knife in hand to cut his throat; but when within about twenty feet of him, he raised up his head, snuffed, and shook his big horns defiantly at me. Some blood on his back gave me the idea that the bullet had just creased him, and that he would be up and fight in a minute. Running to a big tree near by, I loaded again and shot him in the head. He was a splendid fellow, and made me forget my disgraceful "buck-fever."

My father was fond of hunting the deer at night on the water. The deer liked the moss that grew in the water, and was always attracted by a light. Placing a candle in the bow of a canoe, and setting up a screen behind it to conceal them, the hunters would paddle noiselessly down the stream until they discovered their game. This was an Indian way of hunting. Father once met Jonathan Alder and his Indian wife—known in the early history of Ohio—in their bark canoe, engaged in this sport. When I was about fourteen, he took me on such an expedition. We chopped down an elm-tree, made a canoe of its bark, and, just after dark, put out. Father sat in front and I behind, guiding the canoe with a smooth little pole, which I dared not lift out of the water, lest the drops would scare the game. We pushed along that way until we espied a deer. It raised its head; but the light blinded it, and we poled nearer until we could see it wink, when father shot it. The night, the water, the shadows of the forest, and the breathless stillness of the hunt, gave a certain charm to this mode; but somehow it never seemed quite so fair for the deer as the other way.

Scarcely second to hunting was our three-months' winter school. I think we appreciated the advantages, and improved them. But the three months of good times we had together brightened the whole year. Our games were rugged, and our tricks not always the gentlest. One of the latter was to bar out the teacher at Christmas, and dictate terms of admission, which usually were two days' vacation, time to be made up by him, and a treat at his expense of a quart or two of whisky. Some of the boys would take too much; so this treat fell into disrepute, and apples were substituted for it. Barring out, however, was continued until about 1825, when some of the parents who opposed it, joined forces with the teachers from New England, who were indignant at what they styled "a Western outrage," and put an end to the practice.

Spelling-matches between neighboring schools excited great interest. The school on Glade Run and ours once met half-way. Each side put up its picked ten. We were gaining rapidly, when the man who gave out the words was caught cheating us. This raised quite a disturbance; but we chose a man who lived on their side, in whose honesty we had confidence, and the contest went on, our side winning and my brother Robert bearing off the honors.

Our course of study included "the three R's" and orthography. One of my teachers, Edwin Cone, I recall with great pleasure. He was a good man, and inspired his scholars to do good work. When about eighteen, I was sent thirty miles to Marysville, Union County, in "the Big Woods," to study mathematics with a Mr. Phelps, the county surveyor. In the four months I was with him, I went as a hand occasionally, and thus secured practice as well as theory. This was of advantage to me in early times in Illinois.

Two years before this, the first Sunday-school ever held in our place, Georgesville, was organized. The exercises consisted mainly of learning and reciting chapters of the New Testament. Outside of the large towns, Central Ohio was slow in planting Sunday-schools.

CHAPTER II.

CONVERSION AND CALL TO THE MINISTRY.

IN the month of September, 1830, I attended a camp-meeting near Beech's Woolen Factory, in Madison County, where I joined the Church, and made my first public attempt to seek the salvation of my soul. My name was put on the class-book as a seeker on probation. I was fully resolved to seek until I found peace to my soul; but some way I dreaded the class-meeting, and feared it as though it would prove my ruin. But when the leader, Henry Clover, spoke to me with kind words of encouragement, and assured me that no sincere seeker was ever lost, my feelings completely changed. From that moment I have believed the class-meeting to be one of the greatest means of grace in the spiritual economy of our Church. I sought earnestly, embracing every opportunity to go forward for prayers; and when the camp-meeting was held again on our circuit, thanks be to God through Christ, I was made a new creature; my burden was rolled off, and I rested sweetly in my Savior.

This peace was destined to be of short duration. I was the only young person in my acquaintance who was even attempting to be religious. There was to be a social gathering, with "innocent plays." I found I had not given up the world. I was riding in the woods after dark, and the tempter pressed his arguments upon me: "No harm could come of it;" "Some Church-members frequented such resorts and allowed many such things;" "If I denied and separated myself from all such amusements, I would be a castaway from young society, and the subject of reproach." I concluded not to be so particular as to cause persecution to be hurled at me; a middle course would meet the case. Just then the Spirit left me as plainly as it came when I promised to forsake all sin and live for God and his cause. My hair seemed to rise, and I felt to see if my hat was not going off my head. Darkness pervaded my mind, and I repented of my wickedness and struggled back into the light. But that settled the question of worldly amusements for all time.

This was the fall of 1831, and I was in my twentieth year. After a long deliberation, my father had concluded to move to the prairies of Illinois. It had been thought that only what could be fenced could be farmed, and that the scarcity of timber would, therefore, limit the cultivated land to a small area. Nevertheless, we decided to go at least as far as the Illinois River. We had one large wagon, of the kind called later "prairie schooners," with four horses—which, as being the eldest of the eight children, I drove— and one two-horse wagon, both well-stocked with camp equipage, provisions, utensils, etc.

On the 6th of October we started on the journey. We went to the west line of Ohio; thence to

Greenville, White River, near Strawtown, Ind.; through "the Wilderness" and Wabash Prairies, to Danville; across a branch of the Grand Prairie to Bloomington, Ill., then a hamlet of about twenty-five houses; reached Pekin, November 6th, just one month out, where I saw my first steamboat; thence crossed over to the neighborhood of Canton, Fulton County, and settled near where Fairview now stands.

The journey was uneventful. The summer had been unusually wet, and the roads were very muddy. It was not uncommon to spend a week in going forty-five miles. The Wilderness was a flat beech-forest, forty miles with but one house, and no bottom to the roads; that is, it was mud down as far as we knew. Teams, with families camped, looked like a small camp-meeting. One evening, after supper, I strolled out among the groups of men around their camp-fires. The general topic of conversation was the depth of mud, each claiming that he had seen the worst. But one fellow said: "All that you have seen is nothing. I was looking ahead, and saw a plug hat on the mud, and thought I had a prize. As I got nearer, it seemed to have a man's head in it, which said, 'Let me alone, I have a good horse under me!'" That closed the conversation on that subject. I do not remember any bridges, but plenty of poles everywhere to pry out with. The sloughs on the Wabash Prairie were almost as bad as the Wilderness.

We spent the winter in looking over the country, with the view to a permanent location. In those before-railroad days, the great object was to settle on a navigable stream. We purposed settling on the Illinois or the Mississippi. Accordingly, a Mr. Day, my father, and myself, set out, about January 1, 1832, to examine the country up along the Mississippi. It was an almost unbroken wilderness. We passed Swartz's Grove, near where Abingdon now stands. In Monmouth there was only one house, occupied by a Mr. McNeal, the recorder of Warren County. Thence we went to Ellison Grove, Mr. Jarvis's, and stayed at Mr. Wells's. The next day we visited Pence's Fort. Mr. Pence and his family I shall not forget. My father would have bought his farm, but the title was uncertain, as the land was military.

We dared not cross our horses over Henderson River on the ice, as a January thaw had set in, and we feared the ice would go out. So we left them, and walked up the Mississippi to the Upper Yellow Banks, where New Boston was built. We found three houses in Mercer County, two of them contending for the above town-site. Two young married couples had moved out just before to a point eight miles east of the river, said to be a good place for a settlement. We walked out there. Meantime it had snowed about eight inches, and turned desperately cold. The newly married men had cut hay and hauled some logs for their house before they took their wives up, in the time of the thaw. They had raised their house up one story, cut out a place for the chimney, built a fire, and made clapboards as fast as they could, putting poles across inside. The roof was made of four courses of three-feet clapboards. On each side of the fire-place was what we called a Jackson bedstead, made of hickory poles, which answered a good purpose and was fashionable in those days. A blanket served for a door. It was stormy, and we asked to stay. They said: "You see we are caught in the storm just as you are; but we will do the best we can for you." They made us a bed on the ground-floor. After we had got into a sound sleep, one of the oxen pushed away the blanket, walked in and put his nose on my father's face, which aroused him. He threw up his hands, and the ox threw up his horns against the clapboard roof, which we thought was all coming down on us. But nobody was hurt, and after driving out the ox and securing the door with a pole, we managed to get some rest and sleep, notwithstanding the night was severely cold.

In the morning we had for breakfast fried pork, corn-bread, potatoes, and coffee made out of burnt corn-bread. Before night we longed for more of it, for we traveled all day till after dark without a bite to eat. We held a council of war that morning, and decided that we would make for Pence's Fork by the old lead-mine road, rather than go back the way we came. I have thought it was thirty miles through the grass and eight inches of snow. But there was no house this side, and we determined to go through. My father had been afflicted with sciatic rheumatism in one limb; and after tramping

about eight miles, he began to suffer and to fall behind, Mr. Day pushing on, and I about half-way
between them, with feelings which, though fresh, I
have no words to express.

We reached Pope River, and stopped to rest a
little. We had no means of building a fire, or we
would have stayed there. The frost was flying,
with a hard west wind. Father was compelled to
rest a little, and said: "You and Day go on, and you
get a horse and meet me." All I said to him was,
to keep in the road, which could be seen on the
bottom, the grass being tall on either side. It was
quite late in the afternoon, and a hard snowy road
twelve miles or more. Mr. Day and I started side
by side. It was for life, as I hardly expected to see
my father alive again. Before we got half-way,
Mr. Day proposed to slacken his pace and let me
go on. I reached the fort at dusk, and young Mr.
Pence saddled a horse and was off on a lope as
quick as possible. I could not have gone, as I was
all overdone, sweating, shivering with the cold;
but my anxiety was not abated until I saw my
father. He was met about five miles back. He
said that after we left he felt a little rested, and
walked on and felt better, but was so cold that he
grew sleepy; and when he got on the horse he had
to hold to the mane to keep from falling. Mr.
Day only got in a short time before him. Father
was shaking with cold, so that we had to help him
off. Mrs. Pence brought him a good cup of coffee;
but he shook so with cold and fatigue that it had
to be put to his mouth. He was soon warmed,

and found that he was not frozen, except that his nose and one cheek were frost-bitten. I had never been so tired and cold before, never had such a burden rolled off, and never experienced such thankfulness.

That was one of the hardest day's travel I ever have had, and I feel yet that it was through the goodness of God that I was enabled to endure it. We rested a day or two, and returned home, and settled as above stated.

In the spring of 1832 the renowned Black Hawk war broke out, about the time grass was so that stock could live on it. Almost all the young men, and some of the old ones, volunteered as rangers to fight Indians. I was anxious to go, but we were new-comers, and much depended on raising a crop. Rails were to be made and hauled, and my father thought he could spare neither a man nor a horse; but promised that, as soon as we could get the spring work done, I could go. He thought there was not much danger, and staid all alone on his place. There was not a man within six miles who did not leave at times. He said that when we saw a man running, and crying, and saying the Indians had killed all but him, then it would be time enough to run.

Some time in June, Major Foster, a recruiting officer, with a number of men that had come in on furlough, was to start up to Gum's Fort, on the waters of Henderson River. I took gun and ammunition, and a good horse, and joined them at Canton.

About a dozen men of us set out for the seat

of war. Mr. Westerfield, a man of good repute, came an hour behind, and concluded to overtake us, but had only ridden about one mile north of Canton, near the house of Captain Barnes, when he heard a man, who afterwards proved to be one familiarly known as Father Thurman, chasing a coyote wolf with his horse and dogs, hallooing at the top of his voice every jump. Mr. Westerfield heard it, but could not see for a skirt of timber; and as big Indian was on his mind, he turned his horse back for town, and cried at the top of his voice, "The Indians are killing Barnes's family!" and everybody believed it. In a few minutes a fort was commenced, and word sent to every family near but Mr. Barnes. Of course every body ran to Canton. Creeks were out of their banks. One horse was drowned, and some members of families that were in delicate health were injured.

It is strange how scared men will act. The first man Mr. Westerfield met was a Mr. Coleman, who had a store and horse-mill, a lame boy attending the mill, just across the road. He did not even call his boy; turned the key on his store, mounted a horse which a customer had hitched to the rack, put his plug hat under him, as there was no saddle, and galloped down the road with Wester-field, crying the alarm. About three miles down the road they met a Mr. F——, who, on hearing the news, was so scared, that he ran into his house, took what change he had, left his wife and family, and never stopped until he got to Ross's

Ferry, on the Illinois River, and actually rode into the river to meet the ferry-boat, such was his fright.

It is plain to be seen that men ought to know the facts before they give any alarm at a time of excitement. As my father and family lived eight miles out, and Barnes's place was on the road, they heard nothing of it till they heard both sides at once, and kept quietly at their work. I was out fifteen or twenty days, saw the rangers and country, was well persuaded that the Indians would rather be west of the Mississippi River, and concluded not to volunteer, but returned to hear. of Westerfield's defeat, as it was called.

Several times during the summer it was reported that Indians were within a few miles of us. I will mention one more scene. There was what was called Babbit's Settlement, north-west of Canton some twenty-five miles. Five or six families had quietly stuck to their farms. One of their number, a Mr. Cox, went out to hunt a two-year-old colt that was not bridle-wise, and got back with it just at dusk. In his absence, two or three soldiers on a furlough from the army, called to stay over night. As he came near the house, he heard strange voices, and at once thought it was Indians, and was sure they had killed his wife and children. In his grief and alarm he struck out for Canton on the colt, crying, supposing his wife and children were brutally murdered. About half-way, with a man he had met, he passed Mr. Zebulon Foster's, waked them up, and told them that the Indians had killed his family. When asked for particulars, they swore it was true, and started at half speed. Well, the family got up a yoke of oxen, notified a widow and family, and started the same way at midnight. Mr. Cox alarmed the people with his cries and tears as far as he could, and by nine o'clock they had sixty men with arms to go out to war. In the meantime, after she had given the soldiers—the innocent cause of all this alarm—their supper, Mrs. Cox became very uneasy, fearing that her husband had been thrown from his colt and killed or crippled. She induced her guests to go in search of him in the night. They soon got tired and rode on to Canton, and hearing of Mr. Cox's trouble, found him and told him that his wife was very uneasy about him, and that he had better go home. This was the end of another Indian scare. As the road was three miles from our place, my father fortunately did not see the man, or he, too, would have been constrained to flee for safety.

This was a summer of almost constant excitement. Black Hawk and his band were whipped, and fifty miles of territory ceded to the United States on the west side of the Mississippi River, all that was then thought we should ever want.

Illinois having proved to be wonderfully rich in soil and natural advantages, about this time experienced a great influx of population and a wonderful rise in property.

We read in the papers of the first railroad in

New York. I asked my father what he thought of such a project—flat iron rails for steam-cars. He thought a moment, and said it might pay between large cities, but the expense would be too great to build through the country. The old gentleman lived to ride on such a road from Illinois to the Rocky Mountains.

From 1834 to the spring of 1837, times were good, and speculation ran high. But the awful crash financially, in 1837, broke up thousands. Only men that had a surplus of money and were out of debt, stood the shock. No money could be had on credit for less than twelve per cent, and property and produce were not worth anything to speak of. I hauled one load of good wheat thirty-five miles to Peoria, and could get only twenty-five cents a bushel. Pork was sold from $1.25 to $1.50 a hundred pounds. The farmer had to run all over a village to sell a few pounds of butter at six cents a pound, and take it in calico. Eggs were three cents a dozen.

Everything but the Churches stood still. The Methodist Church was far in the lead. We had valiant men that led the hosts of Israel—Peter Cartwright, Peter Akers, John Sinclair, Henry Summers, the Hobarts, the Haneys, Wilson Pitner, Peter R. Borein, John Morey, and a host of others.

There was no regular circuit preaching in the northern part of Fulton County, Illinois, till the fall of 1832. Then the Rev. Peter R. Borein came to us in the spirit of his Master. It was his first circuit. He acquitted himself well, and was known only to be loved and respected. Just before his arrival, Brother Carter, who was a kind of missionary among us, held a camp-meeting at Canton. I suppose the ground is all covered with buildings now. He was assisted, I think, by Rev. A. D. West, a located preacher, Brothers Jordan and Joel Arrington, all of precious memory. Attendance was large, and much good was done.

I had been under a heavy cloud for a year, although I had often walked five miles to class-meeting, and always took part in the prayer-meetings when asked to do so. I resolved at this meeting to have the cloud of darkness raised, and to seek and look for all that God had in store for me through Christ's all-cleansing blood. Hard was the struggle, and not until Monday morning at the altar, almost in despair, I looked away from self and all but Christ and him crucified. Just then I was enabled to receive the blessing at his hand; was taken from the mire of sin and unbelief; a new song was put in my mouth, and I made no apology for shouting, "Glory! glory!" for a full salvation to my soul! I started for a local preacher; but he escaped me. He told me afterwards he was too cold to meet one so baptized by the Holy Ghost. I believe the whole work was done at one blast, as I never could question the fact that God could justify and sanctify at the same time; and I believe it is often done.

But I soon came down from the mount of transfiguration, and was confronted with one of the most fearful temptations of my life. I was cutting house-logs, my brother hauling them. I could more than keep him going, and improved my spare moments reading my Bible. I opened at Job, and read the book through. The thought of his trials, and that mine should be like them, brought great distress upon me. I looked backward and forward over life, and feared I should not be able to endure the test. All at once the thought came: "I am fully prepared, and it would be better to die now, and go to the land of the blessed and sing the songs of heaven forever." And knowing no other way to get off honorably, I set in to pray: "O God, if it can be, consistently with thy will, take me speedily to thyself, while I feel thou art mine and I am thine." For a time my prayer was a constant entreaty to him, until it became an agony. I often thought of the Apostle Paul's three prayers for God to take the thorn out of his flesh. His faith and zeal moved his Lord to give an answer, and stopped his intercession. So in my case, God put an end to my prayers for death. While kneeling at the root of a tree, far from any one but God and the supplicant, while in an agony, wrestling like Jacob of old, with the desire to get away from the trials of earth to an eternal home, just behind me I heard a voice, saying: "Your work is not done; go ye into all the world and preach the gospel." The boy, seeking to be liberated by death, instantly turned around to see who was there; for it seemed impossible that any one should be near. Suffice it to say, it turned the seeker's mind to meditation on a subject to which he had never given a serious moment of reflection before; and never again did he try to bring death by prayer.

Soon after this I was prevailed upon to take a class, by my pastor, Rev. Peter R. Borein, although it seemed to be a great undertaking. I tried to live a Christian life, and thought much on the subject of the ministry. I had an overwhelming sense of my inability, arising from my lack of educational advantages; and had often said that I would rather be anything than a poor Methodist preacher. Soon after this I was licensed as an exhorter, my license being written by Peter Cartwright. This was the first step toward preaching. I was also one of the circuit stewards. Our members, and the people generally, were at fault as to pastoral support, and I used to stir up their minds on that subject.

We came to the third quarterly meeting. Revs. N. G. Berryman and Rufus Lumery were on the Canton Circuit, with Rev. Henry Summers presiding elder. The quarterly conference was composed of nearly forty members. The claims of our preachers were hardly half paid, the presiding elder in the same condition. As there was no missionary money for him, and he had to take his pay in proportion with the preachers, he had the unpleasant task of holding up the claims of needy preachers on each occasion. On the present occasion we were brought to a stand. In our history no preacher had received all of his scanty allowance. Hard times were pleaded as an excuse. The writer made his first breeze in quarterly conference by moving a resolution that a bill be made out against each class, according to their numbers and ability, and that each leader collect it or pay it, and for once pay our preachers in full. We had a mighty stir; but all except one leader agreed to try, and on the fourth quarter we met the claims. I had to put up ten dollars out of my own cash.

In our early settlement, the people were thrown together from all quarters of our country. We became acquainted with Zebulon Foster and family, who had been among the first settlers of Fort Washington, now Cincinnati, Ohio; and our acquaintance resulted in my marriage with Miss Harriet Foster, his youngest daughter; and his youngest son, Harvey Foster, to my oldest sister. We were married by Rev. H. Summers on the 4th of December, in the year of our Lord 1833. I, of course, felt that the best of the bargain was on my side, and, in fact, have never had reason to change my mind. She was of a sweet disposition, a member of the Methodist Episcopal Church, and walked worthy of her profession. Our marriage resulted in five children—three boys and two girls.

In 1844 I took my family to Wisconsin, and settled in Potosi, where, on July 14, 1847, my wife died in full assurance of hope; and where I buried by her side, two months later, our youngest daughter, a babe of thirteen months. Our other children reached maturity. My wife's death almost crushed my spirits. In addition to this, I was financially broken up, and had nothing but my hands to depend upon. I was working lead-mines, or rather, prospecting. My misfortunes, however, were only temporal. I had faith in God's goodness and promises, and did not think for a moment but that the Giver of all good gifts would help in the hour of distress.

Very soon I struck a streak of mineral, which brought several hundred dollars, and greatly helped me financially ; and, indeed, we never were without the real necessities of life. My loneliness drove me to thoughts of marriage. There was a widow about my age near by. I proposed marriage, and was accepted. It transpired that she had been twice married before—the last man dead, the first one still living, and that they had never been divorced. I was not informed of the facts in the case. Of course matters came to light. Our union was not congenial before, and when the situation was understood, I felt it wrong to live in that relation. I expected a separation, and in nine months obtained a divorce in Lancaster, Grant County, Wisconsin. But I have never forgiven myself. My marriage was too hasty. I did not give myself time carefully and prayerfully to ponder my steps. I would say here that the divorce was not got in order to marry again. I felt that I had disgraced myself with my family and friends, and was brought very low in spirits. Our preacher, Rev. F. Smith, of Wisconsin Conference, came around, and I told him to take up the case, and have a committee of Church members to investigate the matter—as I was class-leader—so that the Church might be relieved as far as possible. He did so, and they acquitted me. Although I suffered severely, I found no place for repentance for my great mistake. Sorrow was upon me such as I never felt before. I was humiliated in life and in the sight of God.

Soon after this, we left Potosi, and went to Lost Grove, near Mineral Point, as I was still prospecting in the lead-mines. I took my Church letter as an exhorter. Rev. Henry Summers, presiding elder, was an old friend, and helped me, as I was a stranger. Soon the way opened for me to exercise my gifts as an exhorter in my own neighborhood and in other places, and the brethren gave me license as a local preacher, notwithstanding I objected. I thought I was as far along as I ought to go, but was overruled. I feared they had almost spoiled an exhorter. This was in 1849. Here I was enabled to make enough to rise out of all my financial difficulties. My sister Rachel kept house for us, and, as a family, we were all at home, with my brother Robert, as we were in company mining, and were as comfortable and happy as we could be under the circumstances.

In the fall we moved to Mineral Point, so that my poor children could have the benefit of a good school. We carried on our work in the mines, and frequently tried to preach.

This year, Rev. J. M. Snow was on the Mineral Point charge, and he had a plan that embraced all the local preachers, and by which, every four weeks, I was to preach in the old stone Church in his presence. My first attempt I well remember. All the week I could not get my mind on any subject. The time came, and the attempt must be made. After the preliminaries, I announced the text. Suddenly I became so blind that I could scarcely see or utter a word. After trying for some minutes, I said, "Brother Snow, you must preach." But he said, "Go on," and I tried again; but soon said, "I will quit," and sat down. As I retired, I saw that everybody's eyes were straining at me. You may believe that the preacher felt as if he could have crawled out at an auger-hole, if there had been any. Brother Snow talked a little, and dismissed. As the people left, it was discovered that three or four penitents were weeping, and not willing to leave without prayers. We continued with them till they were all converted. Then the preacher in charge said he had been blessed, and was looking for a revival. Then the Sunday-school superintendent got up, and said that he had been praying, and that his prayers had been answered. Then Brother Dyer got up, and said he felt like a poor boy at a frolic—he had not a word to say.

But be it said, to the glory of God, that the meetings were continued, and there were more than forty souls set at liberty. The series of meetings which was to have begun in two weeks, started that night. It was a good work, and my own family shared largely in the blessings that

God showered upon us. They called it my breakdown. Although I failed often, I never so entirely failed as at that time. It was a great trial. The next Sunday evening, in the same place, three hundred crowded the house. When I announced the text, I looked up, and every eye was on the preacher. He said: "I suppose you all remember last Sunday night's failure; but I am not convinced that there is no preach in me yet." This brought a smile to many a face, and we set out with unusual liberty.

Soon after this, Rev. E. Yocum, presiding elder, called on me to go as a supply to one of his circuits; but under the circumstances, I declined, and my brother Thomas and I started to Yellow Stone to our mines, with a good buggy animal; but she became frightened, and kicked all about our heads, and tore almost everything to pieces. It looked like a providence that one or both of us were not killed; but neither of us was hurt.

I had been gloomy all day, and after the above escape, felt worse, and slept but little through the night. Next day I was with a hired man, helping to sink a prospect shaft. I was in the ground about thirty feet, but was exceedingly sad, and grew worse, until I had no power to work. My feelings were awful. Panting for breath, I sat down in the shaft, and said: "O Lord, what ails me?" Just then a hundred promises which I had made, that if ever the way opened I would go and preach the gospel, rushed to mind; and now, though the way was open, I had refused. Two things were in the way. The first was that divorced woman, and the belief that, if I went, the cause would be injured and myself disgraced. Then came this text: "If you eat any deadly thing, it shall not hurt you." The other was the fact that I had one son at Lawrence University, and wanted to educate the other children, and my prospects were fair to do so. Then came the words: "Every one that hath forsaken houses, or brethren, or sisters, or father, or mother, or children, for my name's sake, shall receive a hundred-fold, and shall inherit everlasting life." The response was: If deadly poison will not kill, I will leave the children to God's care, and go. The best of the bargain on my side—eternal life.

It was now all settled. I put pick and shovel into the tub, stepped in, and said, "Hoist," and my man took me up out of the pit. He asked me what it meant. I told him I was going to quit work for awhile. When we got to the cabin for dinner, I said to my brother Robert: "I am going to try to preach the gospel." He said, after a moment's reflection, quoting Davy Crockett: "Be sure you're right, then go ahead;" and go I did, and reported myself to the presiding elder. He sent me a note with directions where to meet him, and instructions to help Rev. A. H. Walter on the Wingville and Lancaster work; altogether a different direction from where I was first asked to go. This suited me better. The work went within seven miles of where I had lived, and Lancaster was where the divorce was granted. The reader may guess how any one would feel, six months after, to be in the court-house well-filled with people, as there were no church buildings in the place. The writer relied on the promise—poison will not kill you—and suffice it to say, we had a good meeting. The people seemed well pleased to see me, and I thanked God and took courage.

When I went on that work with Brother Walter, it was four months till conference. In that time we received over one hundred into the Church, most of them happily converted. Brother Walter was quite a revivalist. The head of Platte, in Clifton's settlement, and Fenimore were the best works. We began a meeting at Franklin, a mining town. After a week's time, some difficulties arose in the place, and Brother Walter said we had better quit; but I was to stay another day. The school-house had been crowded, and a certain young man took a chair to have a seat. A rowdy fellow said: "What are you going to do with your chair?" He replied: "I am going to the mourner's bench." He answered: "I will bet you a quarter." Jim as readily replied: "I will stand you;" and they put up the money. Sure enough, when the call was made, up he came with others; but we were none the wiser of his object. The next day the saloon-keepers had their fun. A friend told me of the situation. We had the appointment given out for the evening, and I was prepared as well as possible, and did not think he could hurt me while I was in the line of duty. When the time came to call seekers, I spoke of the meanness of any man that

would come on the bet of a quarter; such a creature would sell his soul for a sixpence, spend it for
whisky, and go to the devil at last. But several
came, and the same fellow came again, of course,
for he had money at stake. I said: "Sing a verse."
At the close, the preacher stepped up to Jim,
slipped his hand in his collar, and said: "You came
here last night on the bet of a quarter." He replied: "But I did not spend it for whisky."
"Well," said the preacher, "I believe that is your
business," and pulled him up, and said: "You put
for the door, or I will put you out at the window."
The fellow said: "You asked me here for prayers,
and I want you to pray for me." The preacher
said: "You must pray for yourself." "I can't
pray." "But you *must*, I will teach you; say, God
have mercy on me, a sinner." By a little squeez-
ing of his neck, he was induced to say the prayer,
but spoke very low. He was asked to pray louder,
and said his prayer so that all in the house could
hear. He did not cease till we closed.

The house was crowded; but while the above
scene was passing, you might have heard a pin
drop. That fellow never troubled us again, and a
talk was given on the principle of such a course.
The man who bet with him, came and apologized
to the preacher, and promised to do so no more.
Some good was done. The writer was pastor a
year after that, and never again was intruded upon
by rowdies. This was the spring of 1851. After
about four months as a supply, the quarterly conference proposed to recommend me as a suitable

person for the traveling connection. On account
of my age and the circumstances that surrounded
me, I felt quite safe in the thought that the conference would not take me. Their decision I would
accept as settling the whole question. I had but
one request to make the presiding elder—not for
a good appointment—but, if I was received, not
to send me away from where I was acquainted.
But, to my surprise, I was admitted into the Wisconsin Conference and appointed to Elk Grove
Circuit, a part of it in the same county, Platteville District—my old friend, Elmore Yocum, presiding elder.

Chapter III.

ADMITTED TO CONFERENCE.

I WAS the first admitted of the class of twenty-three, in the year 1851, at Waukesha, and I thought it would have been more appropriate for me to have been at the other end. The next Sabbath I was on my work. Found about ninety members and probationers. Brother Samuel Leonard had preceded me. We had eight appointments on the two weeks' circuit, three on each Sunday, all kept up. We had three good revivals, not by might nor by power, but by the Spirit of God. During the year we doubled our numbers with converts. We had one camp-meeting, which I shall not forget. E. Yocum, A. Brunson, and Brother Fraser, a good local preacher, did most of the preaching.

During the progress of the meeting we had some rain; but at Potosi, where my divorced woman lived, a cloud burst at the head of Snake Hollow, causing a flood to do much damage. She, being alone, was alarmed; ran to a near neighbor's, and it was thought that, on her return, some drift-wood caught her; for in the morning she was found in a drift, one-quarter of a mile below. Poor, unfortunate woman! if she had remained in her house, the sad occurrence would not have happened. She was the only one drowned.

This was a year of hard work; but it paid well spiritually, both for myself and the Church. I had many good friends; but as I was well known, and had some interest in the mines, they thought the preacher was rich. I received a single man's quarterage—one hundred dollars—with four children and sister Rachel to provide for; about half enough to keep us. Elias, my second son, was taken with white-swelling, which made him a cripple for life. Doctor's bills and all, three hundred dollars to square accounts it took for the year, over and above all I got on the charge.

Our Conference this year was held at Fond du lac. I passed the first year's study, and was continued on trial, and appointed to Franklin and Wingville Circuit, where I had been a supply, to help Brother A. H. Walter. Found good friends there, who had borne with me two years before. Among others, there was an old Brother Lincoln. He would shout at meeting or at work. Rev. S. C. Thomas, presiding elder, came to the charge to hold quarterly meeting. Brother Lincoln would say, "Glory!" as the service went on. The new presiding elder stopped, and said: "If that brother can refrain from shouting, I would be glad; but if he can't, let him shout." The brother said, "Glory to God for the privilege of shouting;" and of course he made use of his privilege. He was a good blacksmith, and every time he laid down the hammer he would say, "Glory!" On one occasion, a man brought a bad horse to be shod. The horse had been tried and given up. He swore he would take him to old Lincoln. Lincoln knew nothing of the horse's wickedness, took hold of his foot, and was thrown a somersault on some old irons in the corner of his shop. He jumped up, clapped his hands, and said, "Glory to God! he did n't hurt me a bit!" and took up the horse's foot, and shod him. The wicked man said Lincoln had a right to shout as much as he pleased. I noticed his obituary; his last word was a shout of "Glory!"

Brother Henry Wood preceded me here, a conference classmate, a good man and true. He has since passed to his reward.

We had revivals at several points on this circuit; the largest at Newman's Mills, in a stone school-house. After it was over, I remembered a dream I had some time before. In my vision I was fishing, saw quite a school of fish, and had them in close quarters. At first I could not catch any, but finally succeeded in making a large haul. I held meetings for two weeks; no one would make a start, although the house was crowded every night. I did my very best, but at the end of two weeks I knew not what to do. After we had a few prayers, I concluded to divide the house. The stove was in the middle. I talked a little, and told the singer, Thomas Kirkpatrick, to select a hymn. I then proposed to divide the house; all that were trying to serve God, and any that would seek the salvation of their souls, to come to the front; and all that were careless and wicked to take the other end. It seemed they were mixed. Both sides started, and they passed each other. It was a solemn scene, a comment on the great day and the final separation, every man taking his place in heaven or hell. I gave out meeting for the next night, and dismissed the congregation. God worked meantime, and when the invitation was next given, fifteen came at once, and within a few days over forty. It was what we called a good meeting. Some hard cases were converted and joined the Church.

We visited an old man and his wife. They had been members long before, but were careless. The man was honest; said he knew when the Spirit left him, and after that had never felt concerned for the salvation of his soul; was altogether without feeling on the subject. I asked to pray with them. They had two farms. The man said: "This place belongs to the old lady. I have nothing to say." The old lady said: "You know this is your house as much as it ever was." He said he did not control it; and both cared so little that they would not say they were willing, only: "You can do as you please." I said: "Let us pray." They were quiet, but the old man did not quit smoking his old pipe. I asked them to come to meeting, but neither promised to come. I left them to do as they pleased.

I saw the fulfillment of my dream. It was very hard to get the work started; but when the penitents came, it was all at once. We had nearly one hundred conversions on the circuit that year.

Our conference in 1853 was held by Bishop Scott at the town of Baraboo. Quite a pleasant session. All of our class present were admitted. There was a camp-meeting of some interest, held at the time of the conference, a half mile out of town. Chauncey Hobart was to preach the missionary sermon. I fell in with him on the way out, and he was shaking like an aspen-leaf. I asked why he was so nervous, as he was accustomed to preaching. "O," he said, "it is easier to get a reputation than to keep it." He was a six-footer, and when he began to speak, it seemed to me he twisted down a little; but began to rise as he proceeded, and before, or at the close, his length was all there, and, in addition, his long arms reaching up toward heaven, having the full attention of the whole camp-meeting, and of the conference in the bargain. He was sick, and not able to leave when the preachers left. I have always thought that it was the overstraining of his nerves and the labor of delivering that sermon that caused his sickness, and detained him for several days.

I received my appointment at the above session to Fayette Circuit, with Brother B. Crist as colleague. It was a large four weeks' circuit. We had a pleasant year working together; enlarged the circuit, had a good revival at Willow Springs, and some interest at other points. Had a good camp-meeting. Rev. S. C. Thomas, our presiding elder, with Brother Haughawout and others, were on the ground.

It seemed that we had more than our share of difficulties to settle; and, in addition, in the winter the small-pox broke out at Centerville in one of our best societies, and two members died. We could have no services for months. Then the cholera broke out in August and September, in different places on the work, and cut off nearly twenty. This cast a gloom and fear over almost all classes of people. At Wiota, all of one family died, and the neighbors got together and burnt the house with the dead bodies in it. This was before the days of cremation, so far as I know, or it would not have looked so horrible. In cases of burial, it seemed that the people thought the bodies could not be interred soon enough after death, and it was doubtful if some were not buried alive. At Fayette, where we lived, three of one family died; only one little girl was left.

Brother and Sister Benson, both members of our Church, were called away. The mother was taken first. I visited her. She was in extreme pain, but was resigned to the will of God. In twenty-four hours she died. I was with her to the last. It was warm weather, and at nine o'clock in the evening we sent out for help, as she was a large woman. Only Aunt Polly Journey came. My sister was at home with my sick daughter, and I sent for her. Nathan Woodberry also came, and as the bedroom was too small, we carried the corpse out in front of the house, and laid her out. Two or three had been dispatched to dig the grave. Her husband had sent to have a coffin, as he feared the people would want to bury her without one. But he need not have feared, for scarcely one could be got near the house. Mr. Woodberry got a wagon and team, and we went a half mile for the coffin. It was not quite done. This was Monday night, and I tried to preach three times the day before. I lay down in the shavings and slept till the coffin was done, when I was awaked and ready for service. About day-break there were just enough of us to perform the burial of the poor woman so suddenly called to death. Just before she breathed her last, the little boy was taken down, and within twenty-four hours he was buried. I was not there, as I had been called to attend a funeral.

On the next Monday I was sent for, to go and see Brother Benson. He was at his brother-in-law's, one and a half miles away, down in the timber, and had the cholera. I carried him some medicine, as the doctor could not go. We worked over him all day till about dark. His brother-in-law and I were the only ones to attend on him. We tried to encourage him, but he seemed to expect to die. He suffered intensely, and about dark breathed his last. His brother-in-law said: "You are older than I; you must stay, and I will go for help." He went to the village, and no one would go; all prayed to be excused. Sister Nancy Smith, a good and brave woman, said if the men would not go, she would raise some women to go. This stirred two men to go with Woodberry. By the time they got the coffin it was dark.

It was a rainy night, with thunder rumbling. I was left to myself, and laid him out as best I could; wrapped him in a sheet, and sat down on the opposite side of the room, musing all alone. Just then he began to move his hands and one foot. I went to him and spoke to him, but he was dead; the cramp worked on his nerves. He moved one hand up to his shoulder, and the other downward; raised one knee six inches. His limbs could not be moved any more. All the light we had was a little old tin lamp—hog's-lard for oil—and that almost gone. I could find no more about the house, and the light was not larger than a man's finger-nail. As it was after midnight, I looked up toward the road. It was raining, but presently I saw a light coming, and sat down to see how they would proceed, when they drove up to the door, which was open. One of them said: "I guess Brother Dyer is gone." I stepped to the door, and spoke. They seemed much relieved, came in, and asked me what we had better do. There were men digging the grave. I told them I did not wish to bury him so soon, nor in the night. He had been moving since we thought him gone. We put the corpse into the coffin, and laid the cover over all but his face; then we went home and slept. In the morning I took my horse and buggy, and asked several to go with me, but without success. At last we met Brother Horace Woodworth, a Free-will Baptist preacher, and he did not refuse. He and Brother John Ethridge, and Brother John Roberts, took the corpse in their wagon, and buried it in daytime beside his wife and child, assured that they were safely landed together in the heavenly home, to die no more.

I would say just here, that I had always been afraid of the cholera till it came where I was; but then I could discharge any duty that I was called to perform without any fear whatever. On the night referred to above, the man that was with me took asafetida about as thick as cream every little bit, and offered it to me; but I told him I dreaded it as much as the cholera. I felt, and still feel, great thankfulness to God for his sustaining grace.

During this year we had three appointments for each Sunday. I was called on to preach at a funeral on Sunday morning. It was not in the direction of either of the services. The messenger said they wanted it early. I told him if they could meet me at their school-house at nine o'clock, I would be there. This would enable me to get to my appointment at Fayette at eleven, a six miles' ride. They were all on hand, and we were not long preaching the child, through the great atonement of our Lord Jesus Christ, to eternal rest, and in giving the parents and weeping friends a warm exhortation to be sure to meet it in heaven. At half-past two o'clock I preached at Vanmeter's, and at half-past five at Yellowstone, near Brother G. Hall's. I went home with Brother Robert and family for the night, and we all slept so soundly that a thief got in through the kitchen window, and stole brother's gold watch and chain, a few dollars in change, about sixty dollars' worth of silver-ware, and, to cap the whole, took my boots, the finest pair I ever had made— French calf-skin. I could get nothing to wear home but a pair of buckskin moccasins. We closed up the year satisfactorily to the most of our leading members, and considerably enlarged our circuit.

Our conference was held this year, 1854, at Janesville. Bishop Morris presided. We had a pleasant time. The old Fayette Circuit was divided, and the southern part formed into the Wiota or State Line Mission. I was appointed there, and lived at Wiota. The circuit extended down the Picatonica River some ten miles.

About the first of the year my horse got away, and I was inquiring after him, and night came on. Went to a house, and they sent me to a local preacher's. I asked to stop. He said they had no accommodations. Brother Ed. Russell. was with me. I told him we could sleep on the floor, or put up with any sort of fare. He still persisted. So we had to plod our way four miles through the dark to Winslow. He did not ask my name, and I did not tell him. We went off singing a hymn. When he found out who we were he never forgave himself. I thought I would teach him not to turn away strangers. We found the horse, and got home, and made or formed the circuit. There had scarcely ever been a preacher over most of our work.

Many of the people were, or thought they were,

infidels. Of course they were practically without Christianity. We took in the town of Gratiot, a small place, where they were nearly all professed infidels. They had a neat little school-house. The first time we had service, there were twenty-five or thirty in attendance. The preacher was a stranger. After we closed, one whom we will call Mr. C——, stepped up and introduced himself, and invited me to his house; said I would be welcome to such as he had, for which I thanked him. I can not afford to lose the incident, and do not wish to give any offense, as this was the beginning of a social acquaintance. We could not agree as to the Bible and religion; but I retain a warm regard for him and his family, and my prayer is that God will yet save him and his. When I called he wanted to feed me, but would have no blessing nor prayer at his house. He had a large table, and stood at the end, talking incessantly, and carved and helped our plates. By this time I concluded to say nothing. After supper he talked infidelity, got the folks almost all to bed, then politely offered to light me to bed. Next morning at breakfast it was the same way. When I left he asked me back.

Some time after this we had a two days' meeting. Brother Lawson, a local preacher, was with me. On Sunday, after service, we both went to take dinner, but no place for a blessing. He was very pleasant. I had to go in the evening to Chapman's school-house to fill an appointment. When I was about ready to go, I said, "Mr. C——,

I have partaken of your hospitality, and as there has been no opportunity to pray, if you will permit me to pray before we part, I will feel grateful." "Well, Mr. Dyer, I have said there should be no praying in my house." "I can't help that; I felt it my duty to ask you, and I wish the privilege." "It won't do any good; things will go on just the same; but if my friends are willing, I will not object." A neighbor was in, his mother-in-law, an old woman, and the hired girl. His wife told her to call in the children and shut the outer door, but not the partition door, for that would make too close quarters. That done, I knelt and prayed with the family, and I think that all felt better. The next time I came he requested me to ask a blessing, and we had prayer, and passed the year the best of friends. When the new preacher came on, he introduced himself to him, and invited him to come to his house, but added: "I don't want any prayer; when Mr. Dyer was here he prayed, and they got it all around that I was converted." I hope he has been before this, for I desire to meet him in heaven.

I was deeply exercised and earnestly prayed for help, and to be guided by the Spirit of God. About the first of December, 1854, while committing myself to God for success, I dreamed I was fishing with a seine, in company with others. We caught fish, and divided them into piles. I thought I got a good string of them; but when I got the last one, it was so large that it reached down and covered all the rest. A Baptist preacher preached every other Sunday, and a Primitive Methodist preached occasionally, and I in the evening. But the Baptist preacher made fun of a Methodist revival, and the other engaged elsewhere; so I went it alone the first week, and was having some stir among the dry bones. The Baptist preacher came and seemed pleased, and was evidently uneasy, for we had two converts of Baptist families. He helped, and the meeting resulted in thirty conversions; and when we came to divide the converts, I took in eighteen at nearly the close, and the others got seven. Still there were three that had not come in. They were beset in almost every way to join the Baptists; but, on the eve of closing, Brother Chapman asked me if I was not going to give another chance to join the Church. "Yes," I replied, "if I thought any one wanted to come in." He said there had been quite a desire to have him join one of the other Churches, but he had made up his mind from the first to join the Methodist, but had put it off for fear it might check the progress of the meeting. But now he and his family would join, if we would take them. When I got him on the string, I thought of my dream. This was a most gracious revival. To God be all the glory. Brother Chapman had found fault because we made too much noise, or preached too loud.

At the end of the first week I took Sister Rachel to be with us Sunday, and went to stay over night with him. Before retiring, he laid the Bible down, and said: "You read and let your sister pray; she do n't pray quite so loud as you do." This was before he had made a start to seek his soul's salvation; but when, a few evenings after, he came late with Mr. Richardson, and stood at the door, the invitation for seekers being given, he said audibly: "Richardson, let's go." Richardson said he would not. "Well, I have made up my mind to go." The crowd gave way, and he never stopped till he reached the stand. He prayed loud and strong, till God in mercy met him; and as soon as he felt the burden of his sins was gone, the love of Christ filled his soul, and he exclaimed, "Hallelujah!" like rumbling thunder. Let me say, it was a quiet meeting till then. Chapman honored God and his cause as long as I knew him, and was one of the most consistent shouters, at home and everywhere, I ever knew; and if I am so blessed as to reach heaven, I will hear him in glory. Bless God for the prospect! There was a Brother Fleharty here, who had been an early settler in Wisconsin, and had exercised his talent as a local preacher, and was very useful and devotedly pious for a number of years, but for some cause had ceased to preach, settled here, and had no connection with the Church. He liked to have me come and stay with him. He attended our services, and his youngest son, a young man, professed religion and joined the Church; with which he was well pleased.

He related an example of answer to prayer. Being acquainted with both of the parties, I related it to my family at home, and my second son, E. F. Dyer (about fifteen years old), laid up with white-swelling, wrote the account for the papers, as follows:

In the early settlement of Southern Wisconsin, a certain Brother F—— settled in the mining district, on the head-waters of Platte River, and proceeded to erect a mill; during the erection of which, he became somewhat pressed in money matters, and concluded to use twenty dollars that had been placed in his hands by a blind man for safe-keeping. He thought, certainly, "I can raise twenty dollars at any time on a short notice;" but the money was called for very unexpectedly, and was wanted on a certain day, as the owner was going to leave the country. Brother F—— went around among the neighbors to try and borrow the amount; but the old adage, "He that goeth borrowing, goeth sorrowing," was verified in this, and he returned home much dejected; for he was a class-leader and steward in the Church, and thought, what would the world say to his keeping back the poor man's money? He felt that it would be a disgrace to himself, to the Church, and would be a hindrance to the cause of the Redeemer.

The time had all passed but one day, and that was Sunday. The morning of that day had come, but no relief came to his burdened mind; there was scarcely a hope left. He knew not what to do; but a thought came to his mind that he ought to pray for help. He had not thought of this before; but now he went down to the further side of the garden from the house, and there kneeled down, and prayed to that God who had so often befriended and delivered from spiritual trouble, to open up a way for his escape out of this dilemma, and to send relief, that the cause of religion might remain untarnished. As he proceeded in supplication to God, he waxed warmer and warmer; the spirit of prayer came mightily upon him, faith took a firm hold on the Almighty, and the answer came, the mind was set at liberty, and the soul felt shouting happy. Full of confidence in Him whom he trusted, he went home, sat down on the door-step, and, looking up, saw a man coming over the hill toward which the door faced. As he drew nearer, he was recognized as a brother in the Church.

He had been to the village of P——, and was now returning home; he drew near and spoke to F——, who invited him to walk into the house. The invitation was declined; but said he: "I would like to have a few moments' private conversation with you; come, and walk along with me a short distance." F—— rose up and they went together down by the garden. Just as they reached the spot where he had been praying and wrestling so hard, Brother B—— said: "As I came to the forks of the road, upon the hill there, I felt it impressed on my mind that you were in need of a little pecuniary aid; and I thought I would just call by and see." Now it was just the same time (as near as could be calculated), when F—— received the answer to his prayer, that good Brother B—— was at the forks of the road. The result was, he received enough from his friend to cancel the debt, and have a six-pence over.

I will give an incident in my visiting, for it was my custom to visit every family within two or three miles of my appointments; and, as all were strangers to me, my constant prayer was that God would make me useful at every house. I called on Mr.— no matter: I found him and one of his friends in consultation; told him who I was and what my errand was. He said he would not say whether he believed the Bible or not; but his friend did not claim to believe it. I talked morality and religion to them, and was about to go away, but said I would like to have prayer with him and family before I left. He positively said he would have no prayers in his house, and I was just on the eve of starting, when his wife opened the door and said dinner was ready. He invited me to take dinner with him. He was a Virginian, and I knew their hospitality, and said: "Mr. M——, I could not eat with a man that would not let me pray with him when I had asked the privilege." He insisted. I told him if he would have prayer first, I would eat with him. He said to his wife: "Had we better have prayer?" She replied: "Certainly." "Well, then, call in the children;" and I both prayed and ate my dinner with them; invited them and they came to meeting, and his wife was forward for prayers.

Another remarkable incident occurred. There was a Mr. S——, who lived in sight of the school-house. At first he seemed to be interested in the meetings, but ceased to attend. We went to see him, but he would have no prayers, and said to me it would be time enough for him to pray when he got sick. I spoke of the danger of such a resolution as that. He was in good health, and working at a well. He was a young man with a family. The meeting closed just one week after. As I reached the neighborhood on my next round, I saw a company at the cemetery, but could not think who was dead, as all had been well the week before. But it was Mr. S——. He had been sick only four days. I understood he prayed, but did not hear that he got any answer to prayer. O, what a warning to all that defer repentance till sickness comes! God alone can tell the results of this meeting. It was his work. I am only glad to have been a humble instrument.

This was a hard year. We had opposition from many that called themselves Come-outers, the followers of Foster and Abby Kelly, at New Lime, Ohio. We took in about seventy-five on probation. In September we had a camp-meeting that I have not forgotten. Some good was done. Many of the baser sort came to mock and make disturbance. While I was holding a prayer-meeting, and some seekers were at the altar, a brother pulled me by the shoulders, and told me that the rowdies were breaking the lumber that we had for seats. Among them I saw a large man at the root of a tree, crowing like a rooster. I took a candle in my right hand and held it above my head, and made for the mocker. He walked back of the tents, and as he walked, pulled off his coat. I said, "My honey, I see you."

By this time he was crossing a hollow, and by the time I was at the bottom of it, and starting up, the first I knew he wheeled and struck at me, grazing my arm, and sending the candle spinning. But without thought my fist struck on the left arm, met his eye, and he was at once down and I had him by the throat. Just then, Brother Moore, a local preacher, said: "Do n't hurt him." I said: "God have mercy on him; for it is hard for me to." He was making loud cries for help. He went off and swore that I assaulted him, and sent an officer, who took me before a justice. I had plenty of friends, and we beat him on the papers, and I got out of the affair easily; and the general verdict was that he deserved all he got, and that I was the man to administer it. Suffice it to say, it was the only fight I was ever in, and I did not want that one, and was careful before and since to avoid collisions of that kind. That night and next day we had a quiet time. Brother S. C. Thomas was our presiding elder at this meeting.

The father of the man that crowed lived within less than a half-mile of the camp-ground. A few days after, he was helping to haul hay, and fell off the load and broke his neck. He was about seventy years old. They had a dance at their house on Saturday evening of the camp-meeting. What good ever came of a dance?

This was near the close of my fourth year in the conference. The next session was held at Racine, Wisconsin. I was elected to elder's orders, and ordained, with several others, by Bishop Janes, at this time, 1855.

This closed my work in Wisconsin, at least for a time. I will speak of the country, as my circuit covered the oldest and first settlements of Wisconsin. My travel had been south of the Wisconsin River, except when I crossed over from Muskoda, and preached among the first at Uncle John McKinny's, and south to the State line, including Iowa, Grant, and Lafayette Counties. This corner of the State is not surpassed, take it every way. The greatest attractions at first were its mines, known as the lead-mines, opened about 1830. Men were not allowed to mine at Dubuque till the fall of 1832, when the Black Hawk purchase was concluded. Mines were worked about Galena and at points in Wisconsin. It was not only a mining region, but a good agricultural country. Many a poor man made a raise digging, and went to farming or into other business. Many of the settlers went up from Illinois. They were called Suckers, because they came first in the spring, and took the sucker-shoot back in the fall. Next were the Missourians. You could tell them by their butternut jeans coats and pants.

Our Church was generally the first in new settlements, and especially here. Father Mitchell and Major Rowntree were at Platteville. This seemed to be head-quarters for Methodists, and from this place they went from one digging to another, and did most of the early preaching. Rev. T. M. Fullerton started in about 1842. He was converted a year or two before, and married Father Journey's daughter, in the Parkison Settlement, where Fayette now stands. The presiding elders were one of the Cavanaugh preachers, Henry Summers, with I. I. Stewart and Brother Whitfield. They held the revival meeting at Snake Hollow, now Potosi. Some sixty were converted, out of whom came three or four preachers. The Church kept pace with the growth of the country. As we traveled over this part four years, we could but think it the most beautiful part of the world—its high prairies, its deep gorges, with diggings on the rough parts, and good farming land on the smooth part. Such grand views! The Platte Mounds near the center, the Blue Mounds, and the good soil, all to be seen from almost any place, were calculated to inspire the mind of the traveler.

CHAPTER IV.

RICHLAND MISSION, MINNESOTA.

FROM the above conference I was appointed to Richland Mission, Fillmore County, Minnesota, some two hundred and fifty miles from the seat of conference. I returned to Wiota, and began to arrange to start. A few days after, I was called on to join in matrimony Dr. W. B. Thurston and my sister Rachel, who had been a friend and sister to me, and next to an own mother to my children, and, for the four preceding years, useful on all the charges, and more beloved than her brother. They were married at father's, within eight miles of Platteville. They settled in Argyle, where they have resided ever since.

I left for my mission, accompanied by my oldest son Joshua. We took a mule and buggy to Dubuque, Iowa; thence a steamboat to Brownsville, the nearest landing to my work, forty miles west of the Mississippi River. Here I found a class of about twenty members that had been organized the year before by Brother B. Crist, the only one on my mission, and the only school-house that I knew of in the Territory at that time. We went from there to Preston. Two families made an appointment. Thence six miles to Brother Martin Kingsberry's. He was a new settler; had two small rooms on a beautiful claim. Brother Kingsberry was a probationer, and his wife a member of our Church, and they gave us a hearty welcome. Before bed-time, he informed us it was their custom to have prayer each morning and evening, and on Thursday evening a prayer-meeting. They both prayed, and we had prayer-meeting that night. This was the first meeting of the kind in those parts, and is worthy of mention because it was the first time I had found it on this wise in my life.

Feeling much refreshed in spirit, we went to Carmona, and from there to near Rochester, where my son left me for St. Paul, to seek an opening in business for himself. I found Rochester was to be supplied by another. There were but few houses in it. Thence I went back to the State line east of Spring Valley, and back by Elliota, to Brother Purcell's.

This week I received a letter from my father with the sad·and unexpected news of the death of Brother Robert C. Dyer, who was two years younger than myself. We had been brought up side by side, and had been much together after we were men. I had feared something was not right, as he was constantly in my thoughts, and every thing I saw in my travels I wanted to tell him about. But I was not permitted to see him again. I hope to meet him in heaven. His death was sudden. He was with a man for a load of wood. Directing the man to drive home, he said that he would go by a neighbor's whom he wished to see. So he took the driver's gun, and when he got to the house, the lady asked him in; but he stood on the door-step, the gun by his side. It slipped off the step, and discharged into his side, near his vest-pocket, ranging up into his stomach. He survived about thirty-six hours. My father and some of the other children were with him. Brother Thomas held him in his arms till he was gone. When I heard the news, with deep sorrow I repaired to a lonely spot to give vent to my anguish by weeping, and to ask God to help me to bear it, and to be a more devoted man and consecrated minister. I thank God for his sustaining grace in this hard trial, and for all his benefits toward me in all my hours of distress.

To return to my work; it was arranged for a two-weeks' circuit, with eight appointments. I found some additional places—among them Brown's Mills—to visit occasionally. I preached from two to three times on Sunday, and served the other appointments on week evenings. During this time, having a few spare days, I took up a quarter section of prairie-land, cornering within a few rods of the school-house, and had a house raised, working on it as best I could.

Now, about the first of December, 1855, our first quarterly meeting was to be held. Saturday two o'clock preaching had been announced. I expected my presiding elder, Rev. N. Hobart, but in vain. I saw the people coming, left my work, and took charge of the services. Here we held the first quarterly conference on the mission. Brother James Graham, C. Willford, Brother Emes, and Leroy Streetor were present.

It was at this time I first held communion unassisted. Here, in the almost wild prairie, we had a gracious time. At the close on Sunday night we took a vote as to the continuance of the meeting, and every evening for three weeks held service. There were forty-two at the altar for prayer, and almost every one made a profession of religion. Brother Anthony Willford was clearly saved through faith, as was his wife. He has been quite a successful traveling preacher, and is still in the work. James Purcell was also recommended to the conference, but never went to his work as I know of. Many others were converted; one C. C. Streetor, who afterwards married my only daughter, and now lives in Colorado. Several that I know of are on their way home.

After a week's rest, I went over four miles to Purcell's neighborhood, and held eight days, and the result was a good revival. Twenty-two joined, four or five by letter, and the rest on probation. On Christmas day we had a good time; the power of God being manifested in the salvation of the people. Brother Purcell had been led off by the Second Adventists, and became cold and somewhat soured. His wife and mother-in-law and four or five children, with three or four of his brother's family, and others to the number of twenty, were forward for prayers; and but two besides myself to pray. The father was sitting back. I called on him to come and pray for his family, and he went to the work, and was blessed, as they all were; and next day we closed the meeting and formed the class, which grew within two years to near fifty.

We formed a class in Kingsbury's settlement of members and probationers—some ten, I think. During the winter our increase was about seventy, This winter—1855 and 1856—was the coldest I had ever seen, or have seen since. In the forepart of December, there came heavy sleet and snow, and it never thawed for over forty days. It was almost impossible to go out of a beaten road, as there was a heavy crust on the snow. I received a letter from Wisconsin that seemed to make it necessary for me to go and attend to some business. I went in February, and as soon as the spring was appearing, we, as a family, moved up into Minnesota. The snow was gone; but we crossed the Wisconsin and Mississippi on the ice at Prairie du Chien. We had plenty of mud on both sides of the river. We were in our house at once. I was soon around to all my appointments, and found things, after a six weeks' absence, quite encouraging. Our quarterly meeting was to be held about the first of June.

We got the camp-ground cleared up on the land of Mr. Eastman, near Lenora, which had been laid off, and the lots put on sale that spring. I surveyed and platted the forty acres, and deeded it to trustees, and got it on record. They were to pay me fifty dollars for it, but I took two lots. The proceeds were for the erection of a church. We made all calculations on as good a time as possible. Rev. N. Hobart, with several others, was in attendance.   It was a great treat to have plenty of help.   I suppose it was the first camp-meeting ever attempted to be held in Minnesota; but I was soon corrected in that, for they had a little one up at Red Wing prior to this; ours was the second.   We had a good, profitable time.   About ten were saved and added to the Church.   It seemed like old times, with our presiding elder, and Brothers Fate and Crist, and others, to help. This was in 1856.

Our part of the country was filling up fast with settlers, and we set in to build our church of stone; but the walls were not nearly up when cold weather came.   Then followed the spring of 1857, and with it the financial crash.   This was much worse here, from the fact that we were all new settlers.   The majority of the people had spent most, if not all, that they brought with them, and had not time as yet to make anything off their farms.   There was scarcely any money in the country; and land that had been bought from the government at one dollar and twenty-five cents, could not be sold for that much, including the improvements.   Nothing was at par, save the salvation of our souls.   Thanks be to God, no drouth, floods, nor financial depression, can stop the constant fullness of the grace that comes from above! But it may retard the building of churches, and break many a good man financially.   Some of the preachers were not exceptions.   I heard one—who had been worth thousands, and was almost too well-off to continue in the work—say that he was brought so low, financially, that he could scarcely get enough to keep himself and family from suffering.

I felt the pressure, but not so severely as many. I had taken with me sixteen hundred dollars, with which I secured two hundred acres of land. My fifteen-year-old daughter and Samuel, my twelve-year-old son, kept house in our cabin, a mile from neighbors, and alone when I was on the circuit. Daughter says that I left no latch on the door, and that she cried for fear at night. But our God seldom, if ever, permits evil to befall us or our families if we keep on preaching the gospel.

We will pass now to the first conference ever held in Minnesota. It was at Red Wing. Our lamented Bishop Simpson presided, to the admiration of us all, both as to his eloquence and spiritual powers. His preaching on Sunday was never to be forgotten by any who heard it. The love-feast was one of unusual enjoyment. The writer made three attempts to speak, and would have succeeded, but a good sister opened her mouth just as he began to rise. I concluded to improve by her example, and be ready next time. Nevertheless, the meeting was power all the way through, and left a bright spot in my memory.

Many of the preachers looked rather careworn, as though it had been a hard year. I may have judged by my own feelings, in part. It was a good, refreshing session. The brethren proposed a spring session of our conference. I, in my feebleness, opposed it, having moved one hundred and sixty miles that spring. Some, who lived along the river, said there was no mud in Minnesota; and the experiment was tried, but only once. We were not entirely unacquainted with the brethren of the conference. C. and N. Hobart, D. Brooks, Jabez Brooks, T. M. Kirkpatrick, John Hooper, G. W. Richardson, and others, were present, and kept us from feeling like a stranger. N. Hobart was presiding elder on Winona District again. Brother Hooper was sent to Caledonia, and I was returned to the same work; only it was called Preston Circuit.

We labored, the second year, with some success. Our last quarterly meeting was a campmeeting, held at the same ground used the year before. The presiding elder was not present, but sent Brother Fate in his place. Brother Lease, of Iowa, was also there. The first and second day, every service seemed to drag, until darkness prevailed. The writer gathered about one dozen select men, and took to the woods for a prayermeeting. After a few words of exhortation, we fell on our knees and struggled for half an hour, when the power of God came down, and victory was felt and seen on every hand. The meeting at once gave signs of life, and grew better to the last. The morning we thought of leaving, the preacher in charge felt that there was an unusual power resting on the people, and called for seekers. New converts and old members started out for their friends. Hardly any seemed able to resist. One exhorter was very successful; had a penitent on each side of him, and looked up and said: "Brother Dyer, I got them all but two, and those ran away." Such a scene has seldom been witnessed as was presented at that altar for several hours—weeping, praying, and praising. About forty were converted.

This closed the conference year; and I left the next day for conference, which was held at Winona; Bishop Ames presiding. This was the first time I had met him officially since the conference at Fond du Lac, Wisconsin; the first conference he ever held. Rev. Chauncey Hobart and some others were present as fathers among us. We had a pleasant session, and I was appointed to Caledonia Circuit.

Just here I would say, the financial crash of 1857 was fully upon us. I had given forty acres of land toward the Church, which was a large share of all I had. Unfortunately several of us went security for a man, in order to help him bring a saw-mill into the neighborhood, supposing him to be reliable; but he failed, and, as it turned out, his father owned all the property, and the security had to pay. I had no money, and so gave a mortgage on thirty-eight acres more to secure my note; and when the mortgage was foreclosed, the father of the man bid the land in and deeded it to the debtor's wife! It was always worth the debt. This, with some other misfortunes, and not receiving enough the two preceding years to support me and my family—as I was a single man and one hundred dollars a year was quarterage—suffice it to say, I was financially burst; actually sold my mule to pay a debt, and started on foot to my circuit; visited all the houses, and talked to the people on the importance of their salvation.

I spent my time thus until near December, when I undertook to hold a protracted meeting at what was called the Red School-house; quite a large one. There I visited twenty-seven families—about all in the school district—and found but one old lady that gave any evidence of saving grace. I saw all but one family. The day before, on my way there, I met a boy and asked him about them, and he said they had gone away. "They expected you would be there," he went on; "and give them the devil."

I heard of a family at the edge of the settlement that was called religious, and hoped to have a good time. The man was a shoe-maker. I rapped at the cabin door, was invited in, and told them who I was and my business, and inquired of them if they enjoyed religion. The lady had been an Episcopalian, but the man said he made no pretense, but had more of religion than men running around to every house and raising such a stir among the people. He had a religion of his own, and reverenced his God. Well, the preacher asked him for a bit of his experience, and how he performed before his God. He gave no response to the questions, only said he would as soon hear a man swear as pray. I said: "We generally ask to pray; but as you would as soon hear a man swear as pray, I will waive it on this occasion." The woman said: "I hope you won't go away without prayer." "Well, if you will kneel with me, we will pray." We knelt, and offered a short and pointed prayer. I noticed that the man kept his hat on. When we got up I asked him how he liked the prayer? "O, very well." "Now, sir, if you had reverenced your God half as much as you professed, you would have taken off your hat while we prayed." "I beg pardon," he said, "and hope you will excuse me; I never thought of it." Of course I squared accounts by a promise that he would come to meeting.

But while I was visiting, some of the leading men got together and resolved to close the schoolhouse, and not let me preach any more. That night, near time for service, I met in the vestibule two of the school directors, one a Quaker. He said: "Mr. Dyer, how long does thee intend to hold these meetings?" "Do n't know." "Well, we have concluded these excitements that thee gets up will hurt our school." I told him that it was thought that religion and education went together, and I was sure that they were not religious enough yet to hurt the school, or prevent the children from learning. "Well," he replied, "Mr. Jones thinks the weather is too bad for people to be called out every night." "I suppose Mr. Jones does n't think it too bad to run opposition twice this week with a dance at his house," I responded. He was a fiddler as well as school director. And so, saying that we could have the house that night, we passed them.

We had a large audience and good attention, and if ever I gave a warm mess, it was on this occasion. At the close, I said if there was any one who wished to have the meetings continue, we would like to have him say so in the congregation. No one said a word. Then I asked the school directors what they had to say. One of them said: "You can have the house on Sunday in the day-time, but not in the evening." "You all three agree to this?" They replied in the affirmative. I gave them a few words on leaving, and said I was about to do as the devil never did, and that was to leave them. We were sorry to do so, as our only desire was to see them converted and saved in heaven. We dismissed and left. I will say that it was a common talk that they had closed their house against the preacher, and secured preaching by a Universalist; and when the hat was passed around, some of them threw in buttons, and so he left. The next year, when the preacher came to the circuit nearest them, they sent a man to ask one of the stewards to have him come and preach for them every other Sunday, and promised to be responsible for their part of his salary. They soon had a revival. I am glad that it turned out well in the end; for I could bear with them, and often prayed that good would be done in that place.

From here we went within seven miles of Caledonia, into a settlement where they had no school-house. One of the houses was large enough to hold fifty or sixty people. We began about the twentieth of December, and the people here were more noble, inasmuch as they heard the word gladly, and we had about twenty-five conversions, and formed a class. We held a watch-night meeting, which was a gracious time. Nine o'clock and a little after midnight there were ten conversions, almost a clean sweep. There was to be a ball at Sheldon during our meeting, but we had captured the fiddler. They boasted that five dollars would secure his services; but he told them he had quit, and would not go. It was said they had poor music, and not enough receipts to pay half the expenses. We went down and found there was a very bad state of feeling among them; but got them all out. Soon all troubles were settled, and a good work was done. Quite a number were reclaimed, and some were converted. We formed a class of sixteen. The good Lord descended in great mercy at both these meetings. One old sister got very happy, and took a good shout. She was in so great an ecstasy of joy that she made for her husband, who was a member, and he got out of her way very quick; he almost ran. I went home with them, and asked him why he ran from his happy wife. "Why," he said, "I am just as afraid of her when she shouts as I am of any other woman."

We took a little rest, and next went over to the South Prairie. Held a meeting for two weeks, and had about ten converted and joined to the Church, through the blessing of God. We felt he was with his people, and sinners were saved and the members built up in their most holy faith.

We had some very good members; Brother Lewis and his wife, good and true, young folks in the Church, and Brother Hate and family, with others.

Notwithstanding that whisky and cards were used freely, Caledonia had some nice people and some religious individuals. One of the hard cases was a man of family. He loved his company, and spent his money. His wife grieved, as he was wasting his living. She went to a neighbor woman whose husband was in the same row, and they agreed to take axes and knock in the door and windows on the west side of the house, as the wind was blowing from that way. The courage of one failed her; but the other, firm in her determination, knocked the window in the first lick, and struck down the door the next. The wind blew the lights out and everything off the table. The whole crew thought it a mob, and jumped out of the window on the other side, and ran away.

At another time a saloon-keeper bought six barrels of whisky, and laid them on their sides, with the ends against the weather-boarding. Somebody—so the same lady told me—bored holes through the boards and into the heads of the barrels at the lower edge, so that there was but very little whisky left in any of them.

The above shows how women and children suffer by drink and cards. This woman was a perfect hater of these things; and to hear her abuse both, one would think she had tongue enough for two sets of teeth. Rev. John Quigley came soon afterwards, and lectured on temperance. Although I never had the pleasure of hearing him, by report he was never surpassed. The above woman said, when she heard him, she was ashamed of herself that she had failed to tell the half, and felt assured that nothing which would stop the traffic was to be considered mean in the sight of God.

I traveled on foot this year, and attended closely to my work, and received but very little compensation. My presiding elder was Brother D. Cobb, and, if my memory serves me right, he got more money than the preacher in charge. But God was pleased to bless the feeble efforts put forth, and graciously revived his work. To him be all the glory.

On this charge there was one of the most diminutive little mills that was ever seen in Minnesota. While we were looking at it doing its level best, two other men, new in the country, gazed on it with astonishment; and one of them who always would speak in approbation of any thing he could, whined out: "Why, it is the most industrious little mill I ever saw; just as fast as it grinds one grain, it begins on another." We turned away from the first mill erected in the county, with the idea of industry on our minds.

There was a man whose name was Job Brown, who built a very good mill in the bounds of this circuit. He was converted at a prayer-meeting held by Brother Wilcox. Mr. Brown had been possessed of wealth, as he was proprietor of Brownsville on the Mississippi. He had been, by his own report, a very wicked man, a leader in almost every sort of vice. And when he was a changed man, he was just as determined to do all he could for the cause of Christ, and was faithful while I knew him. I heard him tell of his dancing, which, by the way, is the mother of most other sins. He and one of his associates had been at swords' points for some time. He was invited by this man into a saloon to drink, and both were the worse of liquor. After drinking, the man said, "I will shoot you with an empty revolver;" put it to his own ear and snapped it first, and then at Brown's head, and again at his own and at Brown's. This way he snapped it four times. The fifth, he put it to his own head, and it went off, and he fell dead. As that was the only load in the pistol, it was concluded that he intended it for Brown, but made a mistake in count and killed himself. This was a shock to Brown, as he saw how close he had been to death.

Some time before his conversion he dreamed that he saw this man, among others, in a large room that was not more than half lighted; but as he had seen him dance, he knew him, and he seemed tired. He soon observed that he could not quite hold up his head, which lolled over first on one shoulder, and then on the other, and his tongue was hanging out of his mouth, and he seemed to be in agony. The dancing was done without music. The sight was so horrible that he waked, and was glad it was only a dream. It had a tendency to arouse him to serious reflection, and was to some extent the cause of his seeking the salvation of his soul. I have for many years thought that dancing causes more of the evils in society throughout the nation, than any other institution the devil ever started; but that if it were done without music, and men and women danced by themselves, it would not do much harm.

This was a short year; for we had met in May at St. Paul. Bishop Morris presided in his usual pleasant manner. He boarded with Brother McClain, who had been acquainted with my father in early times in Ohio. He heard my name, and inquired from where I came. I told him, and he asked me to go and take dinner with him. We went, and had a pleasant visit—all being from Columbus, or near there. The bishop gave an incident that happened when he was stationed in Columbus. They had a good old man that told his experience and conversion, just in the same words, every quarter; and at one of the Church meetings his case was brought up, and they feared it would offend him to tell him that he took too much time. One of the brethren was a good singer, and he proposed when the brother got about half through that he would sing a verse. When the time came, he struck a lively tune, sang his verse, and just as soon as it was done, the old brother jumped up and said he would finish his story; that he always liked a little singing mixed in with his talk. The old bishop had not forgotten how the old man beat them all.

This was a pleasant session. I met Brother

Hoyt here, who had preached at my house in early times, about his first effort. I made no request, and was not consulted as to where I would like to go, and my name was read out for Austin Circuit—the farthest south-west work in the conference.

CHAPTER V.

CIRCUIT WORK.

I TOOK steamboat from St. Paul to Brownsville. Thence we walked, riding when opportunity served, forty miles. We went through my old and last circuit. Saw quite a number of my parishioners, and bade them farewell. I have seen but few of them since. We reached Lenora, and found that everything I had there was gone, or would soon be gone. My oldest son, Joshua, had determined to go west, on the Des Moines River, north of Spirit Lake. And we arranged to send my daughter, in company with Miss Maria Streetor, to Red Wing, to the university, for a time at least. So we broke up keeping house. This done, I traded for an old horse, and of course he was not worth much; but I thought it would be better than to go on foot. Accordingly I set out for Austin.

It was about the last of May and very wet. I traveled along a few miles from the State line. After passing Spring Valley I stopped all night, and it rained hard till morning; when I started, and came to Vanmeter's, at the crossing of a branch of Root River. The stream was out of banks and all over the low grounds. I concluded to try to cross. I went up so as to take advantage of the current. I started in water knee-deep;

all at once the horse and rider were under, except my head and neck. I supposed my horse would rise and swim; but either he did not know how or would not, for his head would come up and he would make a plunge and go clean under again. This he did three times, when, fortunately, we reached where he could stand, the water over his back, but his head out. There he rested a little, and waded out with me. Once out of sight, I took off my clothes, and made a wringer of my hands, and got all the water out that was possible. I had an appointment about two miles distant. The man said he would have had a dozen to hear me, but the flood prevented; so he had seven. I was all wet and had taken my boots off, and was drying my socks. The time came, and the poor Irishman said: "Can't we have a little preaching?" I said: "I can't put my boots on; would it do barefooted?" "Just as well." And it came to my mind that I had not seen so great faith in all the country. I gave out a hymn, and kneeled in prayer. I learned afterwards that it would have been the better way to have stood to pray; as my pants stuck to my legs, and I had to pull them loose, or they would have reached only down below my knees. When everything was adjusted, I took the text: "In those days came John the Baptist preaching, saying, Repent," etc.; and did the best I could barefooted.

The afternoon was fair and warm, and by evening I was well dried. I stopped at the first house beyond the Wet Prairie, crossing a deep creek on a bridge, the water all over it. Three other men were with us, and we led and pulled our horses over, and hauled a wagon over by hand. One tall man got in up to his neck. He was walking on the log that held the poles on the bridge, and had hold of the fore-wheel of the wagon. The tongue took a lunge, and the wheel pressed him off. He went endways till he was all under except his head. He soon extricated himself, got up, took hold again, and said he was not afraid of getting wet now. He was so afraid of getting wet before, that the tongue slipped out of my hand in spite of myself!

The next day, when within less than half-mile of Brownsdale, I came to a broad slough, water two feet deep. About midway my old horse went down to his body in the mud. I got off, and took the bridle-reins, and pulled, and he made a lunge right toward me. I made for the shore, and he after me, and by the time I got to *terra firma*, was covered with black mud. I pulled the dry grass, and wiped my clothes as well as I could, and also the bridle and the saddle and the horse, all in sight of town. While I was in this predicament, I thought this was too much for anybody except a Methodist preacher, who had made his vows to take things as they come, and thought nothing could compensate me but a good revival. I found Brother Moses Mapes, who had supplied the work the preceding year. He published preaching for Sunday at eleven o'clock. By Sister Mapes's help, I was fixed up as well as circumstances would admit, and had about forty hearers, who paid good attention while I tried to preach from the text: "All are yours, whether Paul or Apollos," etc.

I was impressed that there was a revival ready to come to the surface; so much so, that I gave out meeting for Wednesday week in the evening, and announced that if it seemed promising, we would hold extra meetings if we could have the school-house, which was granted. At the time there was a good attendance; but during the meeting I felt great concern; for I said to Brother Mapes: "I thought we could have a revival, by the blessing of God." "Brother Dyer," he said, "you do n't know this people as well as I do. They have had their balls, and run opposition all winter." He gave me no encouragement; but I had gone too far to retreat, and was led to plead with God to guide me in every step, and to help; for I knew that God alone was able to save, and that he could thrash the world with a worm. I came with no self-dependence; and it was well, for if ever a man had need of help, it was on this occasion. For several days, in giving out my appointments, I had a travail of soul. I even had a dream; thought I saw a man up in the air. He was of a dark complexion, riding a black horse; had a whip in his hand, and I thought he made, in his descent, right for me. As I watched him closely, I saw that he was missing his aim; but the feet of the horse seemed close, and I dodged my head, but was not touched. So it appeared to me that there was war ahead, but all would be right with me.

On my return I found a good congregation, and all the indications of a successful work. The next Friday evening the house was crowded, and we made room and called for penitents. About a dozen came at once, and we had one or two converted; a clear work, and everything was going just right. But on Saturday a man brought four Campbellites, all preachers and, it was said, linguists, all but one. Of course I had the house pre-empted at night, but they had a meeting at one o'clock. With about thirty others, I went to hear them, and who should speak but the man I had seen on the black horse with the whip in hand! His talk was almost all in opposition to the different Churches, and especially against the Methodists. He said that he would throw all our mourners' benches out of the window, and he gave it to us generally. When he quit and sat down, he said, if there was any gentleman in the house who had any objections to what he had said, he hoped he would reply. I saw they had debate in them, and he asked the third time, and looked at me. I arose and said if I had given such a harangue as he had, it would have been ungentlemanly in me. He jumped up and said, "I am branded with not being a gentleman," and repeated it two or three times. I replied, "You may wear the 'brand;'" and we were dismissed. They could not lead me away from my fixed purpose in the revival work, to engage in any contro-

versy. I was as careful about that as I was not
to be hurt by his horse's feet, and so dodged it.

At night the house was full, and all of the
preachers were out to see and hear. We took for
our text the words: "That they should seek the
Lord, if haply they might feel after him and find
him." The Lord helped me, so that the trail all
through the subject was as light as day; and at
the close I called for benches, and said: "We had
one full last night, and by God's help to-night we
will have two." Twenty-two came to the altar, and
the meeting was about as warm as I was ever in.
Several were converted. It got too hot for my
Christian brethren. They went out and looked
in at the window. They stayed a few days, and
left. Our meeting closed with about thirty converts, and all but one joined our Church.

During this meeting, there was an old Roman
Catholic who lived in the village. His wife was
a Protestant. Their daughter was the school-
teacher, and our first convert—an accomplished
young lady of more than ordinary ability, and a
power in our meetings. Her father did all he
could to oppose her. After the meeting he would
harass and abuse her every night. I called on all
the families, and with the rest, on Mr. D——. He
was not in. The old lady and daughter were very
pleasant, and we had a good visit. Before I left
I proposed to pray. They consented, and we knelt,
and while in prayer, the old man came in; and
when I rose up he was standing right behind me,
and spoke with his rough voice: "What business

have you to pray in my house without my leave?"
I was taken by surprise, but told him prayer was
becoming at all times, and that I was in the habit
of praying with his neighbors. He replied: "I
won't allow you to pray in my house." I told
him that I did not wish to intrude, and intended
no harm in all that I had done, and would not
pray in his house any more unless he requested
it. "I will never do that," he said. "I want you
to stay away." Of course I was rather glad to
get away, and did not intend to visit him soon.

During the meeting his daughter was taken
sick and went into a spasm, and most of the
neighbors ran in to see her. She sent for me,
and I went. Her father was away at work.
When she could speak she gave her testimony for
Christ, who had so lately saved her from sin, and
given her a clear evidence of acceptance with
him, and a bright assurance of glory. She took
me by the hand and said, "I think I am going
home to heaven soon," and added: "I want you
to preach Christ to lost sinners, and tell the world
how I was converted and how I can meet death."
Her face was shining with a glow of happiness.
She was taken with another spasm, and during
her convulsions her father came. He was wonderfully alarmed. In a short time she came to
herself, and as soon as she could speak, reached
her hand to her father and told what Christ Jesus
had done for her, and talked to him, and made
him promise to repent and be prepared to die.
He was standing at one side of the large chair,

and I on the other. She then said to him: "I want you to kneel down, and the minister to pray for us." He dropped on his knees, and I said: "Do you say I must pray?" He answered, "Yes, sir." With that license, we bowed together in prayer. This young lady recovered, was married, lived several years, and died in full triumph of faith. Glory be to God for such a convert!

There was another lady, a leading spirit in the town, who sought her soul's salvation through opposition. She was reared by a Christian mother, who belonged to the Campbellite or Christian Church, and died happy. When she was on her death-bed, she called her children around her, and gave them her dying charge, and in particular said to them that she knew there was a reality in experimental religion, and that she was in the enjoyment of that blessing, and requested them not to live without this knowledge of sins forgiven. Her brother would come every day and say all he could to stop his sister taking any part in our meeting—would say, "Just *do* religion," and made use of the Bible to prove his position. But at the last of his talk she would say: "You know, John, what mother told us when she was dying; that there was a reality in experimental religion." He never disputed that. We can not but be thankful for a dying mother's advice. It often brings the children to Christ.

I talked with her every day, and was exercised to a great extent, and laid her case before God in earnest prayer, until he was pleased to give the evidence that all would come out right. Sure enough; it did come out right. Near the close of the meeting we had a terrible rain. The ground was covered with water, and we had a small turnout. Three were forward for prayers; the above lady was one. After we had sung and prayed around the three seekers, who were sitting on a seat near the middle of the house, we sat down to wait a few moments. All at once the young woman began to draw her breath so loud that all in the house could hear her. She raised her hands and said, "Lord, take my breath, but give me Jesus;" and looking up, said, "He comes! he comes! O, he has come!" and she gave a shout, the only outburst of the meeting. None that was there had ever seen so clear a conversion.

Next came the baptizing, two weeks after. We had a good man from Vermont, Rev. Dr. Frary, of the Baptist Church. He was too old to do much, but did what he could. His daughter, a young lady of promise, was one of our converts When we came to the baptism, he said to me: "Brother Dyer, do you feel when you baptize by immersion that it is Christian baptism?" I answered that I considered Christian baptism water applied in the name of the Trinity, by a properly authorized person; and as our rules allowed either sprinkling, pouring, or immersion, I was willing to give the subject his choice; it was in the line of my duty to perform it in either way. He replied: "My daughter has made a profession, and I think is sincere, and would like to go with the rest, and

I am satisfied for you to baptize her, since we have had your explanation." I must say I had never seen it on this wise before; nor have I since. There were nine subjects, and there were seven preachers present, representing four different Churches. Our Campbellite brethren had come back by this time. All four of them sat on the opposite side of the creek, where they could see. I heard that they said that it was well done, only one man's nose was not covered. A crowd was in attendance. The Christians only got one that professed at our meeting. They baptized several, left, and did not come back very often.

We have always felt thankful to God for this blessed work; for it was not by might nor by power, but by his Spirit. I have always felt that he verified his promise: "Lo, I am with you alway, even unto the end of the world." He made a way for our escape in every trial, and we had good meetings every time we came to Brownsdale. My heart says: "Ne'er let old acquaintance be forgot."

We had eight appointments on this work. There had been no regular preaching, if any, by the Methodists in Austin. Two men had settled three miles above town—Brothers Clayton and Dobbins—and there was a class there. Here I met the Congregational minister, and inquired if there was any place where I could preach in Austin. He said: "There is but one hall, and we occupy that every other Lord's day, and the Rev. Mr. Gurney the other." "Well, could I have it in the afternoon, say two o'clock?" "That is just the time of our Sunday-school." "Well, could I have it at five or six o'clock?" He lectured every Sunday at six o'clock. "Well," I remarked, "I can come at three, at the close of the Sunday-school; will you be so good as to announce it in your service?" "Yes, he could." I thanked him for his kindness, and preached there through the summer. Rev. D. Cobb was presiding elder. I believe he only missed one quarterly meeting.

In early fall we held a meeting at Brother Sargent's school-house, two miles east of Austin. There were about forty forward for prayers, and most of them joined the Church. It was a blessed time, through the goodness of God. Then we went to the State line, six miles south of Austin, where was a mill-dam, and three miles by water below was another, and that backed the river up to the former, and each had a city. The surveys brought them together, and of course they had a big lawsuit, and were in a quarrel, and accused each other of testifying to things not true. They had a school-house, but it was not daubed. I helped them daub the cracks. We had two members; but they gave me no encouragement, as there was no feeling among them. The people were as far as could be from the possibility of a revival. I could only say: "In the name of God, we will try." The two members were feeble, but would come all they could. We held the meeting two weeks. The house was full every night, but the good attendance was all; and I adjourned in about eight days to attend a quarterly meeting at

Brownsdale. The presiding elder was not there; but, by the blessing of God, we had a good time.

I returned to our meeting. The first night some awfully big dogs got to fighting, and at least half a dozen got up to go out. I requested them to stop, and told them I would rather the devil was in the dogs than in them; let them settle their own fight. It was not long till they quit. We soon saw signs of good. Several were forward for prayer, and only two of us to pray. About the third night we prayed twice around, and were at a standstill. I thought to call on one of the seekers. As soon as asked, he raised his head and began to pray, and was blessed. Called on another, and he began, and the Lord converted him, and they both gave clear evidence. During the meeting we had about thirty converts, and they were almost all brought through trying to pray. One old man was reclaimed who had been a preacher a number of years before in New York. For a few weeks he was very happy, and then took sick and died in triumph.

We went around the circuit once or twice, and then got the use of an empty store-house in Austin, put in temporary seats, and began a protracted meeting. Of course we had the Congregational preacher to help, and the Baptist also. We had quite a good meeting, but not as many conversions according to the number of people as we had in the other places. Organized the first class in Austin, with about twenty members. Held the first camp-meeting in those parts, just above the town, on Cedar River, and took in ten. One rowdy made himself conspicuous. Brother G. W. Richardson came with Rev. D. Cobb, presiding elder, to help. This fellow was forward with others. Brother Richardson told me to watch him; he thought he was there for no good. I asked the seekers to speak. He got up and said he had slept all the time, but did not know why the brethren prayed for him as though he was not sincere. I said: "How could you tell any thing about it if you were asleep?" About this time he was shoved out of the altar, and told to move with a quick step. The presiding elder was in the stand, and said that the man might well be denominated a three-cent seeker, for he said that afternoon he would give that amount to any one who would tell how to become a convert. While I was around there, he went by the name of the three-cent seeker. With this exception, the order was good, and the results satisfactory.

I had no place on this circuit to call home, paid no board, and was welcome all over the work. This was in 1858. People were new settlers; there was hardly any money, and it was a remarkably wet year. Crops were poor. Along Cedar River, where they were usually the best, the floods destroyed about all. The river rose twenty feet in eight or ten hours, and took off all the bridges, stacks of grain, and so flooded houses that, in some cases, the inmates were taken out at the upper windows. One man was awakened, and the water was knee-deep. He had a trap-door to go into his cellar, and it floated off, and, in the dark, he stepped in, but caught with his hands, or he might have been drowned. I had to have a canoe to get my old horse over, for he would not or could not swim. Take it altogether, it was a hard year. I do n't know what we would have done, if it had not been that the lakes all ran over and carried mill-ions of fishes into all the streams. The farmers would fill their wagons in a few hours so full of the best kinds, that the fish would roll off as they drove along. Their tables groaned under fishes fried, and baked, and stuffed. The blackbirds were almost as bad as grasshoppers. I received about fifty dollars in money and clothing in the year.

I remember of a temptation that was presented to me as I was going to commence my meeting in Austin. My coat was not much but lining from the elbow to the wrist on the under side. It came like this: Now you are going up to town, and your coat-sleeves are thread-worn to the lining. But I went and had a good old Protestant Meth-odist preach for me, and I exhorted. I thought I would tell on the devil the first thing, and try to stop him; so I told how it was, and raised my arm up and said: "I am ready to shake the last rag over you." The next day, to my surprise, Mrs. Holt and others took the matter in hand, and made me a present of a new coat, for which I was very thankful, and I have never forgotten their kindness. I do n't know how I should have stood that year through, only that God in his mercy revived his work all around the circuit. Blessed be his holy name!

About the first of May I started for conference, which was held at St. Anthony; Bishop Baker presiding. Traveled about one hundred and fifty miles to the Mississippi, and took steamboat for the seat of conference. Every man that came by land was almost covered with mud, and all wanted a fall conference. Many of the preachers were dissatisfied. We had four or five presiding elders. They had two hundred dollars missionary money apiece, or more, and very little was left for the poor circuits. There was a motion for an addition to the missionary committee of one from each district. It prevailed, and I was appointed from our district. It was the first time I had been in the cabinet, and of course I could not do very much; but you would better believe, the outside places were represented and pleaded for. One place must have some aid, and so they took fifty dollars from a district to which a new elder was to be appointed, and gave it to the poor place; but none present offered a cent off his own district for any poor work. The addition to the committee, however, caused a more equal and satisfactory distribution.

This year I was appointed to Wabashaw, Kashaw, and Reed's Landing. This was a short year, and we had but one revival—at Cook's Valley. It was a very good meeting, considering the thin settlement. A class of fifteen or twenty was formed. We had good congregations, and kept up our work at each appointment—there were only three regular places. Every Sunday morning we preached in Wabashaw, and divided the afternoons with the other places.

I remember in the summer we heard that the river was out of its banks—that was the Zumbro River. Mr. Bolton and sister took me in a buggy to the edge of the bottom where there was a bridge gone, but it was a mile to the main river. I walked the stringers, and went on in hopes the bridge was not taken off; but it was gone, and the river full to almost overflowing. I thought for a moment what I had better do, and concluded to make a raft of some planks that were in the drift. I soon had one I thought would take me; got a long pole and shoved off, but presently found myself in deep water, where I could not touch bottom, drifting down stream. There was an island, and I hoped the current would carry me over; but before I reached the foot of the island there was a tall, fallen tree lying straight across my course, and my raft, in spite of all I could do, went under it. I took my boots in hand, and when it went under, jumped over the tree and lighted on the raft all right, and was carried down nearly a mile. I saw some boys on the west shore in a skiff, and told them they might come and take me off. I left the raft with some satisfaction, as I was nearing the Mississippi River, and was about twenty minutes late for my appointment. But the congregation were waiting for the preacher, and we had a good time. Never was I more thankful to get to an appointment, and have wondered ever since how I got over; but certainly the good Lord was on my side that time.

From this place Brother Crawley, Sister Bolton, and others, went up the Chippewa River on a steamboat, above Durand, to a camp-meeting. When we got to the landing nearest Lake City, about twenty other Methodists got on board; and soon after our boat stuck on a sand-bar, which detained us some time; and at dark we stopped for the night, as the water was so low that they feared to run. There was quite a number of passengers, and some of them were anxious to have preaching. We had Moses M. Strong, a lawyer of ability, with us, and he and I had lived neighbors at Mineral Point. He secured the privilege for me to preach on the boat—the first and only sermon I ever preached on a steamboat. We had a good time, and good singing that echoed from bank to bank.

Next day we landed where I had been directed; but they had changed the place three miles, and we had to go through the woods, and my company began to complain that I had taken them out into the desert and lost them. I thought of Moses, and suspected that I felt a very little as he did; but we got there all the same, and found Rev. C. Hobart, the presiding elder, in charge. He at once asked me to preach. I took the subject of the prodigal son, as we had been lost, but got to camp-meeting all safe and sound. Suffice it to say, we had a good meeting, were refreshed, and returned in safety to Wabashaw; and went the rounds of the circuit two or three times after that.

This was a short year—from May to October. Conference was at Prescott. Bishop Janes presided. It was a memorable time, a season of real enjoyment to most of the preachers. On Sunday there was a good love-feast, and the bishop was blessed in his sermon. I never have seen as general enjoyment in a conference, before or since; everybody was happy in the love of God; almost all forgot the hard times and the losses and crosses that had been endured.

Here I received my appointment to Dunville and Menominee Circuit, with Brother J. S. Anderson. It was a large circuit. Brother Anderson was much discouraged, and went to Eau Claire to quarterly meeting to see the presiding elder, Chauncey Hobart, D. D. The elder did not come, and he made a bargain with the official board to preach for them, and let Brother Thomas Harwood come and travel with me. Accordingly Brother Harwood came. I was well pleased with the trade, but he had been asked to go up to Chippewa Falls and form a new circuit. I had to go to Lake Pepin, and told him I would go and see the presiding elder, and lay the case before him. The elder wrote Brother Harwood to stay with me or go to Chippewa Falls, whichever he chose. We talked the matter over, and concluded it was best for him to go, and I would do what I could alone. I say right here, it worked well for both of us; for he did a good work, and I was told during the year, by two of the official board, that it was the last time they would allow such a transaction.

To show their repentance, after a year the quarterly conference passed a resolution that, if the conference saw fit in their wisdom to return him, they would receive Brother Harwood with pleasure. This year's acquaintance with Brother Harwood was no doubt the cause of his subsequently being a missionary to New Mexico.

We commenced our work in earnest. Dunville, Ogalla, Waubeek, Massey's and Kyle's School-houses, Menominee, Mud Prairie, or Harshman's, and several other places, we included in our plan; preaching three times each Sunday and three through the week. In early winter we began our revival services, first at Kyle's. Held four weeks, with forty seekers, the most of whom were converted and formed into a class. At Ogalla, about twenty were brought in and joined the Church—a class. At Menominee Mills we had a good meeting, and formed a class of over twenty. At Brother Harshman's, a class of about ten; held a week, and took in six new converts. We held meetings a few times at other places, and marked attention was given to the word. At Massey's School-house there was quite a class, and we had meeting over a week. Rev. C. Hobart was with us a few days, and preached to our delight. Several were brought in and joined the Church. We held a camp-meeting at the lower end of the circuit, Rev. C. Hobart, presiding elder, in charge. It was a good meeting, but attended with no such wonderful displays of mercy as are sometimes seen.

I took a trip to Rice Lake, and found only Chippewa Indians, about twenty in number. This was in the summer of 1860. The fallen timber made it impossible to go forward on my horse farther than within a mile and a half of the outlet of the lake. Moreover, the green-headed horse-flies and mosquitoes set him nearly crazy. I should have had to abandon the trip had I not luckily found a logger's stable, in which I left him, comparatively secure from these insects. I went on foot the rest of the way, and found it very difficult to get through the fallen timber and the young growth; but finally reached the lake, about half-way up. I saw two Indian squaws in a canoe, and motioned to them. They were fishing with hooks. I discovered that they saw me, although they did not move. I then took out a half-dollar, holding it between my thumb and finger, and they at once came to my relief. I was glad they did so, for the mosquitoes and green-headed horse or deer flies were almost intolerable, lancing me at will through my thin coat, and setting me on fire.

The squaws paddled me down to the outlet of the lake. The water was about half covered with wild rice, which was quite an item of sustenance for the Indians. I was told that, in gathering it, they ran their canoes right among it. It stood two feet above the water, and was easily thrashed off into the canoe. It was a Godsend to them in this wilderness country. But the squaws did not allow me to get into the canoe until they got the money, and when my fare was paid they quickly rowed me down to the outlet.

Here were about twenty Indians, including squaws and papooses, all dressed in Indian costume, so far as they were dressed at all. Two or three men were the oldest-looking human beings I had ever seen—hardly looked like men. Their appearance made an impression on my mind that has never been effaced.

Now my horse was at Grover's logging-camp, at least one and a half miles below, on Hay River, and the fallen timber impossible to cross, and I could see no way to get there but to have some of the Indians take me in a canoe. There was a half-breed Frenchman who could speak an English word or two. He and two others undertook the trip. While they were launching the boat, I looked out westerly, and through the heavy timber saw an unusually black cloud, accompanied by heavy thunder, coming fast. I watched the Indians and the cloud, and made motions for them to row faster; but about half-way they began to talk, and stopped altogether. I tried to urge them on, but one of them said in broken English, "One dollar and quarter," over and over. I was in a close place; an awful storm coming, and the boat standing still. So of course I paid the bill, and they started, and soon we met another Indian, and they stopped and traded me off, and made me get into his canoe. The terrible storm kept coming, and he got near Grover's cabin, and stopped and gave signs of wanting his pay, and I gave him a twenty-five cent piece, and he barely made out to row me into camp, just as the rain began to come in torrents. Such thunder was seldom heard; but there was enough dry ground for me to sleep on, with some old hay for a bed. I had only a piece of bread and butter for my supper, nothing for breakfast, and about twenty miles to the old Hay River settlement, which was left to the west of me as I went out.

Here was the battle-field between the Chippewas and Sioux Indians some time before. I saw where the bullets had lodged in trees and stumps. There was a settlement of old loggers, who, when the logging camps were moved farther up, staid and farmed. I went around, got them all out, and preached to them as best I could—thirty-five all told. As it was the first service of any kind in that place, they were all attention. There was a Mr. Tiffany, from New York State, who had lived up there many years, who came to the cabin door, and leaned up against the wall almost spell-bound through the entire discourse. I had a talk with him. He told me this was the only preaching he had heard for twenty-two years, and then he heard Mr. Littlejohn, of New York. He had worked upon a creek making shingles so long, that they called it Tiffany Creek. He seemed to be a man of intelligence; but so far they had had no schools or preaching.

From here I made my way to Menominee Mills—Knapp, Stout & Co.'s large saw and grist mills—over twenty miles. I rode into Hay River where it was swimming deep, and got all wet. This was a well-managed company, headed by Captain Wilson, who was one of the firm. The company had quite a town, and carried on the manufacturing of lumber, shingles, and laths. There was also a large flooring-mill. Three hundred men were employed, quite a number of whom had families. All rented of the company, who had a very large store, which supplied their town and the surrounding country. This was a regular preaching-place.

Among the men, there was one who doubtless had some thoughts on an equalization of capital and labor, and was somewhat fond of fun. One day, while there was a throng around the stove, he remarked that he had a dream the night before, which was so singular that he could not get it off his mind. Some were curious to hear it, and pressed him to tell it. He refused, until the request became general, when he said he feared that the company would not like it. He was assured that they would take it all right. Then he began by saying that, while in a sound sleep, he thought the devil came after him and was determined to take him. He prayed and begged, and asked if there was something he could do that might give him time. Two or three things the devil told him, which, if he would do, he would let him off. The first: "You raise that mill-dam and start the water to running up the other way." He did that, and then asked what next. "You carry those mills up to the top of that hill." It was so steep that it would have been as much as a goat could do to get up, but he did it well; and the devil said: "You are a captain." "What next?" he inquired. "Now," said the devil, "I want you to show me a company this side of hell that can sell goods at as high a price as Napp, Stout & Co." He gave it up in despair, for it could not be done. Then he awoke, and was glad that it was only a dream.

The truth was, when they paid their rent and paid their store-bills, men had nothing left. Times were hard all over the country in 1860, and if anything was made, it was by the company. They were the only company that I knew of that did not go down with the crash of 1857.

My first appointment here I shall not forget. It had been set for Sunday evening. I as usual was on hand, and put up at Mr. Bullard's, who kept the boarding-house. The company and the whole town were generous. The stable was free for the preacher's horse, and the toll-bridge was free for the preacher. I walked over to Captain Wilson's before meeting. The conference had not sent the preachers he wanted, and he put in his complaint that the Methodist Church had not used them as he thought they deserved. They had preaching only seldom, and some of it on week-day evenings, and so he had engaged a Congregational preacher, and would dispense with our services. I remarked that I should like to attend the services this time. He assented, and we walked together without a word. But mental prayer was my preparation. When we got to the school-house it was jam-full. I thought if this was the last as well as the first, I must, through the grace of God, do my best. Sure enough, God helped me, and I rose far above myself, and a more attentive people need not come together. At the close I remarked that this was likely the last time, and then told them what the captain had said to me, right in his presence, that they were soon to have another preacher, but that if they wished it, I could come once in two weeks till the other arrived. I asked an expression from the congregation. Mr. Bullard said to Captain Wilson, "I think we had as well let Mr. Dyer come for awhile," and he assented, and we went through the year.

Next morning, Captain Wilson and I met, and he said: "Mr. Dyer, you seem to be a plain, matter-of-fact man, and I want you to make my house your home; and when we get tired of you we will tell you." "Thank you, Captain Wilson, I will certainly feel at home with you and your family." His wife was an excellent lady, and his daughters very accomplished. I must say it was a pleasant home, and a weary itinerant enjoyed it.

This place was a green spot on our charge; all seemed to be friends, and we formed a class. Mrs. Wilson united with us, and others to the number of twenty. I enjoyed visits with Mr. Bullard and wife also. He gave me an incident of one of his Indian friends. This old Indian was taken sick there, and expected to die. It was a very cold winter, and the ground froze four feet. Before he died he requested Mr. Bullard to have him buried like a white man, and he wanted him to buy his squaw two gallons of whisky so she would "cry heap." When it came to digging the grave, the ground was so frozen that it could hardly be done. There were several Indian tents at hand, and one of the Indians offered to take his tent away so that he could dig the grave where his fire had been all the winter, and where it would be comparatively easy to dig. There he buried his Indian friend.

We felt we had many friends on this charge. There were Carson Saton at Ogalla, with others, on that end of the circuit; and Mother Massie and her family; Brother William Massie and his wife. For a number of years William Massie has been an itinerant preacher in West Wisconsin Conference. I don't know but I did something to set him out, because he saw what small talents I had, and yet was able to do some good. There was my old friend Lewis; but while I was there he had not seen his way clear to come out in religion. At Mud Prairie was Brother Harshman.

Here was an incident that occurred through whisky: There was a man brought some of the liquid fire to sell. Three men came with a jug, and got it filled with whisky and molasses about twice. They lived two miles up the Prairie; had a wagon and yoke of oxen; all got in, and the oxen went home; two of the three got out. The woman saw they were deathly sick; she administered warm water and set them to vomiting, which helped them; and about the time they had thrown up their "black-strap," a little boy came, and said: "Mother, there is another man out in the wagon." She went and found him dead. They sent for a doctor; but it was too late to do anything but analyze the whisky. He said enough of it would kill anybody. The saloon-man ran away, leaving the key with a neighbor. All that loved the whisky were in trouble, because of fear. By chance, a Negro came along. The neighbor called him and gave him a glass, and the darkey passed on; and the man followed him forty rods around the corner. He was asked what he was following him for? He replied: "I gave him a glass of that whisky, and I thought if it did not kill him before he got out of sight, I would take some." Brother T. Harwood was here on a visit, and preached at the funeral of the unfortunate white man. How sad to think of the destruction wrought by whisky!

We had a man and his wife who joined the Church this year, and who had some grown children. One, a son at home, came to get me to marry him. He said that his father would be mad, and that I must go to meet him at his brother-in-law's, Rev. Stubbs. After the ceremony, he said he wanted me to do all I could for him; for he must take his wife home, as he had no other place to take her. I went to the school-house, and gave out a prayer-meeting at his father's, and went in advance to see the old folks. O, how mad they were! I gave them all the consolation I could, and told the girls that we must kill some chickens and make a big supper. We caught some; and soon the bridal party came. The old gentleman would not speak to them; but we all ate at the same table, and after this came the prayer-meeting. Quite a number came, and all prayed around; and at last, I called on the mad father, an Irishman, and he prayed for us all, and said: "Lord, have mercy on this new married couple. O Lord, thou knowest I had nothing in the world to do with it." The next morning we found him so far blessed that he spoke to them, and soon ordered lumber to build a house for them, and gave eighty acres of land to build it on.

By this time we were set off in a new conference, called North-west Wisconsin. We were organized at Sparta by Bishop Scott. We were not large in numbers, and but few if any among us claimed great ability; but all were self-sacrificing men, in a new, rough, timbered country, with times hard and many of the people poor. But we went to work. I was appointed to Mindora Circuit; filled all the appointments; held some special services. A few were converted at one point. I was only on the work about four months, when I was taken with sore eyes. I still kept up my work until April; not able to read—could hardly read my letters; stood in front of the light at night; had the lids of my eyes turned over and burnt with caustic, and concluded to quit and rest awhile. I took a note from my presiding elder, stating the cause of leaving my work, and with my youngest boy, who was at school in Galesville University, went by the way of Eau Claire to Dunville. My son stayed with Brother F. Massie until the gathering war-cloud burst, when he enlisted in the Fifth Wisconsin Regiment.

I might have given some names on this work, had not my memorandum-book been lost. Brother Barber was one of the official members. T. C. Golden was presiding elder. I crossed the Mississippi at Reed's Landing, with Brother C. Hobart, D. D. He rowed, and I dipped water, for our skiff leaked. The river was very rough, but the Doctor was a good hand with the oars, and we got over safe, and parted at Reed's Landing. This was the last I saw of him till we met in 1868 at Chicago in the General Conference.

I made my way through Minnesota to Lenora, where my daughter lived. There I closed up my business, or rather closed out and paid out all my effects that had been left, and was minus over five hundred dollars in one place, owed two hundred in another, and had a good horse, saddle, and bridle, a few little things in a carpet-sack—Bible, hymn-book, Discipline of our Church, and a copy of Lorain's Sea Sermons, with a change of linen, and fourteen dollars and seventy-five cents in silver and gold. I received about fifty dollars in the half year, and had collected about fifteen dollars for periodicals. There being a crash with some of our banks, that much was sent back to me from the Book Concern, which I afterwards made good. I traded about twenty paper dollars that I could not pass at any per cent in hard money, for about

seven dollars in a coat. I had gone security on
two notes, paid one, and gave my house and some
lots for over four hundred dollars on the other,
and yet owed about seven hundred, and my cred-
itor wanted me to give him my horse, or wanted
to take it. I had received seven appointments,
and attended to them as best I could; brought
about sixteen hundred dollars to Minnesota, besides what I received. No man can realize just
how I felt, unless he has been at some time in the
same situation. There was no extravagance,
either, except in going security.

CHAPTER VI.

PIKE'S PEAK AND WESTWARD.

I HAD made up my mind to see Pike's Peak; that was, if I could see at all, as I had to wet my eyes and wipe them to get them open every morning. I had a bottle of Sloan's Instant Relief that I used every day, and my friends said, "You will put your eyes out on the plains," and advised me not to go. Added to blindness, my means ($14.75) were scanty; but I had made up my mind to go—if I did not starve on the way—and felt that my Heavenly Father would provide, and that my bread and water were sure.

On the ninth day of May, 1861, I left Lenora on a splendid riding animal. Omaha was my first place of destination.

As I left Minnesota, I could but reflect on the six years passed in that new country. First, I counted up over five hundred penitents whom I had seen at the altar, and most of whom had professed conversion. I had been the first preacher in many places, and formed societies; and in this I praised God for his goodness in making me his instrument in doing some good. Then, looking at my financial condition, I could see no way out; but I had given all my property up, and had one consolation, and that was, that I had intended to wrong no one, and cared less for what was gone than that I was unable to pay at once all claims against me. I held myself fully committed to pay every cent as soon as I could make it. I rode that day forty-seven miles. I stopped with a partial acquaintance for the night. We had seen each other several times. I asked for my bill. He looked down his nose, and said, "Twenty-five cents."

From that to Newtown, Iowa, I made fifty miles a day; rested Sunday at the above place. Before eating, I fed and took care of my horse; but while at breakfast, the landlord saw my mare was about to disturb a sitting hen, and took her into another stall where there was a peck of corn. As the result, she was foundered almost to death. I mention this because the hen worth six cents, a dozen of eggs four cents, and his saving ten cents, cost me one hundred and fifty dollars. I led her a few miles and sold her for a gun, an old watch, and fifteen dollars, a very little more than the saddle and bridle were worth.

I stopped a day at Omaha, and there was a train of eighteen wagons starting for Pike's Peak. One of the men agreed to board me across for fifteen dollars, and haul my carpet-sack and gun. I was to walk. We set out for six hundred miles, as it was called. A Mr. Penny bossed the train. We got to Fremont about ten o'clock on Sunday morning. I was told they would have preaching at eleven o'clock. I staid to hear, and was asked to preach at the afternoon service, and did so. I thought it would be easy to overtake an ox-team, as that was the last settlement between the Missouri River and the Rocky Mountains. I had about thirty hearers. I staid all night, and caught up with the train.

There were a few soldiers at Fort Kearney. I exercised myself with two or three trips out to the Bluffs, four or five miles. I wanted to see a buffalo, but never got sight of one, much less a chance to shoot one.

About seventy-five miles below Julesburg, we came to a house made of cedar logs, just built, and it was on Sunday. Our train stopped, and my company said if I would preach they could get the privilege of the house. It was so arranged. There were others there besides our company of twenty men, which made in all forty very attentive hearers. After it was over, our boys concluded I was disgraced, for it was a house of ill-fame. I replied that if it was, I had had forty whore-mongers to one woman. They did not bother me any more. Those who live in glass houses must not throw stones.

We frequently met with Indians. The poor creatures had learned to swear. What a pity the white men had no better manners than to teach them to blaspheme!

One day we came to a station where there were a number of camps, and a lot of drunken men tearing around. A fat dog belonging to the train began to stagger, and soon died. It was thought he got strychnine. The Indians saw him kicking his last, and offered twenty-five cents for him. They skinned and cooked him, and soon had dog-soup.

Here a drunken man came into our corral and claimed one of our oxen. Swore he would have him, holding his gun at a ready. I stood at one end to help, and had a big ox-gad. He ran toward me. I raised the gad and told him to get out of there, and made at him, and he got out at the nearest gap. I looked around, and not a man was to be seen; they all were scared. This proved quite a brevet to me.

We reached Julesburg, and there took the cut-off—a new road—which a company had opened, having bridged two or three sand-creeks with poles, and put up a toll-gate, and of course advertised the cut-off. This meant—"Do n't follow the Platte River, and you will soon be in Denver." The trail was not yet worn smooth, and it seemed long and tedious.

One day, as we were taking our lunch, a German said: "I believes dese cut-offs is one *cut-on.*" It struck us all, for we began to think it about so, since we were all foot-sore, as well as the oxen, and nothing to break the monotony. The day before we got through, we stopped to water the cattle. I asked my team-boss if I should make some coffee. He was mad, because one of his oxen was not likely to get water, and swore at me. My offer was gratis, for I had not agreed to do any thing, but had done many little things to assist the boys. When I told him he had as well stop his abuse, he said that he did not care for

my profession, and would thrash me. Of course
I told him he could not do that, and said I did not
want to dirty my hands with him, but that he
ought to be slapped in the mouth. By this time
some of the boys spoke to him, and he shut up.
I had got almost through, and had not had a hard
word with any of the company. In fact, I believe
that, without an exception, they would have de-
fended me to the last, if necessary.

Now we came to the last night on the plains.
I had two pairs of pants, about half worn. I had
left my pocket-knife and purse in the pocket in
the pair that was in the wagon that night, and
when I took them out, found the contents all gone.
Well, the loss was small, as it was less than two
dollars and a-half; but it was all I had, and I was
consoled in the fact that I was no worse off than
I would have been if it had been five thousand
dollars. We stopped two miles up Cherry Creek,
above Denver. I took what I had in my carpet-
sack, and, with my gun on my shoulder, walked
into the town, and met my second son Elias, who
had come a year before. He was working in Mr.
Sprague's store in West Denver. That was almost
all of Denver, the 20th of June, 1861. Suffice
it to say, I was surprised to see—so far from any
other place—so much of a village; and I have
seldom, if ever, seen any one since who has not
been similarly surprised when he sets his eyes in
Denver for the first time. Why should it not sur-
pass his expectation, after traveling six hundred
miles across what was called the American Desert,

with only here and there a small sod tenement about seven feet high, all at once to come to the metropolis of Pike's Peak?

Denver was nearly all on the west side, only a few brick houses on the east side, and a few buildings on Blake Street; and Wm. N. Byers, on neither side, as his building was in the middle of Cherry Creek, attached to the lower side of the bridge.

After visiting with my son a few hours, I crossed the bridge where the printing-office was in operation, and saw the name of Byers, which was familiar to me in my youth. I met the man, asked him about his birthplace, and he replied: "Madison County, Ohio." I said: "You were born in 1830, either in February or March." He told which, and it appeared we had been raised within four miles of each other, but I had left when he was only six months old; but soon I met Daniel Andrews, who kept the Chicago House. We had been near neighbors in Illinois.

On Sunday evening I was invited to preach by Rev. Mr. Kenny, the newly arrived preacher for Denver, of the Methodist Episcopal Church. I remember the subject was repentance, and in speaking of the full surrender of a sinner to God in order to his being taken back into favor, declared that it must be unconditional; and as I had just heard of our war being a reality, I illustrated by what terms would be granted the rebels—they never could be received back except on unconditional surrender—and added, that though it might be through fire and blood, it would come. And as there was much feeling on the subject just then, several in the audience rose to their feet in sympathy with the patriotic sentiment. The remarks were more prophetic than the speaker was aware of at the time, but he always believed that such an end of the Rebellion would come.

I swapped my watch for about twenty dollars' worth of provisions—flour, side-bacon, dried apples, sugar, coffee, and salt enough to save it, with a few cans of fruit. Price, on an average, about twenty-five cents per pound. My son gave me a buffalo-skin and quilt for bedding. My mind was bent on a mountain trip, and no time to spare, as I thought of getting back by the last of September. The Phillips Lode, at Buckskin Joe, was the point of the greatest excitement at that time. I joined myself to a company which had a team. They hauled my stuff, and I started on foot for another hundred miles. This was the third day of July, 1861. We reached Apex, at the foot-hills, the first day, which I supposed we would reach by noon. But I was like the man, several years after, that started to the same place before breakfast; traveled till he got tired, and seeing a ditch some fifty yards ahead, he stopped and began to pull off his boots. His comrade asked him what was the matter? He replied: "If that ditch"—about four feet wide—"is as much wider in proportion as the mountains are further from Denver than they look to be, I will have to swim it."

We began to ascend the mountains on the 4th

of July, 1861, and as it was my first mountain trip, I was wonderfully interested. It was so different from what I supposed—timber, grass, shrubs of many kinds, strawberry-vines in full bloom, with an occasional view back across the plains. It was a pleasant day. I indulged in reflections on the wonders of the creation of God; but could not conceive that the signers of the Declaration of our Independence had even a faint idea of the half they were doing.

We reached the head of the North Platte, on Kenosha Hill. For over twenty miles, up the cañon, we had been shut out from seeing much of the world by the towering mountains on either side. We were well prepared, as we reached the top, to be astonished at the sight of South Park, which from this point is a view of grandeur never to be forgotten. Prairies, surrounded with high mountains and interspersed with pine-groves and small peaks—a very Eden Park—are a sight seldom surpassed even in the Rocky Mountains.

On the ninth day of July, we reached Buckskin Joe Camp. Just two months from the day I left Lenora, Minnesota, my eyes had improved a little. Otherways, I enjoyed good health, after a tramp of over seven hundred miles on foot. What a difference between then and now! Then, a half-beaten wagon-track on an Indian trail; now, the passenger sits on a cushioned seat, and rests at night in a sleeping-car! One thing is certain—he can't come as independently as I came on twenty-seven dollars!

I find among my papers "A Short Account of My First Year in Colorado, Commencing June 20, 1861," which I read before the first District Ministerial Association ever held in Denver. I walked from Summit County in order to read it. Governor John Evans, after hearing it, presented me with fifteen dollars. At the risk of repetition, I will give it here: After resting a few days in Denver, having walked from Omaha, Nebraska, and having preached once, I started on the 3d of July for Buckskin Joe, in South Park; and on the 9th saw the Phillips Lode, then the bonanza of the country. On inquiry I found that Brother William Howbert had preached a funeral sermon in 1860, and Brother William Antis had held one service. This was the first preaching in these parts. Rev. William Howbert was on the South Park Mission, 1861.

The following Sunday we selected a shade, with a few logs for seats, where services were kept up for some time, with street-preaching at night. In a short time Brother Howbert preached, and proposed to form a class; and as no move was made, I arose, and said I had often beat up for volunteers, and always felt like joining over again, and now was my time; and gave my hand and name to the Church. Over twenty followed. They formed the first class so high up in the mountains.

The first Sunday in August I walked eight miles to Montgomery to preach, and instead of finding a good number, all were out staking off claims but one man. He asked me to take dinner. We sat down on the ground to eat, as there was not a house, table, or stool, in the place. From there I made my way up to Quartz Hill, just at timber line, where I preached to about thirty attentive hearers, and felt that the Lord was with us indeed; walked back sixteen miles, and held two services; the next Sabbath, visited Fair Play, and preached to thirty, who all gave good attention to the words spoken, as it was the first preaching there. On the 25th of August I tried to preach the first sermon in Mosquito by a camp-fire, as there was no house at the time in the place. For nine weeks my house was made of poles and pine-boughs, so thatched that they turned the rain after being well soaked one night. Worked through the week by the day and contract.

On the 16th of September I set out for California Gulch, having been solicited previously to take charge of that mission by the pastor who supplied it. He agreed to have the presiding elder make the change. But he left in disgrace, and the presiding elder—John M. Cherington—had become a major in the army. I was left on my own resources, in a wilderness country, with six or seven members, and they scattered over one hundred miles! The outfit was a buffalo-skin and quilt, some crackers, a piece of bacon, coffee and sugar, with some dried apples, a tin cup, and an oyster-can; in all, thirty-seven and one-half pounds to pack on my back. I now made my way up the range, about eight miles, to the top of the Mosquito Pass, the highest and hardest range I had then crossed. From here I could see the head of the Platte River, Arkansas, Blue River, and the head of the Grand River; like the Garden of Eden, it was at least the starting point of all these mighty rivers.

As I took a view of those gigantic mountain peaks and deep gorges, the thought came to me, if heaven is above, I am nearer Canaan's shores than ever before. After prayer for our country on both sides, and for myself, alone on the dividing range of our great continent, I partook of my frugal stores, and that night preached at California Gulch, now Leadville. The next day started alone for the Gunnison country, following an Indian trail. Had to wade the Arkansas. Took off my boots, and I thought the top of the cold water would cut my legs off; and that day I saw for the first time the beautiful Twin Lakes. Had not heard of them before. My surprise may be imagined. My path was up Lake Creek, a perfect mountain wilderness, snowy ranges towering on either side. I had not seen a human being for several miles; night was coming on, and I began to look for a camping-place. I heard, just as the sun was sinking behind the snow-capped mountains, the sound of a bell, and soon found five men. They had one burro to pack their food and blankets. I asked for lodging. They said: "If you can furnish your own accommodations, you can stay." I accepted. I had a paper with me with a sermon preached by Dr. Elliott, in St. Louis, on the "Rights of God and Cæsar." It was in war time, and by the fire made of pine-roots it was read, and you would better believe it was a grand treat. Next morning I had breakfast, and started before my company, and at three o'clock was at Kent's Gulch, where there were about one hundred men, one of whom had a family. He had raised his house, and was just covering it with poles, grass, and dirt. I told him I was a bit of a Methodist preacher, and would like to preach in his house. He said: "You can, sir, when I get the roof on." It was announced for the next night, and nearly every man in the diggings came. There were a table and two benches. When the benches were full, the hearers sat on the ground all around the walls, and the next row against their knees, until every foot of space was filled. The tent opposite the door and the space around the door were also crowded. It was as singular a scene as the Savior had, when he broke bread to the multitude. My subject was "Repentance and Conversion." A more attentive crowd is seldom seen, and God's presence was manifest, and the preacher felt that he was standing between the living and the dead. This was the first effort in the way of preaching ever made in all the Gunnison country. One man arose and took a collection of about twenty dollars in gold-dust, and gave me an invitation to come and preach again. The woman said she had no time to hear; must do up her work, and so washed dishes until the text was read. She turned her back to her work, holding her dish-cloth in her hand, and never moved until the discourse was closed. I found three members of our Church, Brothers Gamble, Dunnagan, and Case.

The next day I took my pack and started for Washington Gulch, forty-five miles west, on a dim Indian trail. Near the crossing of Taylor River I overtook a pack-train loaded with food, all but one burro, which had twenty gallons of whisky. Just then we were met by a number of prospectors. They saw the whisky-kegs. Of course they must have some. They caught the burro, one holding it by the head, and another by the tail, and the third trying to get the cork out. The preacher stepped up, and asked if they were tapping the jack. "No," was the reply, "it is the keg." Suffice it to say, they all drank out of a tin cup, and one of them poured out gold-dust into the freighter's hand until he was satisfied. Well, I passed on, and for once got in ahead of the whisky.

That day we passed Deadman's Gulch. At this place six white men had been killed by a company of Indians in 1859. It is said that they fought bravely, standing behind their horses; and it looked as though it might have been so, as I saw the bones of several horses, as well as a part of the frames of six human beings, that lay bleaching in the mountains. They had been slightly buried, but the wolves had uncovered them. Kit Carson was informed by the Indians that several of their number were killed, and some wounded. There was none to tell us of the dreadful scene; the tall pines alone witnessed the ascent of the dead men's ghosts.

We camped near that place. It was very high, and disagreeably cold. Next day I camped, in company with two men, in sight of Minersville, on Washington Gulch. Sabbath, the 24th of September, I entered the town, and shall not forget the scene. One man was cutting and selling beef; others rolling logs down the hill; others covering their cabins; another building a chimney; and still others selling provisions and whisky in a tent. From this stand-point I resolved to announce my appointment.

The first man I spoke to was dressing some grouse. After salutation, I said: "Did not you expect a Methodist preacher would be on hand as soon as you had chicken to eat?" "Well," he said, "I have heard that they were fond of chickens," and gave me a welcome to take dinner with him. The preacher was on hand in time. I stepped out to about the center of the camp, and said: "O yes! O yes! O yes! there will be preaching at half-past ten o'clock wherever the most people can be found together."

As I walked around the camp, I met some going fishing, others berrying, and invited all. Here I met Brother Tindal, of Georgetown. One asked me who was going to preach. I made a bow, and said: "I am going to try, with the help of God." He seemed much astonished. Meeting quite a hard-looking man, I invited him to come and hear preaching. He replied: "It does n't look well for a man to ask people to come and hear him preach." The preacher looked at him in the crowd, and said: "Sir, if I could get such a looking man as you are to come by asking him, I would do well."

The time arrived, and now came the tug of war; for the most people were around the grocery. Forty men and jacks, mules, and ponies. Just now the preacher began to sweat. It was hard to speak in such a place, not knowing that there was one in sympathy with him; but it must be done. I got in front of the tent, under the shade of a pine-tree, and read the hymn, beginning, "Alas! and did my Savior bleed?" and as I tried in the old way to sing it, a number joined in and helped; but some were selling, others buying, and some packing their beasts. At the proper time I said: "Let us pray." After this the poor preacher began to feel better, and the people kept coming in until there were over one hundred. And as the speaker proceeded, he felt that God had verified his promise: "Lo, I am with you alway, even unto the end of the world." I was at the last camp east of California, and had the evidence that God was in the wilderness as well as in the city full, and felt that I could run through a troop.

I will state two things that took place during the service. When about half through, three men got on their ponies in the outskirts of the congregation, and one of them waved his hat and said farewell. The speaker responded for the audience, and also said, "God have mercy on your soul," and they passed away. Soon after this a mule reached his head into the tent and took out a loaf of bread, and started off with it; but was soon caught, tied up, and the bread taken away, so that we were getting rid of some of the stock. Notwithstanding these interruptions, most of the hearers listened with great attention. At the close, I gave out that I would have a camp-meeting at night. There were tents enough, and plenty of pine-knots for light, but that we would have to dispense with the women, for there was but one within a hundred miles of us. We built an extra fire or two, and I suppose there were not less than one hundred and fifty people out to hear the word.

We had services on Monday evening again. It was seed sown in weakness. God only knows the results. A man came to me at the close, and invited me to take breakfast with him; said it was the first sermon he had heard preached for eight years, and several said it was the first they had heard for two years. I met a man here from Wisconsin, and another from Minnesota, whom I had been acquainted with. They gave me about ten dollars.

On Tuesday I started back alone on the Indian trail, and near sunset met a German in Deadman's Gulch, and in sight of the bones of the six men killed by the Indians. He made some inquiries. I told him where we were, and pointed to the bones, and he began to whip his jack and put out; did not want to hear any more. Within a mile

I met a man that had stopped to camp. We agreed to lodge together. I saw at once that he was a Southerner; his speech betrayed him. I was careful to say nothing relative to the war; but he asked me how I stood as to the Rebellion. I told him I was for the Union, and remarked it would not be worth while for us to fight here, as we had no reporter. He said we could talk friendly on the subject; so we did, and parted friendly, after sleeping under the same tree. He was armed, and I was not, save the arms that God had given me, but I felt safe in his protecting care.

Next day I reached Kent's Gulch, and stayed until Monday. I preached twice, and again took the trail across the range to Twin Lakes and Cask Creek. I will here speak of the first preaching on Cask Creek, some four weeks before in a saloon. The owner said I was welcome if I would preach. The reply was: "If you can get more sinners in there than in other places, there is no good reason why I should not try to reform them in that or any other place." I had some fifty hearers. The preacher stood at the end of the counter, and this time Bible and hymn-book took the place of bottle and glass, and the preacher had control for the hour, and seldom felt greater freedom in dispensing the word of life to an attentive set of miners. From my observation, I began to think that scarcely a man had crossed the plains who would not behave in divine service. And as there were no trees without going into the woods, I found room in a cabin to sleep, and after I retired, a man came in and asked me to get up and go with him and marry a couple. Of course I went. I wished to know something of the case in hand. They gave the following account:

The couple had run away from near Denver. The girl's father was opposed to the match. In their flight, they found a justice, and he performed the ceremony of matrimony. The father followed, with help, some eighty miles; and while the bride and groom were eating their dinner on the bank of a creek in South Park, the pursuing party came up and demanded the girl of sixteen. All being armed, the girl stood between her father and her husband until he hitched up, and then, jumping into the wagon, the plucky couple put for the mountains; and the father and company gave up the chase, but told them he knew the justice had no commission. The groom pleaded with me to marry them, so that the father would be better satisfied, knowing that a preacher had performed the ceremony. I thought they were married and that it would do no harm to marry them over again, and so did it. I was out of money, and he gave me two half-dollars.

The next day I visited Georgia Bar, on the Arkansas River; found some fifty men at work panning out the dust; gathered a few, and preached at night. Next morning, as I passed up the Bar, thought it a mighty contact, water against rock. I felt gloomy, and the scene looked so; and just as I passed a cabin, a man came out and asked me if I was the man that preached below last night. "Yes, sir." He said a young man died there last night, and asked me to attend the funeral. Forty men and two women were present. All seemed to be deeply affected, as it was the first funeral most of us had been at in the mountains. He was buried as decently as the circumstances would admit. From there I went to California Gulch, and preached; and, after resting a few days, went to the Gunnison again. Falling in with a Mr. Noah Armstrong, we bought a jack, packed him, and I thought that, as I was on my own hook, it would be well to dig a little, as necessity seemed to demand it.

We prospected over three weeks without success, when a deep snow fell. We were seventy miles from any winter quarters, and the main range to cross, and the snow from three to five feet deep. While we were out, on the first Sunday, my partner said, as we did not work, we ought to have preaching. I told him if he could stand the application, I could preach to him. So he gave it out for one o'clock; and after the preliminaries, knowing my whole audience had plenty at home, and had lost all in the mountains, I commented on the Parable of the Prodigal Son. Suffice it to say, the congregation was attentive and serious. We staid so long that it was with difficulty we got out. We were several days on short allowance, and one day had nothing. We shoveled snow three days and a half to get three and a half miles; but, by the blessing of God, we made the riffle. I reached California Gulch in good health, weighed one hundred and sixty-three pounds, and when I left the States, pulled one hundred and ninety-two pounds. I found out that a man at forty-seven, getting fat, could walk, work, and preach off all the fat.

I stayed at the above place until the 7th of January; held meetings for ten nights; some rose for prayers, but they must have the school-house to dance in, and we had to yield; and then started alone for Buckskin Joe, by the Weston Pass. At timber height I was met by a severe snow-storm. Had a box of matches, but not one would burn. The prospect was frightful. I prayed and dedicated myself to God, and thought that by his grace I would try to pull through. For five or six hours I waded the snow waist-deep, until, almost exhausted, I leaned up against a tree to rest. I never saw death and eternity so near as then. My life seemed to be at an end; but I resolved to keep moving, and when I could go no more, would hang up my carpet-sack, and write on a smooth pine-tree my own epitaph—"Look for me in heaven;" but through the goodness of God, I reached the toll-gate about one hour after dark; and I shall never forget the kindness of the Swede who took me in and cared for me.

From here to Fairplay, called fifteen miles, I gathered up a congregation of twenty-five, and preached at the store of Mr. Sharman. From there I went to Buckskin Joe, and, with Brother Antis, held meeting for two weeks, in the face of every kind of opposition—at least two balls a week, a dancing-school, a one-horse theater, two men shot—and yet, notwithstanding all these things, we had a good meeting. The Church was much revived, and several backsliders were reclaimed. In about four months I traveled near five hundred miles on foot, by Indian trails, crossing logs, carrying my pack, and preaching about three times a week. Received forty-three dollars in collections at different places. Nothing that we ate cost less than twenty-five cents per pound, and we had to carry freight on our backs. Spent about fifty dollars of my own resources, as I had worked by the day and job through the week, and preached nights and Sundays. My clothes were worn out; my hat-rim patched with dressed antelope-skin; my boots half-soled with raw-hide. This is a sample of my work and experiences the first year in the mountains of Colorado.

CHAPTER VII.

IN COLORADO.

ABOUT the 1st of February I started on foot for Denver. We had a stage once a week to Buckskin Joe. Fare, ten dollars each way. I could walk the hundred miles in two days and a half. If I did not make money, I could save some. On Saturday evening I reached the city of Denver, dressed, as far as it went, in miner's clothes, minus a vest. I thought it would be all right to sit back and hear the preacher; but who should it be but Colonel Chivington, in his military suit, with belt, bowie-knife, and revolver. I had taken my seat half-way back. As he passed, he took hold of my collar, pulled me out into the aisle, and said: "Come, preach for me." Of course, by this everyone in the house had seen me, as well as my clothes. I walked up, told him to give out a hymn, and afterwards I led in prayer. It was always best for me to whet my own scythe. I will say nothing about the effort, only that I forgot all about poor clothes.

The next day I was passing a store, and was called in by my esteemed friend, Brother Pease, now of Cheyenne, Wyoming, who made me a present of a vest. I have not been without one since. This gave the colonel a chance to tell an incident, which contrasts the preachers of the past and present, and shows the generosity of a Presbyterian in early times. It was common for our preachers to wear homespun; and their wives often spun, and sometimes wove the jeans on the common loom. I think they do not do so now. Well, all right.

At the first conference of the Methodist Church ever held in the city of Columbus, Ohio, Rev. Russel Bigelow, one of the members, was dressed as above, and present. Rev. James B. Finley was the preacher in charge, and was told by a Presbyterian friend that if he would send him one of their best preachers, he would board him. He sent Brother Bigelow, whose plain garb almost disgusted his host and family. Meeting Mr. Finley, he said: "Why did you not send a respectable preacher?" "You wanted one of our best preachers, and the one sent is to preach at your church Sunday, and if you do n't say he is good or the best you ever heard, I am mistaken!" Sunday came, and they took their pews. The lady and the two daughters kept their veils over their faces at first; but as he began to rise in his discourse, they lifted their veils, while the host, with many others, was unconsciously standing on his feet. I suppose they forgot all about his coarse clothes. Mr. Finley met his friend next day, and asked him how he liked his preacher. He answered: "You Methodists are not fit to have such a preacher!" He took him to a tailor and ordered him a fine suit, which the eloquent Bigelow always kept to wear to conference. Such were the men we had fifty or sixty years ago. There were not ten his equals in the United States at the time of his death.

I made a trip to the Wide-awake Camp, and tried to preach several times, and over to Central City, to help Brother Adriance hold a quarterly meeting, about the first of March. We had a useful meeting.

In the latter part of March, 1862, I received a letter from Brother B. C. Dennis, presiding elder of the Rocky Mountain District, Kansas Conference—at this time Colorado was included in this conference—asking me to take charge of Blue River Mission, Summit County, Colo. I was in Denver, and the next day started on foot. I went by Central City, and the first day out from there it snowed four inches, which made it bad walking. The second day reached Kenosha Hill, remarkably tired. My purse of gold-dust was so light that I feared there would not be enough to pay my bill. I told the landlord that it was possible that my means would not meet my expenses, but wished to stay, and that I would remit to him. He said that it would be all right, and the call for supper soon came. When I sat down, I saw that the food was all cold except a weak cup of tea. After a few mouthfuls, I became sick and left the table, and lay down on a bench in the bar-room and rested, for I was almost given out. After half an hour, another man came in for supper, and while he was eating I went in for a drink of water, and saw hot coffee, ham, and eggs, I thought I would never say anything about pay again until after breakfast. I rested all night, and in the morning ate a hearty breakfast, and gave the host my purse. He weighed out my bill, and I had some left. There were at lest twenty-five miles to walk, and but one house. I took dinner and handed my purse to the landlord, and he weighed my bill and I crossed the range on a snow-path; for, although it was April, the snow was from five to fifteen feet deep.

I reached Georgia Gulch on the second day of April, and was received kindly. There were about one hundred and fifty people in the Gulch, and I found some few that had been members of some Church. I gave out preaching for the next Sunday at ten and a-half o'clock, and at French Gulch in the afternoon. The hall was well-filled in the morning, and there were about forty hearers in the afternoon. There was a friendly Jew at Georgia Gulch, who proposed to raise the preacher something, and took a paper and collected $22.50 in dust; for that was all the currency then. This amount was quite a help, as there were only ten cents in my purse when I got there. There was an appropriation of one hundred and twenty-five dollars from the conference. We had at first five preaching-places for two weeks, and afterwards more.

I saw that what I was likely to get in the new wild country would not board me, as common board was seven dollars a week, and a man had to find his own bed, and do his own washing. I had a chance to buy a cabin in French Gulch or what was then called Lincoln City, and I set up in a humble way keeping bachelor's hall. My bedstead was made of pine poles, even to the springs. The bed was hay, with blankets for covering. I slept well, and rested as well as though I had been in a fine parlor-chamber. My furniture was primitive and limited—a table, and a couple of boards against the side of the wall for a cupboard, six tin plates, half a set of knives and forks, with a few other indispensables; a coffee-pot, a tin cup, and a pot for boiling vegetables—when I had them—and a frying-pan. As to a library, mine had not crossed the plains; but we had a few books to read—the Bible, hymn-book, and Methodist Discipline, with two of our weekly *Advocates* and the *Rocky Mountain News*. I tried to keep up with the times.

The compass of my circuit was not large. The farthest appointment was six miles; and I preached about seven times in two weeks. I formed one class, and then discovered that there was little profit in it, as the people stopped so short a time in one place. I concluded to get everybody out, and then preach the truth burning hot, whether my hearers were in the house or around the camp-fire, or, at other times, under the shade of a pine-tree. We generally had good congregations. The way we got them out was to go along the gulches and tell the people in their cabins and saloons where the preaching would be at night, and then, just before the time, to step to the door where they were at cards, and say: "My friends, can't you close your game in ten minutes, and come and hear preaching?" I tried to adapt myself to the situation, neither showing that I felt above anyone, nor ever compromising with sin or with transgressions, and being ready always to speak for the Lord Jesus Christ.

We cooked by a fire-place, generally baking our bread in a frying-pan set up before the fire. I must not forget to say that we had stools and benches in place of chairs. There was one chair left in my house, made by some one out of crooked pine-limbs, with the seat of ropes. It was so comical that if I had it now, I would certainly place it in an exposition. It was easy enough for an editor.

I tried to make my cabin useful. It was about eighteen feet square, and, taken every way, the best place to hold our meetings. The floor was hard ground. I got gunny-sacks and made carpet, and covered the table with two copies of the *Northwestern Christian Advocate*. And thus I preached to the people in my own house, not in a hired house, as the Apostle Paul did.

The first county officers had been elected the fall previous, and the assessor refused to act, and it was intimated that he was afraid that the miners would not stand it to be assessed; so he, with others, insisted that I should take the office as deputy. I told them the office I held was all I could attend to, and that I did not wish to take the responsibility. But they were set on my doing the work, and I concluded to try. Only one man resisted me, and I made him believe that he was the best man I could get to help me, if there was any resistance. He asked me to dinner, and ever after was one of my warmest friends. When I was through, I charged them fifty dollars, and got it after two years; and it came in good time, as I was then in a close place.

My appointments were Park City (Georgia Gulch), American Gulch, Galena Gulch, Delaware Flats, Gold Run, Lincoln City, Mayo Gulch, and Breckenridge. It was a two weeks' circuit. I preached once at least in Gibson Gulch, and I must say that we had, without an exception, good behavior and good attention. Although we all looked rough, the miners treated me and the cause of Christ with respect. Often after preaching I was greeted warmly, and some of them would say the service reminded them of home. They were generally liberal, although it was not the custom always to pass the hat, and sometimes the preacher, when his pants began to wear out, would think the boys rather long between collections. It was common to give a dollar all around; and to this day I would as soon ask miners for help, with assurance of receiving, as any class of men I have ever found. They were always ready to divide, although at times they would take exceptions to a man that wore a plug hat or noticeably fine clothes.

I made me a pair of snow-shoes, and, of course, was not an expert. Sometimes I would fall; and, on one occasion, as I was going down the mountain to Gold Run, my shoes got crossed in front as I was going very fast. A little pine-tree was right in my course, and I could not turn, and dare not encounter the tree with the shoes crossed; and so threw myself into the snow, and went in out of sight.

This was my regular round on the circuit. We had a new field, one that gave a good chance to read human nature, in the fastnesses of the Rocky Mountains, where moral and religious restraints were absent. The most of the men would go to the bar and drink, and play at cards, and the Sabbath was a high day for wickedness. Balls were the common amusement, especially in winter. The women were as fond of this as the men. Although far in the minority, they were accosted like this: "Now, Miss, or Mistress, you must surely come, as we can 't have a set or cotillion without you." Often the father was left with the children at home; at other times both went and took the children; and then the old bachelors would hold the baby so that the mother could dance every set.

I will give an instance at Lincoln City, at our hotel. They must give a Christmas dinner, and, of course, a dance at night. I concluded to take dinner with them. The host made me no charge, as it would be what we old bachelors called a square meal. As I was about to leave, the ladies pleasantly invited me to stay to the dance. Of course I could not accept the invitation. But they said: "You visit at our houses, and you ought to show us respect and stay." At the last came the lady of the house, and said: "This is an extra occasion, and it will be no harm for you to dance with me; why can't you accept my offer?" The reply was: "You're a lady, but not quite handsome enough for me to dance with." She was taken back at that, and the others laughed, and I got out, as my cabin was only two hundred feet away. They soon fiddled me to sleep. But they danced till daylight, and often drank at the bar. Being full, and having no place to sleep, they went up to Walker's saloon. He made some hot sling, and that set them off. They declared that every man in town must get up, and the preacher should treat the company or make a temperance speech. It was just daylight when we heard them on the street, and as they had always passed me before, I turned the key and hoped they would do so again. But when they found the door fast they said: "If you don't open it we will break it in." I threw it open and invited them in; but they said: "We have come to take you up to Walker's, and you can either treat or make a temperance speech." I requested them to let me eat breakfast first; but they said: "You must go now." I slipped out, leaving the door open, and went ahead of the company.

Soon there were over forty men, and they called a chairman or moderator; but they were too drunk to be moderated. I got upon a box and stated my arrest, and proposed to make the speech.

They said: "Go on." I said: "Gentleman, first I will tell you what I think! There is not a man here but would be ashamed for his father, mother, sisters, or brothers, to know just our condition here this morning." They stamped and roared out, "That's so," all over the house. "And next," I continued, "if we were not so drunk, we would not be here." (Cheers, "That's so, too!" all over the house.) "And if we were a little drunker, we could not do as we are now doing." (Cheers and "That's so!" all over the house.) I wound up and was about to take leave, but the judge said: "I move that we vote that every thing Mr. Dyer has said is true;" and they gave a rousing vote. He said, "The ayes have it," but that I must not go yet; and made and put a motion that they all give Mr. Dyer one dollar apiece; and that was also carried. They took the hat, got twenty dollars, and I thanked them and went home to breakfast.

CHAPTER VIII.

SNOW-SHOES.

AS all the mining was gulch or placer diggings, a great part of the people left in the fall to winter—some for Denver, others for Cañon City or Colorado City, some crossing the Missouri River with ox-teams. Only a few would come back in the spring; for men did not come to Pike's Peak—as it was called—to stay, but to make a raise, and then go back.

In the summer of 1861 a troop of theatrical performers came across to Summit County, and played in all the camps—Sunday morning at one place, and in the evening at another. I thought the devil was traveling the circuit as well as myself. I have thought less of theaters ever since. There is little about them but evil. We had some miners who would go to the dance or theaters.

But the best work done was a revival at Gold Run, in the midst of winter. The snow was about six feet deep. We concluded to hold a protracted meeting at the above place, where we had four members, and only about twenty-five people, all told. From the first, the meetings were interesting. Irrespective of denominations, all began to work in earnest. Seventeen was the average attendance, and about that number were warmed up, reclaimed, or converted. We called it a good revival on a small scale. A more enjoyable time I have seldom had. Among those present were Dr. John McKaskill and wife, and J. T. Lynch, the former of whom were in Kansas the last I heard, and the latter in Utah.

In March, 1863, I received my appointment from Kansas Conference. My work up to this time had been as a supply. Through the presiding elder, L. B. Dennis, I was readmitted. It was a surprise, for I had not made up my mind to stay in the mountains. This decided me to stand the storms and leave the events with God, and do the best I could to build up the Church in this wilderness country. I was put down for South Park, and on the third day of April left Lincoln City and stopped at Mr. Silverthorn's, in Breckenridge, until about two o'clock in the morning, when I took my carpet-sack, well filled, got on my snow-shoes, and went up Blue River. The snow was five feet deep. It might be asked, "Why start at

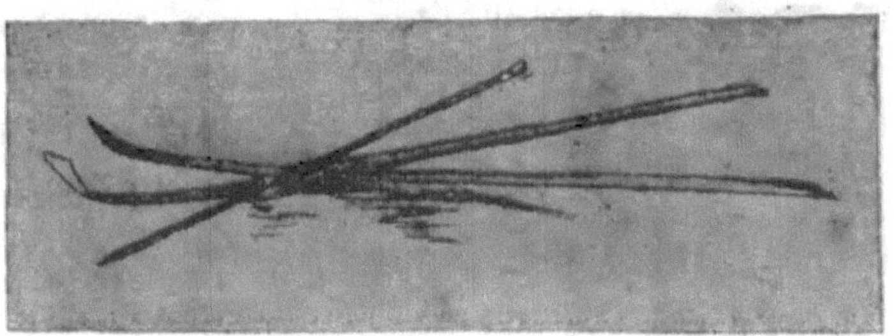

SNOW-SHOES AND STAFF.

two o'clock?" Because the snow would not bear a man in daytime, even with snow-shoes. From about two o'clock until nine or ten in the morning was the only time a man could go; and a horse could not go at all. When about three miles up the Blue River, back of McCloud's, the wolves set up a tremendous howling quite near. I was not armed, but passed quietly along, and was not disturbed. It was not likely, I thought, that the good Lord would let anything disturb a man going in the night to his appointment, although wolves and bears, with some Rocky Mountain lions, were numerous.

I reached Montgomery about nine o'clock in the morning. The snow drifted above the tops of the doors. All along the streets steps had been made in the snow, and served as stairs to get into the stores and houses. There were some two or three hundred people in town, among them seven members. I must mention Brother and Sister Gurton, and Brother and Sister Fowler. I stayed eight days, and held service each evening; on Sunday twice. Two or three professed to be reclaimed, and we all were revived. My circuit embraced the above, with Buckskin Joe, Mosquito, Fair Play, and Tarryall. Buckskin Joe was so called from the nickname given to a prospector wearing a suit of that material.

Tarryall was discovered in 1860. Some very rich claims were opened, and soon all were taken. The news spread, and prospectors by the thousands came, but with no chance to get a foot of ground; so they all tarried, and hence the name Tarryall. From there the prospectors went every way, and some struck pay dirt in the Platte, and called it Fair Play, as they claimed to be more liberal.

This was a two-weeks' circuit. Brother Wm. Howbert was preacher in charge a part of 1860 and 1861, and Brother Loyd in 1862, a part of the year.

Mosquito got its name from this circumstance: The miners met to organize. Several names were suggested, but they disagreed, and a motion was made to adjourn and meet again, the place for the name to be left blank. When they came together on appointment, the secretary opened the book, and a large mosquito was mashed right in the blank, showed it, and all agreed to call the district Mosquito.

In addition to the above places, I went to California Gulch, as that place was not supplied.

Two Mexicans, called Espanosa, who had become enraged against the government of Colorado, came from near Fort Garland, armed to kill as many Americans as they could find. They struck Arkansas River at Hard Scrabble, met Judge Bruce, and shot and murdered him. Thence they went north to Park County, and murdered Mr. Addleman, and from there to near the Kenosha House, where they found two men camped and murdered them. Next, about half-way between Fair Play and Alma, they shot down and killed a Mr. Carter in the road. Just after they had rifled his pockets and taken his pistol and most of his clothes, Mr. Metcalf came along with a wagon and oxen, loaded with lumber. As he sat on the load, they shot at him from a tree about seventy yards off, and gave him a close call—the ball striking right opposite his heart. But the ball struck a pamphlet in his side pocket, and glanced so that it did not hurt him. He of course halloed, and the oxen took fright and ran. They shot again at him, but missed him; and as there was a house in a half mile, he got clear of them. He was the first one that got away from them to describe them. He said they were negroes or men blackened. I suppose he had never seen a Mexican. One of them had a broad-rimmed white hat; and after he was captured, and his hat brought in, Metcalf recognized it as having been worn by the man who shot at him. From the above place they went east to the Red Hill crossing of the Denver road, where any one could be seen coming from either way. There they waited until two men came along on their way from Denver to California Gulch. They shot one dead, and it was supposed wounded the other in the arm. He retreated down the hill to the foot or level, where they caught him and knocked a hole in his skull. This was the last murder they committed. This was late in the evening. The next morning the word came to Fair Play that just over Red Hill there were two men that had been murdered, lying by the roadside.

At this time there were a few soldiers at Fair Play. A number were sent to bring in the dead bodies, and try, if possible, to capture the murderers. Just as the soldiers passed the second dead body, they saw a man coming on the road, whom they at first thought to be a traveler. But seeing them about the same time, and having heard of the numerous murders on the road, he thought they would surely kill him; and dropping his coat in the road, put out south. The soldiers seeing him run, thought he was the man they wanted, and so followed after him at full speed. He, being a man in the prime of life and active, especially on this occasion, made a good race. The word came to Fair Play that they were after the murderer, and another company started on horses to try to head him off. But Mr. John Foster—for that was his name—evaded them all. At one time his pursuers were very close on him, as he passed over a sharp ridge, but he got over before they got quite to the top, and that gave him a chance to turn his course and throw them off his track. After running fifteen or twenty miles, he reached Fair Play in his socks, without coat or hat. As the people saw him in his plight, they halloed: "There comes the murderer!" But I recognized him, as he kept a "Methodist hotel" in California Gulch, and kept in between them and him until he got to the first house. The door being open he went in, and it was some time before he could relate his feat, as he was very short of breath and badly scared, and did not know till then but it was the murderers that had been running him so close. After a while his pursuers came, feeling mortified that he got away from them; but when the facts were known, they felt relieved, for although they had been outrun, they had been saved from killing an innocent man.

I shall not forget that week or ten days of intense excitement. Everybody was alarmed. The five murdered men were buried at Fair Play. The sickening sight of the dead, and the thought, Who would be the next? set the few inhabitants into almost a panic. During the time, word came that a man was harbored at a ranch some fifteen miles east, and a company went over about night and demanded him. The family would not let them in. They guarded the house. There was a shot fired from within which killed a mule. When daylight appeared they gave the inmates just a few minutes to surrender the man, under the alternative of having the house burned. They went in and took the man, and made the ranchman give property to the full value of the mule, and ordered him to leave. They took the prisoner near to Fair Play, and without trial or jury, hanged him, although he denied being guilty of any crime for which he deserved death. But poor Baxter had fallen into the hands of hard men in an evil hour. This was a mob, and nothing better ever comes of such work.

But to return to the pursuit of the Mexicans. The people started a company on their trail from Red Hill. As they had two ponies, they were easily trailed south, and finally were overtaken at breakfast in the chaparral. The pursuers waited for them to go out of the brush to get their ponies. At last only one of them went out, and John said to Joe: "Can you shoot him?" He said, "Yes;" and with his deadly rifle, brought him to the ground. The Mexican tried to shoot, but was not able to do it. One of the avengers, whose brother had been shot by them, craved the privilege to finish the wounded man by shooting him in the head. The other Mexican ran, and got upon a pinnacle of rocks that hung almost over where they were. While Mr. Lamb, who shot first, was stooping over the dead Mexican, to see whether he had shot him as he intended, the other Mexican shot at him from the rocks, the ball passing through his hat-rim, ranging down through his clothes, but fortunately doing no harm. He then made his escape back to near Fort Garland, but was afraid to be seen. He got one of his nephews, and they took up their residence in the mountains for some time. They would come into the settlements on the sly for provisions. A woman found out where they kept themselves, and told it. Mr. Thomas Tobin took a company of five or six men, and went in search of them. As there was a bounty for their heads, both were shot—the old man falling dead in his tracks; the young one, although mortally wounded, running some distance before he expired. That ended the Espanosa trouble. What I have given was most of it done on my route of travel, so I had a good opportunity to know the facts. It was a hard blow on Park County. One mother yet lives to mourn the loss of her son; and sorrowful traces remain in the memory of all the inhabitants. It was a most daring and deplorable outrage.

CHAPTER IX.

COLORADO CONFERENCE.

DURING the alarm occasioned by the murderous raid of the Espanosas, I went around my circuit once. I had been two years traveling in the Rocky Mountains, and had carried no weapons but a pocket-knife, and used that mostly to cut shavings and my broiled meat. Some of my friends advised me to arm myself, or to stop for a time; but I could not see it. I told them I would trust to getting along when the murderers were not watching; and while they had got weapons from every man they had killed, if they got me they would find no pistol to add to their arsenal. First, I did not have money to buy a pistol; and, in the second place, I had been sent there, and my appointments were out, and for two years I had passed all sorts of men, and often slept alone under the shelter of a pine-tree, when I had reason to believe the Rocky Mountain lion and the savage bear were my nearest neighbors, and had never been molested. I felt that I was still in the hands of that same God whom I tried to serve; and that He who had kept me from being a prey to the wild beasts, would keep me, if it was best, from these unknown murderers.

So I started from Fair Play to Mosquito on foot; and about half-way I saw the clotted blood of Mr. Carter, who had been shot in the road two days before. I stayed at Fair Play two or three days, where my exciting experience, above recited, occurred. I filled all my appointments, saw no danger, and was scared only once. As I left Fair Play for Montgomery a slight fall of snow made the pine-trees all white. A bush about five feet high stood under the cover of a larger one, and so had no snow on it. It showed dark on the snow. Just as I passed where the Mexicans had killed Mr. Carter and shot at Mr. Metcalf, I saw the bush, and as it was partly hid behind the body of the tree, it looked as though it might be a man looking for a victim. While I was walking in the road, and had my eye fixed intently on the object, a prairie-dog, within three feet of me, at the side of the road, gave a sudden bark. It was so close and unexpected that I jumped as high as I possibly could; and right there had all the fun to myself, as the dog had gone into his hole. It made an impression on my mind that will not be forgotten. What an alarm it would have made if I had gone back, and said I had seen a man crouching behind a tree! The murderer had not been caught, and such a report would have aroused the whole community. A man should never allow himself to be mistaken, and start a false alarm, especially at such times.

When this excitement finally died out, I preached generally three times on Sunday, and sometimes twice in the week, averaging four sermons a week. Besides, I managed to have a little time week-days to work. Thus I got me a pony, and concluded to prospect some in Pennsylvania Gulch, which had been abandoned. There were several cabins unoccupied. No one lived nearer than two miles. I packed my blankets and provisions, and took the boarding-house for a parsonage, and worked as I could get time for three weeks. Once during the time we had a week-night meeting, and I rode back home through the dark, and staked the pony out to grass. My house was thirty-six feet long and fifteen feet wide; had a door in one corner, and the chimney in the opposite end. I felt my way to the fireplace, lighted a match and set some pine leaves and limbs in a blaze. There were six bedsteads along one side of the house. The springs were pine poles. All at once I heard something try to get up through the poles. My first thought was that it was a Rocky Mountain lion. I caught the poker—a stick four feet long—and struck at it twice, but failed to hit it. But when it got to the end of the room it made for the door, and I took it a back-handed lick and knocked its brains out, and it went heels over head against the door. I heard the quills rattle, and then knew that it was a porcupine.

As I was not successful in mining, it was more convenient to settle in Mosquito town. Very soon I was notified that Bishop E. R. Ames would be in Denver to organize us into a separate conference, and that closed my brief connection—only about four months—with the Kansas Conference.

In order that the reader may have a better notion of our peculiar experiences among the rough men of the frontier and mining camps, I will here give a few instances: With Brother Wm. Antis I held a protracted meeting in a mountain town for two weeks. During the time, there was a ball that was wont to be called respectable; but a man that kept a house of ill-fame went. One of the would-be leaders ordered him away. He went home, and the next morning the fellow who ordered him away took his gun, went to his house and asked for him, and fatally shot him as he rose up in bed. I took dinner at the same restaurant, and sat opposite the murderer. He ate but little, and every nerve trembled. He skipped the country before night.

We had quite an attendance at the log church. Some were reclaimed and some converted, notwithstanding they had a dancing-school each week, a ball as often, and a theater.

I visited many families. In one place the parents were over forty years old; a boy sixteen. When inquiries were made as to their religious experience, the woman said she belonged to the Baptists. I assured her the preacher was glad to see a member of any Church, and invited her to help us; but she replied that she could not, because she was taking her first lessons in dancing. Poor woman! In the spring she left son and husband, and took up with another man. The dancing-school referred to was the first institution of learning I heard of in these mountains.

Jealousy was excited to such an extent by these dances that separations were frequent; and the women generally left, sometimes deserting several children. I was in a small town one morning, and there was a man whose distress was apparent to all. On inquiry, we saw another man with his wife, already seated in the stage. She was leaving him alone, as there were no children. He, however, got a seat in the same stage, and went to Denver also. The dishonest wretch kept her a few days and left her. But her husband took her again, and went to the States. The sequel is not known.

But there was another case in the same place, where the woman did not fare so well. The writer one Sunday was preaching, and was led to speak against the evils so prevalent; among others, of men persuading the wives of their neighbors to go to the dance with them. I described a case almost exactly that had occurred the day before, but had no knowledge even of the ball. The parties were all there, and of course were mad, and almost ready to fight. The better part thought I was too personal, so I apologized like this: First, I knew nothing of such a thing occurring so lately; and, in the next place, the evils of dancing were such a curse to community that no man could say too much against it, or against the sin of creeping into their neighbors' houses and leading silly women away from their families and thereby destroying the peace of the household. This case turned out thus: The woman left for Denver with a wretch in human form. He kept her a few weeks and left her; and the poor thing was without friends, and, it was said, died in a barn. The evils of balls will never be revealed until the great day of accounts. I used to say that the people must not expect anything from a preacher but opposition to dancing, since John the Baptist lost his head through the flirtations of a silly girl. But I always felt incapable of doing the subject justice.

14

CHAPTER X.

ROCKY MOUNTAIN CONFERENCE.

IN 1863 Bishop E. R. Ames organized in Denver what we called the Rocky Mountain Conference, now known as the Colorado Conference. The bishop said he was opposed to organizing with less than two districts, although there were only about eight appointments. Oliver A. Willard and W. B. Slaughter were the presiding elders, and I was appointed to South Park, which embraced Park and Lake Counties and about twelve members scattered over the whole work.

I had walked one hundred miles to be at the conference, and returned on foot to my work, without any missionary aid. The bishop preached in the theater at Denver, and took up a collection. He told the audience that he would leave the money in the country among the people; so he divided it among needy preachers. Out of $71.60 he gave me $20, which just about paid my conference expenses. Mr. J. W. Smith gave me a cabin, and I set to work to keep bachelor's hall. Gulch-mining was the principal dependence. The water failed in many places, and there being some excitement in Idaho and Montana, about one-third of the people left for the bonanzas. What members remained were so poor that they could not get away. This was about the state of the case with the parson. Winter was approaching, and with what little could be expected from collections and all I had on hand, I had not more than half enough to carry me through. I bought three sacks of flour at fifteen dollars a sack, and had to trust Providence for most of the rest. I preached four times a week.

About midwinter I found myself without means, and so sought work, but could get none, unless I would work on Sundays, which was out of the question when necessary, except to prevent actual starvation.

In the forepart of February, a man came to me who had the contract to carry the mail from Buckskin Joe to Cache Creek by Oro, California Gulch, a distance of thirty-seven miles. He had carried it as long as he could on a mule. It was once a week, and he offered me eighteen dollars a week to carry it on snow-shoes. I thought at once: "I can preach about as often as I have been doing, and am not obliged to go on Sunday." So I took the mail, and crossed the Mosquito Range every week, and preached three times a week.

Right here let me tell how I came out. This was war-times, and the currency was greenbacks. In California Gulch and Cache Creek they were drifting out gold-dust all winter. Gold was on the rise, so that an ounce of dust brought over forty dollars in greenbacks, and so I added exchange to my business and became expressman, and got the per cent agreed on. One man gave me five dollars each time, and I carried all he had to send.   At one time I had enough dust to bring in Denver thirty-seven hundred dollars in currency. Suffice it to say, I made over three times more expressing than my wages for mail-carrying. I boarded myself, or paid my board, received forty dollars on the circuit, and at the end of five months, had twelve hundred dollars; and a Brother Fisher, who had three hundred dollars, missionary aid at Colorado City, drew half, and left for Kansas.   Bishop Ames ordered Brother Slaughter, the presiding elder, to pay me the remaining one hundred and fifty dollars.   This was the first year of my itinerancy that I made any money.   We had four quarterly meetings, but sickness and stormy weather prevented the presiding elder's attendance.   No effort was made to raise his salary, except when he attended.   Brother Slaughter was a good man, every way acceptable; but his health was poor, and the country was almost too new and rough, and he left before the next conference.

Now for some of the incidents in the mail-service. The mail's weight was from twenty-three to twenty-six pounds, with from five to seven pounds of express matter. The carriage was on snow-shoes, over an Indian trail that was covered from three to twenty feet with snow. My snow-shoes were of the Norway style, from nine to eleven feet in length, and ran well when the snow was just right, but very heavy when they gathered snow. I carried a pole to jar the sticking snow off. Suffice it to say that the winter of 1863 and 1864 was a remarkably hard one, and the spring held on until June, with terrible snow-storms. I was the first to cross the Mosquito Range with a horse. That was the third day of July. I carried a shovel, but did not have to use it. The mail-bags went the trip across and back every week. I had for two weeks a substitute. There was no cabin from Mosquito to California Gulch, and no one living between the Gulch and Cache Creek. At first I had no company, say the first month. After that I often went in the night, as it thawed in the day so that it was impossible to travel, and passengers sought to go with me. A man came up from Denver, and we had a hard trip. He begged me to stop. On top of the range he lay down to sleep, and it was with difficulty that I could get him up. I knew that if he went to sleep, chilled as we were, he would never awake until the judgment. We finally reached Oro City at breakfast-time. That man was one of the leaders of a mob that caused the death of a number of better men than he was. One of his victims was my son.

Again, I was coming over, and at the foot of the pass, at the head of Evans Gulch, I overtook two men. One, an old man, was given out. I saw at once that it was death with him without a desperate effort. It was seven miles back, and farther ahead, to a house, and the wind piercingly cold. It seemed impossible to make him believe he could walk either way. The snow and wind were blowing so that a man could hardly stand. I determined to get him over the range and down as far as the timbers, and build a fire and keep him from freezing. We told him what could be done, and he would not even try to get on his feet. I took hold of him, and when he was about half up his hat blew off, and the last I saw of it it was about thirty feet up, and the wind making sport with it. He had on a soldier's overcoat, and as the hat went off the cape blew over his head. We tied it fast with a handerchief. He had taken off one of his gloves, and it was so frozen he could not get it on. I gave him a mitten, took his arm, and got him about three hundred feet up the mountain, and he sat down. I went back and got the mail-sack and his and my snow-shoes. The snow was so packed on the west side of the range that we carried our shoes. I passed him three hundred feet, laid them down, and went back and helped him up, and when we got to the load, he sat down, and I carried them as much further and helped him to the top, which was a mile and a quarter, and said to him: "Now you shall walk alone." He started, and after going a few yards, he said: "Anybody can walk down-hill." Suffice it to say, we all got into Mosquito by nine o'clock. The old man's fingers and ears were frosted a little. He was going to Montana, and said, if he struck it big, he would remember me. As I have never heard from him, I suppose he had poor luck.

Again, there were three men—one was Dr. Hewett, a friend and acquaintance; another a boy about sixteen years old. As the men were not used to such trips, I took pains to go slowly until we reached the top of the range. The boy complained of cold. I kept my course to the pass, as it was in the night, by the slope of the mountain, and stopped several times, and waited a little until I could see or hear them coming. The boy said he was cold, and they could take care of themselves. We saw them no more, but thought they were coming, as one of them had been over before; but they lost the course, and the doctor missed his footing and slid down the mountain about three hundred feet, to a bench that had caught considerable fresh snow, and enabled him to stop. If he had gone twenty feet further, he would have been carried five hundred feet to the gorge below. His two companions stood just where he started, and called loudly for him. He heard them, but was unable to make them hear. He shot off his pistol, and they succeeded in making a connection, got safely to Bird's-eye Gulch, followed that to the Arkansas River, and went down below the mouth of California Gulch, and next day at noon reached Oro City, hungry and weary.

I was very uneasy. I arrived with my boy by three o'clock, took a sleep, and, about one hour before they got in, started with a man to the range, to try, if possible, to find them; for I feared something had befallen them. But we could not even find their tracks, as the wind had covered them with snow. So I went back to Mosquito; heard nothing of them, and told where they left me.

The news got back to Denver. The friends of one of them were preparing for a funeral, when they heard, to their great joy, of their safety.

Another time, for some cause, the stage failed for a week to come from Denver, and the next time we had two weeks' mail, and four passengers bound for California Gulch; and we were obliged to go mostly in the night, while the snow was solid. At the hotel, while at dinner, the passengers inquired for the mail-carrier, and I was pointed out to them. One, an Irishman, said: "Is this Mr. Dyer?" "Yes, sir." "Well, we are glad to see you. We want to go over, and we would n't go with anybody else, as we have been told you are so well acquainted with the range." "Be assured I am glad to have the company of four such strong young men, as I have two sacks to take over; and if you join together, it will be easy for you to carry one, and I will guide you all safe over." He at once stopped his blarney, but the others were willing to accept the proposition; but as soon as dinner was over, the Irishman began to make fun of his comrades; said he would not carry the mail, and could go just as well as anybody, and that they did not need a guide. In due time we all set out, and he took the path ahead for three miles, until he got to the crossing of the creek. He undertook to cross on a pole, but fell, and came near falling into the water. He got up, and started to find another place to cross. We all crossed over safely, and he had to come back to get over. By that time we were ahead of him, and the trail was hard to see. He got lost, and cried aloud. I answered him, but we kept on, and when he came up he was all in a sweat. There was a brother Irishman along, who said: "Now you have got to carry this mail-sack." He was willing enough. Just above timber, we had about one mile of snow, say six inches deep, and water under. He wore shoes, and his feet got wet, and it was freezing cold. When we got to the steep part of the mountain, he asked me to wait until he could change his socks, as his feet were wet. He made the change, and we had gone but a short distance until he began to cry, and said, he was a ruined man, that his feet were frozen—"Boo-hoo! boo-hoo!"—and a little further on he threw himself down on the snow, and said he would not have come for a thousand dollars; that his feet were ruined. He cried and prayed, and said, if his friends only knew where he was and how he suffered! I told his comrade to pull him up on his feet, and make him come along, or he would perish. He took his hands, and raised him, while he was crying like a boy of five years' old, and said to him: "What the d—l do you want your friends to know? I do n't want mine to know where I am!" and so he led the man who "could go as well as anybody, without a guide." We got over, and down to the nearest timber, and built a fire. When he came up, his friend took his shoes and socks off, and said: "Your feet are not hurt— they are as red as a turkey-gobbler's gills." The poor fellow sobbed and cried clear across, with his feet aching, but not frozen. We got both sacks of mail through by three o'clock in the morning, and felt pleased to have a sack carried; and the music, crossing the range, even yet prompts a smile.

We will close this account of our mail-service by mentioning two or three lonely trips. Once, leaving Mosquito at two o'clock in the morning in a snow-storm, when near timber height, plodding our way on deep snow, all of a sudden I felt a jar, and the snow gave way under me, and a noise struck my ear like a death-knell. I thought it was a snow-slide, and turned as quickly as possible up the mountain-side. About a hundred and fifty feet ahead, I came to a crack six inches wide, and the snow had settled about six inches. It will easily be believed that I felt better on the upper side of the break. A week after, there was a snow-slide right from that break that filled the gorge below.

At sunrise I was near the summit of the range, very weary, and sat down under a large rock. I looked through the snow-storm to the east. The sun rose clear, but across South Park the wind was furious and full of snow. The sun penetrated the storm so that the wonders could be clearly seen. While the wind was blowing the snow from the north-west, there would small whirls start low down, and rising, grow larger, until they would be of enormous size. The main storm passed between them as though they were not connected, even as the mighty current flows past the whirlpool in the water. Although my situation was very disagreeable, I could stop a few minutes and gaze

at this astonishing Rocky Mountain scene, sitting
in the storm to watch its wondrous ways.

Soon after this I started earlier; but it proved
to be too much so, for when I reached the other
side of the range, there was snow for two miles,
and it would not quite bear me. Sometimes I
would go three steps and sink to the waist in the
snow, and then three steps before I could get on

CAMP-FIRE ON THE MOUNTAIN.

top again. It made the situation very serious.
About midnight, after reflection, not fearing human
hands, and believing that the wild beasts would
have more good manners than to touch it, I set
up the mail-sack on end in the snow, and made
for the nearest timber off to the north, as I had
seen a small spot of bare ground there when I
passed before. But how to get there! Well, I
rolled and crawled until I reached the timber,

where I pushed over a dry stump, and soon had a fire to warm by. I had time for thanksgiving and prayer, even if I had no supper. Cutting some pine-boughs, I made a bed and took a sleep, and it was daylight when I awoke. My first thought, after thanking God that I was as safe there in his hands as anywhere, was whether it had frozen so that I could walk. I started, and had not gone more than three steps when I went down to the waist. I knew it was softer near the edge. I crawled up and tried again, and it bore me. It was hardly fair light when I reached the mail-sack, found it just as I left it; the wolves had discovered it and gone within about ten feet of it, and had walked around it until they had beaten quite a path in the snow, but never touched it. It is worthy of note that the mail-carrier had an appetite when he reached Oro City!

We come now to the last incident. I left California Gulch about the middle of March. It was thawing, with alternate snow and sunshine, until about one o'clock. The snow stuck to my shoes so that traveling was very heavy. None but those who have tried snow-shoes when the snow sticks to them can understand how soon it will tire a man down, knocking the snow off at every step. It was so this time. When within a few hundred feet of the pass at the head of Evans Gulch, I looked to the north and saw a black cloud just coming over. The wind that preceded it gave evidence of its terror. No pen or tongue can describe its awful appearance. I fastened and tied up my neck and ears, and took its bearings with reference to my course up the mountain, about how it would strike me, so that I might keep my course in the snow. But when the storm struck me, I could not have stood up had I not braced against my snow-shoes, which I had taken off and held in position for that purpose. .I had thought I could keep my course by the bearings of the storm, but when it struck me, it was in a perfect whirl, and I had nothing left but the shape of the mountains, and by this time the snow was so dense that it appeared to be a white wall within ten feet in any direction.

I found myself unable to make more than fifty yards before resting, and had to hold my hand over my mouth and nose to keep the snow out so that I could breathe, bracing with my snow-shoes in order to stand. On the west side the snow all blew off, so that I had to carry my shoes. About the third stop, I came to a large rock, and braced against it; and in the midst of the awful surroundings, poured out my soul to God for help, and felt encouraged to try, in his name, to make the trip. I could not travel against the wind, so I had to bear to the right, which brought me on the range south of the old Indian trail, where there was no way to get down without going over a precipice. I hoped that the wind would abate, so that I might make the trail. But I could not see anything in the whirling snow. It took my breath, and I concluded to retrace my steps; for I felt that to stay there or go forward was equally

to perish. I made a desperate effort, but started
east instead of west. I had gone scarcely three
rods when my foot slipped off the precipice. I
threw myself back in the snow. The air was so
thick with snow
that I could not
see how it was.
I could not tell
whether the pitch
was ten feet or
fifty. The cold
wind seemed to
be feeling for my
heart-strings, and
my only chance
for life was
to let myself go
over. I took my
long snow-shoes,
one under each
arm, holding the
crooked end in
each hand for
rudders, and be-
lieved that if I
could thus keep
my feet foremost,

A FEARFUL DESCENT.

I could go down alive. I said, "O God, into thy
hands I commit my soul, my life, my all; my
faith looks up to thee;" and then, with com-
posure, I let go; and, as might be expected, there
was a great body of new, soft snow for me to fall

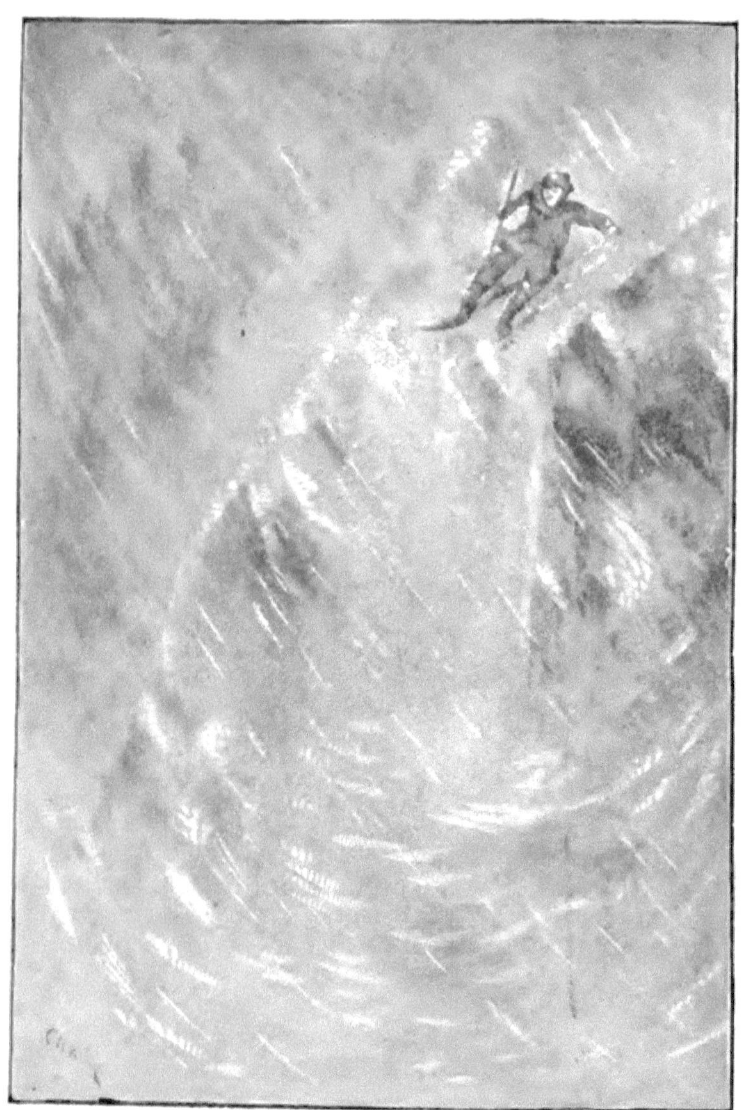

A FEARFUL DESCENT.   Page 175.

" My feet were foremost, and I went at railroad speed."

in. I have never been certain how far it was. It was soon over, and I was buried in six or eight feet of new snow that had just blown over. My heels struck the old snow, which must have pitched at an angle of more than forty-five degrees, and my weight carried me, and according to former desires, my feet were foremost, and I went at railroad speed. My snow-shoes must keep me straight. I was covered with snow from the start. I raised my head so that I could breathe, and when I had got near one-half mile, I began to slack up, as I had passed the steepest part, and soon stopped.

I now discovered that I was on the horse-shoe flat between the range and the timber on Mosquito Creek. I got up, but could not see ten feet, the snow was so thick. But I knew if I kept down the mountain, I would come out all right. Putting on my snow-shoes, I soon came to timber. The first tree was the top of a large pine, standing just at the foot of a precipice. It was well that I saw it in time to turn my course. I took down Mosquito Creek. The snow covered almost all the willows and brush, and the wind pressed me so that for rods there was no need of taking a step. My shoes ran like skates. The snow began to abate, but darkness was closing in on me.

When I was within one mile of my cabin, I saw a pool of water in the creek; and as I had been fearful for some time that my feet were frozen, I thought of Job when his sons had been out frolicking; he sacrificed for them for fear they had sinned. But it looked rather rough to go in over my boots in order to draw the frost out, when I still had hopes that my feet were not frozen. I reached my lonely cabin, started a fire, and my feet began to hurt. I soon had them in the spring, and held them awhile, but it was too late to cure. I got my supper, but did not sleep much. Next morning an old brother, whom everybody called "Uncle Tommy Cummings," brought a little balsam sapling, and we shaved off the bark, and poulticed both of my feet. The third week I was able to carry the mail. Half my toe-nails sloughed off, with considerable of the skin. For two weeks I was confined to the house, busying myself reading and doctoring my feet. I sent to H. A. W. Tabor, our store-keeper—now ex-senator—and paid him sixteen cents a pound for corn to make hominy, which I considered a luxury.

Our provisions were all drawn over the plains with teams of cattle, mules, and horses. We had some sharp fellows that made a corner on flour about this time, and the price was forty dollars a sack. Fortunately, I had one sack on hand in Buckskin Joe. My friends in California Gulch were out, and wished me to supply them. I tried to buy a pack-pony, but could only find a pack-cow, which I purchased and packed, and tied to a post while I ate breakfast.

An old friend, Mr. Moody, volunteered to help me start. We tied a long rope around her horns about the middle, and he took the lead, and I drove. The cow got on the war-path, and bawling, took after him on a down grade. He ran as fast as he could, and I held as well as I could; and the cow jumped as high and as far as she could. The old man did his best, and the old cow would light right at him every jump. Finally he took round the corner, and she after him. Just then the cingle broke, and the pack-saddle with the flour went down right behind her. Then, lack-a-day! she stopped, and did just as cows do when they are about played out.

After this novel scene I gave up the idea of trying to feed the hungry with temporal bread, and confined myself to dispensing the bread of life. Some ministers may say that the above was hardly becoming; but the alternative was, either to leave the work and conference, or earn a living, and I was not educated up to the point that a man is justified in leaving if the people do not pay a good salary.

There are many places now that need the gospel, where there are more people than lived on my circuit, and yet they are not supplied with a preacher of any denomination, because so few feel, "Woe is me if I preach not the gospel!" and so many stand at the corners and say: "No man hath hired me."

CHAPTER XI.

MORE ITINERATING.

I CONTINUED to carry the mail till August, and also acted as agent for the *Rocky Mountain News*. On one occasion I had collected ten dollars, and inclosed it in a letter, and had a number of other letters in my pocket to put in the office at Laurel or Buckskin Joe. I turned over about one thousand dollars in dust to the expressman, and mailed all the letters, save the ten-dollar one, which fortunately I missed. They started for Denver, and I for Breckenridge; but when they got to McLaughlin's Ranch, they were met by six or seven men from Texas, who claimed to be soldiers—"Secesh," of course. Some of them had been here before, and I suppose they thought that if they were to commence hostilities, the Southern element would fall in with them and raid the country. They rode up to the stage, cocked their pistols, and ordered a surrender. Of course there was no resistance, and the Texas roughs took possession, and with an ax cut spokes out of the wagon-wheels, opened the mail-sack and ransacked its contents, broke the express box, and took dust and amalgam to the tune of two thousand, more or less.

When Wm. Berry, who carried the mail from Summit County, reached Hamilton, four miles from there, some one told him of the robbery. He had a lot of dust which he wisely hid in the stable, and started ahead of them to Denver to tell the news. They followed on to the Junction House or near there, and camped where there was a high peak, well adapted for a look-out. They hoped to be joined by friends; but neither rebels nor Union parties paid any attention to them. The former were afraid, and so were the latter. Finally they broke camp and marched west, stopping for the night somewhere between Slatt's and Georgia Gulch. A company of miners from Summit County came up with them just after they had unsaddled their horses, and fired on them, killing one and wounding another in the arm. They all fled—one of them mounted, the rest on foot. The boys took the spoils, and but little of the money was ever accounted for.

We heard of the robbery at Breckenridge the same evening. In the morning I started for South Park by Montgomery and Buckskin, and reached Fair Play before night, thirty miles. They had heard of the raiders being routed, and supposed they would flee through the Park. Thirty-five of us made up a company. By this time it was dark. We had a wagon loaded with provisions. The company crossed the Platte River west of town on poles and piles of washed rocks, tailings from sluicing for gold. It was rough and in the night. When the roll was called, three were missing. We reached the Platte River just where Mr. Hartsell now lives, another twenty miles, and made for Hamilton. We disagreed about the proper course to go for them, and I took across the Red Hill to Fair Play. I got in at sunset, having walked about what was called eighty miles in the two days, without sleep. This was my entire experience in fighting rebels. The next day was Sunday, and I got about twenty-five hearers and tried to preach to them.

The rebels made their way south. One was taken in a cabin between South Park and Cañon City, and the remainder at Mr. Toof's, at the junction of Beaver Creek and the Arkansas River. They had become hungry and called for breakfast. They were at once recognized from the description as the mail-robbers; and while their meals were being prepared help was secured, and they were surrounded and captured while eating. They were turned over to some soldiers and taken to Denver. After examination there, they were sent to Fort Lyons for further trial. I saw them put in the wagon at the door of the old jail in Denver, well ironed. I noticed one of the guards next them, Abe Williamson, who had been ordered to give up the lines as stage-driver at McLaughlin's. They had said to him and Mr. Wm. McClelland (expressman): "We will run this institution." As the wagon was starting, I said: "Abe, you watch them." The reply was: "You *bet*." But it is said that down somewhere north of where Colorado Springs now stands, the prisoners tried to break away. That was the last of them. Those were times of war and excitement, not only by secession but by Indians. Although we suffered from the red-skins, we had no sympathy from the East. The New Englanders seemed to think that the Indians had as good a right to kill us as the anarchists think they have to throw dynamite among them.

This was near the close of the conference year. I went to Denver, and on my way met Mr. McClelland. He did not feel like running the stage unless he could have a guard. He proposed to sell, and we made arrangements. He turned over the contract to me. I at once thought, "How will you run this thing and preach on a circuit?" and I answered: "I will get rid of mail-carrying in three weeks, and be ready for conference." Sure enough, I was satisfied that my calling was the best thing for me, and the only right course to pursue. During the time I paid thirteen cents a pound for Missouri corn by the sack in Denver. But I sold out, and was ready for conference. Although I lost a house that cost me $150, I cleared about $100 in the rounds.

This was a memorable summer. The Indians were on the Plains, and there was no traveling without guards, and no mail for almost three months. When it did come, by the same mail I received two letters from the States; one had come straight, the other around by San Francisco.

On one of my trips with the mail all Denver was on a craze. The people were building a fort out of town, but not so far out as where the center now is. They had bought a log cabin, and were raising it. I noticed that they had their gloves on in warm weather. I laughed at Colonel Chivington, and said to him that a few old squaws would upset the fort. He replied: "If you were not in the mail service, and made light of and discouraged our movements, you might find yourself in the calaboose." But he could take a joke, and so I had no prison-pen experience for my history.

It was to be expected that the people would be alarmed, when just out on Running Creek there were two families almost exterminated. One woman, near to confinement, was ripped open, and the child taken out, and the Hungate family brought into Denver killed and mangled. Those who have not seen such a sight do not know the effect it would have on them. They would want to be killing Indians or getting away at their best speed. Of course, Colonel Chivington needed only say to the boys in blue: "Remember the Hungate family!" and it made a Sand Creek battle.

We saw these things in the light of self-defense. While our Eastern friends would say, "Poor Indian!" my own observations have been that many of the whites were killed, while the red man went free. When they killed Father Meeker, with a number of others, and took his wife and daughter prisoners, they were not whipped, but got scared and left. Father Meeker undertook to do them an act of Christian kindness, but he went before they had been whipped. It is impossible to have a sinner converted unless he is first convicted; and it is just as impossible to tame and educate an Indian until he is subdued. My prayer is that all wars may cease, and that the red men of the forest may be civilized and Christianized. When this is done, will there not be cause for a jubilee? May God hasten the time!

This year was full of hard toil, both spiritual and physical. One excitement followed another; but out of all dangers, God, in his infinite mercy, brought me safe to the end of another conference year, which was unusually long—about fifteen months.

Bishop Clark was to preside in the summer of 1864; but, as stated above, the Indians had made it impracticable, and the conference was put off till fall. W. B. Slaughter, through ill-health, had left the Southern District, and O. A. Willard had not yet returned from the East. At the appointed time we assembled at Denver. We consulted the brethren, Colonel Chivington, Governor Evans, and others, and it was considered best to go to Central City, the place chosen to hold the session, and go through with the business of the conference. This we did, the writer acting as chairman in place of the bishop, and B. T. Vincent being secretary. We had a pleasant time, no conflict except over the report of the Committee on the State of the Country. There were two reports—one to stand by our country, the other to stand by President Lincoln. Brother Chivington was there, and spoke for the Lincoln side. He spread himself, and made the strongest and most eloquent speech I ever heard him make. But the other report was adopted; there being no real difference in patriotism between the two. This closed the conference year, 1863–64.

A few reflections as to the past year. It had five quarters. I was sent forth without any missionary help. It was not just. My good friend, Bishop Ames, before I left, on parting, said: " Brother Dyer, I hope you will do well in the mountains. I am told you are highly esteemed out there; and it is well for you to know that you are appreciated. It may do you good." It was a desperate case; but I resolved to go and do what I could, survive or perish. I received about forty dollars from the work. When winter came I left my pony on the range, in the valley, and took it on foot and on snow-shoes, as above stated. The result was, that when I settled up I had cleared very nearly a thousand dollars. This I have related before, and recur to it here to show what can be done even in forlorn hopes. As already stated, I had left the States in debt, and with no way that I could see, except God would especially help, ever to pay out. The first thing was to put aside about eight hundred dollars for this purpose. Then I took three hundred, and bought eight cows. W. L. Bailey kept them on shares, and I paid no attention to them. But it was known that Brother Dyer had some cattle. Soon I heard that he owned a herd of cattle, and I found that if a preacher in our Church had anything ahead, it was only a detriment to him. It was used as an excuse to give him a poor appointment; and to excuse the people for not paying his salary. I confess that I did not always feel very happy over this, especially when so many abandoned the work because of the scant pay, and so many others because there were not enough good appointments to hold out.*

My short experience in the place of a bishop—Brother B. T. Vincent was the cabinet—was satisfactory, except as to my own and one other appointment. From my personal knowledge, I thought one brother ought to be moved; and kindly told him so, and spoke of a better appointment. But he would not consent, because he could not endure to have the news go back East that he was moved the first year. So I returned him; and the result was a failure.

As to my own appointment: I was willing to go to the southern part of the territory, and take it as a circuit, instead of as a district. But I was overruled. However, as I was alone—Brother Peter Smith having failed to report as a supply—I concluded that the name of district might stand,

---

* From my observation in a new country there has not been equality enough in the division of our missionary money. It is too often given where eight hundred dollars can be raised on the work, while other places are neglected on the outposts, where a little help would enable them to have a preacher. Also, that it is a grand mistake to suppose that preachers who can not sustain themselves East will succeed on the frontier. Really there is no frontier; and Colorado and the West require the best talent and consideration.

but that I would travel it as circuit preacher. Within its bounds were South Park, Oro City—which is Leadville now—Colorado City, Cañon City, Pueblo, and all south to Trinidad. The last half of the year, Brother John Gilland preached as a supply on the Oro City work, including all the settlements to South Arkansas River. The Missionary Committee allowed to Denver District twelve hundred dollars, and to the other appointments about the same as the year previous; South Park District five hundred dollars, and the presiding elder was well satisfied. Our collection on the work was about one hundred dollars.

From those who had traveled there, I was led to feel that they ought to have the gospel in New Mexico; and now, as I had the opportunity, I concluded to extend my district so as to include that country. This was in the latter part of March, 1865, and the mountains were almost impassable. Accordingly, I left Pueblo for Captain Craig's Ranch, twenty miles on the road to Trinidad. I called on the captain, and told him my name, and that I was a Methodist preacher, and wished to stay with him for the night. He replied: "Your denomination does n't stand very high with us at this time; but 'light." Notwithstanding his Southern proclivities, he was very pleasant; showed me his fine improvements and ranch; gave me the best he had; told his cook to put up a lunch, as it was about sixty miles to the next settler. I wished to go through, but it snowed hard, and the roads were heavy. At the Pishapah Creek it was dark. I could not see the road; had nothing for the pony, and but little left of my lunch. So I hitched up for the night, gathered some dead brush, built a small fire, sat on the saddle, and covered up with the saddle-blanket. It snowed till it was nine inches deep. It was a good time to reflect, for it was next to impossible to sleep. Daylight came at last. I started on; but such a snow to ball up on the horse's feet has not often been seen.

At eleven, reached Mr. Gray's ranch, and was kindly taken in and cared for. Next day, Sunday, with his consent, I gathered in some neighbors, and preached to about thirty, one-third Mexicans. It continued so rough that I stayed till Tuesday morning, and went two miles to Trinidad, where I found a few Mexicans and one white family. I stopped over night and talked to them who could speak English. The Mexicans "no comprehenda." The next day, with two gentlemen, I crossed the Raton Mountain, and as they could speak Spanish, I learned at least six Spanish words, and all I could about the priests. It seemed that the priests were a thrifty lot. They would not marry the poorest couple for less than sixteen dollars.

We saw the tracks of two footmen in the snow, and soon met some folks who told us the footmen were a Mexican man and woman running off to get married. I thought now was my chance, and told my companions that I could marry them. One of the men rode on to overtake them. We came to the foot of the mountain where he had corraled them on a bare spot of ground. All things being ready, and my companion acting as interpreter, I went through with the ceremony, and gave my hand to the bride, wishing her much happiness, and then to the groom. He took hold with a mighty grip, and raised my hand and kissed it on the back, and handed it to the bride, and she kissed it too. No wonder I was taken aback, as it was the first time I had ever been saluted with a kiss on the back of my hand.

I wrote out a certificate in full, stating my residence and Church, and my interpreter translated it into Spanish, with the names of the witnesses, and we all felt happy. They asked what was the charge. I thought of the old prophet when his servant came back after following Naaman. It was no time to make charges, and I told them I never charged poor people anything.

The next place of note was Maxwell's. He had a large house and ranch, surrounded by Mexicans and Indians. I stayed with him over night. I was used well, and entertained free of charge. Got some information as to the settlements. He told me there were several families down the Cimarron Creek, and advised me to visit them, as they were Americans. It was Sunday morning. I rode seven miles, and collected about twenty-five people, and preached to them. This was the first Protestant service ever held on the now famous Maxwell Land Grant. And from here I made toward Santa Fe, by way of Las Vegas. Found

ADOBE HOUSE OF THE PUEBLO INDIANS.

"This house was purely Pueblan, and was originally designed for a fort."

Page 189.

but two or three Americans, but quite a village of Mexicans. Passed through three Mexican towns to San Jose, and reached Santa Fe. I found a Baptist minister, the only Protestant preacher in New Mexico. He introduced me to Judge Watts, a very intelligent man. He took great pains to inform me in every respect, and taught me some of the usages of the Pueblo Indians. They had been taught to read, but had degenerated, only some eight or ten of them being able at that time to read.

As Santa Fe was one of the oldest places in the United States, when the Indians were whipped and taken prisoners, the Romish priests baptized them—they not being able to resist. This was missionary work.

Tradition said that Montezuma was born near there in a large adobe building that I had passed sixteen miles east; but others said it was in an old building about as far north from Santa Fe. The honor certainly belonged to one or the other of these two places.

The Pueblo Indians raised stock and grain on a small scale; lived in villages. Generally they had one large house of adobe in the center, and over one hundred feet square; six or seven stories high, each story not more than eight feet. Each story was drawn in all around, say eight feet, terracing the building to the top. Small square windows were in each story, without glass or shutters, and no door—after the first story, a ladder on the inside, and a square hole in the corner with a lid to cover it, and this repeated to the top story. I visited one, and made signs as well as I could to be shown the inside. A young man took me up the ladder, first on the outside of the lower part, and then inside up to the fourth story, and showed me that there were no more ladders. In the third story there was a young squaw sitting beside a flat rock, on which, with another stone, she was rubbing corn to make meal. This was the most simply constructed mill I ever saw. The dusky miller seemed to think she was competent for the task, and offered no apology, either for the mill or her garb, although she was not more than half covered with clothing. She smiled pleasantly, and kept at her work.

This house was purely Pueblan; and was originally designed for a fort or refuge in time of war. My conclusion was, they needed Yankee civilization as well as the gospel.

I was entertained over Sunday, and preached for the only Protestant minister in all New Mexico, to about forty hearers. The next day they were to commence a new adobe roof on the house. The contractor undertook to put a self-supporting roof, and take out the posts that held the old one. He got it completed, and they held a church meeting Saturday evening, and announced Sunday services; but in the morning the roof had fallen in. It was in the night, and no one was hurt; but the people were discouraged, and shortly after, the preacher left for the East. I made my way toward Taos. There were but few Americans;

traveled one whole day without seeing a man that I could talk with. It was in time of Lent, and in almost every village the people were doing penance. Some carried a joist sixteen feet long, two inches thick, and twelve broad, with a piece of scantling nailed across, the hind end dragging on the ground. They were all sizes, down to those small enough for children—eight or ten years old—to carry. At one country church I saw a dozen or more boys crossing a field, quite a number of women in company. They were heavy laden, and one boy fell under the weight of his cross. A woman ran and helped him up, and he staggered on to the church, where they all threw down their heavy crosses and went in. It was a strange sight, and I was never more astonished than to find that we had people in the United States who were so low and heathenish. I was more than two days among the cross-bearers.

Coming near a church, I saw three men standing in the road. One had a large cross on his shoulder, and was naked, except a rag around his hips and a green veil over his face. As he walked with his heavy cross, he lashed his naked back with a long-tailed cactus. The other two men had each a little book, and one would suppose that it might have been a ten-cent revival hymn-book. At any rate, it looked as though they were singing some kind of a dirge for the poor fellow carrying the cross. I rode along-side of them, saw blood on his back, and running down on the cloth that was around his hips. I wondered if this was in place of a revival, as it was taking up the cross and giving blood for their sins, and his two brethren singing a penitential song. I passed on to the church. There must have been a hundred crosses laid up against the house, and as many people as there were crosses. When the three whom I had left came in sight, these began to shout. One man had a large horse-fiddle. He ran up on the church by means of a ladder, and began to tune his fiddle. My horse was so badly scared, and jumped so much farther than I thought he could, that he came well-nigh landing me in the church-yard. But I gathered as he ran, and went on. It was the first horse-fiddle I had heard for forty years, and I trust will be the last.

Next came preparations for sleeping, which were in the same room. Their cochones were piled around the wall, and were made ready on the floor, which was the ground, covered with blankets in place of carpet. The cochone is what we call a mattress. It is a foot through, of pure wool, and well stitched. Although it was on the floor, it was a grand relish to a weary traveler, and I slept well with an old man whose looks indicated a hundred years. I thought of what some had said of a country where the people never died, just dried up and blew away. I saw several that looked as if they would never get away unless they were blown away. I never slept with a man that seemed so near eternity as this man. There were three other beds in the same room. I awoke early, and found my bedfellow was alive. After that the first sensation was brought about by rubbing my eyes with the same fingers that had been used at supper to dip the bread in the chilicolorow, which was red pepper boiled with a piece of meat. It seemed that sparks were coming out of them thick. I thought it a good joke on me for not washing my hands. I called for a fire to be made, and the man told his wife to make it, which she did at once.

We had much the same for breakfast as for supper; and I rode twenty miles to Red River, where I found an American. He had boiled pork and potatoes; and if he did have a Mexican wife, I called it a square meal. I overtook an old Mexican with a blanket tied around his neck and his bosom full of lambs, illustrating how lambs were carried in patriarchal times.

The Mexicans were kind, and in the out-settlements—as a rule—made no charge. They expected something, however. A few were half-educated or half-Americanized, and they would charge from three to four dollars a night. It made me think that half an education was worse than none. I called on one family, and they seemed to take great pains, and soon had supper. It consisted of good coffee, bread, a little tolay, which was parched corn ground up and wet, and chilicolorow. The provisions were set on a stool in the center of the room. There were no chairs, as they sit down flat when they eat. I looked around, and the man noticed it, and folded up a blanket for me to sit on. I sopped the bread in the chilicolorow, and it was very hot. The coffee was good. I had to use my fingers, as there was neither knife, spoon, fork, nor plate. Being hungry, I took to the bread and soup, not being aware of the meat at the bottom of the dish. When I quit the woman came and put her fingers into the soup and took up the meat, and offered it to me. I thanked her. I might have taken it, but she stood up above me, and it looked comical that I should take it from between her fingers with mine. But fingers were made before forks.

I inquired of the man if those Penitentes were better than the rest of the nation; and found that they were the worst cut-throats among them. Their priests told them that they need not punish themselves if they would behave. Not a year passed but one or more killed himself. Serious injury was a common thing. The severest punishment was the most applauded, being considered the most effectual. This heathen practice comes from the Roman Catholic Church, as penance is one of their seven sacraments. Of course it is practiced among them to this day, but not so publicly.

I learned this lesson, that the Roman Catholics were reformed more by Protestants than by any other means, in their schools and all other features of civilization. As a proof: There has been more improvement in the last twenty years in New Mexico among the Romanists than for three hundred years previous, when Catholicism had it all its own way. Hence St. Paul's advice to provoke each other to love and good works. By the grace of God we are doing it. From all I could learn, New Mexico was completely priest-ridden; a wedding or a funeral was as bad as a fire.

I made my way back to Colorado. My pony gave out, and I had to swap for a fresh one, and had to pay as boot half the worth of either of them. When I counted up, I was out about one hundred dollars on the trip.

CHAPTER XII.

SOUTH PARK DISTRICT.

THIS summer, 1865, the conference was held at Denver by Bishop Kingsley. The following brethren were in attendance: O. A. Willard, presiding elder of the Denver District; J. L. Dyer, South Park District; George Richardson, O. P. McMains, B. T. Vincent, Wm. W. Baldwin, C. H. Kirkbride, and Chas. King, besides John Gilland, supply in Lake County, and Wm. Antis, in the Denver District—ten, all told. We had a pleasant meeting. Near the close of the conference Rev. George Murray appeared and was admitted. At the close of the conference we made known to Bishop Kingsley the condition of New Mexico, and urged him to secure a suitable man, one who could endure hardships, and who had other qualifications as a missionary, especially among the Mexicans, as there were comparatively few Americans. He listened with attention, and promised to consider the matter and speak to the bishops. But a man who could preach or teach the Spanish, and whom they believed to be competent and trustworthy, could not be found.

The writer took the whole conference, with the bishop, to a photographic artist and had their likenesses taken, at a cost of twenty-five dollars. He thinks more of the picture now than he ever thought he would; and is sorry that Brother George Murray was not there in time to be photographed with the rest, as we were so long time co-workers. He took charge of Colorado City, Cañon City, and Pueblo, with Florence, Beaver Creek, and Fountain City in his circuit. The districts remained as before, and no change was made in the presiding eldership. Empire was chosen for the seat of the next conference.

This year I kept the same head-quarters, and preached in the mining camps whenever I could spare time from the district. I also visited Summit County, as we had no single man, or man of a family, suitable to take the work. It was hard times, as the grasshoppers ate up everything in the shape of garden stuff or crops; and it was about as much as any of us could do to make a living. Many of the people were so poor that the preacher ought to have had something to give them. It was not the custom to pass the hat every time we came together. After service I met a man who asked me about the congregation, and said that if he had had a piece of money to throw in he would have been there. When I told him that there was no collection taken, he said that I was behind the times; for at Central they took the collection every time in advance.

This was a year of affliction to me, as I had two sons in the army. The youngest was back, minus one foot; and Joshua, my oldest son, the last heard of him was that he was left at Wilmington. He had been sent, with others, from

Andersonville Prison in a starving condition, and could go no farther. We could hear nothing from him, and the supposition with me was that he was dead. All we knew was that he was sick and almost starved. He was a young man with good habits, the oldest of my family, and I had hoped that he would be my comfort in coming years, if God in his mercy saw fit to save my unprofitable life. I was far separated from my children, and often felt as though it would be a great joy to have some of them where I could see them, and take a rest and visit them. Nothing but a sense of duty to God and the cause could have kept me in Colorado.

In December, 1865, I made my arrangements, and started for the States, to try to settle the facts relative to my son. I came to Denver. The Indians were hostile on the Plains. No company with a less number than forty armed men was allowed to start. I bought a rifle and a navy-revolver, some blankets for bedding, and got a passage with a mule-train to Omaha. The mules proved to be weak and worked down, and of course made slow time. I made myself useful in taking care of the sick till we reached Fort Kearney. There we struck a man with a light carriage. I made a bargain, and went with him to Nebraska City.

In due time we arrived. My baggage was laid out of the wagon, and as I looked for help to get it to the hotel, only a minute, my pistol was gone. It was under a blanket, and some thief took it. I made some inquiries, but got no clue to anything. I was very unwell, as I had a desperate cold, and was laid up for a day. Then I made my way to near Fall City, where my brother Thomas and family, with father and mother, had stopped on their way to Missouri. There I rested. Thence I went to St. Joseph, where I took the cars for Quincy, Illinois, and went as far north as Leonora, Minnesota, to see C. C. Streetor, my son-in-law. No tidings had been heard of my son's whereabouts. But in a few days a paper came from some friend who had taken the names of all the soldiers that had shipped on the steamship *General Lyon*, from Wilmington, North Carolina, which was blown up off Cape Hatteras, and all the crew and passengers lost. His name and regiment, 1st Minnesota, were in the list. We may conjecture, but all in vain—it never will be known—just what was the cause. Some murderer may have put an explosive in the coal that caused the disaster. But we shall have to wait till God calls on the great deep to give up its dead; then all secrets shall be made known. This affliction was a severe stroke on us all, but we could only say: "Our Heavenly Father, who knows best, has suffered it to be."

As I had never been east of Ohio, I concluded to take the cars for Boston and New York. After I had been in the latter place, and looked over many of the sights, I went to the depot for Boston. They were not ready to give tickets, and as I stepped out, a man—I suppose that he saw I was somewhat green—asked me where I was bound for.

I told him. He said he lived there, and was going on the train, and that he was waiting for some silk goods. Just then a man ran up, and they talked a little. He went to settle the drayage, and offered a draft. Of course they could not make change. "Could you let me have five dollars till we can get into the office?" I took out my pocket-book, and he grabbed it, and slipped around the corner, and that was the last of him. Just then I realized that I was in New York City, and that he had played the confidence game on me. There were just two hundred and sixty dollars gone. I reported, and hunted a policeman, but it was dark. We heard nothing more of him.

Next day I went to the bank, and got a small draft cashed; and left with the belief that there were more thieves in New York City than in any other place in the country. It waked me up when it was too late. I had been amused at the thought that Peter Cartwright, D. D., had been fooled out of some money in the same way; but I felt more serious on this occasion.

I took in Baltimore, Washington, and Philadelphia; visited Bishop Simpson, and had my fill of the East in the short time that I spent there; so that from that time on I never wanted to go East, either to make a visit or acquire a home. I returned by cars through Pittsburg, and, with but little visiting, came to Atchison, where I took the stage for Denver. My ticket cost one hundred and twenty-five dollars, and meals one dollar and fifty cents each. This was the latter part of

April, 1866. I visited in Illinois, Iowa, Ohio, and Minnesota. This was the only vacation I ever took; and have been almost all the time since in Colorado and New Mexico.

I was soon on my work. The same day that I reached Denver, Brother Willard left for Omaha. I tried to preach at all my regular appointments and at many of the mining-camps. There was a great portion of my district among mining-camps and new settlements. My lot was cast in a country where the people, most of them, had come to make a raise financially, and then leave. On this account it was almost impossible to keep up organized societies. Most of the work in the mines was done in the summer, and in the fall most of the miners would scatter. I resolved that they should have a full gospel, and gave them the words of Christ as to the condition of unforgiven sinners and those who were determined to enjoy the sinful pleasures of this world.

After faithfully preaching the truth, I was told by many that I was behind the times; that Methodist preachers had quit saying anything about eternal punishment and the horrors of hell. I thought that it was at least partly a slander, and that I would tell them we had the same doctrines that we had fifty years ago; that the fault was in them; that when they were young they read the Gospel, and it was preached faithfully; that they believed its truths and trembled; but that they have resisted its force and the Spirit's strivings till they were hardened and brought to think the preachers have changed, when the change was in their own hardened hearts.

But, after all that can be said, is not the assertion too true of many Methodist preachers? They smooth the word for fear of mortal man. And in the revivals, instead of drawing the line like the old prophet, and calling penitent sinners to the altar for prayers, they say: "Just rise up where you are." Where the terrors of the Book are kept out of sight, convictions are slight and conversions not generally clear. In the Testament, Christ describes the torments of hell and the glories of heaven and eternal happiness. If there is anything in the call to the ministry, it means both; for the Lord said: "Go ye into all the world, and preach the gospel to every creature; he that believeth and is baptized, shall be saved, and he that believeth not shall be damned." This is the call, and any preacher who leaves out half is unfaithful to it; and if he does not believe fully what Christ said, he himself is an apostate.

In the summer of 1866 Bishop Baker held our conference at Empire. He was rather feeble in health, and as he was in a high altitude when he reached the seat of conference, he was paralyzed so that his speech was much impaired. He was not able to preach. Brother Charles King, preacher in charge, treated him with the greatest care, and the cabinet met in his room at the parsonage. I was the only presiding elder, and acted as chairman for him, and went through the business. Brother Baldwin went with others to his room to be ordained elder, and, to relieve the bishop, I went through the ritual service as far as to the laying on of hands. At the close of the session in the school-house, I read the appointments, and we all left refreshed for our work. Brother King conveyed the bishop to Denver, where he stayed with Mr. Burton, an old acquaintance, till he was able to take the stage across the Plains. I think he never entirely recovered his former strength. We love to remember him, for he was a man of sterling qualities, and in his case we can say: "Blessed are the dead which die in the Lord."

This year just closing was a period of hard times. For several seasons the grasshoppers made almost a famine among the farmers, and the mines were not so productive as to make much excitement. Such a state of things made it hard on the people as well as on the preachers. None but those who are acquainted with the rise and fall of mining-camps can give any idea of this country in its early days. This year Wm. M. Smith was appointed presiding elder on the Denver District, which embraced the best appointments; while South Park District, to which I was appointed, took the south and south-western parts of the State, the most thinly settled. It embraced Summit County, and ran south and west to the line of New Mexico. In all this region there were to be only four preachers, viz.: Colorado City and Cañon City, George Murray; Dayton, supplied by Brother John Gilland; Pueblo, C. H. Kirkbride; Buckskin and Summit, to be supplied.

We arranged to hold quarterly meetings every round at both places on Brother Murray's work, as the two places were forty-five miles apart. Formerly we had had about forty members on the Buckskin charge; but now all except about eight had left, and they were poor and discouraged. After consulting the brethren, it seemed best that I should make my home at Buckskin, and serve that charge all the time that I had to spare from the rest of the district. This I did, to the best of my ability. On this part of my work, I preached four times a week.

In traveling over the district, I visited many places not included in any of the charges, and preached to the people. After meeting they would say, "This is the first preaching we have heard in this country;" and some said, "It is the first for several years." This year I visited Fort Garland, and found one company of soldiers, about one hundred souls, and no chaplain. I asked the captain if I might preach. He replied that a chaplain had been there with Colonel Chivington, and only succeeded in inducing five to hear him. Not discouraged, I said: "Well, I am a bit of a Methodist preacher, and if you will help me, I believe we can fill your room." He said he would use his influence, and the preacher went around and invited the people. At the time appointed, nearly one hundred hearers were present, and only one left before dismission. At the close the captain came to me and said he would not have believed, had he not seen it, that the boys could have been kept still that long to hear preaching, and that he was glad he had the service.

About four miles out from there lived Mr. Thomas Tobin. He was a Missourian, and belonged to no Church. His wife was a Mexican and a Roman Catholic. I obtained the privilege of preaching at his house, and had about thirty—three-fourths half-breeds and Mexicans. I had found that the Spanish always had the Americans to translate the discourse to them. So I took the text, "Repent ye, therefore, and be converted," and contrasted our way with the Catholic's way; we confessing to Christ, and he forgiving us and letting us know the blessed fact for ourselves and not another.

I left an appointment to come again, but before I got around, Father Machbeuf, now bishop, who was the only colleague I had in that part of the district, met Mr. Tobin, and made him promise not to let me preach at his house any more. Tobin thought that this was hardly fair, for though his folks belonged to them, he liked our way the best. The priest taught that none but Catholic clergy could solemnize marriage, or do anything right.

At Saguache I found a small settlement, and held a two days' meeting at the house of Mr. Ashley, a family from Kentucky. They were Baptists, and good people, but had hardly heard of a Protestant preacher being in the country. They kept me, and it seemed like home in the wilderness. On Sunday the power of God came down, and nearly all were in tears. The lady of the house broke out with a grand shout, the first ever raised in the San Luis Valley. I called for seekers; three came, and two, I believe, were converted. We had there a foreigner, I think of Jewish descent. He sat near the door, and looked first at the door, then at me, and then at the scene among the seekers. A man by the name of Fullerton, and a Mr. Woodson, who had Mexican wines, were present. The former was reclaimed, and I hear that he is preaching. I could but thank God and take courage. It was about twenty-five miles to any other settlement. The men mentioned above lived neighbors, were farmers, and had wheat and oats. A severe hail-storm beat their crops into the ground. Indians were more numerous than white men. Old Chief San Juan came along, and expressed great sorrow at their loss. For him it meant, no biscuits this year. He said: "There is some good in it, but we can't see it. You must not complain, for the Great Spirit has permitted it. If you complain he might send the thunder and lightning, and that would kill men, even as the hail had destroyed their crops." The old man had never heard a gospel sermon or seen a Bible, and believed there was a happy hunting-ground beyond this life. In order that his son, who had been killed, might have plenty of horses in the happy hunting-ground, he sent his braves, who shot about one hundred and twenty-five head out of the herd. Our Savior said: "I will send the Spirit, and he shall enlighten every man that cometh into the world." The old chief must have got his share.

From here we made our way to Poncha Pass, the nearest settlement; thence to California Gulch, where Leadville now stands; and so across the Mosquito Pass to Buckskin. I visited the South Arkansas River, where two families had moved—six men, two women, and a little girl. They were living in tents. The women said they must have preaching that night. Meantime I concluded to go up on the mountains, where the iron mines are. The river was low, and I forded it. But the day was warm, and the snow thawed so that, when I got back in the afternoon, the river was out of its banks. When I got into the main stream, it was very rapid, and my Mexican horse would not go in more than knee-deep. It was near one hundred yards across. I called for help, and the men came down and asked what they could do. I had seen a new clothes-line at the camp. They brought it, and tied a stone to one end, and threw it to me. I tied it to the bridle; they pulled, and I whipped. The mustang had not got more than the length of himself, till the rushing water knocked his feet out from under him. As he rolled over, I slipped off, and shoved him as far as I could. They pulled, and brought him angling across against a high bank. I thought it was a good thing to know how to swim. They had only brought him to the bank, when I swam in, and ungirded the saddle. They had a big rope, and threw it over his head; then helped me up, and we all took hold, and pulled the pony out. He went to eating grass as though his experience were an every-day occurrence. I got dry clothes from my saddle-bags, and set about drying up.

After supper, while I was sitting by the fire barefooted, some one said it was time for the preaching. I rose up, and began to sing one of our old hymns. After prayer I took a text, and preached them their first sermon, barefooted. This was about two miles south-west of where Salida now stands. From here there was no house for fifty miles east, on the way to Cañon City. South, the first ranch—Curber's—was distant twenty-five miles. West, so far as I knew, there was nothing to the Pacific Ocean; north, up the Arkansas River, twelve miles, to Brown's Creek settlement; fifty-two miles to where Leadville now stands. The country was thinly settled, and I preached wherever a few could be got together. It was not known then that I had on my district what was destined to be the richest mining-camp in the United States, if not in the world.

Nothing of much importance was done till fall. We held a camp-meeting near where the town of Alma now stands. It was the day of small things, although, by altitude, it was the highest camp-meeting ever held. There were three tents and a wagon or two. We had only about eight members. Brother Cummings, Brother Hubbart and wife, were there, with others; Brother Bates and wife, Baptists, and an old Presbyterian brother, all good and true. Brother John Gilland, of Dayton charge, Twin Lakes, was with us. We had a good time in our social exercises, and enjoyed the opportunity of being together. Some came twelve miles. Few know how we appreciated those seasons, after our long exile among people taken up with sin of every grade, none even to sympathize with us and cheer us on our way. I have heard since that Brother Hubbart's oldest daughter, now the wife of Brother A. J. Smith, of our conference, received her first impressions at this time; but there were no conversions that I know of. Brother Cummings and Brother Hubbart, I trust, are in that better country, where congregations are large, and never break up. I love to think of the few with whom I shared privations, dangers, and religious joys in the Rocky Mountains.

It was my practice to go around the camps and invite all to come and hear the word. I would say to the boys at cards: "Can't you get through with your game in twenty minutes, stack up your chips, and give us a hearing?" Frequently they would all come; and they always conducted themselves with propriety. Indeed, I never found it otherwise in these mountains.

I tried to preach as often as four times a week during this conference year, and, where we could, three times on Sunday. About the first of November, in the morning, I was at Buckskin; at Montgomery 2.30 P. M., and at Breckenridge in the evening. This was twenty miles, and across the main range. Just as I got on top of the Hoosier Pass it began to snow, and snowed so severely that, although I was on time, there was no service at night. Next morning it had not abated, and, for fear of being blocked in, I started back with a little lawyer in company.

At Hoosier Gulch we rode into an empty cabin, and started a fire. My partner's gloves were wet, and his hands ached with cold. He made a face ugly enough to shed tears. We started on, and I loaned him my mittens, his gloves being unwearable, and went bare-handed. Suffice it to say, we got down the mountain somehow to Montgomery, and stopped with my old friend Mr. Ray. With great labor we reached Buckskin, eight miles, before dinner.

Leaving my lawyer, I rode to Fair Play, as there had been a trail broken, sent my horse to Bayley's ranch, and, having made me a pair of snow-shoes, concluded to go that way. I started from the south bank of the Platte, at Fair Play, on my shoes, supposing that I could stand walking as in the past; but having ridden on horseback all summer, I soon felt the effects of the change. At six, I reached Platte crossing, and expected to find a foot-log, but it had been washed away. There were two crossings, ten rods apart. I started down the creek. The snow had covered everything; and as I passed over some willows, I broke one of my shoes; but got to the ford, and saw that there was no way to cross but by wading. It was after dark. I sat down in the snow and took off my boots and socks. The stream was running full knee-deep of slush, and was about sixteen feet wide. I waded across, wiped my feet as dry as I could with my handkerchief, got my boots on, and made four miles through the snow to Garro's Ranch. I was tired out, and so hungry that I could have eaten anything. My condition was anything but enviable. But it was go or perish. The snow was a little packed by the wind, which was on my back, and helped me a little. I could make only about one hundred feet before having to rest. I was warm except my feet. I had one snow-shoe, and could scrape the snow off the ground to make a place to stamp my feet so that they should not freeze. I got within a mile; stopped to rest. I dug a trench in the snow long enough to lie in. The wind blew the snow and the scales I had knocked off over me, and it seemed like being buried alive, the clods being shoveled in on the coffin. I soon got out of that hole, and at last, near eleven o'clock, steadied myself by the door-knob with one hand, and rapped with the other. Mr. Garro jumped out of bed with his revolver in hand, ran up-stairs, hoisted the window, and cried out: "Who's there?" The reply was: "It is Dyer." He was astounded, and hurried down-stairs without shooting, brought me in, and set me supper, with hospitality so royal a king might envy it.

I remember yet how thankful I was to the good Lord that I got in; and how good that hay bed felt, and how greatly refreshed I was the next morning. Nothing but the grace of God, and what little grit I had in me, ever got me through. Mr. Garro saddled a pony, and sent his boy part way. Four miles out the snow was only six inches deep; and I got to Mr. Sam Hartsell's, where he now lives, about one o'clock, ten miles distant. He had just killed an antelope, and we had a good dinner. He put up a lunch for me, as I expected to reach the Thirty-nine-mile House that night.

The snow was not deep at Hartsell's; but when I got three miles up in the timber it was full knee-deep again, and by the time I got within two miles of the house I was well-nigh given out. I saw a log and a dead pine-tree by it. The bark was loose, and I concluded to camp. Soon had a fire and my lunch; rested and felt happy. I scraped away the snow, put some bark down to make my bed, lay down, and looked up at the bright stars of heaven. They seemed to sparkle as though they were laughing at me. I kept up the fire, rested and slept a little, and was up and off by daylight, reaching the Thirty-nine-mile House just at breakfast time. The mail-carrier from Cañon City was there. He had come the day before, and thought the snow was a sufficient excuse to go back. I told him it might do for him, as he was working for Uncle Sam; but that I was ruled by a higher Power. I gave him three dollars to let me ride an extra horse he had with him back to Cañon, as that was the place of our quarterly meeting. There I rested a day, was well cared for by the brethren, and, after a good meeting, went home with Uncle Jesse Frazier. O, what a good place to stop! Aunt Jesse would always make one feel as if he were with his own mother.

From there I went down the Arkansas, calling pastorally at many of the houses, preaching at Beaver Creek and at Pueblo. At the latter place I found Brother Kirkbride in not so agreeable a situation as I would have liked. He had been teaching school; and the two occupations did not work well together, for he had forgotten to announce the quarterly meeting. Fortunately I was there on Friday, and so went around and invited the people, and we had quite good congregations. I took up a collection of fifteen dollars, and gave it all to Brother Kirkbride. This was before the presiding elder had his salary separate from the preacher in charge.

From Pueblo I went up Fountain Creek to Bannister's settlement, and gathered up about thirty-five, and preached to them. Then I went on to where Fountain City now stands, and preached at Searles's; thence to Colorado City, where we had quarterly meeting with Brother Murray. Here they made fifteen dollars or more, and I turned almost all of it over to Brother Murray, as I knew he was in more need than I at that time. Sister Murray took quite an interest in the collection, and gave five dollars herself. When we arranged it, she said she would not take so much interest next time if she was to get it back. It was hard times for money. Congregations were small, and the preachers had as much as they could do to come out even. We had a number of preachers come and go back because of the work and pay.

I concluded to return by way of Denver, and took the stage in the evening. I hoped to find congenial company, since it was an all-night ride. But the passengers were two deeply colored discharged soldiers. Adapting myself to the situation, I inquired where the gentlemen were from. "Fort Union, New Mexico; we been soldiers." "Did you get your discharge?" "Yes, sar." "Where are you bound for?" "Denver; to see our uncle and kinsfolks." "Your native State?" "Kentucky, sar." "What Church are you members of?" One said he was a Baptist, and the other a Methodist. This was good news. "Now, can't you sing some of the old hymns that used to make us happy?" One said that if he had a book he could, but he couldn't "'membah." The other said he could 'membah some, but he could not read. I named several hymns, and finally one of the soldiers struck up:

> "How tedious and tasteless the hours,
>   When Jesus no longer I see."

We all sang with energy and spirit, hymn after hymn. Following a hymn, one of them said: "I 'sperienced religion twice under dat dah song." We kept it up for seven or eight miles. After our ten-o'clock supper I tried to have more singing, but we all felt too drowsy. We reached Denver about sunrise, entering on the east side of Cherry Creek; but not striking Denver till we got to Larimer Street—that was all there was of the now great city.

CABIN AT MOSQUITO.

"How glad I was to get back, stand my snow-shoes up against the house,
strike up a fire, sit down, and warm a little."

Page 215.

After two or three days, I got to Buckskin, a trip of four hundred miles. I caught some rides out from Denver, where there was plenty of snow. I had been gone three Sundays.

I spent the winter traveling on snow-shoes, preaching on an average four times a week. I had a cabin, which I called home, at Mosquito; the post-office being called Sterling. I cut my own wood, and had an old-fashioned fire-place to sit by; a few books to read; a bedstead made of poles, and a bed made of the tops of fir-trees, and finished out with a hay tick—a very comfortable outfit. There was one window, containing six panes of glass, ten by twelve inches, affording plenty of light, except on stormy days, when it was necessary to keep the door open, if the wind would allow. I could enjoy the hospitality of friends at my various appointments, but when I got around I wanted some place that I could call home. The above was my home, or answered that purpose. How glad I was to get back, stand my snow-shoes up against the house, strike up a fire, sit down, and warm a little; and then, if there was not any bread to warm up, and satisfy my hunger, to take flour and baking-powder, and make a delicious cake! I generally baked it in a frying-pan before the fire. By the time it was baked, the meat was fried, coffee boiled, and with a can of fruit or some dried-apple sauce, the table was set, and I was ready to thank God and eat!

CHAPTER XIII.

AMONG THE INDIANS.

THE winter of 1866–67 was remarkable for snow and its continuance in the spring until April.

Just six months from the former trip, I started from Fair Play on my snow-shoes again; this time for Brown's Creek, in Lake County, by the salt-works. The first house was Mr. Weston's, twelve miles. His friends wished to send them their mail, with some other little articles. He could not go on snow-shoes, and so, with his wife, he had been there all winter alone. The sun thawed the snow so that it stuck, and made heavy traveling. I had to wear a veil, to keep from getting snow-blind, the dazzling light being so intense; but I got there to dinner all the same. Mr. Weston was out splitting wood near the door, and did not see me till I was close, and spoke. He was taken by surprise; but before I was within two rods of him, he exclaimed: "Did you bring me any tobacco?" I could not tell him, but gave him the package, and sure enough they had sent a plug of the dirty stuff. This shows that tobacco-chewers think more of the weed than of their victuals.

The next day I stopped with Mr. Charles Hall at the salt-works, and preached. I found it bad traveling, as the snow would not bear a man, and it was almost impossible to run the shoes. When I got down to Trout Creek, I met about seventy-five Indians. They invited me to stay all night with them. It was late; but I chose to stay alone, and went two miles and camped by a log. I built a fire, and slept some. In the morning I discovered two Indian tepees within less than a hundred yards. I suppose they had gone to sleep before I camped. They proved to be quiet neighbors.

I met my friends, Brother Gilland's family, G. Sprague and family, with others. We had quarterly meeting, and went up to the hot springs, since called the Haywood Springs, which I had laid claim to by discovery. Thence I went to the Twin Lakes. It was thawing, and I saw that Lake Creek ran through the lake just as if it had its regular banks. It had cut a channel through the ice, and paid no attention to a lake of a mile or two across, but just went in and through and out as it pleased. This was a very hard trip, but I was soon back to my cabin at Mosquito.

That spring—May 20th—I took stage from Fair Play to Denver. I got as far as Hamilton—just above Como—all right. There were some five passengers in all; Mr. Cy. Hall—the rich and clever Denverite of to-day—driver. I was in the front seat. Mr. Hall said: "You sit back, and let Billy Berry sit here; he knows the road better than any of us." It had already begun to snow, and the old packed snow was about two feet deep. The horses and sled sunk about six inches. It snowed almost straight down, and was foggy. We

had not gone more than a mile till we lost the
road. It was about four miles to Michigan Ranch,
and we traveled all day till near sundown. We
knew the creek ahead, and Tarryall Creek behind,
and a hill on each side, and in all this time never
saw either. It looked as though we were elected
to make a hotel of ourselves. Unexpectedly we
heard the report of a gun a mile away. We answered with strong voices, and made toward the
sound. We got in about sundown, and stopped
for the night.

Next morning, before we got to Brubaker's
Ranch, crossing a slough, the water had begun to
run under and over the snow. Right in the middle the horses went down, and the water almost
ran over them. It looked as though they would
drown. Mr. Hall got to the first span, but most
of the passengers were a little sick just then.
However I worked out to the leaders, and kept
their heads out of the water until we got them
loose from the sled, in which sat three men quietly
looking on till we got all the horses out. We
took a long rope and tied to the tongue, hitched
the horses, and pulled out. We stopped at Hank
Farnham's to warm. I was wet to the waist with
snow-water. This was staging—sledding, in fact—
almost the last of May.

I have not seen the snow lie so long since. I
think settling a country changes it from its wild
nature, and from snow to more rain. I have tried
three States before this, and it was so in them,
and will be here. Occasionally we may have deep

snow and hard winters, but I trust that we will be like the man who got married; he said that he made up his mind to take things as they came.

I kept up the work on circuit and district till conference, which was held at Colorado City about the 20th of June, 1867, by Bishop E. R. Ames. There was a good society at the above place, including many of whom I love to think as tried friends—Rev. Wm. Howbert and family, Brother Gurtin and wife, Brother Templeton and family, White Roberts, Brother Brown, Brother G. Murray, preacher in charge, with his wife, whom I met on horseback, going forty-five miles to camp-meeting. These and other hardy frontiersmen ought ever to be remembered for their integrity and perseverance, contending against drouth, grasshoppers, Indians, and the devil, six hundred miles distant from the eastern settlements. They had been a year or two in the gorges of the mountains in search of gold, and had spent all they brought across the Plains from their homes. Now they had set themselves to making farms, which so far as could be positively known, was as uncertain work as prospecting. Four-fifths of all were broken up or badly in debt. Such was the case with myself. Surely the energy of these early settlers made it possible for this to become a State, with all its wonders of wealth, its telegraphs, railroads, telephones, splendid cities, and the boundless prospects of its future development.

These brethren at Colorado City determined to build a chapel. We called it a Methodist church.

In fact, it was as much credit to them as the Lawrence Street church was to the people of Denver. They expected to have it ready for the session of the conference; but after straining every nerve, it was found impossible, at our quarterly conference three weeks before, to finish the house in time. We resolved to have a camp-meeting near the village, under the shadow of Pike's Peak, and hold the conference on the ground; and so we gave it out. This was probably the first camp-meeting in Colorado. Rev. George Murray was preacher in charge, and the writer had charge of the district. I was there two or three days in advance, and, with the neighbors, we erected a pulpit, seated the ground, and had all things ready for a camp-meeting conference. But the Cheyennes and the Arapahoe Indians were on the war-path, and the majority of the few members of the conference were in the Denver district, a distance of seventy miles. Thirty settlers armed themselves, and, with Bishop Ames, made their appearance in due time; and, notwithstanding a good old brother was raising pickets around his store to fight the Indians if they came, we were all happy and felt secure, both soul and body.

Our conference was very harmonious; all the regular business was carried on in the altar in front of the stand. We had about ten tents. Pueblo had one tent brought from a distance of forty-five miles, and Brother Fowler, from Cañon City, had one from the same distance. Our preacher's tent represented the whole territory. I must mention the neighbors, or some of them: Brother and Sister Garten, the latter, gone to glory. Brother and Sister Brown had a little boy baptized by the bishop in his full name. Brother Brown sometime since died happy, and the evidences he gave of the power of religion will not be forgotten by his neighbors. Brother Howbert, a local preacher, of precious memory, now gone to rest, was there, as was also Brother Templeton and wife, with others of equal worth. All were interested in the proceedings of the conference.

I mention one incident in connection with this conference. Brother McMains brought the bishop from Denver in his carriage safe to the bank of the Fontaine qui Bouille, a rapid stream. The bishop cautiously took his carpet-sack in hand and crossed on a foot-bridge, and as Brother McMains was fording the stream, his horse made a lurch and upset. He lost his carpet-sack, with no other damage except a wetting and the loss of a suit of clothes and a flask of wine for sacramental purposes. We made up his loss, at least in part. The carpet-sack was found soon after, but the finder thought it a good thing to drink the pure wine.

It was a pleasant meeting. The bishop enjoyed his home on the ground, and the brethren were pleased to entertain the conference. The bishop's preaching was refreshing and helpful. One day the friends got teams and took the whole conference—except the writer, who remained to preach—to see the sights in the Garden of the Gods. It was a scene such as no Methodist conference had ever beheld before, and which is still admired by all travelers. After we had come together, Brother Smith told me that they had concluded to send me to the General Conference, as we were entitled to a delegate. I was surprised, as I had but two preachers on my district that had a vote, but thanked him for the intended honor. At the proper time it was bestowed upon me. Brother Smith, of the Denver District, was elected alternate.

At the close of the conference, the bishop concluded to take a trip with me around my district, of which I give an account, substantially the same as furnished by me for the *Central Christian Advocate*, and printed in that paper in the early part of 1880. Rev. George Richardson accompanied us. We procured a light wagon and camping equipage. I was the driver, and Brother Richardson rode his gray pony and carried a gun. The first day we reached Pueblo, a distance of forty-five miles. We had the mountains on the west of us with Pike's Peak in full view all day, and on the east the vast plains inhabited only by Indians, and they rather hostile. The bishop enjoyed the wild and grand scenery, and made us feel that we had no ordinary traveling companion. He drew out of us, a little at a time, an account of our early life and times. On our arrival at Pueblo, word was given out that the bishop would preach; and as he was the first bishop that had visited that region, all came and heard with interest. On Wednesday, we made our way to

Cañon City, the time spent much as on the day before, the snow-capped mountains towering up in front of us, and I can say that forty-five miles was never gone over so pleasantly to me before.

Rev. George Murray, preacher in charge, had gone from Colorado City to Cañon City by the Ute trail, and announced that the bishop would preach there on Thursday at eleven o'clock, and there was a good congregation, some having come as far as ten miles. And Bishop Ames preached a very forcible discourse. The morning was spent in viewing the grand scenery, the irrigating ditches, wheat-fields, and lastly, the town, which was somewhat dilapidated. There were several store-houses for sale, and we raised the question as to our ability to buy one, and one was selected. The bishop then asked us if we could buy it; we told him the people were not able. He said: "If you had five hundred dollars donated [that was one-third the price], could you reach it? I will give you that amount out of my own money, provided that no part of the property shall ever be sold to pay any part of the original debt." We agreed to it, and Brother Murray began a subscription, and was to report to us at Denver. His report was favorable, and the bishop gave me a check for five hundred dollars. It was a gift in time of need; and if the contract has not been kept, it was not my fault. It has all been sold, but I believe the greater part was applied to a neat church in the place that is self-supporting. For years it answered a good purpose; the store-room was seated for church, and rooms in the rear for parsonage.

After service we started, several persons escorting us several miles on to what was called Devil's Gate, a passage between two large rocks. The bishop spoke kindly of all the people and of his host, T. Macon, Esq., and his family. We began to ascend the mountains, and that night pitched our tent for the first time on Currant Creek. On Friday we traveled all day, and camped in the lower part of South Park. It was a pleasant night; we had supper and prayers, and slept well. In the morning we ate our breakfast on the ground, the whole company seeming to enjoy the simple fare. A stretch of eight miles of prairie gave us a good start, and we were trotting at fine speed, when we saw, some two miles to the right of us, six armed Indians, riding at full lope, and, from the appearance, intending to head us off. The bishop inquired of me as to their object, and he was assured they were friendly—for the Utes were friendly with us at that time—and that they would beg us for something. The bishop directed Brother Richardson to take his gun in hand and be ready for an emergency. But as soon as they were within speaking distance they lowered their guns and sung out at the top of their voices, " How! how!" and called for biscuit. We had none for them, and they soon fell back and left us. A few miles further on we passed through a camp of about fifty more of the red-skins and as many ponies.

After dinner we rested an hour, expecting to reach Cache Creek that day. But we had the Arkansas River to cross, and I will say just here that in 1867 there was more snow in the mountains, and it lay on later, and the mountain streams were higher than they have been since or for several years before. We soon reached the river, and found the bridge there. It was made of hewed logs, with rocks laid on the end of them to hold them in place. The water passed just clear of the stringers, but when a wave washed under the bridge the water would burst through. When safely over this most angry-looking river in the world, the bishop remarked that if there was any other way to get back he did not want to cross that bridge again. That night it was swept away; we were the last to cross it. Fearing that we might not reach the "diggings" at Cache Creek that night, and as I knew a house one mile off the road, they deputized me to get a loaf of bread. When I returned to the road again, I saw a party ahead with the same-sized wagon, and I followed after them; so we were parted for a few hours; it would be hard to tell whether they or I was the most uneasy. But we came out right, and reached Four Mile, a rapid stream without a bridge, and we camped in company with Mr. Pitzer. Mountain streams are always lower in the morning, as the sun thaws the snow during the day.

This was Saturday evening, and the bishop spoke as to the propriety of traveling on Sunday. I said to him: "We have made an appointment for you at the Twin Lakes at two P. M. to-morrow, and it is my rule if I could not make it on Saturday, I would finish it on Sunday." "Well," he said, "I am under your care, and will leave it with you." We forded the creek on horseback, and concluded we could cross by doubling teams; so we hitched the wagons together, and had both span of horses to the front wagon, and I rode one of the leaders. The bishop sat in a chair and held on to a seat in front of him. The water ran into the wagon and washed it down stream a little, but we put every horse on his nerve, and by the blessing of God we brought our valuable cargo through safe. Passing down the stream a short distance, I pointed out where Rev. Rufus Lumery was drowned five years before.

We now began to ascend the Cache Creek hill. It was very steep, dug into the side of the hill with not a foot to spare on the outside, and the roaring Arkansas River almost under us. Just as we reached the top I pointed over and said: " Bishop, there I was called on to attend a funeral, the first in Colorado." He said: "You watch those lines." (I thought it was as much as to say, There might be another funeral.)

We soon drove up to Cache Creek, and the people gave us such an invitation to stop that the bishop asked why we could not; but our appointment had been sent to Twin Lake, and we passed on. At Lake Creek the family there said it would swim us; there was a foot-bridge to cross on, and I thought it would be crossed about a mile above. The bishop hired our equipage carried over while we were crossing the wagon. Both horses had to swim, and it ran over the top of the wagon-box; but when I got back, our loading was adjusted and we pushed on to Dayton at the lakes, the county seat of Lake County. The bishop said he was surprised to see so many out to hear the sermon; there were sixty in the log court-house. My son Elias lived here, and the next morning he furnished us with two cans of peaches and a quart of cream for our dinner.

When we were taking our dinner the bishop said it was a small but delicious present, and he appreciated the spirit in which it was given. The same house in which he had preached was afterward carried six miles to Granite.

We were on our way to Ore City, or, as it was commonly called, California Gulch, now the famous Leadville, but we turned up north to Colorado Gulch, six miles west, and stopped with Captain Cree, and our company was well entertained. The bishop went with the boys and saw them pan out some of the pure dust, and he took care to say that economy and prudence were of great value, as they were blessed with the precious metal. The 2d of July we turned east to the Arkansas River, which was nearly a quarter of a mile wide; the main bed of the stream was bridged, being covered with poles, rather loosely laid on. Bishop Ames requested Brother Richardson to ride ahead of the wagon, and when he reached the east end of the bridge, his horse grew afraid, and that stopped us on the loose poles, the river running at a terrible rate just under us. One of our ponies slipped his hind-legs through the poles to the gambrel; but strangely enough, got them out again, and the driver gave a most unearthly yell for Brother Richardson to get out of the way. We got out of our dilemma, delighted and thankful to be safe across. Brother Richardson and the bishop accused the driver of being angry when he halloed so loud on the bridge; but they were told that it was a case where, if it needed thunder and lightning to make a move, it should have been put in.

Concluding not to go to Ore City, as it would be several miles out of our way, we turned for Weston's Pass to cross the mountain, as we were now headed for Denver. Before we reached the top of the range, the axle dragged in the snow, and sometimes nearly up to the wagon-box. When we had passed over the summit, we came to a drift of snow six to ten feet deep, and it would not bear us. We camped at timber-height, and the query was, How shall we get over? The driver proposed that we be contented, and in the morning it would be frozen, and we could go on the top. The bishop took for his part of the work to cut pine-boughs to make a soft bed for us. In the morning we were up early, so as to get over the snow before the sun softened it; we led the horses, and pulled the wagon by hand till we got within about fifty feet of the edge, when it went down to the box. But we had a long rope, and by the aid of this we pulled out with the horses.

We had no more snow to hinder us, and passed through Fair Play on to Buckskin, and when we came in sight of the dilapidated town, the bishop asked if this was the place I had made my headquarters. We answered: "Yes; but you may depend upon it I would not have made it here. Why, this is the place you appointed me to in 1863, to get my support without aid from the Church. I walked to Denver to get it, one hundred miles and back." I had been telling him of taking a contract to carry the mail on my back, and walking on snow-shoes, and that I made more that way than I had in all the time I had preached. He said, "I am glad you do so well, and that you preached three times a week, too;" and added that it was difficult to know much of such a country without seeing it. But I did not attach blame to him. Brother and Sister Bates entertained us here.

On the Fourth of July we started for Denver. Before we got to Tarryall Creek we heard that a horse had been drowned in a crossing a few days before. It was a small stream, was muddy and rapid. The council said stop; but the bishop took off his coat and said if we were thrown out, there were plenty of willows to catch hold of. We crossed safely; and when asked why he was more afraid of that creek than worse ones, he replied, "Because it had a bad name." From here the streams were bridged, the roads good, and we passed along pleasantly until we reached Denver.

When we parted, after a day's rest, the bishop said he thought we had had a pleasant and eventful trip, and asked me if twenty-five dollars would cover all the money we had spent, and he said he would pay it to me. I will say that we had a good time; we enjoyed the bishop's company, and have always felt thankful that he consented to go round with us. I doubt whether any of our bishops ever had a rougher or more romantic trip in the States or Territories. He has gone, no doubt, to rest from all his labors. We love to think of all our associations with him. He gave me more of my appointments than any other of our bishops, and I always judged him to be a balance-wheel in council with our bishops.

Chapter XIV.

THE GENERAL CONFERENCE OF 1868.

A FEW days after conference, W. F. Warren came, and was employed on the Fair Play work. He did good service for a number of years, and left for the California Conference, to improve his wife's health. As Bishop Ames returned, he met Brother Warren, and talked discouragingly to him. But after several years, he saw Brother Warren, and heard his report, and said that he had feared it was a mistake in his coming, but now saw that it was the Lord's doings. Brother Warren has been remembered pleasantly among us for his hard and faithful work in our conference.

In the fall of this year, as we had no church in South Park, and as Montgomery was almost depopulated, while Fair Play, having been made the county-seat of Park County, was improving a little, I bought a building formerly used as a hotel in Montgomery, designing to convert it into a meeting-house in Fair Play. It was a hewed-log house, two stories high. The windows had almost all been broken out. Two men who had ox-teams, agreed that if I would build, they would haul the house on to the lot. I paid one hundred dollars for the building, hired a man to help me pull it down, paid my board, and got it ready.

The teamsters went one trip, and would not go again. They were not members of any Church. We had but one member in the town, and he worked by the day and job for a living. We were in a close place. I looked for some one to haul the stuff, and found a man who said it was worth one hundred and twenty dollars, but that he would do it for one hundred. When the job was done, I gave him the money out of my own pocket. By this time, Brother Warren and wife had come. I found a part of the provision, and he and I went to work. We were both log-house carpenters, and with the days' works that were given, in one month we had the building up and ready for use. It was forty by twenty-five feet. We took off fourteen feet on the rear, and that answered for a parsonage till Brother Warren got one built. The front would hold all the people in town. It was comfortable, and no man paid over twenty dollars in cash or work, save myself and Brother Warren. Best of all, we dedicated it free of debt.

Before this I had done most of the preaching in private houses and stores. Mr. Hitchcock had often set out seats in his store for services. I remember at one time, early in the spring, the people had gathered. They had arranged for me to stand in front of the end counter, and right above was a sign: "Good Whisky." I saw the situation, and said: "I never can preach under such a sign as that." Mr. Hitchcock said: "Mr. Dyer, I will take it down; the whisky is all gone." He pulled it down, and I preached to about thirty people.

This time I left Brother Warren a church to preach
and live in, and he was looking for a revival.   He
asked me how many would be a good work in
Fair Play.   The reply was: "Three would be a
good thing in that place."   He said he could not
ask the Lord for less than twenty.   But he did
not then know the Rocky Mountain sinners as well
as he did afterwards.

He worked earnestly there and around the circuit for a month, till we held our quarterly meeting, which commenced with about twenty hearers.
There was no special revival; and while I was
gone, somebody reported that Brother Warren had
a lot of silver-ware that he had stolen from an old
widow woman down South, as he had been a soldier.   I took occasion—when we had our largest
audience—to speak of slander, and referred to the
lies somebody had raised about the silver spoons.
Of course I extolled the preacher for having been
a soldier, and having received an honorable discharge.   I happened to know how they came by
the five or six old silver spoons.   Sister Warren
had fallen heir to them from an old grandmother
from England.   "Such a lie," I said, "is a disgrace to your town, and so far as I am concerned,
if I knew who it was that started the slander, I
would run him clear to the head of Salt River."
I mention this to show how our early preachers
not only had hard times financially, but in other
respects.   Brother Warren was a young preacher
of average pulpit ability, and untiring in labor.
The roughs went so far as to shave his horse.

Sister Warren was a patient, Christian woman, and I believe was the first lady that ever made a vocal prayer in Fair Play. Although it was a hard place for a preacher, they stayed over two years, and did good service.

The winter was now upon us. Our travel was much the same as before related. One of our quarterly meetings was held at what we called Cottage Grove, half-way between Alma and Fair Play. We had quite a turn-out for the times. I agreed to make the coffee and find the sugar, if the ladies would furnish the rest of the lunch. It was a good dinner. I borrowed a wash-boiler, dug a trench for a furnace, set on the boiler full of water, put in the coffee in little sacks, made a good fire under all, and gave a boy a quarter to tend it while we were preaching and administering sacrament. It was ready when the benediction was pronounced. Our table was fifty feet long. We had the credit of making good coffee. After we were through, the collection was taken. My old friends, Mr. Hotstettler and Mr. Bates, carried the hats, and when they counted the money, there were eighty-five dollars. They all felt well over the amount. I never liked taking the collection before the preaching was done; but I hope to be excused, because we only took it once a quarter in old times, and that at a quarterly meeting; and that even after James B. Finley or Peter Cartwright had preached with their usual power. But our later preachers think it best to take it every time *in advance.*

On one of my rounds I called at Fort Garland.
I had preached there before, and expected to do
so again. But now they had a chaplain. I called,
and introduced myself. He seemed pleased to see
me. I told him I had been there before, and had
all the soldiers to hear me, and would take it as a
favor to have another opportunity. But he thought
it would be impossible to get the soldiers together.
I told him how we did it before, but he made it
out impossible. I saw he was not willing to allow
me even to try. In our conversation he made it
plain that *The Church* had all the forts under their
care. He mentioned as a strange thing that, down
in Kansas, there was one Methodist chaplain. I
remarked that I had known two others who had
joined the Episcopalians to serve in that capacity,
but that we thought when they left we could well
spare them, and that where they went they would
be but little, if any, better off. I asked if he had
many to hear him. He claimed only moderate
congregations. From others I learned that two
and three were his usual number. I have had the
pleasure of extending the courtesies of my pulpit
to Roman Catholic priests and Episcopalian clergy-
men, but never have been permitted the use of any
of their places of worship. A few miles further on
I preached to six or eight hearers.

This was the year to take collections to pay
the expenses of the delegate to General Conference. Thirty-six dollars were paid to me. I was
anxious to see my parents and children and other
friends. I took stage at Denver City on the

twenty-eighth day of March by the Smoky Hill route. It began to snow as we left Denver, and by the time we got to Kiowa it was blowing and drifting so that we were obliged to stop for two nights; and cooked, ate, and slept in the hostler's room. When we got off again, we had gone only two or three miles when we ran into a snow-drift, and all was fast. After the driver and conductor had vainly tried to extricate the team, they most humbly acted on my advice to unhitch the horses and make the Kiowa stable horseback, leaving the stage to be shoveled out the next day. The lead-horse was a fine one. I unharnessed him, and took the lead-strap. He made two or three long jumps and was out. I got on and took a circle, and got back to the road, and was at the stable as quick as he could lope it. I had left the three men with a horse apiece, and after awhile they came. The next morning we took all the shovels and got the stage out, and went on slowly, breaking our way through, having several times been brought almost to a stand.

We took five days to go from Denver to Coyote. We reached the latter place at 1.45 A. M.; called at several tents, asking for some kind of a bed. At last a man said, if I could sleep with two others in a bed, I could come in. I lodged with them till about daylight, when I discovered it was a saloon. He charged me a dollar; and I found a restaurant, and paid a dollar for breakfast. At eight o'clock I was off on the train. I may be excused for this description, as I was the first delegate and the last delegate from the Colorado Conference who will ever have such an experience.

I made but little stop till I got to my father's, twenty miles south of Pleasant Hill, Mo., where he and my brother had settled some time before. Brother had died, and left his widow and children with the old folks. While there, Sunday came, and I tried to preach. Father, being hard of hearing, did not go. A man asked in my presence if the preacher was coming. I was pointed out, and he replied, "I thought that was the old gentleman," meaning my father! After we got home, father asked my sister how John preached. She said that she had heard him do better. He replied: "I suppose he is failing." I thought it best for me to leave for some other parts, for I had not thought of anything but being in the prime of life, as I was twenty years before.

I went on to St. Louis; and from there made my way to Illinois, Wisconsin, and Minnesota. My daughter lived in Minnesota, and at Juda in Wisconsin my son was keeping a drug-store. So I had quite a visit, take it all around. I reached Chicago the evening before the conference opened, and stayed at the Sherman Hotel. I went to Clark Street Church, where a full attendance of delegates were shaking hands. I found nearly all had been there the day before, and had selected their seats. It looked as though all the seats were occupied. I was quite near to the platform, and remarked that if some good-looking delegation would take me in I would be obliged. Brother

Baker, of an Eastern delegation, invited me, and I felt at home with them. It was convenient, and better than I could have done if I had been there the day before.

I soon found that I was on all the committees, or allowed to sit in many of them, as I was the only delegate from my conference. I concluded not to try to be conspicuous in conference, but to attend every committee that I felt interested in; such as those on Boundaries of Conferences and Indian Affairs. Some of our Eastern brethren were going to take charge of the Indians in love, neither watching nor coercing them. I gave the committee my experience among them, and when the report came before the conference I made an effort to speak, but Brother Fisher, of Nevada, got the floor. We had talked it all over; our experience had been the same. If I could have made a speech on anything it would have been on the red-skins, for I knew their treachery, and that the time had not come to make bosom companions of them.

Our bishops had been forming mission conferences down South, and many of our best men thought the delegates therefrom ought not to have seats in conference. Others equally good thought differently. Dr. Curry opposed them, and, with others, made strong speeches. I feared at one time that they would be rejected; but Dr. McClintock took up their case. He convinced me that he was the most cultured man on the conference floor. He won the day, and the delegates, although some were colored, were admitted. I had been out on mission long enough to believe we ought not to be kept out.

The next and most important thing was lay delegation, which was hotly contested. Dr. Curry made the strongest speech against the change, and Dr. McClintock for it. I voted with the latter.

The next was boundaries of conferences. Our conference was small in number; and I had been doing all I could to induce our bishops to send missionaries to New Mexico, as it belonged to our country, and I had seen its degraded condition, resulting from wearing the yoke of Catholicism three hundred years.

I blocked out a map of Colorado Conference, to include all of New Mexico and the southern part of Wyoming Territory, feeling that they must take the interest that they ought, particularly in the Spanish work in New Mexico.

At the close of the session Bishop Simpson asked me if we could have our conference two weeks earlier, as about thirty Eastern members of the General Conference had secured passes to the end of the Union Pacific, and it would be pleasant to go in company. I thought a moment, and said to him: "That will give me time to hold one quarterly meeting, and we have Brother Warren to recommend to be admitted to our conference." So he changed the time, and we had all in readiness; and the session was held in Golden City, Bishop Simpson presiding.

CHAPTER XV.

NEW MEXICO.

WHILE the bishop was writing the appointments, I noticed he put me down for New Mexico. He had inquired of me about that work and the people; but the thought of going there rather set me back. I felt my inability to do what ought to be done in that mission, and gave him my view in the matter; that a man for that place should not be old, but one calculated to take hold of the Spanish work and elevate those who were starving for the gospel; withal, an educated man. I urged him, if possible, to send such a man. He replied: "You preach to all the Americans; do what you can, and see where and how the Mexicans can be improved."

My name was read out for New Mexico District; and that year I took in Trinidad, being the first Protestant who ever tried to preach there. This appointment was not taken without at least some knowledge of the labor, privation, and dangers attending a Protestant preacher in that field. I had already found that it was not Mexico, but New Mexico, the outside or fag-ends of an old Latinized nation, that had been ridden over by Romish priests. Being the first discoverers of our American continent, their Church, I supposed, had lost almost all but form and ceremony, and had been backsliding ever since. And I was going into the most illiterate part, where the majority had learned no law save what the priests taught them, confession and mass, payment of a portion of all they had or could raise to the Church; nothing to elevate them to a higher state of civilization or make them men and women in our nation.

But some of the better-to-do among the Spanish had sent their boys East to be educated. The inhabitants were scattered, and the early emigrants from different parts of the United States had married among the natives. Notwithstanding the Romanists had generally proselyted the children, the men held to their former attachment to home and American institutions. We could depend on most of them for help in all directions. They were especially anxious for English schools to educate their children. I saw that it was necessary, as they were now one of our Territories. Kit Carson was among the foremost in creating an influence among the natives in favor of our Western States. Mr. Maxwell was also active. He was an American, with a Mexican wife, and, by long acquaintance and association, influential among that people, and with the Indians. He made Mountain Peak his western boundary. It is almost a wonder that he stopped where he did, as no others of equal prominence had yet come West. He generally had whites, Spanish, and Indians on his claim, of which much has been said.

As to my appointment, after all it may have been for the best, to take a man who was used to mountain life, who would ride a pony on an Indian trail, and feared nothing when conscious that he was right, and had orders to march in the name of Jesus.

My small amount of luggage was in Lake County, such as books, bedding, and cabin outfit. To go to New Mexico was to leave almost all that I depended on for a living. I had one-half of the Hayden Ranch on the Arkansas River, where I expected to make me a home and a fortune; but the land was not surveyed, and could only be held by being on it or by representing it. I concluded to deed it to my son, as there was no chance to sell it. I was also the first claimant on the Haywood Sulphur Hot Springs. I thought I would risk them; but while I was in New Mexico, an old Georgia doctor came along and jumped my claim.

It only took a few days to pack a pony with those things most needed, having another to ride. Soon we were in marching order, going through Poncha Pass and San Luis Valley; one house on the route between South Arkansas River and Fort Garland, seventy miles.

The first time going over into San Luis, I met a number of Indians. I saw that they were all mad; and as I did not care to camp near them— they were strung along all the afternoon—I traveled till after dark and camped without any fire; took my lunch, lariated the ponies on good grass, and slept comfortably. In the morning I got breakfast, as I had in my pack bread, crackers, coffee, sugar, cheese, dried fruit, and ham, prepared to live anywhere. I met a man that day who said the Indians were so mad they would not talk; that there had been a quarrel between them and the whites at Saguache; and a company of soldiers had gone up and settled the fuss. The Indians had left mad.

On the second day I camped a short distance from Fort Garland. I stopped over night at Cal-avery. This was the last place in Colorado on my trail. They announced me to preach, and about ten Americans, and—it being a new thing to hear the strange *padre*—about thirty Mexicans gathered in the court-house, fifteen feet square, and a dirt floor. Two or three prominent men helped to sing, and one kneeled in prayer. There was good attention, and toward the close the preacher waxed warm, and several of the Mexican women wept— one so that it was noticed all over the house. A young man who could talk both languages, went home with the woman, and asked why she cried so. She said she thought the strange preacher had some friends that were lost, and he was plead-ing for help, and she thought the man that kneeled in prayer was engaged to help him, and she felt so sorry that she could not help crying. (The young man said to me at the close, "This looks like a revival;" and he learned the above and told me next morning.) The Mexicans are a kind, sympathetic people; will divide anything with even a stranger, especially in the rural parts.

I will relate an incident that occurred as far from civilization probably as any on record. Some fastidious people would not allow such a scene to be described or written, but the facts are never fully stated without the lowest and the highest. I have no desire to burlesque these people, but to help elevate them in every department of life to experimental Christianity. It was for their salvation through Christ Jesus that I was out there among the sheep-herders. I had followed a trail all day from Calavery till near time to camp, and was looking out for wood, grass, and water. Soon I saw smoke a mile ahead, and concluded to go and stop with whomsoever it might be. I rode up. There were two men and two women and a two-year old boy. I asked partly by signs if I could stop for the night. "Si! si!" that was "yes." I got off, and put my ponies out. They had a half-faced camp made of poles, and a fire out in front. I camped on the outside or back of their fire. I soon had my supper ready, and was hungry enough to relish it. Their evening work was done, and they were interested in me so much as to offer me some new sheep-cheese. I thanked them, told them I had cheese; but, in kindness, they pressed me to take some of theirs that had just been made. I ate some of it, asking no questions. In due time they retired to rest in their camp, and I on my side of their fire. I rested well, notwithstanding the bleating of the ewes and lambs, as my bedding was sufficient to keep me comfortable, even on the ground among the sage-brush. When I awoke, they were all up.

As soon as possible I put my coffee on, and

Page 244.

MEXICAN INDIANS.

"There were two men and two women and a two-year old boy."

repaired two hundred feet to the corral to see the men milking the ewes, as it was new to me. The sheep were crowded so close that the ground could not be seen. The men would push their feet in, and press the bucket between them to the ground, and milk. The bucket was well-nigh full. As I watched the milking with growing interest, a sheep discharged a quantity of sheep-saffron into the milk. The man with his hand caught some of it, but let the balance remain, and kept on milking, and I kept wondering that the cheese they gave me tasted as well as it did. While I was preparing my breakfast, they brought in a bucket of milk, and the woman set about straining it through a piece of blue blanket, which seemed to be very necessary, as there was a handful of the digested grass caught. Just then the little boy cried, and the other woman caught him up on her hip, and walked around, and the little fellow began to make quite a stream of water, and as she turned, the stream came across the back of the women straining the milk. As she was thinly clad, it felt hot, and made her jump, and drop the strainer with its contents in the milk again. We thought it well that the stream did not reach quite far enough to go in with the strainer. The traveler was quite well instructed in the sheep-cheese business. But there is still a wonder that it tasted as well as it did.

We were soon ready to start, and must be out one night more before reaching Elizabethtown, where we expected to stop. I had quite a good

Indian trail all day; but in order to have good wood and water, I was after dark reaching camp.

Just at dark, I got on top of a timbered mountain, and the shades of night, with the timber, compelled me to light off my pony, and lead and feel for the path. The big owls began to hoo! hoo! and the wolves to howl as if there might be a score of them close by. It was lonely. I thought they might be scared; but as a howl coming in contact with a howl would lose its force, I started the old long-meter tune to—

> "Show pity, Lord; O Lord, forgive;
>   Let a repenting sinner live."

I happened to strike the key just right, and the hymn echoed from mountain to mountain, and seemed to fill the woods. The owls stopped, and the wolves shut their mouths. Daniel did but little when he looked the lions out of countenance.

The next day I reached Elizabethtown, a mining-camp of several hundred, mostly Americans. Here I made my head-quarters for the year. I held a meeting for two weeks; had one member to help—Brother Simon Tyrer. (I had preached at his house in Wisconsin in 1851.) At the close of the meeting, seven others joined, and the above was class-leader, the first that I know of in New Mexico. This year I preached at Trinidad, Red River, Cimarron, Taos, Mora, Tipton, and Walters, and at Cherry Valley. Early in the spring I went to Santa Fe, Las Vegas, and Tuckalota. At Santa Fe I found Dr. McFarland, a Presbyterian preacher, with a small congregation. I helped him about two weeks in a meeting, as he was there teaching and preaching. I advised all to join his Church. He thought there were about twenty-five converts. One man obtained the blessing while I was preaching. I mention this, as it was the second occurrence of the kind I had known in my ministry.

This year I selected the La Junta settlement for a high-grade school, and made a request for Rev. Thomas Harwood and wife to take charge of the same; but they deferred coming until 1869. I have always thought it was providential that they came. Bishop Ames failed to find a man, and I was in great anxiety, with constant prayer to God for help. I took down a coat that had hung by the wall for months, and found an old letter from Brother Harwood, saying he could not come. But as I looked it over, it seemed to me that if I would write again, he would change his mind. I did so, and received the welcome news that he would come; and there was a warm greeting and meeting. I had not seen a Methodist preacher in New Mexico before. He took my place, and I have reason to thank God that the result has been so good.

During the year 1869 and 1870 I traveled almost all over New Mexico, making my home at Santa Fe. I preached at Albuquerque, Socorro, and Fort Craig. I fell in with a company of about thirty prospectors—many were my acquaintances— at the crossing of the Rio Grande, seven miles

below the above place. I had a hearty welcome
and two or three invitations to dinner, as they had
it messed out on the grass. You would better
believe I was glad to overtake those whole-souled
miners. I had expected to cross the Hornatha—
that is, the desert—alone, but in addition to my
little outfit, they had plenty, and I was made welcome to all I wanted.

The Apache Indians were frequently on the
scout. If sighted by them, it was necessary to
outrun them, kill them, or get scalped. There
was a reach of ninety miles, with but one house,
and that guarded by about fifteen soldiers. Our
boys kept guard at night. At the Lone Rocks,
twenty miles above Fort Selden, the company
spread tent-cloths over two wagons, and I tried to
preach to them in that desert place, the very spot
where the Indians at various times had leaped out
from behind the rocks, and scalped the weary
traveler. This was a farewell to my hearers, as I
have never seen one of them since. We parted
at Fort Selden. They went into the mountains,
and discovered the mines at what is now Silver
City. They offered to bear my expenses if I
would go with them. But my expenses were paid
by the Church, and I had set my face to Las
Cruces, where I gathered about forty, and preached
to them.

The next day I went to Masea, and called on
a Mr. Jones, and was used with the greatest hospitality. He took me around town to give out
my appointment for that evening. We entered

many saloons, and he treated the crowd, and as often asked me to drink. But as I always refused such offers, I did so on this occasion. When he had taken about the fourth dram, I said to him: "We had better go home." He said: "Why?" "Because I am afraid I will have to carry you." He thought there was no danger. That evening we got out forty or fifty to hear preaching, and they all gave good attention, and requested me to preach again.

From there I made my way to what is now New El Paso, in the Corner of Texas, and preached to about the entire American-speaking people— say thirty—and visited El Paso in Old Mexico, and ate of their delicious grapes and other fruits, in that dilapidated old city. I saw but two or three that spoke English. As I made my way back across the prairie to Franklin, I overtook a cart full of grapes, hauled by a burro. I was made welcome to eat, and did so until we came to the wine factory. A trough was filled with grapes, and an old Mexican—with his pants rolled up, and his toe-nails large enough to scratch the contents to pieces—trod the wine-press alone. I could but think, as I saw the wine run through the hole in the trough behind the old man, "How many would take a cup of that wine, and boast of its purity, and lick their lips for more, if they could see how it is made?" This was in September, 1869.

From there I returned to Masea—a grand old town for fruit—and as I came up I stopped at Fort Selden, and preached to the soldiers—two companies, one of colored men, the other white. They arranged seats at the liberty-pole; the colored company took their seats near the preacher, the whites stood afar off; but the preacher felt in the spirit. The evening was fine, the full moon arose—the largest that I had ever seen, it appeared to me—and the sound of God's truth echoed from valley to mountains, and the people, black and white, were attentive. Things were strange here. They lariated their hogs by the nose, let the dogs run loose, and grubbed their hay with a mattock by the ton. But I paid my fare, say three dollars, and left for the Hornatha again, with a Mexican mail-carrier, and at night reached Jack Martin's, about half-way.

At night I preached to the family, hired men, and soldiers, in the plaza, by moonshine. At daylight a messenger came with the news that the mail-carrier from Fort Craig, that was to meet us, had been killed by the Indians, which made a lively excitement through the day. It was thought dangerous to start; but I told them if they were killing men last night they would not likely be there the next night, so now was the time to go; and by evening the carrier and myself started. We rode until some time in the night, when the Mexican must stop and take a nap. He slept, and I watched. He had a pistol, and I had none. I thought if the Indians came, I would take his weapon and shoot till he waked up. But I had to wake him. About sunrise we came to the spot where the Mexican was killed. The blood had run profusely, but the body had been taken to a Mexican town, on the east-side of the Rio Grande, about seven miles from Fort Craig, and they were preparing for the funeral. Here we learned that it was a Mexican, who had a grudge against him, that had killed him, and that the Indians were clear of murder for once.

I got to Fort Craig safe, stopped for the day, and preached in the evening to the soldiers. The colored soldiers attended best, and made the fort echo with two or three good old hymns. I preached once between there and Socorro. Here there were a few Protestant Mexicans. One old brother seemed wonderfully rejoiced to see a Protestant preacher. The day before, while riding alone, along the sands of the Rio Grande, I became melancholy. The strange and almost desert country oppressed me. I became restless, and could not account for such feelings. Just at dark, after some inquiry, I found a place to stop where they talked English. The host, who was a generous Scotchman, showed me a room, and in a few moments returned with a basket of fine grapes and peaches, and bade me help myself. But my mind was so distressed that, before I could eat of the fruit, I took my hymn-book, and asked God, on my knees, to show me a hymn that would give comfort or duty. I opened the book to the hymn:

> "Blow ye the trumpet, blow
> The gladly solemn sound."

Somehow, in my condition, it gave duty and comfort. Next day I called all together and preached, and as there were several Mexicans there, and they could not understand English, through an interpreter I asked one of them to select a hymn, and close the meeting in their own way, as they had Spanish books. When he began to read, I was told to turn to the hymn:

"Blow ye the trumpet, blow."

I thought, Now I have it in Spanish as well. After prayer, the old Mexican took my hand; said he could not understand English, but he knew my preaching was in the right way.

From here, with but little delay, I made my way to Santa Fe, where there were several letters awaiting me. One gave the account of the death of my mother, and it occurred on the same day I had been so wonderfully distressed. I give this circumstance as it occurred, and the reader can draw his own conclusions as to the seemingly singular coincidence.

After resting at Santa Fe, I visited Elizabethtown, Cimarron, Red River, and La Junta. Here Mrs. Harwood commenced teaching, which resulted in the elevation of many of the children in the region round about.

March 7, 1870, I started for Fort Wingate. After passing Albuquerque, I found no Americans to speak of till I reached the fort, where there were two companies of soldiers. They had just received orders to go to Prescott, Arizona. After preaching twice, Colonel Evans, in command, offered me a free passage with them to

Arizona; but after expressing my thanks to him for his kind offer, I declined. I concluded instead to go to Fort Defiance, just over the line in Arizona, where I preached three times. Here I found the Rev. Mr. Roberts, sent by the Presbyterian Board, assisted by Miss Gaston, as teacher among the Navajoe Indians. The Navajoes were more proverbial for stealing than killing people. But the squaws' loom-made blankets were the best known. The loom would not cost more than seventy-five cents in work. They wove by draft any figure given them, and silk neck-ties as well, on the same loom.

Brother Roberts undertook to keep a few sheep. He hired a boy to herd them. Some Indians came by; one caught the boy, and held him, while others caught two sheep, which made them a feast. At another time they came at night, got a ladder, and climbed on to the fourteen-foot wall of the corral, and took the sheep over with a lariat. Well, he sold his sheep, and went to farming. He planted corn, and as soon as the cob formed on the stalk they pulled and ate his crop, and he did not get even green corn. All this time he was preparing to preach to them; and, as one would naturally suppose, his first text was, "Thou shalt not steal." I have not learned his success. This was the beginning, and we can but desire the Navajoe tribe to become enlightened and as perfect in religion as their squaws were in weaving blankets and neck-ties. This was the outside camp, as far as I could learn, that was accessible, unless I had gone with the army. One year after, I was sorry I did not go, as our Church had no preacher there.

My next trip from Santa Fe was about one hundred and seventy miles south to Fort Stanton, one hundred and six miles of the way without a house. There was a mail carried once a week. I was not there on the right day, but was told the carrier went alone a part of the time, and I concluded to try. It was forty-five miles to the first water—a spring on the side of a mountain. At an hour, by sun, I reached a grave-yard, with some half dozen graves; but could find no water. As I was looking for it, I saw a Mexican, with a keg of the article most desired on a burro. He showed me the path up to the spring, a mile from the camping-ground. After horse and rider had satisfied themselves, I found ten or twelve Mexicans camped at the foot of the mountain. I learned that those who were buried there had been killed by Indians. The campers were anxious for me to stay; but I could not feel safe alone with them. So I fed my horse all the corn I had with me, ate my grub, and just at night started on a dim road at a good speed, and went about twelve miles and camped. I built a fire and tried to sleep, but was too cold. After several efforts, I got up, moved the fire, put in sand until it was tempered about right, spread one blanket under and the other over, took a good sleep, awoke, and found my kind Preserver near. My danger and deliverance had been greater than I knew.

About ten o'clock I met four men, well armed, who inquired whom I had seen. I told them of the campers, and described the outfit. They said it was well that I had left them, for some of them were not too good to kill a man for the clothes he wore, and that they had stolen cattle. I reached Fort Stanton that day, about five o'clock; and as I had no fire-arms, they asked me which way I came. "Well, did you not see Indians?" I told them "no." "Well," pointing the way I had come, "day before yesterday there were three Apaches walking along on that hill and looking down into the fort." The men I met brought back the thieves and cattle. I was well-nigh tired out after my long journey; but I told them my name and business, and they used me with great hospitality.

As I visited among them, I found a man who was living with a woman with a contract that they should be married as soon as they could get a preacher to tie the knot. I married them, and the groom gave me ten dollars. After preaching to a large turn-out, one of the captains got up an extra good dinner and invited me to dine with several of the officers.

Next day I started for Ashland down the Rio Benita. I stopped at a grist-mill, and preached to eight Americans and two Mexicans. For fear of Indians, they locked my horse up in the mill, and barred the doors of the cabin with timbers prepared for that purpose. The next day I started with a Mexican to Ashland. He was armed; but after we got a half mile from the mill, he kept about one hundred yards behind, evidently afraid to keep by my side. But we reached town without trouble. Here they seemed glad to hear a sermon. Word was sent around, and a mixed congregation came together to the number of forty-five. At the close, a collector stood at the door and received gifts to the amount of thirteen dollars for me.

Next day, Monday, I went with some cattle-herders to their camp, and preached to five; and the day following I got to Boska Grande, where I preached to about thirty men. I never said "collection" at any place; but in the morning the store-keeper where I preached called me to the counter and gave me fifteen dollars. He said the boys had left it to my credit. This was generous, and as it should be. How much better they must have felt to give without being asked! I am sure the preacher felt better.

From there I proceeded up the Pecos River, forty-five miles to old Fort Sumner, where there were eight or ten persons, and most of them Mexicans. I only stopped over night. My way was still up the river. I turned east to Fort Bascom. There were but about fifty people. They turned out well.

Thence I went to La Junta and Fort Union. Visited with Brother and Sister Harwood. They were commencing to build the main part of their present school-building at Tiptonville. This was near the close of my travels in New Mexico. I would have been willing to go to Misea, Las Cruces, and to Franklin or El Paso, with some other points, leaving Brother Harwood all the Mexican work; but Bishop Ames said it was too far away, and that he could never follow it up. So I submitted to the powers that be, and came to Colorado again, having traveled a little over ten thousand miles on horseback in two years.

During the year 1868–69 I had made up my mind that Rev. Thomas Harwood was the best and safest man that I knew of in my acquaintance for the New Mexican work. We had traveled adjoining circuits in the North-west Wisconsin Conference, and helped each other. Afterwards we were separated. When the war became hot, he left his work, and volunteered as a private. A presiding elder, one of my class in the conference, went as chaplain. Although a strong preacher, he was not popular with the regiment, and Brother Harwood was chosen in his place, and acquitted himself creditably. After the war, he took work in the conference again.

This matter of supplying New Mexico had been a special subject of prayer and thought, and I could not feel like asking the bishop for any other man. And now that he has been there nineteen years with his faithful wife, hard at work, preaching and teaching, I am confident that the blessed results have justified my decision. Until Rev. S. W. Thornton took the American work in 1884, he had charge of that as well as the Spanish work. Mrs. Harwood, equally well qualified to do her part in teaching, has been equally successful. The last Minutes I saw gave over eight hundred converts to our Church, all taken from the Roman Catholics; something over twenty native preachers, among them one Romish priest. To God be all the glory.

Bishop Machbœuf, our old priest and bishop of the Roman Catholic Church, came from New Mexico to Colorado in 1860. He was considered a great worker, and can be compared with Brother Harwood in making proselytes. Brother Harwood had the advantage, for he had a good wife to help him. I have been a close observer, and I have known but few taken from us, only where fathers and mothers have been so blind to the religious interests of their children as to put them under the control of the Sisters of Charity, so called.

I forbear to say more, as Brother Harwood should give us a history of his own times and hardships. I have given a short account of what I saw personally. I am aware that some of my sayings have been disputed, but the history is so plain and well-known that it can not be successfully refuted. The people in New and Old Mexico are not to blame for their condition so much as are their religious teachers. I have seen men by the dozen go to Church in the morning, and by eleven o'clock, the same men carrying their chickens to a pit to have a cock-fight in plain view of the priest's house. They were communicants, and yet I never knew one of them to be brought to account for violating the Sabbath. My prayer is that God will convert and reform that whole country. Indeed, it is rapidly becoming enlightened and improved in every way.

CHAPTER XVI.

MARRIAGE.

AT the close of the first year in New Mexico, I rode my pony from Santa Fe to conference at Central City, Colorado, a distance of four hundred and fifty miles. Bishop Kingsley presided. He was on his way around the world, but died suddenly and was buried at Beyrut, Syria. I well remember when I read the account of his death. I had just returned from a long trip to Tiptonville, and my *Advocate* told the story. I felt the loss severely. It was a mystery why such a man, so full of usefulness, should be taken, and I left. I was lonely and sad. But God knows best.

In the summer of 1870 our conference was held at Pueblo, Bishop E. R. Ames presiding. Brother Harwood was sent to the New Mexico work, and I was put on the Divide Circuit—all south and east of Denver, beginning at Petersburg, Bear Creek, Littleton, all up Cherry Creek, and the settlements on Running Creek, and Kiowa and Bijou Basin—a four weeks' work. I was in the cabinet when it was named, and told the presiding elder to call it Littleton, or by the name of some post-office; but nothing but "Divide" would do. I had several letters and other matter sent to Spring Valley, eight miles from any appointment. I was asked to preach in the school-house in West Denver, but made no such arrangement. The presiding elder said: "I suspect I will have to interfere to keep you out of Denver." I gave them no trouble; formed a class at Petersburg, and at Fonda's School-house, on Cherry Creek, during the year. We held a camp-meeting at or near Isaac McBroom's, which was well attended, resulting in some good.

On the seventh day of November, 1870, I was married to Mrs. Lucinda P. Rankin, of Cherry Creek, Douglas County, Colorado. I had been a widower over twenty years, and had never seen the time that I thought I could live and support a family without locating. But since I could almost keep myself, I thought it was a poor woman who could not help a little. So we were married, and, by God's blessing, lived happily together until she was called to her reward.

That year I took up a homestead, and in 1871 our presiding elder divided my circuit, and gave a young man he judged to be of great worth the best half. But before the year was out, the youth left without credit to himself or anybody else. It seemed to be hard to accomplish much on this charge. The settlers were ranchmen. Stock was ranging far away, and the loss of a cow was more seriously felt than that of a human being. If a man were killed, it was looked over, and the murderer allowed to escape justice. But if a man stole cattle, he was almost sure, if caught, to be hung. Trial by court was too slow and uncertain. For instance, there were three men taken for stealing cattle. They confessed that they were out on the Plains, and being destitute of provisions, had killed a heifer to live on till they got in. They were willing to pay for her; but some persons took them from the place of their trial to the dividing ridge between Running Creek and Cherry Creek, and hung them all on the same tree. I was not at the trial or the hanging, but passed by the day after they were taken down by the sheriff and buried. Tracks were to be seen, although I had not heard of the hanging at the time, but thought it looked as if some one or more had been hung there. I mention the above to show how far many had been led from the way in which they had been educated; and that it was hard to succeed at once in the religious reformation of such people.

What is Elbert County began to be settled in 1860. In 1870 I found the settlers there very hospitable. It was a mixed community. The first who came were lumbermen, to secure the valuable timber and the ties; then the owners of herds of cattle, sheep, and horses; then the ranchmen proper. The settlements were not close, and social gatherings not large. The devil, however, always introduces dancing, which ruins the morals of old and young. And all these years there had been no missionary among them.

I found one saw-mill where they were willing to have preaching on my regular round. I included it in my plan, and missed but once. On one occasion, when I had come at my regular time, I found that they had given out a dance for that night. A young man from New York State had come out for his health, and could play the fiddle. At the hour, the dining-room was full, and I preached as usual, and gave out an appointment for two weeks. There was a board partition between the dining-room and an office with an open window. Just as I was dismissing, the New York invalid drew the bow across the catguts very hoarsely, and directly I was out of the house they were dancing. It was an insult; but I went back to my next appointment. I had been asked by several who had heard of the above, if the report that there had been dancing after preaching was true? I could not deny it, and remarked that it was a new wrinkle in my history; that I had been in pineries, mining-camps, and in other rough places, and this was the first time I had received such usage.

On my return, I put up my horse at the logger's boarding-house, and went up to the mill-office. The proprietor and fiddler, with several others, were in, while cooks and dish-washers were looking through the window. I knew there was another ball on hand. I said: "Mr. ——, do you expect to have preaching to-night?" He replied: "I thought you would not preach for us any more, as you said we were worse than any people;" and he related what I have above stated, and more with it. "I made the appointment in good faith, and because I thought you were in great need of the gospel. I have preached in several States and three Territories, and never had even a backwoods fiddler to insult me as this fellow did!" "Why, his Church allows dancing." "Can't help that, sir. If he doesn't know any better than to act as he did at the close of our service, he had better go back and learn how to behave." "We will dance, all the same." "Very well, sir; then I will serve you as the enemy of all souls will never do, except you repent. I want you to know that there are plenty of places to preach without coming here again, where you don't want what you need most; that is, the salvation of your souls." I bade them good night, and going to the public house, began preparing to depart. The host protested that it was dark, and I must not go away, and was welcome there. So I concluded to stay.

After a half hour, a young man came in and said: "Mr. —— sent me to say that he will have all out to hear you preach at eleven o'clock in the morning." At first I said, "No." But he said they were all whipped, and wanted this difficulty stopped. I sent him to see if they would be on time. He was soon back; they were sure to come. The turn-out and attention were good. The case was like this: The loggers and teamsters hired their men with the express understanding that they could only dance on Saturday nights, so that they could rest on Sunday. They said a man was worse than nothing after dancing all night; the next day he would whip the horses and mules, and accomplish nothing. I have thought

dancing the most enticing of all evils—the cause
of separations and breaking up of families, and
the starting point of almost all grades of sin for
young and old.   Yet it is called innocent.   If we
are trying to promote a revival, the dance is the
best means to dissipate all serious reflection.

I tried to do all I could to stop vice, and faithfully preached the Word wherever a few could be
got together.   Yet one decade without gospel or
religious example or associations has a wonderful effect on people, even those who have been
trained well.   It seems almost impossible to turn
them again to righteousness, while the children
lose all interest in anything that is moral, and
have an utter disrelish of religion.

We found numbers that had been members of
different denominations, who had lost almost, if not
all desire to live religiously.   Judge how pleasant
it was to visit the few who had not bowed the
knee.   Brother Wm. Bonafield, on Running Creek,
was such a one.   He was a fervent and consistent
Christian.   Just previous to our acquaintance he
came near being killed.   A young man who had
been in the army with his son, called on them
frequently, and became anxious to marry one of
the daughters, and asked the old gentleman for
her.   He evaded, and said he never wished to go
into such arrangements without consideration.
He talked to his daughter on the subject.   She
said she had no idea of such a thing, or of having
anything to say to him on the subject.   After
a short time he approached Mr. Bonafield again.

The girl was called, and she gave him to understand that she was opposed to his requests. Mr. Bonafield told him that her decision ought to let him off on this subject. But he replied: "If you would say she must, she would be willing." He answered: "I never do such business."

A short time passed. Mr. Bonafield kept a dairy. The weather was rough. He looked out on the range and saw most of his cows, and a man riding among them. He thought nothing of that, as men were often riding over the range. When the time came to go after the cows, he felt strangely opposed to going for them, and told his wife so. After a short time, the same man he had seen among his stock rode down to the house, and proved to be the same man spoken of above. He rode up to a log fence fifty yards from the house, and called to Mr. Bonafield to come out. As the latter neared the fence, he drew his pistol and said: "I am going to kill you." Mr. Bonafield jumped back and threw himself around to retreat, when the wretch fired, the ball grazing the skull just above the ear, felling Mr. Bonafield. By this time the family were nearly all there, crying: "You have killed our father." He rode off with the impression that he had killed him; but Mr. Bonafield soon got over the shock. It was a close call. The would-be murderer escaped, although quite a sum of money was spent to secure his arrest. A few years later Brother Bonafield was thrown from a wagon in the same yard, by a wild span of horses, and so severely hurt that he died in a few days.

We lived on the east side of my two weeks' circuit. I spent one Sunday on Cherry Creek and the next at Kiowa and Running Creek. It was over twenty miles to Kiowa. I left on Saturday, went sixteen miles, and stopped with a friend, so that I could reach my appointment in time. I rode on Sunday about three miles, and had reached Running Creek, and was going up the west side when I heard the report of a pistol some fifty rods across the creek, followed by distressing cries. I turned and rode in a lope up to the house. There lay Mr. Miles Malden, crying with anguish, pain, and prayer commingled. He was lying in front of the door. When I reached him there was one man there; and two or three of his children, who had run over from his mother's, some sixty rods, were crying. He said he would certainly die. I exhorted him to make a full confession of his sins to God, and surrender his all into his hands.

The circumstances of the shooting were these: This Sunday morning he was going to his mother's; as he passed the house occupied by a family which had formerly lived on his place, the woman, who was alone, asked him to come in and address a letter for her. He went in; she gave him a stool to sit on; and when he was about half-way through writing the address, she shot him in the back, near the spine. He fell over, and O, what pitiful cries! This much I gleaned from his answers to my questions.

I stepped up to see if there was any letter. His little girl, about twelve years old, grieved almost to death, passed me, and handed it to me. I saw what there was of the direction on the envelope. I opened it, and found a sheet of paper with only the half of a name of a town on it. I kept the envelope and paper. It showed me that what he said was true. The stool was thrown over; blood scattered about, and the woman was gone.

Before this his mother was there, and the scene was one of horror. Other neighbors came in, and assisted to move him where he could be taken care of. It was said by some of the neighbors that the woman that shot him had been shooting at a mark, claiming that she wanted to be in practice so that she could shoot an Indian if one came along. I afterwards learned that some one had told her that he had talked about her, and that she had become enraged and determined to take his life. He lived some time, but was helpless. His faithful mother attended him to the last. The woman was arrested and tried; but she was finally acquitted.

Another reminiscence: In November, 1871, we had announced our quarterly meeting at a school-house near Brother Bonafield's. It was the middle of the week; and as it was the first time a presiding elder had ever been in Elbert County, Brother B. T. Vincent took his good wife along. On Tuesday it began to snow and blow, and kept it up till Wednesday in the afternoon. At the eleven-o'clock meeting there were fifteen present, including the preachers—all young people but two. The presiding elder preached, and after the sermon there was a speaking meeting. We all went home with Brother Bonafield, and stayed till morning. In the morning snow was up to the axle of the buggy. I piloted Brother and Sister Vincent till he thought he knew the road. It was wide and plain, snow only two feet deep. But the parson took one of the numerous lumber roads, lost his way, and traveled nearly all day, but finally got in. It is the most memorable experience of their Colorado life.

After I left them, just as I got to the edge of Cherry Creek to cross, where the brush was thick on each side of the road, some one shot off a heavy charge close by my side. I was jarred, and heard the bullet whistle. My pony jumped and ran, and I could not check her for seventy rods. My first thought was that it was some one shooting rabbits; but as I had been over there a day or two, and it was known that I was to go home that day, and was a witness in that murder case, many thought some one was waylaying me at that narrow crossing who felt that his cause would be more favorable if I were out of the way. But God only knows.

This was a memorable quarterly meeting to me, as my father was sick, and it was feared near unto death. I wrote to the presiding elder to see if the time could not be changed; but he said the time was set, and he had arranged for it, and we must have it.

I reached home on the afternoon of the 30th of November, 1871, and started next morning from home for Bailey, to see father. I went the near way by Sedalia, up Jar Hollow by Smith's saw-mill, crossed straight over to the head of Buffalo Creek, and struck the Platte near where Esterbrook Station now is, on the South Park road; rode all day—part of the time without any trail, the snow knee-deep. After dark I came to a bachelor's cabin, where I was made welcome, but was overwhelmed with sorrow at the news of father's death. In the morning I went on. It was very cold, and I attempted to cross the North Platte on the ice. It bore my pony till about the middle, when it broke through and gave me a thorough wetting. I reached the house with clothes frozen stiff. Father had died about the time I had heard that shot at Cherry Creek.

Mr. Bailey and my two sisters thought best to inter his remains near their house, at least for a time. He had been a member of the Methodist Episcopal Church over fifty years; a firm believer in the Scriptures as explained by Wesley, Watson, Fletcher, and Clarke. When the latter differed from the former, he liked Fletcher best. He was at our house in the previous summer, and we had sacramental services. It was seven miles home. Before we got there he said that he was tired; it was too far for him; but he wished to take the sacrament, since it might be his last opportunity. Such it proved to be. We are not without good hope that he has reached the heavenly home, going from a mountain wilderness to the fair fields of glory. I was reminded, when I could not see my father alive, of "Let the dead bury their dead; follow thou me." It was only thus that I was comforted for not having been with him before he died. But having tried and failed to secure the postponement of quarterly meeting for that purpose, I felt that my orders, though severe, must be obeyed.

I spent two years on that work; averaged four times a week preaching and exhorting. The rides were long. Received in all eight hundred and forty-six dollars for both years. It cost me two hundred and forty dollars more than I received. Having married a wife, it cost me more to live than when single. We had several conversions, and formed two classes.

At one place we began meetings in a school-house. The second night two arose for prayers. The third night, just about the time to start to meeting, a blizzard—heavy wind and fine snow—came up, too severe to be encountered. But a dozen of us got there, and I tried to talk a little, and proposed to have two or three prayers and quit. But a young lady came and kneeled at the altar, and though the wind blew in the snow till it was two inches deep on the floor and we were all white with it, she never stopped praying or rose from her knees till the blessing came. Then she shouted all the snow off her in a few minutes, and we sang, "Jesus washes white as snow." Outside and inside it was white as snow that time. We all went about twenty rods to the nearest house, and stayed till morning. The storm was so severe that all kinds of stock were scattered, and many sheep and some of the herders frozen to death. We gave up the meeting.

I always thought if a preacher could get off the second year with fair credit, he would better be changed. So at conference, at my own request, I was changed. My new field was Evans, Platteville, and Fort Lupton. I moved about eighty miles to Evans. The house had a leaky roof, so that when it rained there was water more than two inches all over the floor. The floor was good, even if the roof was defective. An inch auger soon relieved the floor, but I concluded to vacate. Fortunately, Governor Evans's house was unoccupied, and he gave me its use rent-free for eight months. The governor was apt to be kind to a preacher.

We gathered a small class at Evans, and had our services. There was a good hall in town, which was used for preaching. There was a colony of old Covenanter Presbyterians, and quite a number of Come-outers from them. Once in two weeks I preached in the hall, generally to a crowded house. I kept up seven appointments in the two weeks' circuit. I was down as far as Corona once, and preached their first sermon.

One of the appointments was at Bailey's School-house, three miles down and across the Platte River. One cold and snowy night in the winter, after preaching to about twenty-five, I started with a span of Mexican ponies. They were wild and chilled, and dashed off at full speed. It was so

dark that I could not see their heads. They had
to turn the corner of a fence to get into the road,
and I suppose that, when they got to the turn,
they took such a sudden and swift whirl that I
was thrown off my seat and out. As I went I
thought the wagon was coming over too. I struck
on the frozen ground below my shoulder, cutting
through both my coats, but fortunately not breaking the skin. I lay unconscious for an hour. The
first thing I knew, I was almost up and trying to
stand on my feet. I saw a light at the house,
some twenty-five rods away, and managed to get
there. My face was bloody, and I was a sight so
frightful that they had to ask who I was. The
principal hurt was between my breast and my
back-bone. Doctor Bedell was sent for, and my
wife came with him. I was hauled home the
next day, but it was two weeks before I could
help myself.

This was the worst jar I ever got. I feared it
was worse than it turned out to be. I only lost
three weeks, the longest time I had ever lost from
sickness. G. H. Adams, my presiding elder, visited me, and said it would take a longer time for
me to get up on account of my age. That was
reasonable, but one of the first places I went was
to his house in Greeley. I had a pleasant talk
with his excellent wife. He had two carriages.
His hired man hitched two horses to one, and he
wished to take the other up town for repairs. He
and I sat on the back seat, holding the pole of the
other carriage, and pulled it easily enough till we

reached the railroad-crossing. Carriage number one was on top of the grade, and started rapidly down the other side; carriage number two was on the other side of the grade, and the sudden jerk tipped the seat we sat on, and out we both went backwards, one on each side of the pole. It was a solid fall on our backs, with heads down grade. I got up first, and said: "If I am old, I beat you up!" As the good Lord would have it, neither was seriously hurt.

This was the most pleasant circuit I had traveled,—the country level, and the people congenial, with some good Christian families. I must mention Sister Williams. She was known as "Grandma Williams." She had come at the earliest date, and settled on the Platte River when the only neighbors for miles were Indians. She had wool, but no spinning-wheel. She looked at the grindstone, and conceived how she could utilize it. She put on a wire for a spindle, and turned the machine and spun yarn enough to knit mittens and socks for her family. There is quite a difference between then and now. Our ladies who come on the cars do much, although many neither sew nor spin, even on wheels, machines, or any other contrivance, having found out more congenial ways to make clothes and money. But "Grandma Williams" can not be too highly admired for her ingenious machine and inexpensive clothing of her family, and, best of all, for her noble Christian character, even among the Indians.

That summer we had a pleasant visit from my

sister Rachel and her daughter Bertha. She had helped me to keep my children together when I was in need of help, through to the fourth year of my ministry. Being rather feeble, she came for a recreation, as well as to see us. We concluded to take a trip to the mountains, as I could attend to some things out there that had been neglected, besides seeing my son Elias, whom she had helped to raise. Started up through my circuit, preaching at three places on our way. We had to cross the St. Brain. There had been rain in the mountains. The crossing was reported to be all right. Just at dark we reached the creek, and drove the ponies in. They were just done drinking. We had a colt following. My wife must have a rope tied around its neck, for she thought it would have to swim, and she would hold the end of the rope and lead it. Just as I was adjusting the lines to ford the river, I heard a shrill voice: "Hold on! the creek is swimming." It was the same man who had told us it was all right. So it was when he crossed; later he heard of the rise above, and knew that it would be about dark when we would get there. So he made all haste to overtake us, lest we should all be drowned. He was just in time. In another instant we would have been in the deep and swift stream. We backed out with difficulty. I have often thought of the favor he conferred on us, doubtless directed by the overruling providence of the Lord.

When we crossed the next morning, Sunday, the water ran over the wagon-box. At eleven we were on hand at the services, and on Monday went on south to see the rest of our folks. Back the next Sunday on the bounds of my circuit; for the conference of July, held at Greeley, 1873, was just at hand, presided over by Bishop Andrews. As my work was long, Evans was taken off, and Erie, Lupton, Platteville, and other places attached. The conference session was pleasant.

CHAPTER XVII.

A MOUNTAIN TRIP.

WHILE my sister was visiting us, I took her, my wife, niece, granddaughter, and Brother Washburn, a member of our conference, on a three weeks' mountain-trip. We left the valley at Morrison in a light wagon, with tent and provisions for camping out. We went up the Turkey Creek road, which was a good one, provided one did not slip off; otherwise he must take a sheer fall, in places, of hundreds of feet, almost perpendicular. Of a mule-team and wagon that backed off, only fragments were left. We passed safely till within ten miles of Bailey's, my brother-in-law's. There we had a long slope of moderate grade, and let the ponies take a long trot. The fastening to the axle on the upper side broke, and the ponies letting out, had a natural tendency to run the wagon off on the lower side. I was soon thrown out. Brother Washburn no sooner had caught the lines than the wagon turned over, smashing the mess-box, and mixing up our provisions and outfit generally. The ponies stopped in a bunch of willows. Finding ourselves unhurt, with the help of some mountain boys we gathered up the fragments, loaded and wrapped up, hitched the scared ponies, and went our way, rejoicing that it was no worse, and reached Bailey's without further adventure.

Next day was Sunday, and my father's grave was there under the shadow of the pine-trees. We concluded it would be best to have preaching, as there were about fifteen people. Brother Washburn preached, and afterwards I talked some. It was a solemn service.

The next day, taking sister and her two children, we made our way to South Park, which, as one approaches it on the old wagon-road, at the point of Kenosha Hill, is as grand a view as one will ever see in the mountains. As we neared Jefferson Creek, Brother Washburn, who was walking, jumped on to the hind end of the wagon to ride across. But as we were almost over, he lost his balance and fell back into the creek. It wet him thoroughly. He got out and asked what creek it was. I replied: "It is Jefferson, but we will call it *Wash*-burn after this!" We had our sport at his expense. We passed Fair Play, and went up Four Mile Creek and Horseshoe to timber height. We left our wagon, borrowed a burro or two, with pack-saddles, and went by the pass between South Park and Iowa Gulch—known now as Horseshoe Pass—to where my son Elias was working what he called the Dyer mine.

Mounting the women and girls on the ponies and jacks, we took up the dim, steep trail. When we began to descend over slide-rock, and no path to speak of, the women screeched out in affright. No persuasion or commands sufficed to keep them on. Off they jumped, all but the little girl, who sat composed on the jack without a bridle. The sure-footed little beast picked its way carefully. We led the other animals; traveled slowly, but made it over, and camped with the men that night. I visited my son, who was killed the next year. The badgers or porcupines made havoc with the straps and bridles that night; and the next day we got back to our tent. I will say here that the Dyer mine was not opened up enough to pay well. After the death of my son, I sold his half of it to Mr. H. A. W. Tabor for three thousand dollars. Two years later it was sold for sixty thousand dollars.

From here we made our way around to Mosquito District, where I had taken a claim in 1861. Elias came over with us. I hauled a half ton of ore to Hill's works at Alma, where its worth was estimated to be thirty-six dollars a ton. I asked what he would treat it for. He said: "Thirty-five dollars a ton." This would not pay. I let it go for less than cost. It has been worked since; but not to so great profit as many others.

By this time it was Sunday, and as we were camped near Alma, I was invited to preach. I found many whom I had known in other places in the mountains. From this point we made our way to the valley and back to my circuit. I preached at Erie, Valmont, St. Brain, Platteville, Lupton, Brighton, and occasionally at other schoolhouses. This was my second year. The circuit stretched over quite a territory. The congregations were fair. The two years were pleasant to me, and, so far as I knew, to the people also.

A few were converted and joined the Church. I received between six and seven hundred dollars each year, out of which the closest economy enabled us to save about seventy dollars a year. The people were not of the wealthy class, and were as liberal as they ought to have been.

I was appointed by Bishop Bowman, at the conference held at Colorado Springs, 1874, to Monument, a new work and newly settled. The Indians, grasshoppers, and drouth had almost used them up. There were about a dozen members, and a few of other denominations. No house could be had at the time; and for a month or more we had to go into the back end of a bowling-alley.

I went around my circuit—about six preaching places at first—and, seeing no chance to get any other house, I went to work, got a good lot given and some subscriptions toward building a parsonage. I engaged in the undertaking with a will. Some gave team-work, but generally I had to drive the team; and paid a little over fifty dollars out of my own purse. I put up a frame sixteen by twenty-four feet, with one partition nine feet in height; inclosed, and lathed and plastered it. I had some slabs given to me, and put up a stable to hold my ponies and cow. When we got through we were comfortable and not in debt.

While living in the old alley there came a hard storm of wind, which at every· blow rocked it a foot. Mrs. Dyer sprang up, dressed, and wanted me to get up. I was tired, and thought there was no danger; but she lighted the lamp just as the stove-pipe came rolling down. That brought me to see how the old thing reeled to and fro. I went out and propped it with poles so that it did not quite blow over. Next morning almost every house in the little town was propped. A car, used by some railroad men for cooking and sleeping, was turned over, and several of its occupants had their heads tied up. But our new parsonage was all right.

For two months and a half I attended to three appointments a week, all on Sunday, and yet lost no time from work on the parsonage. Counting the work, the parsonage cost over three hundred dollars. It was on a good lot, and we felt that we had a right to be thankful and somewhat proud to have so good a house. To be sure we were not able to get seasoned lumber to lay the floor, but we keyed up the green lumber, and had carpet, and got along comfortably with that. I speak of this to give some idea of how matters were then and now.

We had a small frame church, which had been built by Brother Warren, who had formed a society some two or three years before, and before the railroad had been thought of. But when it was made, they put the depot two and a half miles from the church. We preached in it all the time, and it was fairly filled with attentive hearers, as was the school-house at Monument, where we lived. Near the holidays we commenced a protracted meeting, and held a week before the work began among the people. In two weeks we had about twenty conversions, and about the same number joined the Church, and good was done all around the circuit. We enlarged the circuit to include Table Rock, a good settlement, prospected the country generally, and had hopes that it would be a good circuit.

At the close of the year's work, our conference met at Central City, Bishop Haven presiding with his usual acceptability. I was read out for Monument, the second time. Being acquainted, I started in at once, and held a meeting at Spring Valley, and formed a class; and near the holidays commenced at the old church another effort for revival. We had about the same results—a refreshing time—things went pleasantly and quietly.

When the 4th of July, 1875, came, we had a dinner and some speaking—a very pleasant time—in a grove. I remember how comfortable I felt in realizing what liberty and blessings we had in our United States, and how thankful we ought to be for them, although they had cost the blood of so many of our friends. About that same time, at Granite, in Lake County, they were interring my son, who had been murdered by a lawless mob—of which dreadful tragedy I heard the next day. The particulars I will relate at the close of this year's record. The shock of this affliction almost overcame me. My boy was gone! What should I do? Temptations arose like a torrent, and naught but vengeance presented itself. But the Spirit whispered: "Vengeance is mine; I will repay, saith the Lord."

I had a thousand thoughts to investigate as they came. It was intimated if I wanted help to take redress, I could have it. But that would be mob-law, and the guilty might go clear, and some innocent man be killed. It would not be right, nor would it restore the dead to life. I could only go to God in humble prayer for help in this time of awful conflict, and he was indeed my consolation and a present help in time of trouble. I determined to do what I could to have law enforced upon the guilty; by God's help to do my duty, and to take him for my refuge. Soon I was able to say: "Though he slay me, yet will I trust in him." And so I prepared for my Sunday's work. But continually the temptation would come: "As they have taken life, only life for life can repay;" and as I was well acquainted with every hill and gorge in their county, I could see just how it could be done with but little danger to myself. The thought came: "But little justice has ever been meted out, by a course of law, in this country." And then, when almost roused to desperation, this other thought would come: "But I have a right to protection *by the laws* of our land; a right I not only inherited—my ancestors fought in the past—but purchased anew by the valor of my own sons, who shed their blood in the last war; so, not by violence, but by law, must I be protected and righted even in this." But no one can understand the conflict through which I passed, except he be placed in the like circumstances. After the lapse of almost twelve years, I thank God that I was enabled to bear up, and to resist the terrible temptation that had well-nigh overthrown me. All this conflict was before I had heard anything beyond the fact that my son was shot in the court-house. I kept up the work of my charge as well as I could. Monument, Spring Valley, and Table Rock, I concluded, would make a good circuit in the near future. This year the grasshoppers ate up everything, and some of our Methodist folks moved away. The new presiding elder seemed to judge things from the depot. If the town was small, he swapped off and let the charge go. Well, it never seemed the best thing; but if the Presbyterians or other Churches can and will save as many souls as the Methodists, it will be well.

These were hard years of labor and affliction, never to be forgotten. I received $904 in the two years, all told, and it cost me $170 more than I got. Even the parsonage I built they let run down, and finally sold it for fifty dollars. A more careful and minute inspection of the field by the presiding elder would, I verily believe, save many promising appointments to our Church.

CHAPTER XVIII.

LAKE COUNTY OUTRAGES.

WHEN I came into the mountains, in 1861, Lake County included all the territory west of Park County. My first visit was in July of that year. I was well acquainted with its mountains and gorges as far as Gunnison, and equally well acquainted with the early settlers. To say the least, they were a fair specimen of miners in the early days of Colorado. I believe I had their general good-will as I preached to them. I felt at home among them, and, indeed, called it home from 1866 to 1868, during which time I helped to get some settlers into the lower part of the county. It must be remembered that Chaffee County has been taken off since. In 1867 I was elected probate judge of the county. I did not want the office for honor or profit; but the majority of the people called me to it. I served them about one year, and then resigned, having been sent by the conference to New Mexico.

I had reason to respect many of the citizens. Few professed anything but to take the world as it came, and that generally proved to be a very rough way. Below the Twin Lakes the settlers were mostly ranchmen. All seemed to go along fairly; but tale-bearing, a lie once in awhile, land-claims and surveying land, in some cases entering land fraudulently, irrigating ditches—the depraved heart, full of covetousness, made great use of all these to stir up strife. Out of very trivial causes great dissensions sometimes arose. I mention one case, because it led up to the murder of my son: Mr. Elijah Gibbs, a very straightforward man, moved into the neighborhood. The disposition of the older settlers was to domineer over the new-comers. If they submitted, all right; if not, then there were means to subdue their haughty spirits. So when Mr. Gibbs drove up and tied his team where a gang were threshing, he was soon astonished at seeing his team hitched to the machine, his permission having neither been asked nor granted. He indignantly and, I fear, profanely ordered his team put back, under pains and penalties. From then on there was bad blood between these parties, aggravated by conflicting land and water claims. Mr. Gibbs and Mr. Harrington quarreled over a ditch in which they were jointly interested. Almost a pitched battle ensued, but neither was hurt. That night somebody set fire to Mr. Harrington's out-house. He got up, and ran out to extinguish the fire, and was shot and killed by some person unknown. There is no question but that whoever did the dastardly deed should have been hung. The circumstances of the previous quarrel pointed suspicion at Gibbs. As soon as the word went out, a party gathered and went to hang him. But he and some of his friends were armed, and declared that it could not be done; but that if they wished to try the law they could do so; and if Gibbs was found guilty, justice would be permitted to take its course.

A warrant was taken out, and he was tried and acquitted. He went back and went to work on his ranch, intending to live the suspicion down; but those who first went to hang him, to the number of fifteen, filled themselves with strong drink, went to his cabin, and ordered him to come out and be hung like a man. Gibbs was alone, except his wife and little children, and a neighbor woman with her little child; but his courage and presence of mind did not desert him. Barring the door, he prepared to defend himself. His besiegers piled brush against the back of the house and fired it, to drive him out. The result not being satisfactory, using Gibbs's favorite race-horse as a shield, they made another pile against the door. Through a hole at the side of the door Gibbs saw what was going on, and realized the imminence of his peril. When one of his assailants struck a match to fire the pile, he opened with his revolver on the crowd, shooting two men. A third was wounded, but with shot. As no shotgun was discharged from within, it is likely that in the excitement outside a gun was accidentally fired, with the result stated above.

Discovering a man at the back of the house climbing on to the yard-fence, he shot at him through the window. He heard the ball strike, and thought it hit his pistol-scabbard, and that the man was one of the leaders. It turned out, however, to be a man who lived with one of the leaders, and he was wounded in the fleshy part of the hip. I believe this man recovered; but the other three died in about three days, two brothers and an uncle. I heard they expressed sorrow for the course they had taken, and said they did not blame Gibbs for the defense of his family.

The excitement was past description. Gibbs's friends thought it best for him to leave. So, with two or three othrs, he started. But his would-be murderers collected and pursued him, bound to take him dead or alive. Gibbs's party made their escape through the mountains—sometimes hearing their pursuers—to Monument, where they had acquaintances, with whom they left their horses, and took the cars for Denver.

When Gibbs's baffled pursuers went back, they formed what they called a Committee of Safety!—after they had got three men killed and one wounded. Everybody said that Gibbs had done just right in defending himself, and that if he had killed more of them it would have been well. The press of the Territory also sustained him. This "Committee of Safety" gathered all they could on their side, including a lot of tie-cutters, some sixty men all told. They seized horses to ride, and they arrested all who did not think or do and say as they did. Head-quarters were at Nathrop's mills. As the suspects were brought in, the committee questioned them as to their opinion whether Gibbs murdered Harrington. This was all the reason they claimed for their tyrannical procedure.

Among those hauled up was my son, Probate Judge E. F. Dyer. They acted roughly with him; asked if he believed Gibbs shot Mr. Harrington, etc. He told them he did not. When he was forty miles away at work, he heard that Gibbs had done it; but had then said that he could not and would not believe it unless it was proven on him. He had known Gibbs ever since 1860, and firmly believed that he was innocent of the crime alleged against him.

Of course the "committee" were furious. He had a pistol on his person, and could have used it, but determined that he would not unless his life were in danger.

A notice, signed by order of the committee, to leave within three days and to resign his office, was served on him; but as they had taken his horse, and as he could not walk in the snow by reason of a stiff knee from white-swelling, he did not obey. So the second time they brought him before their august presence. He insisted on the return of his horse, and finally they brought it, and he started. A few miles out, as he was going up a gorge, he was stopped by a guard of two armed men. Their orders were to let no one come out or go in on that road. One of them had been befriended by him, and gave him permission to go to Granite. He headed in that direction, but soon turned toward Fair Play, avoiding the road for some miles. It was hard traveling, as the snow was deep, and the weather cold, in mid-winter. Some time in the night he reached Fair

Play. Thence he went to Denver, and visited us at Monument.

The mob of safety procured government arms, and ran off about forty of the inhabitants. It was their gentle policy, when their prisoners would not answer the questions satisfactorily, to hang them awhile in order to subdue their refractory spirits. One of their victims, a Mr. Marion, I saw while his neck was yet sore. Some had to leave home and property, some stock on the range. One or more women died from the terrible excitement. A Mr. Hardin, the outspoken proprietor of a pack-train, cursed their infamous conduct, and was soon thereafter found by the roadside murdered, together with his dog, whose paw the ruffians had clasped in the dead man's hand.

And all this where there were laws, and courts, and officers to prevent such outrages, or to punish their perpetrators! But it appeared that judge, governor, constable, sheriff, like Gallio, "cared for none of these things." I had a talk with the governor, and asked him to send men to put a stop to such proceedings. He intimated that he had heard from the other side, and paid no attention to my plea. I said, "Governor, if you won't do anything to stop such a state of affairs, I am keen to tell you that I have no use for such a governor, and our country has much less use," and left him. I concluded that it was a political dodge, and that he wanted to be on the strongest side, even at the price of not fulfilling the obligations of the highest office in the Territory. The mob carried all before them, and always managed to have a grand jury that was on their side.

At the first meeting of our representatives, I thought to get a bill passed to attach Lake to some other county for judicial purposes. I went to as many as three Republicans to help me after the governor refused. They either wished to be excused, or refused outright to take a hand in it. I felt that I had some claim for help in such a time of distress and violation of laws; but I got the cold shoulder. I met Judge Miller. He was acquainted with the case; said he would draw the bill, for he believed E. F. Dyer was a part of the government. After having been refused by my own party, I met Mr. Andy Wilson, a Democrat, and he took the bill, and at the proper time, presented it. As soon as it was filed, a delegation came down from Lake and defeated it. This was from the upper end of the county, before Leadville's boom, when the county was weak. Not many of them had anything to do with the mob, but did nothing to stop it. When it took such proportions, they, or most of them, would rather let murder go unpunished than to saddle the feeble county with the expense of prosecuting the offenders. And as soon as news of the defeat of the bill got to Oro, a meeting was called at Mr. H. A. W. Tabor's store, the largest house there; and resolutions were adopted commending S. Y. Marshall and others for the defeat of the "*infamous*" and "*nefarious*" act!

Of those connected with the mob, so many

have died suddenly or been killed, either by their own hands or the hands of others, that I have heard even wicked men say that it looked as if the Almighty had followed the guilty with his judgments.

After Harding and others had been shot down, the governor sent out General Dave Cook, a detective. A Mr. John McPherson, who had a club-foot, and did not go around with the mob, but wrote letters to papers in their defense, justifying them, was able to be of great service to them, by pouring oil on the troubled waters, and contributing to the impression made on General Cook's mind that, as everything had quieted down, well enough were best left alone. Whether money was used I do not pretend to say. Some affirmed that while the leaders were manipulating the detective for a favorable report, Uncle Jesse Marion, whom they held in custody, and whom they had hung once or twice, managed to give his guards— who were so much interested in the conference with Cook, that they left him for a few minutes— the slip, and taking down the Arkansas River, made his escape. I saw him after he got to the valley. His neck was yet sore from the rope. He seemed to think Mr. Cook would not have been so ready to report favorably if it had been his own neck that was sore.

As to Mr. McPherson's accusations about Brown's Creek, and the dishonesty that had been unearthed there by those who had been engaged in setting fire to a house over women and little children, and in killing men and hanging others to make them tell what they wanted told,—they are not worth notice. How the governor could reconcile his apathy whilst this lawlessness continued—during which ten or twelve were killed outright, and a whole county terrorized—with his official obligations, I leave the reader to decide.

When spring came, Judge E. F. Dyer returned to Lake County. Mr. Marion—whose escape from the mob, after having been run up by the neck, is given above—also returned, and swore out warrants before the judge for all who had taken part in the outrage. The culprits gathered all they could—nearly thirty men—and the sheriff with them, as he in character as well as ability was more in his element with a mob than anywhere else. They came with guns and pistols, and entered the court-room armed. The judge ordered them to divest themselves of their arms, and they laid them off in the back-end of the court-house; after which their cases were called. Jesse Marion, the principal witness, and others, were not uninterested spectators while the crowd was gathering. From what they saw and heard they feared to go to the trial, and court was adjourned till eight o'clock the next morning for want of evidence. The judge slept over a store, with some others, and was told by the sheriff that he could not leave that night. Mr. Gilland was there. His mule was watched through the night, and without doubt, if he had attempted to get it, he would have been shot. He was advised to leave, and did so, slipping out over the hill, and walked to Fair Play, through the mountains, twenty-five miles, and reported the situation.

At eight o'clock court was called, and the accused were dismissed for lack of evidence. They all went out. Mr. Hayden stopped with the judge a minute. Some one called him down on purpose. He went, and as soon as he left, five men from the crowd went up the stairs at the back-end of the building. The judge was sitting in an office-chair, and three or four shots were fired. One ball struck the chair, another went through his arm above the wrist, and on through the window. One man on the outside heard him cry: "Spare my life!" But he must have made toward them, and been caught by some of them near the door, as the pistol was evidently put close to his head—the hair being all burned around the bullet-hole, which was just behind his ear. They all went down the steps, and mingled among their crowd, which was waiting for them at the foot of the stairs. A man looked through a crack, as it was a log house, and saw the tragedy, and was the first to reach him. But the judge never spoke, and breathed his last in a few minutes. Another man, Mr. Woodard, standing above on a bank, only a few feet away, saw them come out, and knew them all. He was imprudent enough to tell what he saw, and not long after was shot off his horse and killed. The man who shot him resumed his abode with the mob. It was called "self-defense." So it was—to the mob.

An officer was called, an inquest held, a verdict rendered: That E. F. Dyer came to his death by unknown hands. The mob terrorized the community, for only about half their number were brought by a warrant; the rest came armed to prevent those accused from being tried. The inquest was virtually in the hands and interest of the mob.

. One of their number was mysteriously shot several years after in his own store. I will narrate the circumstances as I heard them. He had a young man hired to herd for him, said to have been a nephew of Mr. Harrington, the first man murdered in the annals of the mob. He came into the neighborhood some time after his uncle had been killed, and was heard to say that if he ever discovered his uncle's murderer, he would be avenged. After working for Mr. Nathrop for some time, he quit, and went to the store to settle, and must have settled with Mr. Nathrop. He was the last one seen in the store before Mr. Nathrop's dead body was found lying on the floor. The young man rode to Buena Vista, a few miles distant, and danced most of the night, and in the morning left on the cars. A reward of several hundred dollars was offered for his arrest, but he has not been heard of since. He could easily have been taken; but the people feared that Gibbs was back, hunting his oppressors. The mob all feared Gibbs a great deal more than they did the devil, and so let the youth escape. Nathrop was the wealthiest man connected with the Lake County mob.

My son was murdered at eight o'clock A. M., July 3, 1875. The few people that were at Granite buried him in the usual place of interment, where there were a number resting. Among them was Brother Rufus Lumery, an itinerant preacher, who preached to us at my house when Elias was four years old. But I was not satisfied to leave him among such a set of murderers. So, some three years after, my son Samuel and my son-in-law, C. C. Streetor, went with a wagon nearly one hundred and fifty miles, and removed his body to Bailey, Colorado, where they disinterred my father's remains, and bore both bodies to Castle Rock, Douglas County, and buried them side by side. I considered this our duty. But unless it were a duty, I would never do so again, for the reason that it brings all the feelings of a father or a son back afresh. I learned by this experience that a metallic coffin does not last long. Father had been buried only six years, yet his metallic coffin was rusted full of holes. The other was pine, and sound. They opened it, and the corpse was natural—only a speck of mold on one cheek. God only knows how hard a trial this terrible tragedy was to me. After the lapse of all these years, the memory of it rushes over me like a flood. Yet I would infinitely rather endure my suffering than what his cruel murderers must have experienced. One was so crazed that he drowned himself. Another had what was called the "horrors," and finally miserably died. God's curse was upon them all. Be it so!

CHAPTER XIX.

LAKE COUNTY OUTRAGES—CONTINUED.

A STRANGE fascination holds me to this dreadful scene. No wonder. My son, educated, bright, wayward it may be, but honest and fearless—to have been so wickedly torn away from me! O, the weary, weary months of anguish; the alternate flashes of revenge and forgiveness; the bitter struggles between wrath and mercy! God have pity!—even now, when I retrace the efforts to traduce his character, made by his cowardly murderers, my old blood boils! My son was not perfect; but his sins were against himself, and his last letters show how his better nature was dominating.

We give first the newspaper report of the foiling of the lynchers, as printed in the *Rocky Mountain News:*

Elijah Gibbs, who was, last October [1874], tried for and acquitted of the murder of George Harrington on Coon Creek, in June, arrived in town yesterday afternoon, by the Denver and Rio Grande Railway. He had telegraphed to Sheriff Willoughby to meet him at the depot; but, the latter not doing so, he went to the store of W. T. Lambert, who is a connection, to whose house he proceeded shortly after. About seven he went over to the jail, where he intended to pass the night as a matter of precaution, lest some of his friends, the vigilantes, might be lurking about Denver. He was met at the jail by a *News* reporter, to whom he gave, substantially, the following narrative:

Last Friday, about midnight, I was aroused by a party of men coming to my house, and knocking and kicking violently at the door. I asked who was there, and was answered by the question: "Is Gibbs at home?" I answered I was, and then some one said: "Get up, and come out; we want to see you." "Would not morning do as well?' I asked. "No, we want you now. We will give you ten minutes to get out of the house. We will give you fifteen to get out with your family. If you are not quick about it, we will burn you, house and all."

Gibbs made no reply to this cheerful manifesto, and the party then, with much cursing and calling of names, went around to the north side of the house, where they began making preparations to fire. The house, apparently, is an ordinary log cabin, with a dirt roof, the door and one window being on the south side. The assailants tried for a full half hour to get up a blaze; but the logs, being old and full of water, did not ignite readily, and all their efforts were fruitless. Finally they knocked the dirt off the roof, and endeavored to set fire to the thatch, but it would not catch, and at last they gave up the job in despair.

Gibbs, meantime, had been unable to take any active part in the drama that was being enacted, owing to there being no window on the side which was being fired. At one time, he thinks, he could have killed two men who were spying around the south side, but refrained from doing so, as he wished to get a shot at a man named Coon, who, he supposed, was the leader, and they stood in the way of his fire. Before he could do so, however, Coon got out of reach, and then the party came around to the south side of the house, and began piling hay and wood against the door.

When they got a pile of combustibles about four feet high together, Sam Boone lit a match and was about to touch it off, "when," says Gibbs, "I shot him. It was when he was stooping, the match in his right hand, a double-barreled gun in his left. The ball entered here [pointing to his right breast]. I fired from a chink in the boards which blocked up the window, with a six-shooter. Boone was about eight feet distant. Boone fell, after being shot, crying, 'Boys, he's got me.' All in front of the door then jumped back, and then one of them cried, 'Charge on the door.' They all bunched together, when I fired twice, hitting two men in the legs. The gun of one of them went off as he was falling, killing the other Boone. That he was killed in this way is shown by the fact that I had no shot-gun, and fifty-four shot were found in his body. After these four fell, all stampeded. As they started to run, I counted eleven, which, with the four on the ground, made fifteen. As they crossed the fence to the west of the house, I fired with my rifle, hitting the revolver of one, but not hurting him. I then told the women I would save their lives by going to my father's, who lived about half a mile to the east, in a direction nearly opposite to that taken by the vigilantes. We got there safely, told him what had occurred, and he sent a messenger to Brown's Creek to give the alarm. In about an hour and a half word came that help was at my house. I then went home and found thirty of my friends there, who told me I had killed and crippled three men."

Incidental to this narrative, Gibbs said that, contrary to report, he had no knowledge of the vigilantes' intentions, or he would have had his friends with him when they came. As it was, he was alone with his family, consisting of his wife and three children, and a Mrs. Hutchinson, who had one child. They remained in the north room of the house, which was divided by a partition in the middle, during the assault, and were comparatively out of danger. Illustrative of the deadly designs of the attacking party, the next morning a musket, with a charge that measured five and a half inches, was found, together with a double-barreled shot-gun, containing twenty-one buckshot in each barrel. After Gibbs and his friends had discussed the situation, the former went over to Brown's Creek, and gave himself up to Constable Birchie, who guarded him till Monday, when he was examined before A. B. Corwin, a justice.

Mr. Corwin was present during the foregoing recital, and here gave his version of the examination. He said that Mrs. Hutchinson was sworn, and told identically the same story, which was further corroborated by the testimony of ten of the surviving vigilantes, who, in addition, in almost as many words, justified Gibbs's conduct. The result of the examination was that Gibbs was dismissed, on the ground that what he had done was done in self-defense.

But his acquittal did not help Gibbs much. The sympathizers in the sentiment that led to the tragedy of which he was held not responsible, resolved not only to treat him as responsible, but swore that the justice who acquitted him should, with him, experience the fate of Haman. It was not pleasant, either, for Gibbs's near relatives and intimate friends to be around, about this time; so he and his brother William, Justice Corwin, and one Lewis Gilliard, made up their minds to make a virtue of necessity, and vamose the ranche. Accordingly, after the trial, which was over while the sun was yet high Monday afternoon, the quartet, heavily armed with a brace of revolvers and a double-barreled shot-gun apiece, struck out for Denver. They had got but about fifteen miles on their journey, when, on the edge of South Park, some thirty or forty men "ran onto them," as Gibbs expressed it, and chased them about the same number of miles. It was midnight when the *rencontre* took place, but the moon, then not much over the full, made everything as bright as day, and the dark forms of the pursuers could be distinctly seen as, spreading out in the form of a fan, they came sweeping across the plain.

Gibbs's first move, after calling on the rest to separate, was to run down a gully towards the east—they had been running nearly due north—till the party had passed on. His brother William, who had been the first to discover them, made off in another direction with the two remaining, and soon the chasers were left some distance in the rear. But not for long. They soon came dashing up again, and the pursued quartet, who had come together again, were obliged to lighten themselves of their provisions, blankets, surplus clothing, in short, everything but their arms, to make good their escape to a mountain in the near distance, where they resolved to stand and sell their lives as dearly as possible. Their thinking to unload their cargo, however, enabled them so to accelerate their horses' speed that the alternative was not needed, and at daylight their pursuers were left far behind, as worn out and hungry they rode in on a ranch at the head of Curran Creek, from whose owner they demanded, in Gibbs's graphic language, breakfast, food for their horses, and a house to fight in.

The two former were soon forthcoming, and then they rode on till, at sundown, they arrived at Welters, in Hayden Park, where they passed the night. The next day they deliberated as to whether they would take the Bergen Park or Colorado City road, but in accordance with Gibbs's own suggestion, they finally determined to plunge right into the brush, and all were soon lying along the sides of the mountain at the head of Dead Man's Gulch. They heard the reports of two guns, and rocks at times rolled down the hill apparently aimed at them; but they saw no more of the avengers of the two Boones. When about fifteen miles off Colorado City, they stopped to rest, and passed the night at Welch's. Yesterday morning they came up to Summit, where they left their horses and took the train. The entire distance traveled they estimated at one hundred miles.

Gibbs's intention is to return to his ranch, which is some seventy miles north-west from Cañon City, when the feeling against him has subsided. He has one hundred acres under fence, and sixty in a good state of cultivation, which he thinks too good property to be scared away from by trifles. Speaking of trifles, Gibbs is particularly anxious to say that his friends, the lynchers, did not humanely wait, as was reported, for his wife's confinement before putting their plans in execution. She is at this moment in an interesting condition, and the fight and excitement consequent upon the attack, nearly brought a premature delivery, with all its attendant consequences, on mother and child.

A VIEW FROM THE INSIDE.

SOUTH ARKANSAS, COL., Jan. 30, 1875.

REV. J. L. DYER:

DEAR SIR,—We are very glad, indeed, to receive a letter from you. I almost arrived at the conclusion that you had thrown off on us; and I would not blame you much if you had discarded me at least, for you know I used to be an inveterate joker, and not always very choice of language. We are all usually well, and pleased to know that you and yours are in a like condition.

Times here have been very exciting. The two

Boones and Finly Kane were killed. Gibbs escaped. The pursuit, the forming a Vigilance Committee, the arrests made by them, the reprimands to some and the expulsion of others, the arrest of C. M. Harding for burning Mr. Cameron's premises and horses—and still not yet finished up—has kept us all in a great commotion and excitement, almost up to the highest pitch. Mrs. Hugh Mahan died recently, and the report is that the present excitement was the sole cause of her death. Jake Erhart was arrested; so was Fred Bertschey.

Your son Elias was arrested, and invited to leave the county because he would not attend more strictly to his own business, but on every occasion would voluntarily vindicate the character of Mr. Gibbs, so much so that he made himself odious to friend and foe. The committee requested him to leave for the good of his health. Perhaps he has seen you before now. He was not injured personally, though his feelings may have been injured. You need not apprehend that the people have any desire to do any personal violence to him, though they did choke a few with a rope; but I guess they will live through it, as the last seen of them they were leaving this valley as if they had very urgent business to attend to on the other side. Elisha Gibbs and all of his personal friends made their escape.

The committee have unearthed a nest of fearful vipers. You would hardly believe were I to tell you the particulars of what was found to exist in the shape of a secret organization for the purpose of preying on the people by cattle-stealing, taking up estrays and branding them, branding calves that belonged to their neighbors' cows, butchering their neighbors' beef, slandering their neighbors, and what not; and then uniting together to swear each other clear; and all this in the neighborhood of Brown's Creek, that robbers' roost, where congregate all the unclean birds that have fouled and defiled Lake County for a long time, giving her a bad reputation abroad for no fault of the county at large.

If Gibbs and his friends have any regard for their lives or self-preservation, they will never return to this county. No doubt, when this excitement subsides, all of the less obnoxious exiles can return with safety. It would only be a waste of breath for any one to endeavor to convince any of the well-disposed citizens that Elijah Gibbs is not the murderer of George Harrington, or at least contrived and aided in the act. It is proven to the satisfaction of all that the aforesaid secret organization knew more or less about the murder, and the rope is none too good for them. If the trees of the forest would be made to bear fruit this winter it would help society, at least in the vicinity of Brown's Creek, amazingly. The people have all dispersed and gone home, to be called out again when necessary; and I assure you they have done a good work, in my humble opinion.

Mr. Henry Skews attended the funerals of the Boone Brothers and that of Finly Kane. I believe him to be a very good young man, but very nervous and easily excited.

I have written enough for this time. Please write again. Come and see us, and bring your wife.

From your ever true friend, J. McPHERSON.

To show how my efforts to secure law and order for Lake County were received, consider this correspondence to the Fair Play *Sentinel*:

ORO CITY, February 23, 1876.

EDITORS SENTINEL, — A mass-meeting of the citizens of Oro City and vicinity was held on the evening of the 21st ult., at the store of H. A. W. Tabor, for the purpose of extending to the Hon. J. Y. Marshall the congratulations of the people of Lake County for the able and satisfactory manner in which Mr. Marshall discharged his duties as representative of the Eleventh District.

The meeting was called to order by Wm. McDermith, who, in a few brief and appropriate remarks, stated the object of the meeting. Captain Sullivan D. Breece was elected chairman, and I. P. McCreagh secretary. On motion, the chairman appointed a committee of three to draft resolutions, consisting of Major DeMary, Maurice Hayes, and I. P. McCreagh.

The following resolutions were reported, and unanimously adopted:

Resolved, That the thanks of this meeting are due, and are hereby tendered, to the Hon. J. Y. Marshall for his able representation of the Eleventh District in the late Legislative Assembly of the Territory of Colorado, and in particular for the important service rendered by him to the citizens of Lake County in defending their rights against the infamous and nefarious attempt to strip them of their privileges and make them in judicial affairs a mere appanage of another county.

Resolved, That we hereby express our unqualified approbation of the conduct of our representative in the late Legislature, the Hon. J. Y. Marshall, and assure him of our firm faith in his integrity and ability, and with feelings of pride and pleasure tender him our warm congratulations and thanks. (Signed),

H. M DeMary,
Maurice Hayes,
I. P. McCreagh.

The secretary was then ordered to send copies of the proceedings and resolutions to the Hon. J. Y. Marshall and the Fair Play *Sentinel* for publication.

On motion, the meeting adjourned, amid hearty expressions of good-will toward the Hon. J. Y. Marshall.

Sullivan D. Breece, President.

I. P. McCreagh, Secretary.

The following was clipped from the *News:*

Judge Dyer, probate judge of Lake County, arrived in the city last evening. He left Fair Play Monday morning, and rode his pony to Denver. He was met, shortly after his arrival, by a *News* reporter, to whom he related, in easy and pleasing language, the exciting particulars of the recent tragic occurrences on Chalk Creek. From his recital—which, by the way, is only confirmatory of the account telegraphed the *News* on Monday—it is apparent that the lower end of Lake County is at the mercy of a mob, who are responsible for the reign of terror prevailing there at present.

Judge Dyer stayed at J. G. Erhart's last Tuesday night. He had been down into the San Luis Valley, and was going to Granite to hold court. Wednesday morning, as he was preparing to continue his journey, four men, armed with guns and revolvers, and mounted on horses, approached and ordered him to accompany them. They acted, of course, without a show of authority, and carried their point by force, jerking the judge a little when he demanded to see their warrant. He was taken five miles, and lodged in the Chalk Creek school-house. He was not alone, for others had been gobbled up in the same way, and the victims were increasing in numbers all the while. The prisoners were removed from the school-house to a log building near by. All through Wednesday and Thursday the crowd of victims was continually augmenting. They were being gathered in by the guards from all directions. The mob had runners out all over the county. They were after everybody suspected of believing Elijah Gibbs innocent of the murder of George Harrington. Citizens were marched three, four, and five miles, over hills and through the snow, and lodged in this improvised calaboose. It was a sort of "round-up," similar to the cattle "round-ups" in the stock-growing districts. During Wednesday and Thursday about thirty citizens were brought in as prisoners by the mob.

Meanwhile an inquisition was in progress in another cabin close by. The court was run by a lot of fellows styling themselves "The Committee of Safety." Twelve men were impaneled as jurors. There was no judge, and all were equally officious. Among the so-called jurors were Benjamin Smith, Benjamin Schwander, William Craft, and James Demming, the latter county treasurer. John D. Coon and Josiah Weston played a leading part in the prosecution. The cabin was crowded with the friends of the court, most of them armed, and a guard stood at the door, with a gun in his hand. The victims were examined singly, and each was sworn to secrecy, not only as pertained to the proceedings, but as to who constituted the jury, court, and tribunal, as well as the audience. Among those who were arraigned on Wednesday and Thursday were Judge Dyer, J. G. Erhart, Fred Bertschey, a Mr. Evans, Frank Anderson, Elias Gibbs (father of Elijah Gibbs), Thomas Morgan, Leslie and Ernest Christison, William Richardson, Dr. J. N. Cowan, Thomas Fletcher, Jesse Marion, Thomas Gilland, Lewis Cowan, Anderson Geary, John and Milton Gibbs (half-brothers of the slayer of the vigilantes), and a Mr. Harding. The Gibbs brothers are mere lads, aged thirteen and fifteen years. Mr. Erhart is a prominent and much respected citizen, who represented the county in the Legislature two terms, and has filled the position of county commissioner several years. 'Frank Anderson is a school-teacher, and Fred Bertschey is a constable; but the mob paid no respect to position.

The principal object of the inquisition was to

ascertain whether the prisoners sympathized with Elijah Gibbs. Judge Dyer was asked if he thought Gibbs innocent, and he replied emphatically that he did. Some of the victims declined to answer certain questions, and they were ordered by the court to be hung up by the neck until they could answer more cheerfully and willingly. Among those who were brought to time in this way were William Richardson, Jesse Marion, and Anderson Geary. They were raised from the floor several times, and were finally discharged. Judge Dyer was discharged from custody Thursday evening, but, finding his pony gone, was obliged to remain in the neighborhood over night, and the next morning he was hauled up before the sham court again. After consuming some time in a re-examination of his case, he was handed a written sentence, of which the following is an exact copy:

Chalk Creek, Lake County, }
January 29, 1875. }

Judge Dyer,—You are hereby notified to resign your office as probate judge, and leave this county within thirty days, by order of the Committee of Safety.

The judge's pony having been restored to him in the meantime, he rode over to Trout Creek Friday evening, and was accommodated with lodgings at the house of a friend named Barney McQuade. Saturday morning he started for Fair Play, but was soon halted by a couple of armed guards, who, notwithstanding he produced his passport, in the shape of an order to "git," were determined to hand him over to the inquisition. Upon promising, however, to go straight home, he was allowed to pass, and he continued his journey to Fair Play. One of the men who stopped him is named Diedrick, who is said to have deserted from the army. The judge, hearing that all the roads were guarded, to prevent anyone from escaping and reporting the condition of affairs, took to the hills and pineries, and, by avoiding all ranches and stations, reached Fair Play Saturday night, himself and pony panting with fatigue.

Judge Dyer thinks there are about seventy-five persons concerned in this reign of mob-rule. They are all residents of the lower end of the county, and the strictest measures were enforced to shut out communication with the people of California Gulch, by guarding the highways, and arresting anyone who attempted to pass. Miss Minnie Simpson, step-daughter of the elder Gibbs, was stopped by a guard while on the way to the post-office, and a letter which she held taken from her. The mob have also seized and destroyed the record of proceedings in the examination of Elijah Gibbs for the killing of the vigilantes. John Gilland, an old man who is seriously ill, got his walking-papers the day Judge Dyer got his.

Judge Dyer will lay the foregoing facts before his excellency, Acting-Governor Jenkins, this morning, accompanied with a request for executive interference for the restoration of peace on Chalk Creek, and the protection of law-abiding citizens.

The following extract was clipped from a country paper, name and date not preserved. It shows the spirit of the vigilantes and their sympathizers:

A gentleman who has just arrived from Lake County informs us that Gibbs, the assassin of Harrington, has returned to Lake County, and has with him a band of fifty armed roughs. The respectable portion of the community were notified by parties in Denver that Gibbs was about to return to revenge himself upon them, and they have organized a force of one hundred men fully armed to resist him. Our informant states that the night he stopped at the residence of John D. Bale, on the Upper Arkansas, it was expected that an attack would be made upon the house before morning, which, however, was not the case. It is expected that a collision will take place between the two parties somewhere near Granite. The sympathy that Gibbs has received from the newspapers of certain portions of the Territory has, of course, induced him to return on a murdering expedition. So much for making a martyr out of the vilest cut-throat that ever went unhung.

A LETTER FROM JUDGE DYER.

CASTLE ROCK, COL., February 8, 1875.

DEAR PARENTS,—I write you from Sam's. Came up from Denver to Clint's last night. Am intending to go back to Denver to-morrow. Have had a terrible time of it, but begin to see our way out. Am intending to proceed against them for attempted assassination, and for damage, as some of them have means. Gave your note to Sam, and what McPherson says. I did believe, and do believe, Gibbs innocent of the crime accused of; but minded my own business, and did nothing but my duty as a good, law-abiding citizen, and nothing but what a Christian might do with a clear and approving conscience. I have done nothing that you or any of the connection need blush for, nor what you would not have felt compelled to do under the same circumstances. I am proud and glad to have been able to assist the suffering innocent, even in as humble a manner as I did. My advice and influence has been after the teachings of Christ, and I feel that God approves all my words and acts in this matter. I feel that I have lost and suffered more than the rest of the friends; but I believe that good will come of all; and I have learned not to distrust God or his ways, but have full confidence that, somewhere in all the boundless future, he will make all even, and give me that rest for which I long. The path of duty is the path of safety. I feel it, and shall act accordingly. Many good people are praying for me and my work; and they can do no more, for their hands are tied. I pray constantly to be able to work without fear, and with malice toward none.

Will be to see you as soon as I can, but can't say exactly when; but in the meantime, believe me, I will endeavor, by the help of God, to do all my duty and nothing wrong.

If you have the time to write a line to Denver, it would reach me.

Yours very, very truly, ELIAS F. DYER.
All of us are together to-day.

ANOTHER LETTER FROM THE JUDGE.

GRANITE, May 30, 1875.

DEAR PARENTS,—I received yours this morning, and have to say was made very glad thereby. Have not written fully because I could not; did not know myself. Have been from one end of the county to the other since. Just got around last night. Probably your dream may signify a fact. We are divided as to course of action. I was and am ready to issue warrants, though I do not think it advisable; but unless others will swear them out, I do not feel justifiable in issuing them on my own responsibility. All my reasons, or our reasons rather, I can not give on paper; but it does not take much of a stretch of imagination to guess a good many of them.

I met but one mobite in the lower end of the county. They are all afraid, and many of them are leaving. This is the worst point in the case. Too many of the bad characters will get out of the country. Perry Hutchinson, Ira Wing, and Smith Steele have cowed them. The mob had a meeting, and voted to kill four of our men. Perry went to the leaders, and told them that when the first trouble was made, every one of the mob would be killed like dogs. They denied any knowledge of the affair, and said if any wrong was done they would be as innocent of the matter as he. He told them it did not make any difference; they were the men he and his friends would kill first. So they are in a terrible predicament.

We may be too slow, but I try to do justice to all. God forbid that I should act from malice, or put my feelings before the judgment he has given me. I am not very pious yet—not so much so as I hope to be—but there are, and always have been, some principles of rectitude born in me which I fear to do violence to.

If we are too slow and easy, I will be the sufferer; but my conscience will be clear. If a man errs in judgment, God may forgive, but men never do. If a man errs from conscience, God can scarcely forgive; men always do, if he succeeds. So that you may see that I know where I stand, and that I comprehend the situation. However it may turn out, I will get many curses and but little commendation, *but know that I do not weaken.*

With many considerations of respect for judgment and action, Your son, ELIAS F. DYER.

JAMES H. JOHNSTON'S LETTER INFORMING THE JUDGE'S FATHER.

GRANITE, LAKE COUNTY, COL., July 3, 1875.

REV. JOHN L. DYER:

DEAR SIR,—It becomes my painful duty to inform you of the death of your son Elias F. Dyer, by the hand of an assassin or assassins, at about half-past eight o'clock this morning. He had just adjourned his court, and lingered behind the crowd, and by so doing he lost his life. He was killed in the court-room, shot through the head and arm; but, strange to say, no one knows who did the deed. Some parties were there in a moment, but he could not speak, and only breathed a few times. The citizens here are so shocked; and I myself am the same, so that I can scarcely write. An inquest was held, but nothing that showed any light. He will be buried to-morrow. We will bury him as well and decently as we can.

You all have my heart-felt sympathy in this your sad bereavement. If, after calming down, I find out anything further, I will let you know.

Elias left two letters with me. He had a notion he would be killed, I think, and probably in the letters he has given you some idea. One of the letters is addressed to you, the other to Miss Loella Streator. I will mail them all now.

In sorrow, yours truly, JAMES H. JOHNSTON.

The following is the letter written by the judge on the morning of his murder:

GRANITE, JULY 3, 1875.

DEAR FATHER,—I do n't know that the sun will ever rise and set for me again, but I trust in God and his mercy. At eight o'clock I sit in court. The mob have me under guard. Mr. Gilland is missing this morning, but I do not think harm has befallen him. God bless you, my father, in your old age, and in Sam and his boy—in all your children—but you know John bears the name. Bless him and his forever, O my God!

My love to all friends, and I say I am proud to be your son. There is no cowardice in me, father. I am worthy of you in this respect. God comfort you and keep you always. I am, in this one respect, like Him who died for all; I die, if die I must, for law, order, and principle; and, too, I stand alone.

Your loving and true, and, I hope in some respects, worthy son, ELIAS F. DYER.

The *Rocky Mountain News*, two days later, contained the following dispatch from Fair Play:

This place is the scene of terrible excitement over a tragedy that, used as all are here to deeds of blood, strikes the entire community with a horror not felt for many a long day. The feud which has divided Lake County into two factions, each equally lawless, although one purporting to be the representative of order and legal authority, ever since the shooting of Harrington by Elisha Gibbs over a year ago, which resulted in the night attack on Gibbs's house on the 22d of last January, to the mortal harm of two of the assailants, and the final running of Gibbs out of the country, has culminated in the murder of Judge Dyer, of the Probate Court of this county, for no other crime, apparently, than endeavoring to do his duty. The particulars, as near as I have been able to collect them, are as follows: Dyer had issued sixteen warrants for the arrest of the members of the so-called Committee of Safety, and deputized Doctor Dobbins to arrest them. The latter returned the warrants, saying he had showed them to one Burnett, but had no means of bringing him to Granite. Dyer then deputized a man named Sites, who proceeded to carry out the order. He went immediately to Brown Creek, and arrested, first, Burnett, and afterwards Chaffin, a ringleader of the Safety Committee faction, and a man named Moore. Sites then went up the river to make other arrests, and, on returning to Brown Creek, met Weldon, the sheriff of

Lake County, who told him to give him the warrants, as he could make more arrests in one day than he (Sites) could in three weeks. Sites gave him the warrants, and last Friday evening the sheriff of Lake County, with about thirty armed men, came to Granite a little before dark. The mob took Dyer to the court-room. Fifteen or twenty citizens followed, but were ordered back. What transpired in the court-room no one knows. When Dyer came out he was very pale. He immediately went to Johnson's store, and wrote a letter. That night he was guarded, and the next morning the mob again took him to the court-house. A few moments after entering they came out, but shortly afterwards they returned, and, as they were passing up the stairs, four shots were fired. One ball struck Dyer on the arm. When he found himself wounded, he begged for his life; but the assassins finished him by shooting him in the head at the back of the right ear, the ball lodging beneath the left eyebrow. He lived fifteen minutes, and was conscious, but unable to speak. While Dyer lay weltering in his blood, and in the death agony, John D. Coon, a ringleader of the mob, bent over him, exclaiming, "What a horrible murder!" which sentiment is re-echoed by the men hereabouts, who are aching to hang Mr. Coon for his share in the crime. I will endeavor to collect further details of subsequent occurrences as I shall be able to gather them, but do so at the peril of my life, if any of the Committee of Safety learn of my taking such action.

We extract from a country paper, in the interests of the mob, the following:

E. F. Dyer, late probate judge of Lake County, has been killed. He was well known to have been the associate and defender of midnight assassins, incendiaries, and thieves, and to have been the vilifier of the unfortunate wife of his friend Gibbs's victim. He was requested to leave the county by a Vigilance Committee, composed of its best citizens. He returned, and more than likely nothing more would have been said about the matter, had he not on his own responsibility issued warrants for the arrest of a party of men far honester and more respectable than himself. Somebody shot this sneaking scoundrel, and now the Denver press raise a great hubbub about the death of this injured innocent, and the governor offers a reward of two hundred dollars for the discovery of that friend of the people who finished Dyer's earthly career.

Now let us draw another picture. A Negro is captured by the police of Denver, supposed to be guilty of burglary; he is tortured to make him convict himself, and suddenly disappears under circumstances more than suspicious. He is said to have escaped from two well-armed officers. Bah! Everybody thinks that unfortunate Negro was murdered by the officers of the law while trying to extort a further confession from him. Why is not this murder investigated? Where is Governor Rouatt's reward for this Negro's murderer, and why is it that but one Denver newspaper is independent enough to talk freely about the affair? The motes in our neighbor's eyes are always larger than the beams in our own.

Come, gentlemen of the Denver press, bring a pressure to bear, and let us have an investigation as to who killed that Negro. The sins of the citizens of other portions of the Territory are freely discussed in your ably edited sheets; now let us hear about the misdeeds of your own officers of the law.

ANOTHER LETTER FROM McPHERSON.

SOUTH ARKANSAS, COL., September 5, 1875.

REV. J. L. DYER:

DEAR SIR,—It is a long time since I have written to you—not since your last one to me; and that one I thought a little rough. It would not be rough for publication; but written to me personally, I could not see where it fitted at all, as I took no hand in any of the troubles, pro or con, whatever may have been my views; and my opinion was, and is now, that Gibbs knew all about the killing of Harrington; and I so expressed myself. A man can not help his convictions, and you yourself can not condemn a person for his honest convictions, even if they sometimes prove erroneous.

Never having mixed with our troubles, last winter or since, why was I spotted by your son for arrest, *which is seen on his docket? but I did not know until after his death* that I was marked for one of his victims.

I merely remarked that I did not mix myself up in the trouble; and I will qualify that remark by saying, that when United States Deputy Marshal Cook came in here last winter, I did go down to Mr. Bale's to see him, where I found a large crowd who came for the same purpose, some of whom were still hostile to the Gibbs faction. Some said: "This thing has gone far enough. Let us old fellows try and stop it, and have no more of it."

Among those taking this view of the case, and favoring peace, and opening the door to let the exiles return to their respective homes, thus putting things back where they were before, were old Mr. Spaulding, Sheriff Weldon, John Burnett, Peter Caruth, Joseph Hutchinson, Mr. Newman, Noah Baer, Thomas Cameron, myself, and a number of others. Mr. Bale did not make his appearance at the meeting, but said it was all right, and that he had no confidence that the exiles would return and keep quiet. But the balance of us concluded it best to give them a show. Many of them returned, and were not molested in the least.

I am afraid, Mr. Dyer, that the best counsel your son was taking at Denver proved his death, for he no doubt acted after the counsel of older and more experienced heads than his own. Be that as it may, he was killed in the court-roon—as I am informed, for I was not there—no doubt by one or two fanatics. The people did not kill him, nor do I believe that any person of sound mind supposed that the people had any hand in his murder. Then, why are the whole population of Lake County threatened that they will be bushwhacked? "Punish the guilty" is a law of human nature; but why wreak vengeance on the innocent?

Ninety-nine hundredths of the people of Lake County deplore the death of your son, and also deplore the action of the Committee of Safety last winter. For my own part, the news of your son's death struck me with horror and consternation. I thought of his poor bereaved father. I am a father, and can imagine what your feelings were; and I pray to God that I may be preserved from a like situation! A son shot down like a dog by the bullet of a secret assassin or assassins is awful even to think of. All these things are sure to come to light sooner or later. "Vengeance is mine, and I will repay, saith the Lord." Crimes never go unpunished; but the good Lord does not always square his accounts in a minute. He takes his own good time, and his ways are not as our ways. Your son's murderer or murderers will be found out and punished, sooner or later.

We are told that Gibbs and his friends intend to come in here and bushwhack. Well, suppose they do, and kill a few, or burn the buildings of one or two citizens. The consequence would be that a reward would be offered for Gibbs dead or alive, and the people here will contribute, if necessary, ten thousand dollars over and above what the county would give, besides the Territorial reward; and the consequence would be that Gibbs and his band would all be gobbled, and many innocent people suffer. I do not know that even yourself would be very safe.

Recollect, I am only supposing what would be the condition of things were such a thing to take place, knowing the fearful determination of the people here to repel an invasion, either secret or public. But I can safely assure you that no one will be molested here who is peaceable and attends to his own affairs; but the stirrer up of strife and midnight assassin will not be safe here. It appears so, at least. But do not infer from this that I indorse mob-law, for I assure you I do not.

I understand you had secretly paid this county a visit; but we did not see you in this end of the county. I assure you that you would be as welcome as ever, and you always have been welcome at our house, whatever you may have thought to the contrary recently.

Remember us kindly to your family. My wife desires to be kindly remembered to you, and you have her heart-felt sympathy in your recent great bereavement.   Yours, as ever, very respectfully,

J. McPHERSON.

Mr. McPherson was appointed probate judge. The mob took the lead in this selection, and also in that of the grand jury. The first panel, they were afraid, was not surely for them. Directly it was lost. One of the men said he could give every name, and he proceeded, leaving out two or three whom they did not want, substituting others in their place.

Mr. George Henderson administered on my son's estate. It was thought that one thousand dollars would pay all debts. I sold his interest in the Dyer Mine to H. A. W. Tabor for three thousand dollars, in three payments. The first payment was covered by claims, which we allowed. When the second and third payments were ready, bills just covering them were conveniently at hand. It was too plain. I sent to the administrator for the last accounts, and knew that some of them were unjust, and suspected the balance. Samuel—my only surviving son—took Judge Clough, a good attorney, and they went over and looked into the business. Judge McPherson and the claimants were very saucy. Judge Clough showed where they had all overreached or failed to go according to law, and the administrator and his securities could be held responsible. He proposed to remove the case to another county, and proceed against them. This scared them, and they dropped all claims, and let the estate be closed up at once. Judge Clough afterwards told me that they had counted close, for their bills were just a thousand dollars—exactly covering the payment.

It may seem strange that I have never taken active steps to bring my son's murderers to justice. The combination of the guilty and their friends was very strong, as the facts above recited plainly show. To have successfully combated it would have required more money than I could command. Besides, the county was comparatively poor, and the trials would have entailed large costs, so that the tax-payers dreaded and discouraged the prosecution. But after the Leadville boom, when the county had grown rich and strong, encouraged by Mr. —— Hayden, one of my son's best friends, and who was the last with him before the murder, I fully purposed to make the attempt. The mob, however, never ceased to fear; and so influenced the division of the county, and had Chaffee set off, in which once more they were in the majority.

It is not likely they will ever in this world be brought before any tribunal, save that of their own consciences. But murder, unlike debt, is never outlawed. Detectives have taken interest in it. It may be that vengeance is only sleeping.

CHAPTER XX.

OUR WORK ENLARGED.

OUR conference for 1876 was held at Boulder City, by Bishop Harris, a good-spirited Christian gentleman. I had great respect for him as a clear-headed man. He was always chosen secretary of all deliberative bodies of which he was a member. When things got twisted up, he had a way of untangling them speedily and pleasantly. While we had a few moments of talk at the conference, he said to me: "I see you have had hard work the year past, as well as trouble; and you are talked of for a charge where you will have to move one hundred miles by wagon. I will not direct a man as old as you are to move so far, without at least asking him if he is willing to go." I suppose it was the more noticeable, because it had never been said to me on this wise before.

I was sent to Fair Play and Alma, and had several preaching-places besides. It was quite a circuit, and Brother A. J. Smith was appointed by the elder to travel with me. He gave promise of being a good helper; but after a month or two, owing to business complications, left me to take charge of a ranch, and I had another year with plenty to do. The year previous, the work was almost ruined by bickerings and trouble. It took the most of this year to make peace. We had but little advance in Church matters. An eight-days' meeting at Alma resulted in good. I lived six miles distant, and rode home after service, for lack of invitation to stay. One night I paid my fare at a hotel. The next day some one found how it was, and gave them a talk. That night I had about forty hearers, and three invitations to stay. This was the thaw that broke the ice. Hospitality has abounded ever since.

I had a famous climb up Mt. Lincoln. Mine after mine had been opened in that region. The Dolly Varden, working quite a force; the Moose, with scores of miners; the Russia, with twenty, and at the base of the mountain was Dudley, a village with a furnace. A number of preachers, including some bishops, had passed that way, wonder-hunting; but apparently the thought of preaching to the cliff-dwellers never entered their minds. It was, indeed, an achievement to ascend Mt. Lincoln, one of the highest Rocky Mountain peaks. One large company of climbers had put their names in a box which they had elevated on a tall "liberty pole." Governor Bross was so enthused that he sang the doxology. Thenceforth the boys called one peak of Lincoln, Mt. Bross.

I concluded that I would go up and preach. On Tuesday I started on foot five miles to the first mine. Just as I got above timber, the wind met me with a heavy squall of snow, and, although it was some time till night, the air was soon so thick with snow that I could not see from one telegraph-pole to another. I wished the wire had been put six feet from the ground, then I could have held to it. As it was, I felt along the wagon ruts, and could only go a few feet at a time without bracing myself on my pole, and resting for breath. It was almost impossible to make headway against the wind and snow coming down the mountain.

The road went close to the dump of the Dolly Varden mine and the shaft-house and boarding-house. It was so dark I could not see even the dump; but as I turned my face back to rest, I had got past the house and above the dump. I thought the house must be close. I saw the sparks come out of the chimney, and was only three rods from it. My face was dripping with thawing snow, and my strength nearly exhausted. I was let into Mr. Hall's room, the superintendent of the mine. He seemed surprised that I had got through, although he had given out the appointment for me. He made me welcome, and as I started into the dining-room, surprised me by putting a five-dollar bill into my hand. I tried to preach to eleven hearers. Ten of the number each laid down a dollar on the table, and that, too, without being asked.

The next day I called at the Moose mine, where there were sixty men. I told the cook I was on a preaching excursion, and would be there the next night to talk to them. He said he would tell the men. I went on to Australia, the highest mine worked, within three hundred feet of the top of Mt. Lincoln, where I found twenty men. I had a good visit with the superintendent, and preached to them. They were very attentive and respectful, but forgot to carry around the hat. On my way back, I preached to about forty-five; had good attention, and when the benediction was pronounced, one of the number passed a hat, and took up sixteen dollars. Before this, the storm was over, and I was ready to go home to Fair Play.

We give this trip in full, as it was the first preaching on Mt. Lincoln. I was back several times; but, otherwise, services have been few. I want to say here, that in my experience of almost twenty-seven years, I do not remember an instance where a miner or prospector came to my preaching who did not behave himself; and I predict that that mountain will be mined for a century to come. I continued on this circuit till the close of the year, preaching nearly four times a week all over Park County, and a few times in Summit.

There was one occasion when the snow was quite deep. It was at the time of a wedding, when Mr. Charles Walker and Mrs. Miller were married, about fourteen thousand feet above the sea-level. It was at a saw-mill. My old friend, Mr. Hoope, with Gilbert Havens and others, were on hand, with a double bob-sled. When we got well up in the timber, we met a four-horse team and sled. On either side were logs and snow, five feet high. I thought to pass, but we could not. Neither sled could back. A collision seemed to be inevitable. Eight horses were between the sleds. Fortunately, the company that met us had

the couple with them, they having despaired of
my arriving on time. They got out, and the boys
unhooked the horses, lifted the sled up on its edge,
got the horses back, uncoupled, turned around, and
got us to the house a little late, but all right.
The couple were yoked in matrimonial bonds in
the presence of a jolly set of boys, and of one
lady besides. This was nearer the stars than any
wedding I had ever witnessed. The couple still
live and love each other; and by that we may
suppose, the higher the place, the better the wedding. The groom was so well pleased that he
handed me twenty-five dollars. That marriage in
those mountain woods was a grand social time,
never to be forgotten, and that too without whisky,
fiddle, or dancing.

At the conference of 1877 I asked for a supernumerary relation, which the brethren granted.
But I preached occasionally, and made my own
living. I held this relation till the conference at
Pueblo, in 1879, when I was made effective, and
appointed to Breckenridge Circuit. I had spoken
of that county, and its need of a preacher, but
when I heard my name read out, with no missionary appropriation, to an entirely outside and new
work, I felt hurt. To be sent to the hardest circuit at my time of life, and not on an equal footing with other preachers of the conference, was
rough on me, and unfeeling in those who sent
me. But my old-time loyalty stood me in hand,
and I concluded to go and do the best I could
for a year.

The cabinet named the circuit after the county, and the presiding elder did not know where to address a letter to me. Probably he did not know the size of the county, which, beginning forty-five miles west of Denver, extends to Utah, and north to Wyoming. Since then seven counties have been made out of it; and in all of them there are, at this writing, only two preachers of our Church, and they are supplies.

I had been only four weeks on the circuit when the Ute Indians killed Father Meeker and several others, took his wife and daughter prisoners, and scared almost everybody, so that many settlers left. The excitement crossed the range; for, somehow, people will get more excited and run quicker in an Indian scare than they would if Lucifer was right in sight. For instance, at Alma, when the people were badly perplexed what to do, a man got some whisky in him, and concluded to give the people a scare. So he shot a hole in his coat, and rode through town, crying at the top of his voice: "The Indians are coming, two or three hundred strong! Everybody will be killed!" The men were frightened, and began to gather the teams to carry passengers; every horse, mule, and jack was bridled and saddled. Pack-saddles were in demand. Women, frantic with fear, used every sort of conveyance; scarcely bonneted, they rode sometimes two on a pony, not particular if both feet were not on one side. Many also went on foot. The motley crowd whipped past each other, their eyes almost popping out with fear, all bound for Fair Play. Before they got there, the people of Fair Play had heard the news, and leaving their houses, fled to the big, stone court-house. But here were coming all of the population of Alma. And now the women wanted a fort built of the cord-wood, and some of the men to go and see if the Indians were near. None doubted but they were near. And now—before the volunteer scouts could start—see husband and wife embracing each other, as they supposed for the last time on earth; and some on their knees praying, that had never been seen to pray before! The reason of all this was that they believed the report that the Indians were just behind, with tomahawk and scalping-knife.

I have always thought if an old-fashioned evangelist had been there he might have had a profitable prayer-meeting. "But," says a friend, "I don't believe in excitement." But I do; a man or woman must be excited enough to start them in any cause. Men must believe there is danger, or they will not start. This is the reason that our Savior gave the awful doctrine of damnation without repentance, as well as all the invitations of the gospel. Both the threatenings and persuasions must be presented. Hence, convictions are slight, and conversions are not so clear as they ought to be, when our preachers, instead of showing a sinner his danger, "snugly keep damnation out of sight." I hold that a minister ought to present both sides, so that the sinner shall fear the torments of hell as much as he desires the glories of heaven. Many will never come unless they are first alarmed.

But to return. The Indians were not within a hundred miles. The news reached Governor Pitkin at Denver, that they had burned Breckenridge to ashes. He telegraphed to some one to send men across the range to see if it was so. They came in the night. We, being in the outside cabin, heard a noise, but did not know what made the stir; and it being election-day, supposed that to be the cause. So we slept well, while guards were being put out down Blue River to protect the town. Several of the women and children were sent to Denver. And all the while the Indians were keeping themselves as far off in the south-west as possible.

Father Meeker, as he was familiarly called, was a man of good mind, and everybody that knew him loved him. He was progressive, and did all he could for the first colony at Greeley. Then he was led to try to civilize the Ute Indians—a worthy project, but in advance of the time. To begin with, the Indians had never been subdued or whipped. Every once in awhile they would kill a white man, and manage to get off. As in any other sinner, so is human nature in them; unless they fear, they will destroy. The government of course made a raid on them; lost more men and mules and money than they did harm to the Utes. Still they scared them into giving up prisoners and land, and surrendering two or three bucks. Government did little or nothing with the bucks; yet murders that they had committed were worth more than the lives of the whole tribe.

It has always looked to a Western man that the Eastern people cared more for the filthiest red-skin than for a decent white man. They seemed to forget that the soil on which they themselves raise their bread had been taken from the "poor Indians."

Our white population got over their scare, and came back, and all was quiet again. During all this time we kept up our appointments in about a dozen mining-camps. The snow fell deep. Our stages went on runners, hauled by four horses. I rode at half fare. The line from Georgetown by Loveland Pass to Leadville, with its branches, carried me to most of the camps. The stages were generally full, and to be turned over and all thrown out into the snow was not uncommon. I was overset seven times during the winter, but, through the goodness of God, was not hurt. I went over as far as Carbonateville, Robinson, and Kokomo, south-west, and to Decatur, north-east. In January my wife was taken down suddenly with neuralgia in the head, and her life was almost despaired of for a week; but, by God's mercy and Dr. Hendrick's skill and good care, she came through all right in a month, so that I could go around again on my work.

In February I held a protracted meeting in Kokomo. The first night I finally found lodging at an inn. After traveling most of the day and preaching at night, I was weary, and was shown to my room. There was a small room near by, with a stove and table and cards. The door between was partly open. Soon two young couples came up, and began a game of cards. They were full of noisy fun. Evidently the boys beat, and I supposed the game was what they called smut, as the girls would not stand the application, and ran up the hall, the boys after them. I supposed they smutted them, and went back and at it again. I got no sleep till after midnight. In my reflections it was a serious matter to think how I could succeed under such usage as this; but I concluded to hold on and try.

I got some needed sleep and rest toward morning; breakfasted, and paid my bill. The snow was six feet deep. I started out to visit families and bachelors' cabins. Several said if they had a place to keep me I would be welcome. I came to a Mr. Thomas, a Welsh Congregationalist. I thought he was better than our Yankees of the same Church. I went into his cabin, six feet high at the eaves; snow all around and six feet on top. There were steps in the snow to get out to the street. He had a spare mattress in one corner on the floor, which he offered me if I would not be insulted by it. I told him the past night's experience, and that his mattress would be most grateful.

At this place I made my abode for two weeks, eating with the bachelors and among the people, visiting in the daytime, and preaching every night to an average of seventy-five people. A constant storm prevailed. I formed a society of sixteen; one or two joining by letter, and some from other denominations. In the spring they built quite a chapel for the place. But owing to the town's decline, it is now out of use.

From there I went back to Breckenridge, which shortly experienced a characteristic mining boom. A report was spread that about Breckenridge were immense bodies of gold quartz and carbonates, three feet deep. People of all classes came across the range, and, of course, the inevitable dance-house, with degraded women, fiddles, bugles, and many sorts of music, came too. There was a general hubbub from dark to daylight. The weary could hardly rest. Claims were staked out everywhere, and the prospector thought nothing of shoveling five feet of snow to start a shaft. Saloons, grocery-stores, carpenter-shops, and every kind of business sprang up, including stamp-mills and smelters. All classes were excited beyond all good sense. Town-lots, that could have been bought before at twenty-five to fifty dollars, brought fifteen hundred dollars. Corrals, log-heaps, and brush-thickets were all turned into town-lots. Those owning ground thought it worth ten times more than it was. The excitement was almost as great as when they thought the Indians were coming. The preacher thought it time to secure a lot for a church. He canvassed all the town; but none had a lot to give. One was offered away out, but was refused. Giving a back-lot for a church had played out with me. In the fall I bought a lot and a cabin. It was about one hundred and fifty feet deep by fifty wide. The Town Company undertook to change the survey and take about two-thirds of it from me under pretense that the county had a claim on it. They even undertook to fence it up; but when they began, I began too. I hired men to put in posts; but as soon as I turned my back they came to my men, within forty feet of my house, and told them they would send an officer and arrest them. My hands quit. After dinner I went to digging post-holes myself. The Town Company's representative came with two witnesses, and warned me to stop work. I never laid down my pick, but told him I was a man, and a law-abiding man at that, and his were as good witnesses as I wanted; and I warned him before them to keep off my lot and to leave. By this time the witnesses started, and he followed. He was the company's commissioner; and was very good when he found he could not bulldoze me. I gave half my lot to the trustees to build a church on. We carried a subscription paper till I got enough to start on; and went to the saw-mills, got all the lumber I could, and we went to work and put up a house twenty-five by fifty feet, posts sixteen feet high, and inclosed it. I nailed the first shingle, and did more work on it than any other man.

While I went to conference the friends finished the roof and put the floor down; and the next Sunday we had service in the first church on the

Western Slope in our conference, with a good organ. We had had no aid as yet from the Church Extension Society, which gave two hundred and fifty dollars after I left. This was a year of toil, and no pay to speak of—about two hundred dollars was all; and I paid traveling expenses, and did more hard work than I ever did before, take it altogether. I left about thirty-five members. Including the lot, the church cost me all of three hundred and fifty dollars.

In 1877 I was made supernumerary. At the conference held by Bishop S. M. Merrill at Pueblo in 1879, my relation was changed to effective, and I was appointed to Breckenridge. The year's work I have already related. At its close, the conference was held by Bishop H. W. Warren at Georgetown, in the fall of 1880. It was an enjoyable session. It was the bishop's first conference. Feeling the pressure of years and labors, I asked and was granted a superannuate relation.

I returned to Breckenridge, where the boom had begun in March. In about a year most of the excitement in town-lots had passed over; and in eighteen months building had quit, and not long after a fire burned a block, and the camp went down. There has been no building since to speak of, and town-lots have gone back as fast as they went up.

As conference gave me no help, and the people but little—the members being poor—I put in all my time at work in some way. Being well acquainted with the mountains and mining, I was paid good wages for locating claims. When the snow was deep, I went on snow-shoes, always feeling that a preacher had a right to earn his living if he could not get it by preaching; but no right to leave his charge. I could preach three and four times, and work three or four days in the week. In fact, I sometimes earned more by moon-shine labors than I could by preaching. In the summer of this year my wife boarded some men, and helped in that way.

Brother J. F. Coffman followed me. Conference gave him two hundred dollars to start with. He staid three years, and having the office of school superintendent, made out to live. The unsettled condition of mining-camps is unfavorable to the keeping up of religious societies.

My practical knowledge, as before stated, made my services as a locater in demand. Some-times I gave them to deserving young fellows, whom fortune had used roughly. Two such were Candell and Thompson. In the spring of 1880 they came to me for information. Snow was more than knee-deep. They were out of money, ex-cept enough to board them a few days, and put up a log pen, ten or twelve feet square, just large enough for them to stand up in and make a stopping-place. The next thing was a job of work. I was employed to sink holes on some claims, to hold them, and gave them employment. I bought tools for them, and we started up the mountains, I leading. Soon the trail gave out, and we broke a path in snow waist deep. We carried picks, shovels, tent, and blankets. It was hard climbing for the boys; but they said: "If that old man can get there, we must." And we did. I showed them where to dig. That day they had a shaft three feet deep, and slept in it at night.

They worked for some time, making fair wages—say three dollars per day—and then they and myself took up some ground in company. They also continued to work and prospect for themselves through the summer. Thompson found some float mineral, and followed it up to where it came up to the grass roots, and sunk a hole on it ten feet deep, and threw out several hundred pounds of rich mineral, gray copper, worth five hundred dollars to the ton. He staked his claim—one hundred and fifty by one thousand five hundred feet. He did not know how rich it was, and let one Parkison have a fourth interest for one hundred dollars, and would have sold the balance for two hundred and fifty dollars, but his man failed to come to time. He kept the location a secret. I had not asked him where it was, but said: "You have got on my claim, I suspect." He replied: "You have no claim up there." I answered: "I prospected up there three years ago, and left my shovel to hold my claim." "Where is your claim?" he said. I inquired if he had been at the head of a certain ditch. "Yes," was his answer. "Well," I replied, "my claim crosses about thirty rods above that." "My claim," he said, "is not within three hundred feet of that."

I rode up, and found my shovel; and just up the hill-side I saw his corner stake, and followed to his works. I was pleased with his show for a lode, and was glad for his sake. Seeing the ground was vacant on each side of his claim, before I left I staked one claim south and four north of it. Unable to do the work myself, I took two or three pieces of his ore home with me, and told an assayer where it came from, and that I had staked the ground adjoining; and as I had to attend to my church building, proposed to let him go in with me, if he liked the show; he to do my work for an interest. He went, and was pleased, and we made a contract. He looked at Mr. Thompson's prospect, and wanting some one to do the work, I suggested Thompson, as he would want to keep an eye on his own claim. He said nothing about buying the claim. When Thompson came in to our house, I told him they wanted to see him; and knowing that he had offered his claim for two hundred and fifty dollars, advised him, if they wanted to buy him out, not to sell for nothing. My wife named a thousand dollars, as it was easier to fall than to raise. He went and asked them twelve hundred; but they offered him a thousand, ten per cent down, and the rest in sixty days. He returned in a few minutes with his hundred dollars, and said it was the first time he had ever had that much at once. Then they wanted to see Mr. Parkinson, but told Thompson not to tell how he sold. Mrs. Dyer said: "You tell Mr. Parkinson to come here as he goes, and I will post him." He came, and then sold his fourth for five hundred dollars, ten per cent down. There were four of the company, and so they had the big thing, and—by doing the work agreed on—three-fourths of mine also.

The ore was very rich—from low grade to a thousand dollars a ton. But one of the parties assayed some of it, and showed me the certificate. It was so low that I never said a word to Mr. Thompson about it. I was disappointed in it. If anybody knew it was rich, it was those who bought it. In a day it was all over the camp that the boys had been swindled, the ore being fabulously rich. And, as a matter of course, the discoverers felt bad over the loss of a good thing. Everybody asked why they did not have it assayed. Because they had no money to pay on a risk, as but very few had received any benefit by the assays, and many considered it money out. Parties told them they were swindled, and that the sale could be set aside, and that on certain conditions they would have it done. What those conditions were I never knew. They were not to have anything except they could prove fraud, and so get the property back. So they went to law.

I had been asked by the assayer if I wished to have some of the Warrior's Mark ore assayed. I replied: "No; I have no interest in the lode." Afterwards he called me in and showed me his report on it, and it was lower than I had thought possible. I thought no more about it at the time, until after the sale. When they had me on the witness-stand, they questioned me as to the assay I had seen. I told them what I knew of it. "Did you tell either of the parties before the sale?" "No." "Why did you not tell them?" "Because I was taken back, and thought it would do them no good." This showed that they were not influenced by the assay. So the purchasers held the diggings, and the poor boys got no more. They were advised to compromise with the first party, but they would not.

Now the company go to work, but soon winter is on, and snow anywhere from five to eight feet deep. Some good mineral was raised; but the water was strong, and they concluded to sell. The price was put at three hundred thousand dollars for the whole, including my interest. I was to have eight thousand, five hundred. About the 1st of January, 1881, I began work on a log house. Had a good horse and sled, six miles away, at Breckenridge. Selected a place to build, and taking my horse, with chain and whiffle-tree, went eight rods, mid-sides in snow, and dragged in the first tree. And so, cutting and hauling logs, and going back home each day, returning to work in the morning with lumber, I finished my house. It was seventeen feet by seventeen, a story and a half in height, shingle roof, two floors, and doors. By the 19th of February I moved my wife and the last of our goods. By that time I had a hole against the bank in the snow to stable my horse. Laid poles on the snow, and put pine-brush for roof, and he was comfortable till his slab stable was built. We were within a half mile of the Warrior's Mark Lode, which was the center of attraction for mining experts and speculators. Men would come, and look, and send experts; and then others would come. All wished to make money. Some would levy blackmail, under threats of spoiling the sale. After all the efforts, the property was not sold.

The weather becoming good, they hired a superintendent and about fifty men, and resumed work. In six months they took out, as well as I could learn, between seventy-five and eighty thousand dollars. During this time, they stocked the property at three millions. After one dividend, it failed to pay any more for a time under the management. I took ten thousand dollars in stock for my part. At this time I began to look at the stock system, and concluded to let that be the last stock I would ever have anything to do with in mining. For these reasons: First, the amount is put at three times its worth; second, there are directors, clerks, and treasurer, president, superintendent, and bosses, all on pay, besides the hands. These, with mismanagement, wire-working, whisky, cards, and fancy women, beat the average lode. After several attempts to get pay out of the mine, a man took the property to work. He had secured more than half the stock, and had the control. He bought mine. I realized two thousand dollars.

I have given this sketch to show some of the difficulties of prospecting, selling, or running a mine. Yet mining is the business of the country.

Chapter XXI.

DENVER METHODISM.

IN April I secured Sister Van Cott for a week, and there could not have been a more general interest awakened among miners and citizens than there was in Breckenridge. Every meeting was well attended, and deep interest was shown from the start. Twenty joined; some were reclaimed and some converted, and the little society was revived. If she could have stayed another week, from all appearances, much more good would have been accomplished. She held services twice each day, and worked incessantly.

Our parsonage was a log house, and she boarded with us. It was the first log house she had ever stopped in. She picked off splinters and sent them East as curiosities, and wrote that she was comfortable, and the snow three feet deep! She is a noble worker, and did more in the time she was there than any preacher could have done, everything considered. The people gave her over one hundred dollars in money, and, as she liked specimens of ore, all that she could carry, besides about twenty dollars in pure gold, in dust, nuggets, and wire.

From here I went to Leadville to conference. Bishop Wiley ably presided. I had not then realized anything for stock, and found it hard

work to live, but felt that I must attend conference at any rate. It was a pleasant one, and, to
my grateful surprise, the brethren gave me the
Fifth Collection. I had promised one hundred
dollars to the Denver University. Found Brother
John A. Clough, the treasurer, and paid it. Thus
the first Fifth Collection in the Colorado Conference went for Christian education. My own advantages had been limited, but I coveted the best
things for my children, and felt a profound interest
in our conference educational work.

I went back to Summit County Circuit, and,
having managed to live through the year, keep out
of debt, and be able to work, I was quite happy,
at an altitude of about ten thousand feet. I never
enjoyed myself better any place.

The following December we moved to Douglas
County, to our ranch, and tried to make a living,
but found it rather hård to do so at my age—over
seventy. I milked seven cows, and had a garden.
I raised corn, oats, and buckwheat, and by dint
of hard work, made a living for two years. But
it disagreed with me. I became such an invalid
that I could not ride on horseback. Of course,
therefore, I could not make much of a cow-boy.
Some time in June we had a terrific hail-storm.
Our garden and corn looked nice, and all at once
the storm came—hail and a little rain. My better-
half ran out with old pans and rags to cover the vines
and save her garden. The lightning was frightful, and the cracking thunder so alarmed the old
lady that she ran into the house, pelted all the

way with big hail-stones. I was doing my best to make the same shelter, but her tragic flight was more than I could stand. I laughed the thunder down. Yet it was well that she got in, for the hail-stones were of all sizes, down to the size of peas, and fell with sufficient force to split shingles and break the windows. The ground was covered to the depth of four inches. All our crop was cut down even with the ground. The hail-covering protected the roots of the corn, which grew again, so that we had quite a crop of corn and fodder. But few can realize the amount of water that falls in such a storm. After all was clear, we heard a noise up the creek, and saw the hail and water coming about four feet up abreast, almost a perpendicular front, and another wave on top of that, till it filled the banks full seven feet high, and it plowed the creek-bed much wider than it was before.

Having passed two summers on the ranch, I was convinced that I was too old or too lazy to work on a farm. I traded it for a house and lot in Denver, and in November, 1885, moved to the new home, Glenarm Street, No. 712. It had never been my plan to live in Denver, but Providence seemed to guide me there. I could not remain idle. So, as the Legislature was to convene soon, the thought struck me that I might be elected to one of the chaplaincies. Hon. Melvin Edwards, Secretary of State, advised me to seek the chaplaincy of the Senate. I had been acquainted with Mr. James Monahan, of Park County, for a long time, with Mr. Chilcott, of Pueblo, and Mr. Irving Howbert, of Colorado Springs, and Mr. Wells, of Douglas—all old settlers and old members. I wrote them, and received promises of their support. I got there easily enough. The position was not lucrative; but it gave me something to do, and I served them as best I could.

In the spring I went to Breckenridge to look after some interests. I found our Church without a preacher, and told them I would stop and preach for them till the presiding elder would supply them. It resulted in my staying the year out. The Church people were few in number, and hardly any well-to-do. Such a place, I am sorry to say, has few friends with the preachers. I tried to do what I could for them.

It was two years before I was relieved. I preached at Breckenridge twice on each Sunday, and at Lincoln about once in two weeks; and on week evenings at Montezuma, Dillon, Kokomo, and Robinson, an average of four times a week. There were three or four hundred people at Breckenridge, and the offices were well sprinkled with gamblers and saloon-keepers. There were about nine saloons, and all had card-tables. They had been in the habit of taking the organ out of the church to their balls. About dark one night I heard something in the church, and ran out. A wagon was backed up to the door, and the organ was almost loaded. I objected, and was told that they had leave from the officers of the Church. But I was firm, and they left without it. I speak of these things to show how little regard people had for sacred things, and what a preacher had to contend with, and the material he had to work on. Some would say that such should not have the gospel preached to them. But I think they ought to have both love and gospel. I told them, in an exhortation, that they were hair-hung and breath-shaken over the gulf of eternal despair. "Howbeit, this kind goeth out only by prayer and fasting." O, may God send men after his own heart, who can thunder his wrath as well as display the glories of his great salvation!

This last two-years' term in Summit County was commenced in my seventy-third year, and closed in my seventy-sixth. I preached three and a half times for each week. At this age I felt it a tax on me too heavy to bear. But where can rest be found? For an old man who has always kept going, to stop is distressing, and time hangs heavy on his mind. Only the grace of God and the prospect of an eternal home can keep him in a cheerful mood.

"O, who would live alway, away from his God?"

I proceed to give an account of the religious beginnings of Denver. In the spring or early summer of 1859 came Rev. Wm. H. Goode, of the Methodist Episcopal Church, sent out to see and report on the condition and wants of the Pike's Peak country. He brought with him Adriance, a young preacher who took charge of Denver, and was the first *appointed* preacher in the country.

But Rev. George W. Fisher, of the Methodist Episcopal Church, was here in advance of the former, and preached the first sermon ever heard in Denver. He was a respectable preacher and loved by all that knew him. Little did he think of the importance that would be attached to that effort, it being the first gospel sound ever proclaimed in our Centennial State. It was an enviable privilege. Angels gave glory to God that one of his servants had broken the silence of the desert with the sound of salvation.

Although I have preached in more new towns in Colorado than any man dead or alive, I would freely give all in that line to have had Brother Fisher's privilege to preach first in this State. Brother Goode was a fine preacher and well respected. When E. R. Ames was elected bishop it was by only one vote over him. He was here a short time, preaching in Denver and other places, and then returned to Kansas. From that time there have been regular services in Denver by our preachers, including Sunday-school work. The first Sunday-school was held in Brother Ritz's house. All present but one or two were men. One of the females told me she was then fourteen years old and the youngest person there.

On the eighth day of May, 1860, Rev. John M. Chivington, presiding elder, with his family, came to Denver, and at once began to build. His was the first brick dwelling-house in the place. The house is standing in West Denver now, No. —. Rev. A. P. Allen, of Wisconsin, took charge of the Denver work; Rev. Mr. Kenny was sent in the spring of 1861, and had charge for one year. At the conference held in Kansas in 1862 he was appointed for the second year to Denver, and loaded his wagon to start across the Plains, apparently in good health, but all at once was taken sick and died in a few hours, ceasing to labor on earth, we trust to rest in heaven. Rev. B. C. Dennis was appointed presiding elder of the Rocky Mountain District at the same conference, and remained two years. He was a good man and a fair preacher, but soon after left for Central Illinois Conference, and has been a successful preacher, and is still in the work.

Rev. O. A. Willard filled the Denver charge in 1862. He was appointed at the conference in Kansas for the second year, and served till the Rocky Mountain Conference was organized at Denver in 1863, at which time he was appointed presiding elder of Denver District. He was a talented preacher. Rev. George G. Betts supplied the Denver charge in 1863, and then went over to the Episcopalians. He was followed by George Richardson. He served Denver one year and Georgetown one year, when he returned to the Rock River Conference. Wm. M. Smith took the Denver charge after Richardson, for one year, and was succeeded by B. T. Vincent, who served the charge three years. As our conference Minutes give the appointments of all our preachers from this time, we will write chiefly of Denver. Brother John Cree, a local preacher, who still is with us, was the first Bible agent, and organized Bible societies in different towns as well as Denver. While he has not preached much of late, he is a good Church worker and has been for twenty-eight years.

Of the pioneer Methodists I remember W. D. Pease, class-leader; H. Ritz, Conrad Frick, Mrs. Chivington, Mrs. Hawkins, Mrs. Tynan, Governor Evans and family, Governor Elbert, A. I. Gill, and Peter Winne. Most of these were official members. There were others, whose names I can not call to mind, as I made only occasional visits to Denver.

Brother Frick was anxious to have a German Methodist Church organized, and at last was successful. The prayers of our German brethren have been answered. They have a good block of ground in a central part of the city, with a fine church-building, a good parsonage, with two other houses to rent—a property that would be a credit to any denomination in the city—with a pastor, and a goodly number of members, and a fair congregation. We glory in their prosperity. Our people at first bought and fitted up a house for worship on the bank of Cherry Creek, which was washed away in 1864. Afterwards they built the Lawrence Street Church; and when it was finished it was the largest church, as well as the tallest building, in Denver. For these times it was a great achievement for so small a membership. Governor Evans, Governor Elbert, and Colonel Chivington were first on the list of donors, while most of the citizens were liberal, and all the members did what they could. There was no collection on dedication-day. From this time the Methodist Episcopal Church took firm hold on society, and with her Sunday-schools has been a power for good. Colonel Chivington is an old man now, and has great reason to be proud and thankful for the part he took in planting Methodism in Denver and Colorado. The Methodist Church is also indebted to Ex-Governor Evans, for he has helped all the societies, and in particular the University of Denver, from first to last. I would like to know how much he has paid. But if he were asked, his modesty would not allow him to count it up; but I think his gifts may be said to be more than forty thousand dollars to the university alone.

CHAPTER XXII.

MINERAL WEALTH OF COLORADO.

AS before stated, I came to Denver without a cent. A man—Daniel Andrews, whom I had not seen for twenty years—called me by name. We started in life on land within one-half mile of each other. He now owned the Chicago House in West Denver, and told me to make my home with him while in the place. We had a good visit. The first morning, as we were at breakfast, a man came running in, his eyes bulged out and his breath almost gone. He said Dr. Birdsall had made a fire assay of some quartz from Black Hawk that yielded such an amount of gold to the ton; and that he knew where he could get two or three wagon-loads of quartz that would make all he wanted. I understood this was the first fire assay ever made in Denver, and to hear them all talk, a tender-foot would think that in a short time gold would not be worth more than pig-iron, it would be so plenty. But seven years' work in the lead-mines in Wisconsin had prepared me to be cautious in swallowing such news. The only lodes I heard of were the Gregory and Bobtail, near Black Hawk. At the surface the mineral was decomposed, and the poor men hauled the dirt with a bob-tailed ox (which gave the name to the lode), and washed it out at the nearest water. This was

1859, early in the spring. They are working those same lodes at the present time at a profit. With these exceptions, the mining was all confined to. gulches and placers.

The first gold discovered was at Russellville, on Cherry Creek, thirty-five miles from Denver. Some parties camping on Cherry Creek, under some cottonwood trees, where West Denver now stands, panned gold out of the sand in the creek. That was a favorite resting-place, and was the commencement of all that is called Denver City. Russell and Spring Gulches were soon struck, near Black Hawk and Central City, as well as the Idaho branch of Clear Creek, Georgia Gulch, French and Gold Run over the range, Tarryall, Fair Play and California Gulch, and many others. It seemed like a providence that these gulches were discovered first, as there were no tools but picks and shovels brought at first across the six hundred miles of desert. By the close of 1862, most of the richest pay was taken out; but some of the gulches and placers are worked yet, and with profit after the lapse of nearly thirty years.

Lodes were prospected for, and many were found. But the miners' "toms" and sluice-boxes had to be laid aside for stamp-mills suitable to the crushing of quartz. Where the ore was rich, the mills paid well, notwithstanding there were but few men who knew much about the business. Thousands of dollars were spent in trying processes of different kinds. The ore was often refractory, and no effort was made to save anything but the gold, until Professor N. P. Hill made a visit to Colorado. He was the son of a farmer, but had worked his way through college, and became professor. He came to examine and report on the Gilpin Grant in San Luis Valley. Not far from the same time, I had been requested to report on the same grant. How near our reports agreed, I am not able to say, but mine was to the effect that the money in it was a long way in the future. Somewhat behind the times, as usual with me. But from my acquaintance with Governor Gilpin's early ideas of our mines, as well as of the great resources of Colorado, I suspect that he put the idea of examining the Gilpin County mines into Professor Hill's head. He was favorably impressed. Many of us thought Governor Gilpin a fanatic. If the word "crank" had been in use at that time, we would have called him a crank. I heard him say in a speech once, that our Rockies were ribbed with gold, and that it would be found in mass and position. Of course we made allowance, as an extemporaneous speaker is hardly accountable for many of his expressions. But after twenty-five years of progress in Colorado, we are led to believe that there was much more truth than fiction in his utterances. The governor still lives to see the wonderful production of the mines, and the many agricultural advancements of Colorado.

We must say that Colorado is greatly indebted to Professor N. P. Hill. He was the first man who conceived the possibility of working our refractory ores to profit. His first move was in the right direction, viz.: to go to Wales and see the Swansea works, get all the information he could, and secure men who were practical workmen in the separation of the refractory ores. By this means, silver, copper, and lead at least were saved. In 1867 he organized the Boston and Colorado Smelting Company, with, it is said, a cash capital of two hundred and seventy-five thousand dollars. He operated first at Black Hawk for several years, and next at Alma, Park County. The results must have been great, as he conceived the advantage of moving to Denver, where at Argo he has been operating for about ten years. The works will astonish almost any one, their capacity is so immense. I saw a report, said to have come from their books, up to 1879, which shows over seventeen millions of the precious metals.

In 1887 the Argo works reported over three millions; Omaha and Grant's works over five millions from Colorado ores. The most prominent of our smelters are the Holden Works, the Pueblo Smelting and Refining Works, the Colorado Smelting Company at Pueblo, the Arkansas Valley Smelter, the Harrison Reduction Works, American Smelting Company, and the Manville Smelting Works, Leadville.

After deducting ores from other States and Territories that were treated at the different works in Colorado, the sum of over twenty-four millions is left for the year 1887. This shows only the gold, silver, lead, and copper. In 1886 there was reported to be more, but the reduction in the price

of silver probably accounts for the greater part of
the shrinkage.

Our mines are certainly progressing in general.
Stamp-mills are numerous. Gold has been discovered from the north line of Colorado to the
south, and its development is only begun and on
the surface, as the country has never—except in
a few camps—been proved to any great depth.
Our mines are only in their infancy. After ages
are past, it will be said the half has never been
told. In 1861 I first crossed the State of Colorado.
I believed even then that the leads were worth
millions more than the gulches and placers that
were then being worked.

Our coal-mines have opened more or less ores
in the whole western side of Colorado. The veins
will average seven feet in thickness, and are abundant. The mines near Cañon City are proved to
be in quantity and quality the best in the State.
Boulder County also ranks high. So does Las
Animas County; and a thousand other places on
the east side as well as the west side of the Range.
Gunnison, and Pitkin Counties, have rich deposits.
There is enough to supply all the Plains, with
Kansas thrown in.

Next come our oil interests. Florence, on the
Arkansas River, eight miles below Cañon City, is
the present center. There the crude material is
produced and refined to a considerable extent. I
have always believed that oil was plenty in Colorado. Mr. Cassady, in early times, struck oil near
the above place, and it was used among us. I

came around on my circuit, and took up a quarter section adjoining his well, and had a cabin built for the sum of fifty dollars, to hold my claim. But before I could prove up, I was sent as a missionary to New Mexico. That ended my oil speculation; but though it is getting late in my day, I may strike oil yet! I have no doubt but many a flow of oil will be struck near to Denver, as well as in many other sections of the State.

Iron of the best quality is found in many parts, but has been more fully developed in the southern part of the State. From my personal observations in twenty-six years of travel, mostly in the mountains, ranging from Wyoming to old Mexico, I am prepared to believe there is no danger of exhausting the supply. The Bessemer iron and steel works at Pueblo—a mammoth concern—we think, is destined to be one of the great wealth-producers of Colorado, as it is located in the very heart of our iron region, and produces the best iron and steel known in our country, east or west.

Our mountains abound with hot springs, the waters being heated by the chemical action attendant upon the decomposition of minerals, and thus having imparted to them many curative properties.

We also believe that natural gas will be found in abundance for all purposes to which it can be advantageously applied. But if it is not found in the depths of the earth, we have the consolation to know that there is no lack of it among our inhabitants on the surface. The first hot spring that excited my interest was on Chalk Creek, about six miles west of the Arkansas River, in Lake County. It was so hot that it would almost boil an egg.

It was here I did the greatest climbing of my life ; and it was for my life, too. After a hard day's travel, in company with Brother Gilland, a local preacher, we undertook to climb a steep mountain, some distance up Chalk Creek. I was in advance less than a hundred feet, when I discovered that my position was dangerous. I had carefully worked my way until it was impossible to get back. So I said: "Brother Gilland, you go back; I can 't. To fall from here would be certain death. But I see a way that I can climb some further; and, if it is possible to get over this point of rocks, I can get up and find my way down some other place." If I looked back, my toes would tingle. It was policy to look up and go up. Through the goodness of God, I reached a place where I could stand safely. But we could not hear each other, as there was a gorge, filled with rocks and timbers, and with rushing and foaming water from the melting snow above. My comrade went back and got my horse, and, with his tones of distress, tried to make me hear. But he waited till evening in vain, and then left for his home to get help. He got in just before sunset, as it was some six miles; but I got in less than an hour after, and saved him from gathering help to go in search of me. He supposed I was dead or lost.

Suffice it to say, I came down at what is now called Haywood Springs. As it was not more than three rods till the hot water emptied into Chalk Creek, which was cold as snow could make it, and as I was tired, and wanted a rest after my hard day's walk, with nothing to eat, I concluded to take a bath, where the mingling of the waters would give the right temperature. I went in close to the creek, supposing the creek water had cooled the hot water, but to my surprise the two currents flowed side by side, the division being not more than the thickness of a knife-blade. While the hot water did not quite blister, the cold water did not quite freeze. I washed a little, but soon got out, and if I had been asked which I had had, a hot or a cold bath, it would have been proper to answer, *both*. There was not a human being within five miles of me, and I had all the fun to myself. I suppose this was the first attempt to bathe in those famous springs.

In a few days I located a quarter section, including the springs for medicinal purposes, raised a log house, and thought to improve the property; but, as was the case with my oil venture, my being sent to New Mexico interfered. The land was not surveyed, and there was no way to hold it but by possession. I left it, hoping that no one would jump it; but an old Georgia doctor took it. At considerable cost, I afterwards got him off. At the same New Mexico move, I claimed half the Hayden Ranch, near Twin Lakes, which I gave away. Either would be a fortune now; but preaching and money-making do not work well together.

There are many hot springs in the mountains. The Poncha are valuable. I visited several in San Luis Valley; and the Calienta and the Pagosa Springs are in New Mexico. The latter are wonderful—boiling up hot enough to cook anything. The Glenwood Springs, in Garfield County, no doubt will be a great resort, as they have the Midland Railroad, as well as the Rio Grande, interested in their development.

In the mountains quantities of hay and oats are raised in some places, and potatoes, turnips, and other vegetables.

Take it altogether, the mountains are rich beyond all that we ever thought of. And why are they not as valuable to our cities as the Atlantic is to Philadelphia, Baltimore, New York, or Boston? Is there any good reason why the cities of the Plains should not become, in another century, as great as any in the United States?

The State of Colorado is about equally divided between mountains and plains. The latter were thought our desert, but now good crops, with and without irrigation, are being raised, and the land taken by pre-emption. Soon all will be settled up—a section, say three hundred miles long by two hundred wide.

A word, here, about our towns. While there will be many fine towns in the valleys and mountains, I will speak only of the leading places, that seem to vie with each other in growth and prosperity.   I first saw Trinidad in the spring of 1865. It consisted of a few small houses; and its citizens, excepting two Americans, were Mexicans.   It has the possibilities of a city—mines adjacent of a superior quality, good agricultural country to the east and south, and its situation such as makes it the entrance to New Mexico.   All it wants in order to make a great town of itself, are men with push. Pueblo, the second place in population in Colorado, has as great advantages naturally as any place in our State.   It is connected by rail with the best gold and silver mines, and is nearer to the best coal and oil.   On the east is the valley of the Arkansas, which can not be surpassed.   It ought to have more smelters; then, with its iron-works, it would grow into a city of wonderful wealth and numbers.

Colorado Springs, also, has good advantages; especially since the Midland brings the mines to it, and the Rock Island opens a direct line to the East.   Its site is not surpassed, and is nearer to the finest scenery than any other place in the country—the Garden of the Gods, Pike's Peak, and the Mineral Springs at Manitou, only five miles away, and Colorado City, connecting the two in a continuous town.   They, too, need smelting works and manufactures; but have every prospect of becoming one of the liveliest and most beautiful places in the State.

We come now to Denver, the capital.   The question has often been asked, why Denver came to the front and took the lead.   It had the first printing-press. William N. Byers & Co. reached Denver April 21, 1859. The first freighters were tired, stopped, and made a trading-post. About this time, Thomas Pollock and Uncle Dick Hooton built the first frame houses in West Denver, as it is now called. But A. H. Barker, Esq., tells me that he built the first log cabin or house in Denver in 1858. Of course there were many tents. There seems to have been no wisdom in the selecting of a site for a large city, or it never would have been on both sides of Cherry Creek, as there was land enough on either side; but there is room enough to make a Chicago as it is. Of the people who came, more stayed in Denver than in any other place. It was well advertised in the *Rocky Mountain News*. Everything was said that could be said for Denver first, and after that the mining and agricultural interests were kept before the public. Many grew home-sick when they found that they could not pick up the gold, and left, cursing the whole Pike's Peak country, and particularly the *Rocky Mountain News* for falsehood. Their children are now returning, time having proven that the half had not been told. We feel it due to the *News* to say that we have not had so good and reliable a paper, take it every way, as that paper was while Messrs. Byers and Dailey conducted it. At first there were no telegraph lines, but Mr. Dailey would ride his pony and meet the stage some twelve miles out, get the news, and come back ahead of the stage, so that the readers of the paper could have it. The news was a week coming, but was just as fresh to the Denverites as though it had been streaked in by lightning.

One thing I have noticed—every traveler has expressed surprise to see so large and beautiful a town. I have thought the long journey across the Plains prepared him to appreciate the sight. When the Union Pacific Railroad was first talked of, it was invited to come this way, but, refusing, left Denver a hundred miles from its line. It was well that Denver had one man of foresight, energy, and financial ability, with a will to build a railroad from Cheyenne to Denver. John Evans, governor of Colorado, undertook the task, and aided by other enterprising citizens, in 1870, connected Denver by rail with the cities of the United States. That was Denver's first great day. Arapahoe County voted bonds with a liberal hand, and the governor was considered a great benefactor. Yet there were some who abused him, and called him everything but a gentleman, because he made money in building the road. This being the terminus of the first iron track, gave Denver a boom that set it beyond the reach of competing points.

But what would Denver be with her many railroads, if it were not for the towering mountains close in her front, stored with the richest treasures that the great Creator ever bestowed on any part of our nation? And all that the towns and cities, from Greeley to Trinidad, have to do, when they get hard up, is to look to the mountains, for there the treasures are abundant and unfailing. Colorado, from north to south, from east to west, has seen her darkest days, and the Barren Plains are beginning to rejoice and blossom as the rose.